Turkeystuffer

Mark Crockett

A
Strebor Books International LLC
Publication

Denise
Thanks and
enjoy the read!

Published by
Strebor Books International LLC
Post Office Box 1370
Bowie, MD 20718
www.streborbooks.com

ISBN 0-9711953-3-1
LCCN 2002100264

Graphic Design: Artful Mouse
Photo: Avery M. Commandest
Typesetting and Interior Design: Big Dog Studios

Manufactured and Printed in the United States

*To
Momma
and
Daddy*

Turkeystuffer

Chapter 1

"Wake up, bitch. Your tests are back."

The force of the slap across her face rocked the old high-backed chair to which Mimi Driver was securely bound with duct tape. The high back of the chair (and her head) hit the nearby wall, narrowly missing a half-filled bag of IV solution that hung from a nail. The solution fed into her petite body through the brachial artery on her bare right arm. The chair seesawed for a moment before settling upright. The duct tape covering her mouth somewhat silenced her scream of pain and surprise.

"You've been busy, home girl. You test positive for gonorrhea and syphilis...now that's something you don't see every day. You also have a nasty case of hepatitis 'B.' Kind of a hazard in your line of work, huh? Oh, and you're pregnant. Congratulations."

Her vision blurred and the general disorientation was coming back to her. The man's voice, muffled by the facemask and clear plastic eye shield he wore, droned on as he read from his checklist while Mimi's tears soaked her swollen face. She had been trapped in this room, bound to this chair, for almost two days. She now knew she was going to die here. He put down the paper he was reading from atop a large, closed Styrofoam cooler behind him, then turned to face Mimi.

"So, what do you say? Ready for a little chat?" he said as he adjusted the drop of the IV cocktail that kept her nauseous and, when he didn't wake her with beatings, semi-conscious. Then, in one smooth motion, he ripped the sodden duct tape from her mouth and stepped back to the cooler. Mimi vomited almost immediately. He opened the cooler while she retched, removed a large plastic cup filled with blood-tinged ice water, and threw it on her face. The shock of the cold water hitting her face caused her to inhale some of the liquid and left her coughing and gasping for air. He threw the cup and wad of tape onto the puddle of fluid on her lap.

"Well, you done?" he asked.

She coughed again, then spoke in a thick, slurred voice.

"I'm sorry...don't do this. Please. I don't know nuthin'. I never saw you...I'll leave town...just let me go..." She hiccupped, then began to whimper.

"That's it?" he asked.

She tried to focus the blur that was her vision. She could hear a faint echo when he spoke as she looked in the direction of his voice. All she could make out in the low light was his outline. He was tall. And green. The clothes he wore were green.

"Don't.kill me"

The slap this time was far more vicious, bouncing her into the wall again and toppling her and the chair to the floor. The force of her fall ripped the IV from her arm, leaving a jagged, bleeding tear. The left side of her face hit the floor with enough force to break her jaw in two places. The pain cleared the muddiness enough that she could see him clearly as he stood over her. He was wearing green hospital scrubs with blue booties covering his feet. He was rubbing his gloved hands. She saw that the gloves were taped to his sleeves.

"Shit, that hurt," he said as he massaged the hand he struck her with. He flexed his hand, then looked down at her.

"Frankly, baby girl, I expected a bit more out of you. I'm disappointed."

He walked behind her, grabbed the back of her chair, and sat it upright. The motion of righting her chair caused a loud, high-pitched wheeze to escape from her bloodied, swollen lips. Crossing to the front of her, he noticed by the lop-sided angle that her jaw was broken.

"No. You've been a party I shouldn't have gone to," he said as he reached into a black backpack behind the cooler, taking out a roll of duct tape and a sharpened Philips head screwdriver with a five-inch shaft. Using the tip of the screwdriver, he caught the beginning of the tape and pulled it out to a two-foot strip. He did this three times. When Mimi heard the tape tearing, she started to moan and began rocking side to side in her seat. He stuck the tips of the tape to the front of his shirt, then tore off a much smaller strip and circled behind Mimi. The sound of the roll of tape hitting the floor behind her stopped her rocking. He held the screwdriver in the same hand from which the tape had fallen.

"I've got to be back at work day after tomorrow, so girl, it's time for us to hit the road."

When Mimi turned her head toward the sound of his voice, he looped the first strip of tape under her chin and fractured jaw, pulling it up and back quickly, stopping her scream before it could start. As she kicked against the tape holding her legs, he secured her head to the back cross board of the chair. Avoiding her struggling and bound hands, he moved to her left side and knelt down. When he put his hand on the remains of her wet, soiled top, her kicking became more frantic. He giggled beneath his mask when he tore a gapping hole in the side of her blouse. As her bruised face started to darken from her efforts, he slid his hand up her side to the space between the fifth and sixth rib. He placed the tip of the screwdriver there.

"This is gonna hurt."

With a loud grunt, he pushed the screwdriver up to its base through her flesh, the intercoastal muscle layer, the parietal pleura, and directly into her left lung. Her chair left the floor for a moment with the force of her struggle, but her bounds held. He quickly removed the screwdriver and placed the smaller strip of duct tape tightly over the hole he'd made. Breathing hard, he jumped up and used the tip of the blood-slick tool to cut her head and neck free. She gasped so hard that he, now backed to the cooler, could hear her fractured jaw crackle with little pops. Her kicking had almost freed her left leg, and he now sat on the floor near the cooler to watch her. Within three minutes, the veins in her thin neck were bulging above her flesh like thick piano wire from the tension pneumothorax he had caused. It took another two minutes for the increasing pressure in her chest cavity to collapse her injured lung to the size of a baseball. Another two minutes collapsed the lung further, pressing it against the heart and great vessels. After two more minutes, the compressed lung squeezed the last beat out of her heart. She died with the left side of her chest slightly bloated from the internal air pressure.

He watched her for another minute before he got off the floor and, using the tip of the screwdriver, cut both of her arms and legs free. With a push, her body fell to the floor face down. He turned her onto her back, stripped off what was left of her clothes, then pushed the chair to the side. He pulled the backpack and then the cooler between her opened legs. Looking at a cheap watch he had taped to the top of the cooler, he started to whistle a tuneless melody. He opened the backpack and neatly started to line up his tools next to the body. Looking again at the clock, he began to move faster. He had a lot of work to do and wanted to be finished before morning...

*   *   *   *   *

It was the cold night rain in the Little Beirut section near downtown Phoenix, Arizona, that kept most of the homeless in the vacant buildings that filled this area of town. Centered between the 7th Avenue Police Precinct and the State Capitol complex, Little Beirut was the no-man's land that even the police didn't venture into after sunset. Dotted with more abandoned buildings and crumbling long vacant schools than the light industry it was zoned for, this was a place that, save for the transients gathered there, you did not go. In the shadow of the largest police headquarters in Arizona, every type of illicit activity known was produced, packaged, and served to an eager clientele. Rape, homicide, and drug peddling were nightly rituals whose remnants were addressed only in the brightness of day (with several squad cars present).

The Montovie Men's Hotel (on the corner of 11th Avenue and Madison Street) and the Drawbridge Christian House (a men's shelter and halfway house on 13th Street and Jefferson Road) held the few men trying to escape the insanity of the streets and stay clean (physically and drug-wise). The only women in the area were the hardcore crack and methamphetamine whores or the very few who followed their men into the nightly shelter of vacant buildings.

One of these coupled men, known on the streets as Chickenhead, was walking in the night drizzle looking for his girlfriend, Mimi Driver. It had been four days since he had last seen her. He was beginning to wonder if she had finally made good on her constant threat to go back to someplace in Texas (he didn't remember where). It wasn't too unusual for her to disappear for a day or two, but in the last seven months, they had gotten closer, and she would let him know if she would "be leavin'" (that's what she would call her tricks) and where he could meet her afterwards. Ten years older than her twenty-eight years of age, he really felt that he needed to look out for her.

Chickenhead had haunted these streets for almost seven years and had no fear of them. Six feet tall and rail thin, his long, dirty red hair stuck out of a taped-up, bill-less black baseball cap. He knew intimately the mindless chaos that lived here and tried to pass on this knowledge to Mimi. She rarely listened. He loved her anyway.

After leaving the Home of the Savior soup kitchen earlier that evening, he walked the street, leaving word with people that he was looking for her. It was almost 3:00 a.m. when he started back to their flop on the second floor of the abandoned Grace Court School on 13th Street. The rain had stopped around 12:30 a.m., and the water and cold had soaked through the three layers of shirts and cheap pants he was wearing. A car passed him. He saw its brake lights brighten twice about a half block ahead and stop just down from a streetlight. Chickenhead stepped into a nearby door and watched.

"Fool," he said aloud. The only people on the streets this time of night you don 't want to meet, he thought.

Wearing a long, dark coat, someone got out of the driver's side, opened the back door, and quickly dumped a large bundle onto the sidewalk. The driver whipped the coat away from his legs, jumped back into the car, and sped off.

Chickenhead knew instantly that it was a body. After the car drove off, he hurried down the block toward the body, staying close to the shadows. A slight drizzle started by the time he reached the body. As he left the shadows for a closer look, he saw that it was wrapped in black plastic garbage bags. The bags were torn where they had scraped the sidewalk, and an acrid, chemical smell stopped him a foot or so from it. And the sight of shoes sticking out of the bottom of the bags. Mimi's shoes. He was on his knees tearing at the plastic and screaming when he cleared the wrapping from her head.

He stared at her for only a moment before he tried to stand, stumbled, then fell onto the ground next to her, whining. Unable to stop himself, he looked at her face again. Above the dull shine of her bloated face, stapled to her forehead, was a twenty-dollar bill...

Chapter 2

Another morning, baby," he said.

Stephen Proctor looked at the framed photo of his wife on the nightstand beside their bed. As usual, he had awakened twenty minutes before the digital alarm clock buzzed. It had been slightly more than a year since the death of his wife, Carol.

He swung his feet to the cold wood floor, then walked through the dark apartment to the kitchen. He turned on the radio on the cabinet near the stove and then pushed the "start" button on the coffee maker. A minute later, just as the coffee started to pour out of the opening, Stephen placed a large mug from the sink under it. The smile on his face didn't reach his sleepy, deep-set eyes. This used to drive Carol up the wall. "Why can't you just wait for the pot to finish?" was her almost daily question. "'Cause that first cup is the best," he'd say, "strong, just like my woman."

After she died, he remembered that morning, days later, when force of habit brought him to his morning ritual. As the coffee poured out, no cup caught it. As the steaming fluid ran onto the hot plate, then onto the countertop and then the floor, Stephen leaned against the refrigerator and bawled.

Absentmindedly, he pulled out his now-full mug and replaced it with the pot. He sipped his coffee as he reminisced. He remembered yanking the unit off the counter, not feeling the boiling liquid splashing him, and hurling it into the wall. The plastic and metal exploded from the force of his throw when it hit the wall. It was months before he replaced the unit, months before he drank coffee in the morning again. When Stephen finally broke down, he replaced the coffee maker with the exact same model that he had destroyed. The morning cup of coffee was now a reminder of something they shared.

At the time of her death, he had been studying for the detective's exam after being a sergeant in the Homicide Division of the Phoenix Police Department. Working and studying kept him going. He could barely remember passing the exam when he took it two months later. His Mom and Dad were there when he received his detective's shield at the department ceremony. Whitney, Carol's mother, was there also. Carol's father, Patrick--wasn't. He blamed Stephen for Carol's death; still does. She was his only daughter, his only child. Hell, Stephen still blamed himself.

The alarm buzzed in the bedroom. Carrying the cup into the bedroom, he set it next to the alarm and pressed the "reset" button on the clock. Turning on the bedside light, then the bathroom light, he removed his boxer shorts and stepped into the shower before turning it on.

Carol had been pregnant. After six years of marriage, he had talked her into having a child. She didn't really want one--he did. She did it for him. The early months of the pregnancy were tough for her, but manageable with the medications and lots of bed rest. Carol was an only child because eclampsia had almost killed her mother while she was carrying her. Whitney's condition scared Patrick so bad that while Whitney and baby were recovering in the hospital after a two-day touch-and-go labor, he got a vasectomy. Whitney and Carol came home three weeks later.

The water in the shower started to run cool. Stephen turned the water off and stepped out. He wiped the mist from the mirror with a dripping hand. Another pet peeve of Carol's--the shower. She'd made him late to work many times with her preference for lovemaking in their cramped bathroom after he'd step out of the shower, dripping wet. She'd take all the towels while he showered and wait. When he stepped out, she'd say, "You have to go through me to get dry, Papa." Tall with skin the color of mahogany and slender with huge, peaceful eyes and dreadlocks--he never stood a chance.

He ran water into the sink, lathered, and began to shave.

When he finished, his heavy sigh warned him that today would be rough. Mornings like this were still tough--after more than a year, the worst time of the day for him. The bad days had finally started to dissipate in the last couple of months. He knew this one wouldn't. He made a mental note to call his shrink after he got to work. Toweling dry as he got to the bedroom, he sipped his coffee as he dressed.

She had refused to stop working up to the day the doctor checked her into the hospital because her hypertension was so severe. Her romantic greeting card company, Gentle Persuasion Cards, was run out of the second bedroom. Even in the later months when she was in so much pain, when her frightening weight gain from fluid retention and her condition kept her bedridden, she still worked. He put a fax and phone line in their bedroom just to keep her off her feet. In the beginning of her sixth month, he got scared and asked her to abort their child; he didn't want to lose her. She cried while laughing, saying after all the shit they had been through, she was going to have this baby just so that she could whip its ass for making her so sick. She died in the hospital while he was testifying in court in Phoenix. It happened at the end of her seventh month. He left as soon as he got the page from the hospital, calling over and over on his cell phone as he drove the twenty-seven-minute ride from the State Capitol to Saint Mary's/Mother of Christ Medical Center in Mesa, Arizona. Despite the bed rest and all the meds, her body had spontaneously aborted their son while she was in her hospital bed. The placenta had ripped away from the uterus, and she and his son bled to death on the operating table nine minutes before he got there and forty-five minutes before her parents arrived, driving up from Tucson for their weekly visit to the hospital.

He pulled his cell phone from the charger on the bedroom dresser and clipped it to his belt. Next he opened the bottom drawer of the nightstand on his side of the bed and pulled out his firearm and shoulder holster. Carrying both in one hand, he finished his now-cold coffee as he reached the kitchen and put the cup in the sink. As he adjusted his holster over his shoulder, he stared at the coffee maker and the half-filled pot it held. He reached over, turned the switch off, but didn't move from the kitchen. Shaking his head, he walked to the front door, grabbing a brown sports jacket off the living room sofa. He locked the door behind him as he again reminded himself to call Amber Bennet, his psychologist, as soon as he got to work.

Today won't be too bad, he thought as he opened his car. Yeah, I'll be cool today. He adjusted the car radio to the Tom Joyner Morning Show, then backed out of the carport.

"I'll do okay," he said out loud this time. And he was doing better...he only had to wipe away the tears once during his forty-minute drive to work...

Chapter 3

The sun was just clearing the skyline when the unit arrived.

"Roger that, dispatch. Car 486 on scene," Training Officer Sergeant Jerome Keller said into the car radio. Switching it off, he turned to his trainee, Matt Woods, a rookie who was experiencing his first day on the job.

"Okay, take a breath, Matt. We're here to keep anybody from fucking up the scene any more than it already is," he said and then added, "We'll leave that to the professionals in the crime lab." He laughed as he exited the car.

Keller's joke fell on deaf ears. Matt looked out the unit at the body on the sidewalk and swallowed hard. He was terrified and failed miserably in trying not to show it. For what seemed like the thousandth time, he wondered what he was thinking when he entered the academy. He took a breath, opened the car door, and walked to the back of the car. Keller had the trunk open and was rummaging through it.

"Okay, Rookie, what's first?"

"Uh, we physically secure the perimeter until the crime lab personnel arrive. Upon securing said area, we do pre-interviews of any individuals that may have useful information to the perceived wrongdoing or action, then triage gathers data in order of importance in a written report to be turned over in my shift report...right?"

Keller closed his eyes and rubbed them with one hand.

"Matt, Jesus, don't quote the textbook verbatim. Try to sneak an original thought in every now and then."

"Uh, right. Okay."

Keller reached in the car trunk and pulled out bright yellow perimeter tape and packing tape.

"Here," he handed both to Matt, "rope off a space of about twenty feet on all sides of the body, and make it about four feet above the ground. And for Christ's sake, RELAX! You're turning fuckin' green."

Keller watched Matt's slumped shoulders as he walked away.

"Fuckin' college-educated idiot! They get dumber every year," he mumbled.

By the time Matt began circling for the second time, another squad car pulled up opposite their car. Matt continued taping everything in sight, oblivious to the two cops leaning against their car, smiling. Keller tried not to notice them. The older of the two approached Keller as they all watched Matt perimeter tape, for the third time, a garbage can.

"So, Pop, how's the kid?" he asked as he slapped Keller on the back. He turned and walked back to his unit, laughing out loud. Keller counted from one to twenty, backward, before he called Matt over. The sound of his name caused Matt to flinch and turn, quickly covering the distance to his training officer. In his haste, he kicked the body as he passed it and almost tripped. He was green as he stood before Keller. His color accentuated the deep red shade of his training officer's face.

"Go-to-the-car-and-wait-for-me."

Matt feebly shook his head and opened his mouth to ask what to do with the tape just as the wind shifted, and he caught the corpse's full aroma. Before he could stop himself, he retched onto the front of Keller's pants. Both officers fell against their unit laughing hysterically as Keller half pulled, half carried his trainee to the car.

*   *   *   *   *

Across the street a small crowd watched as more police units drove up. Chickenhead was in the back of the growing crowd. He was the one who called 911 from a pay phone to tell them about Mimi's body. When the operator asked who he was, he gave her the address nearest the body, then hung up. He wiped the phone and the keypad with his shirttail before walking half a block down from the scene. Standing in a doorway, he watched as the first units arrived. As the crowd gathered, he joined them across the street. An unmarked blue Ford pulled up, and Detectives Stephen Proctor and David Murphy got out. He saw both go under the tape just as someone tapped his arm. He looked down and saw an ashy, dark hand holding a large, steaming cup of coffee.

"Thanks, Jamaica," he said as he took the cup.

The small, bent black man nodded at his friend and took a sip out of an equally sized cup of his own.

"I'm sorry about your woman, Robert. I just heard."

"Not as sorry as the bastard that butchered her is gonna be."

Jamaica nodded his head in agreement. A head shorter and twelve years older than his friend, Jamaica was one of very few people who knew Chickenhead's real name--and could call him by it. They nursed their cups of coffee as the cold morning breeze blew up the street. Jamaica moved closer to him and lowered his high voice before speaking.

"Word is that they found another body in one of the canals in Mesa. Same way...wrapped in black garbage bags. He was black," he sipped his drink. "Found him yesterday."

Chickenhead turned to his friend.

"When did they find him? What time of day?"

"They pulled him out of one of the garbage traps about one o'clock in the afternoon. Some kids saw all the trash piling up and went to look closer. Saw a foot sticking up and called the cops."

"Mimi was dumped about three this morning. It was a big car," Chickenhead took a sip from his cup of coffee, "big enough to hold a couple of bodies."

They watched as a white van pulled up and backed behind the detective's car. The back doors opened from the inside, and two men in navy blue coveralls climbed out. One reached back inside and pulled out a gurney. The words "Medical Examiner" were embroidered in yellow on the back of his uniform.

"Excuse me, sir. I'm Detective Stephen Proctor of the Phoenix Police Department. Did you happen to see anything that might help us?"

Chickenhead turned and looked directly at the detectives. Jeez, this guy is big, he thought.

"Um, no...I just got here. I was walking to the store and saw the crowd."

"Thanks."

Stephen gave him the briefest of glances, nodded, then moved on to the next person in the rapidly thinning crowd. Murphy looked in Proctor's direction, waved to get his attention, then shook his head. Stephen handed a card to the woman he was talking to.

"Call me if you hear anything."

As Proctor and Murphy crossed the street, Chickenhead and Jamaica moved as one toward the woman Stephen had talked to. Just before they reached her, Jamaica grabbed Chickenhead's arm and stopped him.

"Let me talk to her alone."

Chickenhead looked at his friend, then nodded.

Jamaica talked to the woman for several minutes before Chickenhead watched her dig into her pants pocket and hand the card to Jamaica. He talked to her a moment longer before walking back to Chickenhead and handing him the card. Before Chickenhead could speak, Jamaica answered his question.

"I convinced her someone needed the card more than she did."

Chickenhead stared at the card, then shoved it into his pants pocket. He looked across the street in time to see the white Medical Examiner's van leave. The last police unit and the detectives' car followed. He watched them all the way to the end of the block.

"Jamaica. I'll talk to you in a couple of days. I'll...uh, thanks. I'll meet you at the Post Office."

"I'll see what I can find out on this end." He squeezed Chickenhead's arm.

"I'm here for you, bro."

As Jamaica walked toward the State Capitol complex, Chickenhead crossed the street to the now-deserted sidewalk. Next to the gutter were a couple of latex gloves and some loose strips of perimeter tape. He stood on the spot where he had found Mimi's body and stared at the spot on the pavement where her head had rested. The tears welled in his eyes but never fell. About ten minutes passed before a small, thin Hispanic man with a slight limp walked behind him. He stopped a few steps away from Chickenhead and leaned against the garbage can that was still taped in yellow.

"Yo, man. You okay? You need some shit? I got it all. I can tighten you up," he said softly.

Chickenhead didn't move from his spot, didn't turn his head when he answered. "Yeah," his voice cracked, "I need something."

"No problem. Meet me down the street. I'll fix you right up."

The man pushed off his perch, slowly making his way up the street. Chickenhead bent down, touched the cold, wet sidewalk with the palms of his hands, then stood up. He turned and followed the man down the street.

*   *   *   *   *

The caravan of police vehicles made it to the downtown Phoenix City Morgue in record time. As Proctor parked his car, he watched the white van carrying the body back up to the loading dock and stop. When he and his partner exited the car, Proctor saw his boss, Lieutenant Bryan LaPlante, pulling into the back parking lot. Proctor waved at him to get his attention as the commander got out of the vehicle. He nodded to both of the detectives as he walked over.

"Murphy, Proctor," he began, "find out anything at the scene? Anybody talking?" The three men walked over to the loading dock.

"The usual," Murphy commented. "Lot of people looking but no one saw shit."

As the men entered the double doors that led into the chilled facility, Proctor tried to ignore the slow roll of his stomach and the tightening of his throat. This place reminded him of the last time he'd seen Carol's body. Patting first one pocket of his jacket and then the other, he cursed under his breath. He was out of Tums. Again.

Murphy tapped his friend on the shoulder. Proctor turned to

his partner and saw a foil-wrapped stick of gum in Murphy's hand. Thankful, he nodded and took the offering. It was better than nothing.

The men watched in silence as the morgue attendant, dressed in black scrubs and wearing a paper facemask, removed the body from the dark plastic body bag. The attendant weighed the body and put a cardboard toe tag on the big toe of the right foot. He scribbled something on the tag before he wheeled the gurney into the autopsy room. Proctor followed the man through the large shiny metal door that led into the room and saw that a police photographer and a fully gowned medical examiner were already inside.

The attendant pushed the gurney next to a large metal table and locked the wheels of the stretcher by kicking a lever on each wheel with his foot. He and the examiner then, together, pulled the body onto the fixed table. Proctor rubbed his stomach with one hand while he suppressed a burp. His guts felt like they were on fire.

"This is the first time anyone's found a fresh body that this mutt's left," LaPlante explained. "Let's hope we can get something out of it."

Proctor nodded as he stared at the puffed broken face of the dead girl, her half-open eyes sunken in, looking upward toward a ceiling she couldn't see. The medical examiner started to cut away the sheets of black garbage bags that were taped around the body as he talked loud enough for the microphone mounted over the table to pick up his words. The other man reached up to a large, circular halogen light positioned high above the table and turned it on. The man cutting away the plastic halted about two-thirds of the way up the body and stepped back from the table. With a gloved hand, he waved the police photographer over and then pointed to the end of his cut. They all moved closer to the table as the man began cutting again.

"I got something here," he said as the photographer snapped pictures. The examiner gently peeled back the layers of garbage bags. Everyone stared at the large clear plastic baggie lying on the woman's abdomen. After the photographer took several more photos from different angles, the examiner, using a pair of six-inch forceps, carefully lifted the baggie from the body. A crudely drawn picture--it looked like a tracing of a person's hand with a beak and two small eyes on the thumb with two stick feet extending from the bottom of the palm--was sealed inside. The paper was lined notebook filler and wet on the bottom, stained a dull red from a tear in the corner of the plastic. LaPlante took a step closer to get a better look.

"Shit," he muttered, "that's a first."

Holding the foot-square baggie over a large police evidence bag, the examiner placed the baggie into the evidence container as his assistant held it open. The examiner sealed it closed, setting it aside on a tray under the table as he returned to his narration and examination of the body.

"Caucasian female, brunette..." He stopped again. "The 'Y' incision already present..." The examiner looked up at LaPlante. "She's already been cut open and sewed up, Commander."

Waiting for his assistant to get scrapings from under her nails and do finger and palm prints, the examiner gestured for his assistant to help him. Working together, they rolled Mimi onto her side. The assistant held her in that position as the other man scanned the back side of her battered body.

"Very little lividity on the back, buttocks, thighs." They laid her on her back again and, lifting her left arm away from her side, the examiner pointed to the small patch of duct tape he found there. The photographer took pictures of the area before and after the tape was removed. The examiner put her arm back on the table and continued.

"I'm going to try to obtain a blood sample from the sub-clavicle artery."

Taking a large syringe from the work tray next to the body, he made several attempts to draw blood from the area across the top of her chest. All failed to produce the desired fluid.

"Unsuccessful with sub-clavicle extraction. Will attempt blood sample from the iliac artery." Putting the needle down, the examiner massaged Mimi's left leg upward from mid-thigh to the top of her slender leg, hoping to push blood up to the artery in her pelvis. After a minute, he sank the needle into her flesh. On the second attempt he withdrew a small sample. Setting the capped and labeled syringe aside, he moved back to the top of the body. He picked up a large pair of scissors from the work tray.

"I'm now cutting away the thread in the 'Y' incision." He cut through the thread with the scissors and removed the remnants with forceps. "I'm now folding back the opening of the chest cavity."

The two detectives and the commander moved closer to the body as Eric Downly turned his head and opened Mimi's chest like a hinged door. And everyone save for Downly stepped back quickly as the thick formaldehyde fumes caused them all to tear up and gasp for air.

Downly's attendant misted the air above the body with a plastic spray bottle filled with an ammonia solution to help neutralize the fumes and then clicked a switch on the nearby wall. Large air movers hanging over the autopsy area cleared what was left of the fumes.

"Goddamn," Murphy growled, his eyes still tearing, "what the fuck's in there, acid?"

The lieutenant, like his men, coughed, and after the vapors dissipated, edged closer to the table. Downly's talk continued.

"Internal organs, at least for a time, have been preserved in a formaldehyde-type solution." He gingerly probed the flesh and bone mantel within the chest area with the forceps. "Edges of the bones of the breast plate are smooth. They appear to have been cut by a bone saw or like instrument."

Not missing a beat, Downly continued. "I'm now removing the breast plate."

Remembering the noxious fumes from earlier, the detectives and the commander took a quick step backward as the police photographer stayed near the table, snapping pictures. The photographer stopped abruptly and moved the camera away from his face. Proctor watched as both the photographer and Downly stared into the blossomed body cavity. The photographer lowered the camera as he stepped back, pulling at his paper mask with his free hand. He had just gotten the mask off when he vomited into a large stainless steel sink directly behind him. Downly, looking mildly annoyed at the man, placed the plate of flesh on a large tray that his assistant had handed him. With a fluid-drenched gloved hand, he gestured for the three men to step closer.

"Bryan, I think you need to see this. And you probably need to look for another body."

All stepped to within inches of the table's side and looked into the body opening. Murphy covered his mouth before burping loudly and sprinting to the nearest sink, where he too lost his breakfast. Proctor was saved from the humiliation of upchucking only because he hadn't eaten anything that morning. LaPlante, though pale as milk, kept his composure as he stared at the mess of organs--both lungs, heart, and what looked to be the stomach--all having been tossed carelessly into Mimi's chest. And sitting on top of the glistening jumble of insides was a man's severed penis--with the scrotum attached--in a clear, sealed plastic bag...

Chapter 4

It was just before 10 a.m., and he was crashing after four sleepless days and nights of walking, riding buses, and questioning every homeless person he met. He'd been to all parts of Metro Phoenix and back again. Fueled by crack cocaine, the drug Ecstasy, coffee, and anger, Chickenhead was obsessed with finding out everything about the murders that had happened five days ago. This was the second time in the last few days he showed up at the Postal Station for the homeless on Eighth Avenue in Phoenix. With today being December 1st, most of the nine-hundred-plus homeless in the area would be stopping here for their disability or welfare checks or the bi-monthly mailing of food stamps. That flow of people he would not miss.

Standing just outside the door, held open with a cracked 2 x 4, he leaned against the graffiti-covered wall. He shielded his face from the bright morning sun with the small notebook he held.

Chickenhead watched for people coming down the street. The two shirts he wore didn't keep him warm, and he looked terrible. The dark blue of his eyes appeared to float on twin pools of blood, making his dirty, unshaven face look on the verge of screaming. In the last three hours, several people had walked up to the building where he had camped, and most had answered his questions. No one knew anything. He moved off the wall as a large man and a bigger woman approached the station. He was a few feet away from them before he spoke.

"Excuse me, can I talk to you for a minute?"

The man Chickenhead spoke to stopped talking to his companion and looked at him.

"What the fuck do you want, tramp?"

The short fat woman with him covered her slack, toothless mouth and chuckled. Chickenhead stopped about two feet from the couple and held up his empty hand, palm facing down.

"Sir, I don't want money or stuff, okay? I just want to talk to you for a minute, then I'll leave, okay?"

The ugly look of contempt that covered the man's face grew into an evil grin that revealed three missing bottom teeth. He was several inches shorter than Chickenhead but outweighed him by at least sixty pounds--most of it in his huge beer belly.

"Oh, you wanna ask some questions? You must be from the Bum Academy," he laughed. "You must be undercover, huh, boy?"

Chickenhead took one step back.

"I'm sorry I wasted your time, bro."

"Fuck you and get out of my way, shithead."

Chickenhead moved to one side and let him and his smiling partner pass. As they disappeared into the station, he was already talking to another man who had just walked up to the station.

Chickenhead had forgotten about the fat man and was talking to two men near the door when the fat man and his partner exited the station ten minutes later.

"Well, if it ain't Mister Reporter," he shouted. "Don't tell him a damn thing, boys. He's working with the cops on Bum Patrol."

The two men Chickenhead was talking to started to back away from him. Chickenhead turned to face him.

"That's right, boys. His cover's blown. You've been talking to an undercover asshole."

Both he and his woman laughed.

"Bro, I don't want any trouble."

"Didn't I tell you to get the fuck out of my way?"

The big man covered the short space between them in one step, swinging at Chickenhead but hitting only air. He turned to his right looking for the bum when he was hit from below by a kneeling

Chickenhead. The force of the bum's open-handed blow to the fat man's ample stomach lifted him a good seven inches off the pavement and slammed him into the building. With one hand on his stomach and the other trying to steady himself against the building, the fat man moaned loudly as his bladder released down his leg. He made a feeble grab at Chickenhead as the bum sprinted past him. He had just pushed himself off the wall in time to see Chickenhead running back, clutching a length of wood that had held the door open. The fat man turned, trying to hobble away, just as Chickenhead's swing connected with his elbow. The crack of breaking bone could be heard ten feet away. The fat man's scream was cut short by another blow across his head. As he fell unconscious to the pavement, the woman screamed. One quick look from Chickenhead, bloody board in hand, silenced her. Dropping the wood, he crossed to the front of the man, backed away a step, then kicked him in the face hard enough to splatter blood and mucous on the bottom of Chickenhead's filthy jeans. Breathing hard and sweating in the morning cold, Chickenhead walked to the woman. She was shaking and a dark, wet stain was spreading down the front of her soiled dress. He shook his finger in her face, and she flinched as if struck.

"If I hear from anybody-cop-anybody," he pointed at the fallen man, "you get the same, understand?"

The stain on her dress, steaming in the morning cold, got bigger.

Before Chickenhead picked up his pen and notebook, he went through the man's pockets. He took the three tiny vials of crack cocaine and about eighty dollars and some change. The two men who had left earlier were now walking toward him. When they spotted the scene behind Chickenhead, they bolted back up the street. It took Chickenhead almost twenty minutes, using back streets and alleys, to get to his flop on the second floor of the abandoned Grace Court School. Moving aside the canvas covering a second-floor window, he had a clear view of the scene he had just left. In the time it took Chickenhead to get home, a police unit had pulled up. He watched the officer get out of the car and walk to the fat man, who was now sitting up. While he watched, a second unit pulled up and blocked his view of the man he'd beaten. Chickenhead scanned the street. Other than the cops and the fat man, the street was deserted.

Backing away from the window, he removed his blood-spotted pants and shoes. He opened a cabinet, pulled out an equally dirty pair of shiny gray dress pants, and put them on. He replaced the shoes with a torn pair of faded black high-top sneakers. Grabbing his bedroll, some shirts, and a gallon of bottled water, he put everything at the top of the stairwell outside the classroom. He re-entered the room he and Mimi had called home and took a yellowed-with-age plastic bucket from one of the lower cabinets. They had used this as their nighttime toilet. Dumping the contents in the hall, he opened a half-full bottle of bleach from the same cupboard and poured the entire contents into the bucket. He rolled the jeans into a tight tube and placed them in the bleach bucket. Then the shoes. He swirled the bucket for a minute, then put it back in the cupboard. He threw the empty bleach bottle down the hall as he headed down the stairs. Chickenhead exited from the back side of the building and quickly walked across to the bus stop at 13th Street and Van Buren. He was counting out the fare when the bus arrived twenty minutes later. Boarding the almost full bus, he made his way to the last few vacant seats in the rear of the bus. His crazed look and his smell (he had walked through the contents of his toilet) helped to clear several rows near him. Sitting near an open window, he read from his notebook during the twenty-minute ride. Two streets down from his stop, he buzzed the driver and got off the bus.

Crossing Van Buren, Chickenhead stopped outside All Star Military Surplus, took off his shoes, and leaned them against the wall of the building before entering. It took him ten minutes to find and pay for his goods. He grabbed his sneakers and put them inside two plastic bags, then put on the two-dollar flip-flops he bought in the store and walked the two blocks to the Sunny Day Motel. After checking into the motel and paying forty dollars for a room with a kitchenette for the next two days, he threw his stuff in the room and walked to the corner store. Ten minutes later he was locking his door as he balanced two bags of groceries in his arms. By the time he put everything away, he was swaying as he walked through the small room. The fight and the four-day drug binge had caught up with him. Holding on to furniture, he made it to the bathroom with the bag that held his soiled shoes. He put a small bar of hotel soap in the sink, ran hot water in it, and dropped in both sneakers. After undressing in the bathroom, he returned to the kitchen to open a beer. He gulped it down before he stepped into the shower, where he turned the water on full blast and stayed in until it ran cold. Drying off with a small hotel towel, he took the only chair in the room and angled it under the doorknob. He lay on the bed with notebook in hand and quickly fell into a hard, dreamless sleep for the next twelve hours...

*   *   *   *   *

Reading his notes while sipping a beer, he figured there had been, counting Mimi, at least five murders of homeless people in the past nineteen months. He tried to ignore the all-over ache of his body and frowned at the notes he'd taken over the last week. From the hordes of people he had talked to, he pieced together that all of them--four women and one man--had been prostitutes. All except the floater in Mesa were white and had been found by street people. No one, save for him, had seen any of the bodies being dumped. All of the bodies had a twenty-dollar bill stapled to the forehead. One old man with whom he had spent the better part of a day in Mesa (along with a twelve-pack of beer and four 99-cent Big Macs) gave him the most useful information of all. The old man ("just call me Buddy," which he kept saying to Chickenhead about every thirty minutes) had found one of the bodies after midnight a year ago by the Interstate 17 underpass at 7th Avenue. He thought he had found a bundle of clothing until he shined a small flashlight on it. That's when he saw the money sticking out of the top of the black plastic.

Buddy had dragged the body into the bushes near the highway and had cut the remaining plastic to see if there might be any more money. That's how he found the picture he had given to Chickenhead.

It was still enclosed in the large plastic baggie Buddy had found it in and was stained with what looked like blood.

Chickenhead got up and crossed the room to the wall-mounted phone. He dialed Jamaica's voice mail number but got only a buzz on the line. Puzzled, he looked at the phone. That's when he saw the small placard on the wall. It read:

All phone calls MUST go through the operator. No long distance outgoing calls are allowed. Dial #923 to reach the operator. A one-dollar per call charge will be added to your credit card. If you are paying in cash, please see the front desk for instructions. Have a great stay! -- Sunny Day Motel Group

"Fuck."

He put on his pants, a shirt, and his flip-flops, grabbed his room key, and ran to the office. He had to hit the little bell twice before a chubby, balding man appeared from a back room. The man was holding a plastic fork and chewed as he spoke.

"You need to check in, buddy?"

"No. I'm in Room 105. I need to make some phone calls."

"Got a credit card?"

"No."

"Ten-dollar deposit. Cash."

Chickenhead handed him his last twenty-dollar bill and waited for his change. Seeing the morning paper on a chair in the small lobby, he took it on his way out.

Back in his room, he dialed the operator, got an outside line, then dialed Jamaica's voice mail. He left a message with his address, room number, and directions how to get there. Hanging up the phone, he sat back at the table and picked up the baggie, staring at the stained picture inside. He was reading his notes when the phone rang.

"Jamaica?"

"Yeah, man. Where the hell you been?"

"I stayed in Mesa for a couple of days. What did you find out?"

"You need to stay away from here for a few days. Someone got the shit kicked out of 'em, and a couple of his buddies lookin' for some payback."

Chickenhead snorted. "Thanks for the tip. What did you find out?"

"Three or four people got killed here over the last year, then that guy in Mesa. All hoes. All cut open, then sewed back up."

Chickenhead frowned. The cut and sewed part was news to him.

"Cut up like a knife fight or stabbed?"

"Nah, man, cut open from neck to pussy, then sewed back up."

Chickenhead leaned against the wall, dizzy. He had never checked Mimi's body. He couldn't. He just screamed and stared at her face. Then he had called the police.

"You still there, Robert?"

"Can you make it here tonight, Jamaica?"

"Yeah, I think so. Wait a minute. Let me check." He heard him talking to someone about a ride. Then he came back on the line.

"It's gonna be a couple of hours, but I'll make it.

"I'll be up. Later." He hung up the phone.

Chickenhead stood against the wall, still weak from the news Jamaica had given him. Something else...something Buddy had said to him tried to surface. He opened the tiny refrigerator and reached for a beer, then stopped and closed the door. Going to the cupboard above the sink, he pulled out one of the two paper-wrapped cups and tore off the covering. He filled it with water from the sink and drank down three glasses before he felt a bit steadier. Chickenhead sat down at the table and looked through his notebook until he found the page he was looking for. Buddy said he had spent a week locked up at Madison Street Jail right after he found the body. He had overheard a couple of the cops talking to a guard about a body that had been found. They didn't know or didn't care that Buddy was listening. The body was the second that the cops had found near the highway in the last month. One cop laughed and said that whoever was doing in bums was doing everyone else a favor by scaring the rest of 'em to Tucson. He said the way they had been found all cut up made him think of a Thanksgiving turkey. Buddy told him that after the cops left, he had written down the line the cop had told the others.

"Maybe we should just call this nut 'Turkeystuffer.'"

Chapter 5

Barely able to contain his anger, Chickenhead sat in the cold interrogation room and looked at the wall-mounted camera for what seemed like the millionth time. After waiting there for the last hour and a half, his patience was gone, and his ass was hurting from sitting on the unpadded metal chair. This wasn't the first time he had been in one of these rooms, but it was the first time he had come of his own free will. He had cleaned up as much as he could before coming here. His long red hair was washed and pulled back, the ponytail held in place with two rubber bands. His shirt and pants were a two-part tan work uniform he had lifted out of an unattended clothes dryer two days ago at the Quarter Plus Laundromat on 15th Avenue. His socks and underwear came from the same dryer. The brand-new hiking boots he had on were the reward of the last three days of day labor he had just finished yesterday.

He badly wanted a cigarette or gum or anything to calm him down a bit. Chickenhead got up and started to pace under the eye of the wall-mounted camera. He stopped and leaned against the back wall, closing his eyes. He could still see Mimi's dead, bloated face colored a sick black and yellow under the streetlight where he had found her. Saw the twenty-dollar bill--the same twenty-dollar bill he had in his pocket--stapled to her forehead.

He opened his eyes and stood away from the wall. This isn't helping Mimi, he thought.

As he was walking to the door it opened, and a stocky, uniformed officer walked in. He was holding several folders under his arm and a cardboard cup of coffee in his free hand. The faraway look on the cop's face as he entered the room let Chickenhead know this wasn't the person he needed to talk to. The cop looked around for somewhere to set down his stuff when Chickenhead spoke to him.

"Uh, officer, is Mr. Proctor here?"

The cop sipped his coffee before answering. "Hello, sir. I'm Sergeant Makes. Sorry to keep you waiting, but it's been a zoo. What can I help you with?"

The officer stood just inside the open door, leaning on a padlocked, battered gray file cabinet. He set the cup of coffee on top of it and opened one of the folders.

"You said to the officer who interviewed you that you had some information. What is it?" The cop glanced at Chickenhead, then back at his papers. He pointed to the chair. "Why don't you have a seat, if you have something to say."

Chickenhead stared at the chair, then pulled it out and sat.

"Good boy," the cop said. "Now what ya got for me?"

"Sir, I asked to speak to Sergeant Proctor. I was told he was here tonight. I would like to speak to him, if that's possible."

"Detective Proctor is out on a call," he lied, "so you'll just have to trust me with this information. I'll make sure he gets a full report, though." Sergeant Makes pulled a pen out of his breast pocket and started writing on one of the folders.

"Like I said, buddy, we're busy tonight, so if ya got something ta say, let's hear it, okay?"

Chickenhead could feel the rage flowing through his body in waves. *If I go off on this fat fuck, I'll never help Mimi,* he thought. *That piece of shit has to pay.* Thinking of her helped him stay focused. He coughed to try to loosen the tightness that threatened to close his throat.

"I've seen him," Chickenhead said simply.

"Seen who?" Makes asked disinterested. He continued to scribble on his report.

"The guy who's killin' all those people. The whores and street people. Turkeystuffer."

Sergeant Makes stopped writing in his report and looked up at Chickenhead. He quickly closed his folder and pushed it next to his coffee.

"How do you know that name? Who told you?"

Got your attention on that one, you fat bastard, he thought. A slight grin crossed his face and was gone. He ignored the cop's question.

"I saw him dump a body and know of a couple more. You motherfuckers ain't been lookin' for him 'cause he's just been killin' us bums. Not 'til now. Now y'all want him. I've seen him."

Makes' face reddened, but his voice stayed even.

"I asked you a question. How do you know that name?"

"You don't believe me? I'll show you. Give me a piece of paper and a pencil...and a cigarette."

Makes looked at him for a moment, then pulled a small key ring off of his belt. He unlocked and then opened the file cabinet, pulled out a legal pad from the drawer, then closed and relocked it. Taking another pen out of his shirt pocket, he crossed the room and threw both on the table. He pointed to the "No Smoking" sign on the wall beside the table where Chickenhead sat.

"Stop wasting my time. If you got something, show me or get to steppin'."

Chickenhead reached for the pen and pad, pulling both closer to him. He turned the pad sideways, placed his hand on the middle of the paper, and carefully started to trace the outline of his fingers. He heard Makes inhale sharply, but he didn't look up until he'd finished the drawing. Chickenhead was frowning while he added a beak and one eye to the thumb, then completed the picture by closing the bottom portion and adding two stick feet. When he looked up from his work, his frown was replaced by a smirk. The cop's face was the color of paste under the overhead fluorescent lights, and his mouth was hanging open. Chickenhead pushed the drawing across the table to Makes, suppressing a giggle when Makes flinched backward.

"When you find the bodies, you find a drawing like this one, only it's in a large plastic baggie, and the baggie is stapled to the body."

Makes grabbed the tablet off the table. He looked at Chickenhead, then the drawing, then back at Chickenhead as he backed out the door.

"Stay here. Don't move. I'll be right back." Makes grabbed his folders and closed the door behind him. Chickenhead heard the door latch and grunted out loud.

Yeah, y'all real interested now, he thought.

He had just finished the last of Makes' coffee when Makes, followed by Detective Proctor, entered the room. Makes was carrying a folding chair that he slid under the table opposite Chickenhead. Proctor was carrying a small tape recorder that he placed on the table between himself and Chickenhead. Proctor pushed the "Record" button after he settled into his seat. Behind him, Makes had stationed himself by the now-closed door.

"Sergeant Makes said you were asking for me, Mister...I'm sorry, I didn't get your name."

"Everybody call me Chickenhead."

"Mister...Chickenhead, how did you come upon the information you relayed to Sergeant Makes?"

He looked at Proctor, then Makes, and the anger came back. Fuck this, he thought, if y'all want something, it's time I got something.

"I...I would like a cup of coffee, if you have any made, please."

The look of bewilderment on Proctor's face was immediate and followed just as quickly with another...disdain. His next words came through tightly pursed lips.

"Sir, this is not a convenience store, if..."

"No, it's not," Chickenhead interrupted. "It's 'pose ta be a police station, and I came here ta help. Know what I got? I got ta sit here in this cold ass room on this hard ass chair for two goddamn hours while y'all ignored the fuck out of me. Then you send in this asshole," he pointed at Makes, "who won't even look at me but expects me ta spill my guts when he won't even ask me my name."

"Sir, I'm sorry, but..."

Chickenhead pushed his chair away from the table but stayed seated. Both cops' eyes followed him.

"Y'all wanna know how I know this stuff? One of the people butchered was my girlfriend Mimi. I saw her dumped out of the back of a fuckin' car like a sack of shit. You want some information from me? Treat me like a goddamn man."

Chickenhead was holding onto the edge of the table, glaring at Makes and shaking. He looked at Proctor, then looked away. Mimi, he thought, help me...

Proctor cleared his throat before he spoke.

"I'm...sorry." Suddenly, Proctor smelled the perfume Carol had always worn. Just as quickly, the scent was gone.

"I'm truly sorry." The emotion in Proctor's voice erased most of the anger Chickenhead felt and brought his full attention to Proctor. Proctor reached across the table to the recorder and switched it off.

"Man, I'm sorry for your loss."

Chickenhead looked at Proctor for a moment, then nodded. The detective turned to Sergeant Makes.

"Jim, could you get us both a cup of coffee, please? And give us a couple of minutes alone."

After Makes left the room, the silence was awkward for both men. After a minute Chickenhead spoke.

"Thank you."

"You're welcome."

"I...I want to help catch this bastard. She didn't...no one deserves to die like that."

"And we want your help. Do you smoke?"

"I'm dying for one."

Proctor pulled a half-gone pack of cigarettes from his shirt pocket, took one out, then handed the pack to Chickenhead. He fished a plastic lighter out of his pants pocket and lit both cigarettes. They smoked in silence until Sergeant Makes returned.

Makes set both Styrofoam cups of coffee on the table with several small packs of sugar, then returned to the file cabinet and closed the door. Chickenhead added several bags of sugar, stirring the coffee with the pen Makes had given him. He sipped his coffee as Proctor spoke to him.

"Chickenhead...do you mind if I ask you your real name?" Chickenhead sipped his coffee again before he answered Proctor's question.

"My name is Robert."

"Thanks," Proctor said as he extended his hand across the table. "Mine is Stephen. I'm glad you're here."

Visibly surprised, Robert wiped his hand on his pant leg before shaking Proctor's outstretched hand.

"Okay," Proctor said, "do you mind?" He pointed at the recorder. "What you have to say may help us in this investigation. We...I want to make sure we get it all."

Robert nodded.

Proctor leaned closer, then switched on the recorder.

Chapter 6

It was the last of six operations of the day, all hip and knee replacements, with an unscheduled bi-polar hip replacement. His double-gloved, tightly bandaged right hand was singing in pain. His patient was a big woman, well over two-hundred pounds and long-limbed. Her heavy weight added density to her already thick bones. With his sprained hand throbbing, his agony was apparent by the profuse sweat his surgical nurse kept blotting from his brow.

"Doctor Howard, are you all right?"

"I'm fine. Thank you."

Finally clearing the femoral shaft of cancerous bone, he inserted various size trials to measure the size of the opening. He settled on a number three femoral stem to insert into the cavity and prepared bone cement to seal the stem in place. After adding the adhesive to the bone, he picked up the two-pound stainless steel mallet to pound the stem into place. Two blows later, he stopped and stepped away from the operating table. He wiped his brow before speaking to the observing resident.

"Doctor Thompson, I want you to finish this and close up."

"I'd be glad to, Doctor."

Talking the resident through the rest of the procedure and closing routine, the doctor watched as the patient was wheeled into post-op recovery thirty minutes later. After thanking the resident and his crew, Dr. Braxton Howard quickly left the operating room and bee-lined to the doctors' locker room. He removed his drenched cap and mask with his uninjured left hand and dropped both garments to the floor. Slowly, he removed the gloves from his slightly swollen right hand. He winced as he unwrapped the Ace bandage from his hand, and the released pressure brought fresh pain. It had been a week since he had killed and gutted Mimi and the bum in Mesa, and the swelling was just going down. He looked up when he heard the door to the locker room squeak open. He slowly flexed the hand.

"Hey, Howie, you in here?"

"In the back, near the water fountain."

Tony Norwood, his regular anesthesiologist, came around the corner dressed in faded blue jeans and a black polo shirt. He was still combing his damp hair.

"Hey, buddy, you looked a little rough in there today. How's the hand?"

"I'll survive. That last bi-polar kicked my ass."

"You taking anything for that?" he asked as he pointed to the hand.

"Nothing that you'd want to know about."

Dr. Norwood smiled, then chuckled.

"Ooookay...you better get your crippled ass in the shower pronto if we're gonna make the Suns game. These tickets are burning a hole in my pocket, and I will leave your busted-hand self here if you don't get a move-on."

A smile broke the frown on Howard's face as he looked at his friend.

"Shit, you'd do that anyway if you thought I'd let you get away with it."

"How true, how true." He looked at Braxton's slightly swollen hand.

"I take my hat off to you. No way I'd be banging bones all day in your condition."

"No pain, no gain," he laughed, "and definitely no plane."

"When do you pick it up?"

"December 19th, an early Christmas present to me."

"You da man." Tony turned and started walking to the front of the locker room. He stopped at the corner and turned to Howard.

"You got thirty minutes to get your shit together or get left. You're buying dinner. I'll be in the cafeteria."

Tony disappeared around the corner. Howard heard the locker room door squeak open, then close. Turning to his locker, he opened it and took out a small bottle of 50 mg Demerol tablets. He popped two of the industrial-strength narcotics into his mouth and dry swallowed them, then quickly undressed and stepped into the shower room. Fifteen minutes later, he was combing his still wet blonde hair as he walked through the hallway to a bank of elevators. He boarded one, pushing the button for the second floor. He had just walked into the cafeteria as Tony was walking out.

"Hey, glad I didn't have to come back to the dungeon to drag you out."

"Would have been a short struggle."

Tony pressed the button for the elevator.

"Struggle? Boy, I could take your tall, skinny, surfer-lookin' ass out and still have time for lunch."

The laugh from Howard was loud and genuine. By the time they reached the underground parking lot, the narcotics had kicked in, and Howard was feeling no pain. Tony pointed to his car, a sparkling ebony Porsche 911.

"I'll drive. Your high ass is liable to get somebody killed."

Pulling out of the hospital parking garage into the light early evening traffic, Tony floored it to the downtown arena. Two blocks from America West Arena, they hit a wall of traffic that slowed them to a crawl. After sitting in traffic for ten minutes, Tony saw an opening in the traffic and gunned the car into it. He drove back two blocks and parked the car on a side street almost four blocks from the arena. Jogging past the walking crowd, Tony was out of breath by the time he handed their tickets to the attendant. When he looked over to Braxton, he realized the doctor wasn't even winded. Tony snorted.

"Great! An in-shape dope fiend."

Braxton smiled and shrugged as they entered the building. They made it to their third-row, center-court seats just as the announcer began introducing the Suns starting line-up.

*   *   *   *   *

The game was a wash, with the Suns losing to the Lakers 85-102. All through dinner afterward, Braxton smiled at his friend's idle threats of canceling his season tickets.

"You want to hit Majerle's for a minute?" Tony asked as they drove into downtown Phoenix.

"Not tonight. I'm gonna call it a night and soak my hand before it falls off."

"Suit yourself, wussy-boy. You gonna be cool for work on Thursday?"

"Yeah. I scheduled two knees. One is a total, but that's the only banger. The rest of the day is paperwork."

They talked shop until Tony pulled into the almost empty doctors' lot and stopped next to Braxton's Mercedes SLK Roadster. Braxton was opening his car when Tony honked his horn to get his attention. He leaned across the passenger seat and talked through the open window.

"You need to heal up quick. I'm missing the spending money I get from kickin' your ass on the golf course."

Braxton smiled and gave him the finger with his good hand as Tony sped out of the lot. Laughing out loud at his friend, he started his forty-minute ride to his Scottsdale condominium. As he turned onto the interstate highway, he popped two more Demerol tablets. Opening the windows on both sides of the car from his door control, he enjoyed the crisp night air as he drove home.

*   *   *   *   *

Standing bare-chested and in his stocking feet next to a large stainless steel bowl filled with crushed ice and water, Braxton slowly turned the pages of a catalog for his new plane. He was taking delivery of a Cessna 3401 Series One in about two weeks. He alternated between turning pages and sipping from a can of beer with his good hand as he slowly turned the glossy pages he had almost memorized. With a range of 1307 nautical miles without refueling and a cruising speed of 270 miles per hour with a 1/2-ton payload, he could be almost anywhere in the country in hours. He was eager to try out his new toy and excited about the new horizons the mobility would open up to him. He had only killed once out of state, in Dallas, while on vacation there almost three years ago.

That entire episode had been a nightmare. He was unfamiliar with the area and got lost looking for a place to dump the body. Not fifteen minutes after getting rid of it, he made a wrong turn down a one-way street and was pulled over. The cop had been parked in an alley just before the one-way sign Braxton hadn't seen. With his bloodied clothes and tools wrapped in plastic and stuffed in the spare tire well of the rental's trunk, he explained to the officer that he was a doctor from out of town visiting friends. After running his plates and checking his ID, the cop talked for another ten minutes about his daughter's nursing career. He didn't give him a ticket. Apologizing for keeping him so long, the officer gave him directions out of the area and wished him a good night.

As soon as the cop drove off, Braxton started trembling uncontrollably. In the thirty minutes it took him to drive to his hotel, hives the size of quarters covered his arms and back. Too shaken to risk discarding his bloodied clothes and tools, he kept them in his room. It was a long, sleepless night. All of this could have been avoided if he had had more time to examine the area. The plane would solve that problem. A pilot since his teens and certified on fanjets for more than a year, Braxton knew this plane would free him to travel the country on a whim. To scout out areas. To kill more.

He pulled his soaked hand out of the basin and flexed it slowly several times. Between the drugs and the cold water, there was no longer any pain. Deciding to play it safe, he would let his resident do any procedures he had scheduled for Thursday. This was the first time, in all of his killings--nineteen in the last five years--that he had beat anyone to the point of hurting himself. Mimi was a total waste of energy with all her sobbing and begging. He had expected a bit more guts from her.

He dumped the water-filled bowl into one of the twin stainless steel sinks in the professionally equipped kitchen he rarely used. He set the bowl on a drying rack near the sinks and got another beer out of the SubZero refrigerator. He turned off the kitchen lights on his way into the living room. Using two remote controls, he switched on the overhead track lighting and the television, tuning the wall-sized TV to CNN. He lowered the sound to slightly more than a murmur. Pulling a plastic exercise mat from behind a huge chocolate-colored leather sofa, he set the mat down near the TV. He stripped down to his boxer shorts and placed his beer on the floor next to the mat. Settling onto the mat, he took a long swallow of beer, then started the first of five sets of one-hundred sit-ups...

Chapter 7

The three men sat at a table in the center of Lt. Bryan LaPlante's office combing through copies of Chickenhead's notebook.

"Christ, this guy is thorough. I wouldn't want him on my ass," Murphy mumbled as he leafed through the Xeroxed copies of notes. Proctor nodded while reading along with his set.

"Look here," Murphy pointed. "He says he talked to the buddy of the floater they found in Mesa last week. Shit, I was on the horn with Mesa PD this morning, and they still didn't know who the hell the guy was. And here he's got both of their names."

"Make sure you get a copy of these notes to Mesa PD this afternoon," Bryan ordered and turned to Proctor. "What do you think of this guy? Is he legit? A flake?"

Proctor put his notes down and thought for a moment before he answered his boss.

"I think he's pissed and wants revenge. This was his woman who was filleted, and he's taking it personal."

"You think he did it?"

"Nah, no way. My gut says no. He's working way too hard to find this fucker. We're checking his alibi; I don't think we'll find anything. He gave us his place in Phoenix so we'd know where to reach him. And he hates cops and ain't afraid to show it. Lit into both of us in the room."

"I heard." Bryan looked at Proctor for a moment, then turned to Murphy. "Dave, why don't you fax these to Mesa PD. I need to talk to Stephen for a minute."

"On my way." Murphy closed the door on his way out.

"I saw the surveillance tape of the interview with this guy." He pointed at Chickenhead's notes on the table. "Everything okay with you? On this case, I mean? Anything you want to talk about?"

"There's nothing to talk about, Bryan. He kind of caught me off guard with his reaction. He really loves her, and it showed. Reminded me of Carol for a minute."

"All the more reason for me to ask if you're okay."

"Bryan, I'm fine. Really."

Bryan looked at Stephen, then to the notes spread out on the table in front of him.

"Have you been able to get in touch with the next of kin yet?"

"Not yet. We got a phone number from an old booking file of hers for someplace in Houston, Texas. Called a couple of times and kept getting an answering machine. I faxed a copy of what we had to Houston PD this morning. We didn't have the notebook copied then. I'll call them again this afternoon."

They were interrupted by a knock on the office door.

"Come in."

Murphy came into the room carrying several file folders. He handed one to Bryan and another to Stephen.

"Well, our boy is who he says he is." He looked at a sheet of paper clipped to the top folder in his hand.

"Robert Stanley Gibbs, a/k/a Chickenhead. Our file goes back about--," he shuffled a couple of pages,"--five or six years. History of petty shit, vagrancy, trespassing. Did thirty days at Madison in '97 for simple assault. Beat up ah couple of guys he said were stealing from his flop. Listed his address as a general delivery box."

Murphy picked up Chickenhead's notes that were lying on the table and turned several pages before he found what he wanted.

"Same as the one he gave us. Last arrest was the Madison incident. No outstanding warrants. Listed day laborer as his occupation."

Bryan held up his hand to stop Murphy's report. He scanned

several pages in his folder before he spoke.

"Has the coroner come up with anything else on either of the bodies?"

Murphy opened the last folder in his pile.

"There's not much back yet. The tissue samples aren't back yet, but it's pretty obvious the organs were switched between bodies. Ya don't find two-month-old fetuses in most guys. No liftable prints on the floater. There's tons of shit to go through from the garbage he was floating in. Found a picture like Robert drew dry as a bone in a plastic baggie. The lab is still checking to see if anything useful comes out of it. Found a couple of prints on Mimi around her head where Chickenhead tore away the plastic. The rain lasted most of the night and washed away just about anything on the surface. The lab is still checking the plastic she was wrapped in for whatever might have survived. The last thing is that the coroner is pretty sure they both died within a day or two of each other. And the floater had a twenty-dollar bill stapled to his forehead."

Bryan looked at Stephen.

"Did Chickenhead mention anything to you about money on Mimi? Maybe after the interview?"

"Not a word."

Bryan looked through the now huge stack of papers in front of him.

"It says that the hole for the staple was there, but no money. The lab found pieces of plastic in the gutter along the street. It's probably a waste of time, but check out any storm drains near where Mimi was found. Talk to Chickenhead again. Gently. See if he remembers anything else."

Bryan grabbed a pen from under the sea of papers in front of him.

"I'm going to be out of town tomorrow, but if anything, and I mean anything comes up," he wrote down a number, "call me at this number. The operator will patch you through."

"I'll take care of it, Bryan."

There were a stack of telephone memos and several file folders on Stephen's desk when he got back from his boss' office. He tried to clear a spot for the papers he carried and made the mess bigger. He picked up the memos as his partner peeked into his cubicle.

"I'm hittin' the deli. You want somethin'?"

"A sandwich. Anything with pickles."

Stephen slumped down into his chair. He knew that the odds were in his favor that Chickenhead had removed the money from Mimi's head. Knew it without being told.

"I'm outta here."

"Get me a soda, too."

He picked up the phone and dialed the hotel where Chickenhead was staying. The operator connected him to the room. After the twentieth ring he hung up, then re-dialed the hotel. He left a message with the desk for Chickenhead to call him when he got in. He was sorting through phone memos when his desk phone rang.

"Detective Proctor, how can I help you?"

The connection was so bad he could barely hear the caller.

"Is this Detective Stephen Proctor of the Phoenix Police Department?"

"Yes, it is. To whom am I speaking?"

"Hold one moment, sir."

Hold? Stephen shifted the phone to the other ear after the line clicked over to taped music. He looked at one of his memos. It was marked urgent. Circled was an out of state number. He checked it against Mimi's number from the file. It was the same area code but a different number. Someone came back on the line.

"Detective Proctor, are you still there?"

"Who is this?"

"I'm sorry about the delay, Officer. The Mayor can speak to you now."

After a brief pause, the line was picked up.

"Mr. Proctor? Detective Proctor? Are you there?"

"Yes, I am. Who is this?"

"I'm Peter Driver. Mimi's my daughter."

Chapter 8

Thanks a lot, Robert. See you next week."

Chickenhead nodded at the lab tech as he took the thirty-dollar check she handed him for his plasma donation. He put it in his pants pocket, pulled on his denim jacket, and walked out into the early evening cold. Walking the three blocks from the plasma center to Kim's Liquor and Check Cashing, he stopped twice to watch the cars drive toward the entrance of Interstate 10.

That motherfucker's still out there, he thought, still alive. Talking to the cops was a waste of time.

Since his talk with the cops a week earlier, it seemed like his anger wouldn't leave him. He hadn't heard from either detective since he let them copy his notebook earlier in the week. If they wanted his help, why hadn't they contacted him? He knew that this case was probably sitting on someone's desk gathering dust, 'cause the only people dead were a couple of bums. No big deal. And for a minute he had almost believed that cop Proctor. Believed that shit about wanting to help. I want to make sure we get it "right," he had said when he turned on that damn recorder. That fuckin' tape is sitting in someone's desk, he thought. Some rich bitch loses her goddamn poodle, and there would be a ton of cops looking for it. Couple of bums get gutted, that's no big deal. Just another tramp off the street.

Fuck 'em. Fuck 'em all.

He pushed open the door to the liquor store and headed

straight to the display for bargain vodka. Picking up a bottle, he opened the chiller and grabbed a twenty-four pack of cheap beer. He set both on the counter, took the check out of his pocket, signed it with a pen from the counter, then slid it to the clerk, who never looked up from his football magazine.

"Got any ID?"

"My license."

"Let's see it."

Pulling out a tattered wallet, Chickenhead set his driver's license on the counter. It had expired four years earlier. The clerk looked at it, wrote down the state ID number, then pushed the card back to him. As the clerk counted out his change, Chickenhead asked for a small bag. He was out the door a moment later.

While walking to the bus stop, Chickenhead opened the case of beer, put one in the bag, and waited for the bus. Two beers later, he was on the bus going to the motel. Sitting in the back of the almost empty vehicle, the driver paid no attention to Chickenhead as he drank straight from the vodka bottle. In the twenty minutes it took him to get home, he drank half of the bottle. As he entered his room, he patted his pockets and cursed. He'd forgotten to buy any cigarettes. Leaving the beer and booze in his room, he walked to the lounge off of the motel lobby.

"Pack of Old Gold Menthols and some matches."

He lit a cigarette on the way back and stopped in the lobby.

"Anything for Number 105?"

He was handed three pieces of paper. He read his messages on his way back to the room. The first two were from Jamaica. "Call me," was all they said. The last was from Detective Proctor.

"I would like to go over a few things with you. Call me as soon as you get this, no matter what time."

Chickenhead looked at the number written on the bottom of the message. After reading it a second time, he tossed it on the kitchen counter and picked up the bottle of vodka. He took two long swigs from it, carried it to the phone, called the operator for an outside line, then dialed Proctor's number. It rang nine times before the line picked up.

"Hello, you've reached the voice mail of Detective..."

Chickenhead slammed down the phone.

Fuck talking to a machine, he thought, I want to talk to you.

Draining what was left of the bottle, he dropped the plastic container to the floor. He opened another can of beer and emptied it before he threw it next to the bottle. He did the same with two more cans of beer before he tried to call the number again. Sitting on the kitchen counter, Chickenhead picked up the memo from Proctor and dialed the operator. He had to dial the three-digit number three times to get it right.

"Sunny Day's operator."

"I need to make a call."

"Your room number, please."

"105."

The line went quiet for a moment while the operator looked up his account.

"Sir, you have no credit left on your account. You'll have to go to the front desk to renew it."

"Look, I'll do that later. Just let me call now."

"That's not our policy, sir. Please see the desk." The line went dead.

Chickenhead listened to the soft hiss of the phone line for several seconds before he let the phone slip from his hand. It bounced off the counter and fell into the trashcan next to him. He had to cover his mouth with both hands to stifle the half-sob, half-laugh that came out.

"Just like my life, in the fuckin' garbage."

Leaving the phone in the waste can, he opened another beer and downed it in one long swallow. He opened another and carried it with him as he staggered to the bathroom. He turned on the shower with one hand and set the can of beer in the sink as he undressed. Chickenhead leaned against the sink in his stocking feet, reached for his beer, and in his drunken state knocked it over. As he watched it pour into the sink, he began to sway back and forth. Feeling himself falling, Chickenhead over-corrected and banged his elbow on the sink as he collapsed to the floor. With the heaviness of the wet steam closing in on him, he began to beat his fists against the bathroom wall. After a minute of listening to the water falling in the shower, he stopped hammering the walls and lowered his head into his bruised hands. As the small room filled with steam, Chickenhead, for the first time since Mimi's death two weeks before, cried for his loss...

Chapter 9

My daughter's been in and out of mental hospitals since she was a child. It took a couple of years for the doctors treating her to figure out she was bi-polar and manic depressive." Peter Driver turned over a page from the folder in front of him, then sighed and shook his head.

"The last time was in the spring of '91. I had checked her into an experimental research clinic in upstate New York. The treatment...helped. As long as she took her medication and got her treatments, she was fine. But she always, after a couple of months, sometimes as long as six, she would start to feel better and stop taking her medicine. The doctors would call me. I'd try to talk to her, get her back in line. We would start to argue, then all-out fight. This cycle went on for years."

Peter Driver, retired judge and current mayor of Houston, Texas, spoke in a monotone to the people sitting in the Phoenix PD third-floor conference room with him. The dull gray color of his eyes never wavered from the autopsy report on his daughter. He was a tall, stocky man with wide shoulders. But as he spoke about Mimi, the slumping of his body over the pages and photos before him made him look like a broken man.

"Your Honor, we can continue this later if you like," Lt. LaPlante said. "You've been through a lot today."

The mayor never looked up from his papers. He ran his hand over his balding head. Shaking his head, he continued.

"After she got back from the program in New York, she felt it was time for her to move on...to be on her own. I tried to talk her out of it, but it didn't help. Our talks turned to shouts, shouts to fights. It's been just us since she was twelve. That's when her mother--my ex-wife Joan--died of breast cancer."

He paused for a moment, sipping from a glass of water.

"She left Houston three weeks later. She was in Albuquerque for about a year, then started moving around a lot, mostly in the Southwest. The last time I saw her was Christmas of '93. She stayed in Houston for about a week. After she left, I'd hear from her four or five times a year. A letter. A phone call asking for money. The last time I spoke to her was June of '95. The last time."

Peter moved some papers aside to uncover a facial photo taken at the scene. His aide placed a hand on the mayor's shoulder. Without looking up, Peter swatted it away as if it were a fly. He removed the photo from the folder, then looked at Lt. LaPlante.

"I'd like a copy of this, please."

"I'll see to it immediately, your Honor."

The mayor returned his attention to Proctor and Murphy. "Is there anything else that you can tell me about the investigation? Anything that's not in this report?"

"No sir, everything we have is pretty much there," Proctor replied. "We'll update you as we can."

"Thank you, detective." He fingered the photo.

"When can I have my daughter's body?"

The lieutenant leaned forward and spoke softly.

"Your Honor, you know how these things go. We'll do everything that we can to release your daughter to you as soon as possible."

Peter rubbed his face with hands that were shaking.

"Yes, yes, I know..." The irritation in his voice was evident to all at the conference table. "I would appreciate it greatly if you did what you needed as quickly as possible. I want to take Mimi home."

"Of course, sir."

The mayor stood up and buttoned his jacket. His aide rose almost as quickly.

"I would like to see Mimi, Lieutenant."

"Certainly. I'll have Detective Proctor--"

The mayor cut him off with a wave of the hand.

"No. Your people here have work to do finding the monster that did this to my child. Get an officer to escort me." He started to walk to the door. When his aide began to follow, he waved him away.

"Daniel will give you any information you'll need about my accommodation. Have your officer meet me in the hall in a few minutes. Lieutenant, where is your nearest restroom?"

"A left outside of the door, then about twenty feet down the hall on your right."

When the mayor opened the door to the hall, he looked over his shoulder to Daniel. "Cancel everything for the week."

As the door closed, Lt. LaPlante called the desk sergeant and told him to send an officer up. Daniel spoke to Proctor and Murphy.

"The mayor and I have rooms at the Biltmore in Phoenix." He handed all three men his card. On the back he had written their room numbers.

"My cell phone and pager are always on. Feel free to call at any time." He frowned as he looked at the door through which the mayor had just exited. In the moment it took him to turn back to the detectives sitting in front of him, the look was gone.

"Gentlemen, I need not tell you the sensitivity of this situation. The media would have a field day with this back home."

Before Proctor could speak, the lieutenant did. "We're all professionals here," he said as he looked at the card. "Mr. Jacobs, we understand what's at stake."

A pained look crossed Daniel's thin, pale face. He put up both hands in a mock gesture of surrender. Proctor already didn't like him.

"I'm sorry, Commander, my bad. I apologize for the way that came out. We have full trust in the way Phoenix PD will handle this incident." Daniel walked back to the table and gathered his briefcase and the file the Mayor had left. As he closed the briefcase, his cell phone chirped. Taking it off of his belt, he looked at the number flashing on the small screen and frowned. He pressed the unit's "Save" button and turned back to Bryan.

"Would it be possible for me to use one of your offices and a phone for a couple of hours? I have a lot of people to call and reschedule."

"See the desk sergeant downstairs. He'll get you whatever you need."

"Thank you, Commander. Gentlemen," he nodded as he turned to leave.

"One more thing, Mr. Jacobs."

The aide turned back to Bryan with the same pained expression as he had displayed earlier.

"That file you have was given to the mayor as a courtesy of this department given his judicial background. The information enclosed is not for anyone's viewing outside of the people in this room. I'm sure you understand."

Daniel opened the door and looked back at the detectives, then at Bryan. He smiled and showed perfect teeth when he addressed Bryan.

"As you've stated earlier, Commander, we're all professionals here. I'll stay in touch." After the door closed behind Jacobs, Murphy spoke the line that everyone was thinking. "That guy has trouble written all over him."

"And an asshole, too," Proctor added.

"Maybe, but he's the least of our worries. I'm more concerned about the judge," Bryan said. He got up, walked to the door, opened it, and looked down the hallway in both directions before closing and locking the door. Leaning against it, he shut his eyes and rubbed his face as he spoke.

"I did a little reading last night on the judicial career of the mayor. He sat on the bench for sixteen years as one of the nastiest criminal judges in Texas. He sent more people to hard time and death row than any judge before or since. Got the moniker "Pile" Driver from the press for the harshness of his sentencing. And the public loved him. Stepped down from the bench in '94 to run for mayor of Houston. Ran a "For the People" campaign. Won in a landslide against a sitting mayor who outspent him three-to-one." Bryan crossed the room and flopped into a chair.

"Won his second term last year by an even bigger margin and has his eyes set for higher office when his current term ends. Has friends from here to D.C. who have been grooming him for Congress."

"Jesus H. Christ," Proctor muttered.

"Wait--it gets worse. Driver was a lawyer for almost twelve years. Worked as a prosecutor for the City of Houston. Made shit as an employee of the city but a killing as an author. Co-authored five law textbooks that are used in a quarter of all post-graduate law programs in the nation. His net worth is around forty-nine million dollars."

Murphy and Proctor looked at each other, stunned. After nearly a minute of silence, Proctor spoke.

"So, Bryan, to say we're fucked wouldn't be construed as an understatement."

The weak laugh that Bryan used in answering Proctor didn't make either of them feel any better.

"The Judge knows the letter of the law. Hell, he helped write the interpretation of it...and the ways around it. He's also pissed, takes losing poorly, and is rich as hell. Not to mention feeling a bit guilty about finally reuniting with his long lost daughter in the Phoenix City Morgue. I've already heard through a reliable source that he's having dinner with our fair mayor tonight."

The lieutenant was interrupted when his cell phone rang.

"Hello, Lt. LaPlante speaking."

Proctor and Murphy watched as their boss' slumped posture jerked upright, and his eyes opened wide.

"Yes, sir, right away...of course...I understand totally. I'll be finished here in a few minutes. I'll see you with all the files in ten minutes...yes, sir."

All eyes were on Bryan as he straightened his tie and fingered his dark hair into place.

"Fuck, the shit is hitting the fan already. That was the chief, and y'all are pulled off of everything except this case. Have all your other case files on my desk by the end of the day. I've got a meeting with our boss in ten minutes to bring him up to snuff on this investigation."

Bryan stood and started to gather files and paperwork. Both detectives did the same.

"Stephen, when was the last time you talked to Gibbs?"

"About a week ago. I called his hotel this morning and was told he had just checked out."

"What? You're just telling me this now?"

"Boss, you paged me while I was on the phone with the hotel clerk. I came straight here. I didn't have the time to tell you yet."

The commander put the files he had gathered back on the table and pointed at Proctor.

"Find him, Detective. Now. In fifteen minutes I'm gonna have the Chief of Police breathing down my neck once I tell him--and I will tell him--about the notebook. And you'd best believe Driver will know about that book tonight. Get going." LaPlante gathered his folders and left the room.

As the door closed, Murphy put his files on the table and plopped down next to them.

"Welcome to being second-guessed, put under a microscope, and fucked without being kissed. Buddy, we have just been put into deep kimshe."

"No shit."

"I think our first order of business is to find Chickenhead. Quick. Like before the good Judge does."

"No shit," he echoed.

*   *   *   *   *

Peter Driver sat in a locked bathroom stall down the hall from the third-floor conference room and cried for a full twenty minutes without uttering a sound. The tears fell from his eyes, down his cheeks, and into a puddle between his legs. He didn't bother to wipe them away. He knew she was sick, knew she couldn't make it for long on her own, yet he let her go. For five years. To prove a point that now made no sense. That she needed him. Needed his money. He could have found her in a week. But he had done nothing. She was living like an animal on the streets of Phoenix, a drugged-up whore. Beaten, tortured, and gutted, then thrown away by some sick pervert.

He unlocked the stall and walked on unsteady legs to one of

the sinks. Washing his face in the tepid water, he felt as if every splash against his skin was draining him more. He didn't even raise his head from the basin when he heard the restroom door open.

"Um...sir, are you...um, okay?"

Peter looked up and saw the young officer. He read the name on his breast pocket.

"I'm...fine, Officer Woods."

"I was waiting outside...I didn't mean to...to interrupt you, your Honor. The desk sergeant sent me up to escort you...to take you to your daughter."

As water dripped from his face, the mayor stepped back from the sink and looked down on the smaller man. The officer was damn near shaking in his shoes and was sweating bullets. The sight of the man's fear turned Peter's already knotted stomach. He reached above the sink to the paper towel dispenser, pulled out a handful, and wiped the water from his face. His eyes never left Woods' face.

"Officer...Woods, how long have you been a policeman?"

"Sir?"

"How long have you been a cop, son?"

"Um...well, sir, almost three weeks. It's been about three weeks since I graduated from the Academy."

The cold gaze of Peter's eyes caused Officer Woods to look away and begin fidgeting with his equipment belt. He had been told who the mayor was and to treat him accordingly. Peter looked at him for a full minute as he dried his face. Throwing the paper into the trashcan near the sink, he finally looked away from the sweating officer. Driver studied his drawn face and bloodshot eyes in the mirror and shook his head. The repugnance that Woods heard in the mayor's voice made him decide right then and there to look for a new job starting the next day.

"Wait for me outside, officer. I'll be out when I'm done." Woods turned and left without a word.

Feeble-minded, weak people like that are one of the reasons why the world is going to hell, he thought, why the streets have turned into shooting ranges, why thugs laugh at the system. A cop? He wasn't fit to be a crossing guard. Guys like Woods are part of the problem-- a problem that just keeps getting worse.

Peter looked into the mirror and adjusted his soaked tie and jacket.

I'm not going to stand by and allow some fool like that to let this monster get away, he thought. Reaching into the inner pocket of his coat, he pulled out a slim cell phone and a small, worn leather address book. Finding the number he wanted, he hesitated for only a moment before dialing it. The line rang once, then beeped.

"You know who this is," the mayor said. "I need your help on a...personal matter. Get back to me on this line after midnight, my time. I'm in Phoenix. I'll explain everything then." He clicked off the phone. Checking himself in the mirror, he pulled his tie off and opened the top button of his wet shirt. He moved to the door, stopped in mid-stride, and took several deep breaths to compose himself. Once more he started toward the door. This time he opened it and walked out.

Chapter 10

It took Chickenhead several tries to hang up the pay phone. Since he had checked out of the Sunny Day Motel two days before, he had stayed dead drunk. This was his third call to Jamaica in two days, and he wondered if his friend was checking his messages. Pushing away from the island of phones on the first floor of the Bank One building in downtown Phoenix, he staggered toward one of the vinyl sofas scattered throughout the area. He misjudged the distance to the sofa, so when he leaned toward where he thought the seat was located, he fell face first to the floor two feet from it.

The two security guards that had been watching him since he'd entered the building ten minutes earlier burst out laughing as he fell into a heap. Chickenhead crawled the short distance to the couch and tried to sit upright. Using the side of the couch as a backrest, he succeeded on his second try. He felt something drip into his eyes and wiped his face with a rag from his pocket. He stared at the cloth for a minute before he realized he was looking at blood.

Concentrating on moving slowly, he held onto the edge of the furniture and pushed himself upright, steadying himself. He reached down and picked up his bedroll and gallon jug of water. Swaying slightly as he walked, he took small, measured steps to the escalator that led down to the basement restrooms. He placed his parcels on the moving stairs and held onto the rails with both hands. Gathering everything at the bottom, he walked stiffly to the washrooms. He opened the door, went straight to the first sink, and dropped everything into it. Moving to the next basin, he washed the layers of dirt and blood from his face and forehead. The blood still oozed from the cut on his forehead after several attempts to stop it with the flat of his hand. He finally held a paper towel to it. The rectangle of paper stuck to the wound and stopped the flow of blood. A stall behind him opened, and he heard a loud gasp. Turning, he saw a petite, sharply dressed black woman holding a hand over her mouth. It took him a moment to realize he was in the wrong restroom.

"Oh, I'm sorry, lady."

She looked at him with eyes that threatened to pop out of their sockets.

"Please...don't hurt me."

Chickenhead turned his back to her. He pulled several towels from the dispenser, gathered everything, and walked out the door. He had just cleared the corner when he bumped into the two guards who had watched him earlier. The force of their collision knocked the towel from his forehead and the bedroll from his hands. Both guards jumped back as if they had touched an electric fence.

"Jesus...look, guy, you gotta get out of here...you're stinkin' up the place," the shorter one said. He then made a big show of dusting off his cheap, company-issued blazer.

"Yeah. This is no bum Friday," the other, much plumper partner added, "but hey, maybe they need a couple of hobos down at the Bank of America building." He pulled a walkie-talkie out of his back pants pocket. "Ya want me ta check?"

Both men hooted at the joke as Chickenhead picked up his bedroll and walked down the short hall, then across the floor to the escalator. He was halfway up the stairwell when he heard yelling from below. Looking down as he reached the top of the escalator, he saw one of the guards, the short fat one, huffing as he reached the bottom of the stairs. The other one was speaking into his radio as he held the arm of the woman from the bathroom. Chickenhead bolted the short distance to the lobby doors and was out of the building. As soon as he cleared the front of the tower, he forced himself to slow to a fast walk.

Trying not to stumble, he crossed the street against the traffic light and was narrowly missed by a City of Phoenix sanitation truck. With a blaring horn, the driver gave him the finger as Chickenhead broke into an unsteady jog. He looked this time and crossed the street halfway up the block. Chickenhead walked directly to an alleyway between two buildings, looked both ways up the street before entering, and quickly moved to the rear of the L-shaped dead end. He sat his things down, undid his bedroll, and removed a half-gone bottle of vodka and an oversized sweatshirt. After he put the shirt on, he opened the bottle and drained it in one long gulp. He removed the few items left in the center of his bundle and put them in plastic grocery bags he pulled from his pockets. Chickenhead placed the parcels next to his side and sat on the ground against the building. He wrapped the bedding around his shoulders and drew his knees to his chest. Chickenhead closed his eyes to the mid-morning sunlight. After sitting that way for several minutes, he opened a bag that sat next to him and pulled out a dark green tee shirt. He draped it like a hood over his head and leaned his head against his knees. Chickenhead was asleep in fifteen minutes.

*   *   *   *   *

He awoke with a start almost three hours later. Slightly sober, it took him a moment to remember where he was. Wincing, he straightened his legs and massaged the feeling back into them. The sweat from the nightmare from which he had awoken chilled him as he kneaded the muscles in his legs. The dream was the same one he had been having for days. He would be kneeling over Mimi, just the way he had found her weeks ago. The only thing different is that in the dream, after he pulled the plastic from her face, she was still alive. She would scream at him to help her...to get her out of the black cocoon she was trapped in. Just as he tore away more plastic, hands...hundreds of them...would come out of the dark behind him and drag him away from her. No matter how much he fought against them, he couldn't break free. Just as he thought he'd made headway, he saw the man...the man dressed in the long black coat. He stepped out of the darkness, leveled a gun at Mimi's head, and fired. The hands holding Chickenhead disappeared, and he leaped at the man, who sidestepped into a pool of darkness and was gone. Turning to Mimi, he then saw that the top of her head had been blown open by the bullet. But there was no gore, just hundreds, thousands of twenty-dollar bills...all colored blood red.

Trying to clear the images from his mind, he shook his head until he was dizzy. It didn't help. Slowly, using the wall for support, he stood up. Chickenhead waited a moment for the world to stop spinning and then repacked his belongings and walked out of the alley. In the forty minutes it took him to shuffle out of downtown, most of his high dissipated. It took him another twenty minutes, using back streets and alleys, to bypass police headquarters on 7th Avenue. Finally reaching the back entrance to Grace Court School, he pushed open the rickety door and stepped into the semi-darkness of the ground floor. He paused at the bottom of the steps leading to the second floor and let his eyes adjust as he listened to the sounds of the building. Chickenhead heard someone cough upstairs. Heard the wind blowing through the open doors and broken windows behind him.

Slowly and quietly, he climbed up the trash-filled stairwell. When he reached the top of the stairs, he looked up and down the dim hallway. Past the nearest classroom he saw the bleach bottle he had discarded the last time he had been there...almost two weeks earlier. Farther down the hall near the last classroom on the floor, Chickenhead heard the coughing again. He stood at the top of the stairs for a minute longer, then quietly walked to the semi-closed door of his flop. Stepping inside and closing the door behind him, he saw that everything was as he had left it. Chickenhead walked toward the opposite wall to one of the many cabinets, opened one, and smiled. Inside it were two plastic gallon containers of water, and behind them were various cans of condensed soup. No one had gotten into his stash, and for that he let out a sigh of relief.

He set down his bedroll and the water he had carried in on the desk beside him and grabbed the nearest can of soup from the shelf. He shook it several times and rummaged past the other cans until he found a rust-spotted, military-issue can opener. He punched two holes in the lid and, bringing the can to his lips, drained it in seconds. Smacking his lips at the taste of the heavy chicken broth, he took a long swallow of bottled water. He was just setting down the bottle when he heard the classroom door open. Chickenhead grabbed the handle of a sealed bottle of water on the shelf as he turned toward the sound.

The man entering the room was the one he had beaten in front of the post office weeks earlier. In the bright light of the classroom, Chickenhead saw the dark scabs on the intruder's face and the filthy neck brace he wore. The sling that held his broken arm was almost black with dirt. He also saw the two men who squeezed through the door around him. Both men slowly walked to opposite ends of the classroom, then stopped. One--the smaller of the two--walked with a slight limp. He was over a head shorter than Chickenhead and looked emaciated. The larger of the two smiled as he leaned against a paint-splattered blackboard. He was as tall as Chickenhead and looked disgustingly healthy. When he pulled the switchblade from his pocket and snapped it open, Chickenhead knew he had a problem. The fat man stepped into the room.

"Well, well, motherfucker, we meet again."

Chickenhead looked in the direction of the raspy, muffled voice. He saw the fat man try to smile but failed in his attempt due to the thick scabs covering his face.

"Didn't think you'd see me again, did you, boy?" he wheezed. "Yeah, found out where you lived and camped out for a while. Knew you'd come back. Got a few friends I want ya to meet. We gonna finish what your ragged..."

A loud, wet thud stopped him in mid-sentence. Both men who came in with the fat man looked back at the door when they heard the sound. Chickenhead saw the big man's eyes roll up to the whites as he collapsed in a heap in the doorway. On his way down, his head bounced off the side of the rough frame, tearing a long gash in his right ear. Behind him Jamaica coughed, holding a brick in his hand. He switched it to his other hand as he stepped over the fallen man and entered the room.

"Guess this evens things up a bit, huh, guys?"

The man with the switchblade snarled as he bolted toward Jamaica. At the same time, Chickenhead pulled the bottle of water off the shelf and ran to intercept him. Backing away from the man's wild swings, Jamaica dropped to his knees just as Chickenhead swung the bottle in a wide arc, smashing the full container into the man's chest. The force of the blow made the man stagger backward, but he still held onto the knife, slashing wildly as he fell. Chickenhead, stepping in front of Jamaica, caught one of the swings. The razor-sharp blade cut a deep groove across his upper chest and arm, slicing through both shirts he wore and drawing a spray of blood.

Backing away from the falling man, Chickenhead tripped over the unconscious fat man lying in the doorway. Before the man holding the knife hit the floor, Jamaica crab-crawled around his entangled friend and picked up the brick he had dropped. Jamaica grasped the leg closest to him and lifted the brick high over his head just as the man sat upright. He brought the brick down like a hammer, connecting with the man's knee just as Jamaica was stabbed in the forearm. Both men's screams echoed down the hall. The bigger man reared back to stab Jamaica again as the thin plastic of the full water bottle exploded when it connected with his face. The force of Chickenhead's throw and the weight of the bottle snapped the man's head backward, and the plastic and water blinded him. Chickenhead sailed over the fat man lying in the doorway and screamed in pain as he drove the full weight of his injured arm into the man's chest. Scurrying to the side, Chickenhead sat on the wrist of the man's knife hand and rained backhand blows to the man's face until he stopped moving. Chickenhead was breathing hard and with his chest wound burning, he looked across the room at the other man. During the commotion, he had backed into the corner farthest from the melee. He still sat there, shaking with his hands covering his head. Turning to him, Chickenhead rushed to Jamaica, who was leaning against the doorjamb. With his tearing eyes closed, Jamaica held his damaged arm against his chest as blood oozed down his elbow and onto the floor. Gently, Chickenhead lifted away the remains of the torn sleeve from the wound. He ran across the room and returned with a bottle of water. He ripped the top off and slowly began pouring a thin stream of water over the wound, dabbing at it with a torn piece of shirt. His own wound was starting to throb. Jamaica winced through tightly clenched teeth.

"Goddammit, man, that hurts!"

"Jamaica, this is deep. We've gotta get you to the clinic to get this cleaned."

"Me? 'Case you didn't notice, you don't look so hot yourself."

"Mine is just a surface wound, no deep trauma," he lied. "Yours is deep...an in and out wound. You need it cleaned, antibiotics, and closed." Chickenhead slowly raised his friend's arm to shoulder level.

"Try to keep it above your heart for a minute. That will help slow the bleeding. You're lucky he didn't hit an artery or fracture a bone."

"Yeah, right, doctor. This kind of luck we all need."

Running back to the cabinets, Chickenhead opened several before he found what he wanted. Dismissing a wave of remorse, he ripped off the paper covering two of Mimi's sanitary napkins. He pressed both to Jamaica's wound, rolled up the remains of the sleeve, and tied the torn ends over the pads.

"I'm sorry, but that's the best I can do here. We need to get you to the clinic before it closes."

"What about your friends?" Jamaica nodded to the fat man and company.

"They can stay here. I won't be coming back."

Jamaica opened his mouth to reply, but a series of deep booming coughs cut him off. Leaning against his friend until he caught his breath, he looked up and nodded. Chickenhead guided Jamaica around the still prone fat man, and they both stopped at the top of the stairwell.

"Wait here a minute." Jamaica nodded and sat on the top step. Chickenhead stepped on the fat man as he entered the room where he and Mimi had lived for the last time. The other man, thinking them gone, let out a loud yelp when he saw Chickenhead re-enter the room. He quickly jumped back in his corner. Chickenhead opened a small closet near the back of the classroom and took out a large blue athletic bag. Taking items out of various cabinets, he pushed them all into the bag. As he walked back to the door, both injured men started to moan. Clearing the doorway, Chickenhead paused and looked back at the fat man. By the time he walked back to the door, the man was laying in the doorway on his back. Chickenhead looked down into the fat man's glazed, semi-conscious eyes, and hate rushed thick and heavy to Chickenhead's mind. Chickenhead turned to the bag and unhooked one of the bottles of water from a rope on its side. He stood over the unconscious man, raised the bottle over the man's head with his good arm, and held it there for a moment. Then he frowned down at the fat man. He slowly lowered the gallon jug and dropped it at his feet. Kicking the man's foot brought a moan from him. When he heard Jamaica cough in the hallway, Chickenhead returned to his side. Chickenhead opened the large bag, removed a long-sleeved tee shirt, and pulled it over his cut shirts. He removed a long-sleeved flannel shirt, put it around his friend's shoulders, and helped him down the stairs to the front door.

*   *   *   *   *

Housed in a five-room section behind the Home of the Savior Soup Kitchen was the Columbus Free Clinic. Open as part of a block grant from the City of Phoenix and the Saint Mary's/Mother of Christ Medical Association five years before, it was, at the time, a one-year study on transient medical care. Staffed on a rotating basis by nurses and doctors doing pro bono work from various local hospitals, the clinic was always undermanned and overcrowded.

Operated like an urgent-care facility, the clinic was one of the very few safe places in Little Beirut. Though a patrol car drove by the clinic every hour it was open, which was from 8 a.m. to 6 p.m. weekdays, and cops frequently stopped in for coffee, what really kept the area quiet were the residents. This was as close to medical care as the vast majority of the indigent got. And the knowledge in the community was that grant money would evaporate in an instant if trouble visited the clinic too often.

Chickenhead and Jamaica had been sitting in the waiting room for the last hour. It was just before closing time, and they were the last two people to be seen. Jamaica had been taken to one of the examination rooms about ten minutes before, and Chickenhead waited his turn. Thinking back on the last few weeks, all he felt was numb. Twice in as many weeks he had been ready to kill a man out of anger--anger that had now been replaced by a cold, numbing emptiness. He heard the door open and looked toward it. A cop and his partner walked into the Clinic. The last one to enter was talking into his radio.

Tensing instantly, Chickenhead tried to appear calm when the one holding the radio looked at him. Hoping the gesture looked casual, Chickenhead nodded. The cop sleeved the radio in his belt compartment and winked at him. Just then, one of the nurses appeared from the back exam room leading a short-haired, petite girl with an arm in a sling.

"Hey, Patrick," the nurse said, "you gonna hang around while we close up?"

The cop with the radio beamed her a smile showing all upper and lower teeth.

"Hell, yeah. Ya think I'm gonna let my girl walk to her car alone in this shithole neighborhood?" he laughed. He looked back at Chickenhead and winked again.

"Hey, buddy, no offense."

"None taken."

The nurse frowned at her boyfriend, then shook her head. Both officers walked to the back of the building where the staff break room was located. The nurse looked sheepishly at Chickenhead.

"I apologize for my soon-to-be ex-boyfriend, Mister." She looked at the sign-in chart she held. "Mister Gibbs. He's a typical cop. An asshole." She smiled at him, obviously embarrassed for him. Chickenhead returned her smile with one of his own.

"Hey, I can't say as I blame him, but thank you for being so sweet."

"And thank you for being gracious, sir." She looked down at

her papers, still blushing. He couldn't help noticing that she was pretty and about the same age as Mimi.

"Ahem."

They both looked at the girl with her arm in the sling.

"Ya'll, this love connection is nice, but I'd like to get the hell out of here, okay?" she said as she stared at the nurse.

"I'm sorry, Melony. I didn't mean to be rude. Just give me a minute, Mr. Gibbs."

They both walked to the desk and started filling out paperwork. About five minutes later, the nurse came from the desk and offered her hand to Chickenhead.

"On to more important things, fine, sir. It's your turn. The good doctor will see you now. If you'll give me but a moment to lock the front door, I would be honored to escort a man of your stature to our finest examination room."

For the first time in weeks, Chickenhead let out a booming laugh. He took her outstretched hand and shook it.

"Why, thank you, ma'am. I look forward to it."

*　　*　　*　　*　　*

Waiting for the nurse to bring his next patient, Dr. Braxton Howard popped a Demerol tablet into his mouth and dry-swallowed it. He pulled back the sleeve of his lab coat to check his watch and released a string of curses under his breath. If he didn't hurry, he was going to miss his appointment with his doctor. Though his hand was healed and back to one hundred percent, he still felt tired. He had a check-up five days ago and was meeting his doctor at 6:30 p.m. to discuss the results. He was more annoyed than worried. Some of the side effects of Demerol were fatigue and sometimes abnormal thirst, another symptom that had popped up as of late. He needed to find a new high. He heard the nurse coming down the hall and snapped the lid on the tiny bottle of pills. By the time the nurse knocked on the door and opened it, he had dropped the bottle into his lab coat pocket.

"Doctor Braxton, Mr. Gibbs." Chickenhead followed her into the examination room.

"Here is his chart," she acknowledged as she handed the doctor a metal clipboard.

"Mr. Gibbs, have a seat on the table." Braxton eyed the long stain of blood that had soaked through the thin shirt Chickenhead wore as the doctor pulled on a pair of latex gloves.

"Tell me what happened."

"Well, doc," he lied, "I was collecting cans for recycling, and, ya know, I was reaching for some in the bottom of a dumpster and got a ton of grease on my shoes. Hell, I had to leave them there they were so dirty. Anyway, getting out of the dumpster, I slipped. Cut myself on a jagged piece of fence that was sticking out."

Braxton listened to the story with a slight smile.

Jesus Christ, he thought, what's he going to tell me next--the dog ate his homework?

"Okay, let's see how bad this is. Take off your shirts, please."

Both men knew why Chickenhead had lied. Under federal law, any doctor who treated a wound that was inflicted by a knife or firearm had to report it to the police. The clientele of the Clinic got around this by concocting some really stupid stories. And unless it was a gunshot wound, the cops didn't want to be bothered. Too much paperwork for someone who in all likelihood wouldn't bother to show up for his court date.

Chickenhead grimaced as the gowned and gloved nurse helped him out of his shirts. The movement also served to reopen the wound. Braxton put on a face shield, then probed the edges of the oozing wound with his fingers.

"Yes, Mr. Gibbs, nasty fence cut. You're going to need a few stitches." He turned to the nurse. "Karen, can you get me a cleaning kit and a suture tray? Thank you."

To Chickenhead he said, "I'm going to need you to lie down on the table, please," as he gave him a shot of antibiotics.

As Braxton started cleansing the wound, there was suddenly a sharp knock on the door. Chickenhead almost jumped off of the table. The doctor patted him on his uncut shoulder and gently pushed him back down.

"Take it easy, buddy. You're okay here."

A male nurse opened the door and stuck his head into the room.

"Mr. Gibbs, your friend said he'd wait for you in the lobby."

"Um, thank you, sir. Thanks a lot." The nurse closed the door.

"A fellow can collector?"

Chickenhead couldn't help but smile at the doctor's comment.

"Yeah, doc, a friend. A real friend."

Prepping the area around the wound, the doctor draped clean clothes outside the damaged area. After deadening the area with a local anesthetic, he chose a pre-threaded curved needle from the suture tray and started working the wound.

"Doc, can I ask you something?"

"Sure."

"I wonder...does the clinic have social workers? Someone I can talk to about something that's fucking...sorry, something that's really messing up my head?"

Great. Another bum with mental problems. I'll never get out of here tonight, he thought. He closed the first line of stitches and started on the next.

"Well, yes and no. We have psychological counselors available on an on-call basis every Tuesday by appointment. Karen," he nodded toward the nurse as he finished up another line of stitches, "can put you on the list. Right now I think they're backed up for the next couple of months."

The sudden grim look that came over Chickenhead's face bothered Braxton.

What the hell, he thought. I'm gonna miss my appointment, anyway.

"Maybe you want to run it past me, huh? I might be able to talk the boss into pushing you toward the front of the line. I got a little pull with her."

Looking through the clear plastic of his eye shield, the doctor winked at Karen. Her cheeks instantly reddened. As he talked, he picked up the last needle he needed to close the wound.

"Thanks, doc. I hope you can. It's...it's about my girlfriend."

"What? She pregnant? Are you and she fighting?"

"Um, no...she's dead. She died a few weeks back."

The remorse in Braxton's voice was genuine.

"I'm truly sorry, Mr. Gibbs. Was it an accident? Was she sick?" Braxton finished the last suture and cut the thread.

"Um, no. She was murdered. Murdered and left not far from here. I saw her dumped out of the back of a car like a sack of shit."

Chapter 11

O
h, my God! Mr. Gibbs, I'm so sorry," Karen said aghast.
Jesus Christ! He saw me dump the body? he thought
in amazement. It took a Herculean effort to keep his voice steady.

"That's...horrific, Mr. Gibbs. Um, of course. Yes, yes, we can
help you."

"I'd really appreciate it, doc. I've been messed up for weeks.
Can't sleep. Nightmares whenever I do."

Braxton's mind was racing. The bright light in the
examination room felt as if it were burning through his clothes.

"Mr. Gibbs, I'll see to it personally. You come back first thing
Tuesday morning. There'll be a spot open for you." He turned to
Karen, who was removing the cleaning kit and the suture tray.

"Karen, can you get the psych schedule for next Tuesday for
me? I'll need to call the attending to open a spot for Mr. Gibbs."

"Sure. I'll be back in a minute," she said as she picked up both
trays and exited the room.

"You can put your shirts on, Mr. Gibbs."

What else did he see, he thought as he tried not to panic.

"Um, doc...you gonna put a bandage on this?"

Braxton looked at the raw wound and mentally slapped
himself

"Jesus...I'm sorry. Of course...I'm just a bit shook up about
what you've told me. Just a moment."

Braxton removed his soiled gloves as he crossed the room to

the medical supply cabinet. Pulling out bandaging, he returned to the table.

Breathe, he thought. Just stay cool.

Donning new gloves, he started to dress the wound. He finished quickly, took off his gloves, and reached into his pants pocket. The doctor pulled out his wallet as Chickenhead put on his shirts.

"I'm really sorry about what happened. I lost...a sister to a shooting years ago. Look, we're not supposed to do this...but I hope this helps." He pressed two folded bills into the palm of Chickenhead's hand, closing it with both of his hands. Chickenhead slipped the bills into his front pants pocket as the nurse re-entered the room. Walking past Chickenhead, she handed Braxton the schedule he'd ask her for. She turned to Chickenhead and tried to put a smile on her face for him.

"Well, skinny, it looks like you'll live." As soon as she realized what she had said, she turned beet red and clamped both hands over her mouth.

"I'm...I'm so sorry...I didn't mean..."

Surprising even himself, Chickenhead laughed out loud.

"Ma'am, don't worry about it. That's okay."

"Mr. Gibbs, those sutures shouldn't bother you too much. No lifting for the next few days, okay?" The doctor handed him a small plastic bag.

"Change the dressings in a couple of days or after you shower. There are a couple of changes in the bag along with some antibiotics. I also put some aspirin in there for any pain you may have."

Chickenhead nodded at the doctor as he took the bag.

"I'll take you out, Mr. Gibbs," the nurse said quietly.

They both walked toward the door of the room. Braxton struggled to think through the dark cloud that tried to shut down his mind. His pager beeped, and he quickly shut it off.

"Why don't you see me on Tuesday, Mr. Gibbs? Come in after the session, and I'll check your bandages for you. You'll need new ones by then for sure."

"Thanks, doc, that will be great. I'll see you then."

Karen walked Chickenhead down the short hall to the lobby. Sitting in the chair nearest the door was Jamaica, smoking a cigarette. Neither of the cops was in sight.

"I'll need you to sign a couple of things, then we can get out of here, okay?"

"Sure."

After Chickenhead signed several forms at the counter, the nurse left them on her desk as she escorted both men to the door.

"I'll see you next week, Mr. Gibbs. You hang in there." She waved at him after she locked the glass door.

Jamaica gave his partner an odd look as they walked away from the Clinic.

"Mister Gibbs?" he asked. "What the fuck line did you feed her?" He rubbed the thick bandage covering his forearm. "This son of a bitch hurts like hell, and all they gave me is some damn aspirin."

They walked for about half a block before Jamaica placed his hand on Chickenhead's arm, stopping him.

"Man, you okay? You're awful quiet."

Chickenhead looked at his friend and smiled.

"How did you know I was there? That I came back?"

Jamaica snorted.

"Man, you don't need to be no rocket scientist to read your ass. I knew you'd be back with your hardheaded self. I just camped out and waited." Cut off by a fit of coughs, it took Jamaica a minute to clear his throat and continue.

"Doctor said I got a bad cold..better get some soup or somethin'. Anyway, saw fatboy and his buddie's hangin' around a couple ah days ago, askin' a lot of questions. He asked me if I wanted ta make ten, fifteen bucks helpin' him kick your ass. Told him sure."

He reached into his pants pocket and pulled out a five-dollar bill.

"He even gave me some up front. Tried to call your ass at the hotel, but you don't return no fuckin' phone calls."

They started walking toward the State Capitol complex.

"We pulled shifts watchin' for you. Billy--he's the one that had the blade--saw you comin' and told us. Bitches was in such a hurry ta fuck you up, they didn't notice me pullin' up the rear. You know the rest."

They walked past the State Capitol building in silence. Seeing a Circle K convenience store a block away on Van Buren, they started walking in that direction. Chickenhead put his arm around his smaller friend, wincing as he felt his stitches tighten.

"Bro, you saved my ass. Again," he said as he squeezed Jamaica's shoulder.

"Don't go 'Oprah' on me, Robert," he said through smiling lips. "I'm in too much pain for hugs and kisses."

They stopped at the park across the street from the store and waited for a hole in the early evening traffic.

"Yo, Rob. You got any cigarettes? Any cash? I'm starving, and this five ain't goin' far."

"Man, you ain't gonna believe this. The doc that fixed me up gave me a couple of bucks." Chickenhead started digging into his pants pocket.

"I told him about Mimi...he said he lost a sister and wanted to help."

He handed the folded bills to Jamaica. Seeing a break in traffic, they ran across the street.

"I'm gonna get a couple of hot dogs. What do..."

Jamaica stopped at the door of the store, staring at the bills Chickenhead had just handed him. He turned back to Chickenhead with his mouth hanging open.

"Robert, what did you tell that guy?" he asked earnestly as he handed the money in his hand back to Chickenhead.

Alongside Jamaica's five-dollar bill were two brand-new hundred-dollar bills...

*   *   *   *   *

What did he see?

The thought stuck in Braxton's mind like a railroad spike. How many people had he talked to? Did he go to the cops? Did he see the license plate?

Braxton absentmindedly went about his closing duties as his mind swirled into overdrive. Standing in the middle of the floor, he looked around at the clinic that he had been a part of since its inception. The clinic of which he was on the board. The place where he found all of his victims. He flinched when he heard Karen call his name from down the hall.

"Doctor Howard, if you're finished, we're all ready to go."

Straining to sound calm, he answered her as he locked the last examination room.

"Give me a minute. I'm just about done."

His pager beeped again, and he almost flung it to the floor. Instead of destroying it, he switched it to vibrate mode and put it in his shirt pocket. Walking down the short hallway to the lobby, he forced a smile onto his face.

"Sorry about taking so long. Let's hit the road."

Just as Karen punched the alarm code into the keypad, Braxton stopped her.

"Damn, Karen, I'm sorry--gotta get some files from my box. Only take a second."

Karen's boyfriend groaned as Braxton ran to the desk area behind the counter.

"Jeez, doc, we're starvin' over here! Let's go!"

Coming around the counter holding several folders, Braxton headed for the light switches on the wall. He pressed down all four, and the lobby was dark save for the light from the streetlamp's glow shining through the glass door. Braxton rejoined everyone at the exit.

"Sorry about making all of you wait, but I need to look over these this weekend."

Karen quickly punched the code into the backlit pad, and they all exited the building. Braxton locked the door behind them.

"How would you like to join us for dinner, Doctor? We're just going up the street," Karen added.

"Sorry, can't tonight. I've got an appointment to keep. See you next week."

Before she could reply, Braxton was practically running to his car across the street. As he quickly entered the car, he started it and was the first one to pull away from the curb. Both cops watched him drive extremely fast down the deserted street as they started their cruiser. Watching his brake lights brighten as he reached the end of the block, they saw Braxton's turn signal come on shortly before he turned right and disappeared from their view. Karen honked her car horn as she pulled away from the curb, waving her arm out the driver's side window. Her man stuck his hand out of the passenger side of the cruiser and waved back. His partner was still looking in the direction the doctor had taken.

"Sheesh, that must have been some appointment. He was outta here like a bat out of hell."

"Yeah, I noticed. Probably had ta give somebody a shot."

They looked at each other and chuckled. Karen's boyfriend reached for the car radio to call in their meal break as they pulled away from the curb on their way to the diner.

*   *   *   *   *

In the ten minutes it took Braxton to get downtown, he had regained some of his composure. He was very glad that he had thought to get the files at the last minute. If he had come back over the weekend, he would have had to use his own code to enter the clinic. In all the years he had worked there, he had never come in on a weekend. He wasn't about to start leaving a trail now. Especially now. Thankful for the empty streets, he parked under a streetlight and switched off the engine. He picked up the files from his box and immediately threw them to the floor of the car. He had used them as a ruse to maneuver behind the desk in order to get Karen's paperwork from that evening.

Leafing through the stack, he pulled out Chickenhead's file. Scanning it quickly, he came to the section that listed address information. The doctor strained to read in the dim light, and his eyes widened as he started to beat on the dashboard. Chickenhead had filled in that all-important space with a post office box number. Hitting the horn accidentally, the doctor was startled by the noise, and he grabbed the steering wheel, squeezing it to stay calm. With a start, he grabbed the rest of the papers lying on the passenger seat and concentrated on the "time entered" section. Looking through several, he tossed a few sheets to the floor before finding the one he wanted. He held both sheets to the window for more light and saw that the times matched. He focused on Chickenhead's copy, specifically checking the sign-out box...6:08 p.m. Finding the sign-out time on the other sheet, the tightness left his face when he saw that it read 5:49 p.m. This had to be the friend Gibbs was talking about. He read the name as he turned the paper over: Timothy Jamaica Rummains. Looking to the address section, he let out a gush of air. It gave the address for The Montovie Men's Hotel, a men's shelter.

As he reached in his glove compartment for a pen, he felt his pager vibrate. He fumbled in his shirt pocket, and it took him two tries to find the tiny backlight button on the unit. As the screen lit up, he immediately recognized the number--it was his doctor's. A tremor of fear ran up his spine as he looked at the unit. Curious, he scrolled back to check the previous pages. Both were from his doctor. Out of habit, he reached for his car phone, hitting the dashboard. He remembered that he was in his other car, the Mustang. He never drove the Mercedes to the clinic. Anger and fear caused him to grind the gears as he started the car twice. As he pulled away from the curb, he tried to stay focused as he searched the streets for a pay phone. It took him almost ten minutes to find one. And with each of those minutes, he could feel the itching intensify as the welts from an outbreak of hives grew on his chest and back.

*   *   *   *   *

Braxton was seething. He had been sitting in an almost-empty coffee shop across from the Bank One tower for the last thirty minutes waiting for his personal physician, Sherman Topper, to arrive. A hostess from behind the counter approached him, smiling.

"Would you like some more coffee, sir?"

Braxton threw a ten-dollar bill across the change she had left earlier.

"Take this and leave me alone."

Startled, she took a step back before recovering and snatched the bill from the tabletop. He didn't even notice her walking away.

Braxton had been on the coffee shop's pay phone for less than a minute before Topper had hung up on him. After refusing to come to the doctor's office and screaming for his diagnosis over the phone, Topper told him in no uncertain terms that he needed to act like a professional and shut the fuck up. Amazed at his doctor and mentor's tone, Braxton pulled himself together enough to give the coffee shop's location when Topper asked. Topper told him to wait for him, then hung up. Ten minutes after shooing away the waitress, Braxton saw the older doctor park his car across the street through the shop's plate-glass window.

Braxton was on his feet before the trim older man was out of the late-model Cadillac Eldorado. Standing at the table as Topper entered the shop, Braxton barely noticed the doctor's dark gray tuxedo as the stately man walked quickly toward the table. With a direct approach to Braxton, the aged man stared up at him with a gaze that could have cut diamonds. The chill in the doctor's voice held Braxton in check.

"Sit down, Doctor."

With his rage just beneath the surface, Braxton slowly complied. Topper stared at his one-time student, then leaned across the table to within an inch of Braxton's face.

"Do not ever speak to me in that manner again, Doctor. If you can't handle the meds you're prescribing yourself, get professional fucking help."

Topper sat down at the table. Braxton stayed silent.

"Since you are obviously...anxious, I'll get to the point. The reason you're fatigued is because you've contracted Hepatitis 'B.' The infection is well on."

The hard look on Braxton's face shattered as if it were glass. "Your youth and physical conditioning have kept you from noticing the condition until recently. That, combined with the various narcotics that you're addicted to, may also be the reason for your less than pleasant demeanor in recent months."

Still reeling from the bad news, Braxton's voice was barely audible. "How? I feel fine. I took all the precautions. I..."

The hard edge in Topper's voice barely softened as he edged closer.

"You are exposed to blood and body fluids constantly, Doctor. Unsafe sex, contaminated food or water...sharing needles..."

"I don't do intravenous drugs."

"All it takes is one time."

Braxton opened his mouth to reply, then just shook his head. Topper pushed his seat away from the table and stood. Reaching into his inside jacket pocket, he pulled out two pieces of paper. He held both for a moment before looking down at his one-time prized pupil. His own face softened as he set the prescriptions on the table.

Braxton was sitting with his head in his hands. When Topper spoke again, some compassion had returned in his voice.

"Braxton, I wrote a couple of prescriptions for you. Start taking them immediately. They will...help. I'm sure you'll be discreet in getting them filled. You also need to stay in shape--your excellent physical conditioning was one of the reasons it took so long for the symptoms to surface. I have to go--I'm late for a charity ball in Tempe."

Turning to leave, Topper made it to the door before stopping and looking back. Braxton was still seated at the table with his face buried in his hands. Moving back to the table, the doctor leaned across it and placed his hand on Braxton's shoulder. He spoke softly to the younger doctor as Braxton raised his head.

"Braxton, you're not the first sawbones to be hooked on meds, nor the first I've treated for a chronic illness. I've seen a few in my day. You need help, son. And you need it now. Take the next couple of days off and pull yourself together. Call me on Monday. I promise this won't end your career. If we work on this together, you'll come out okay. But you have to want to get help, son--you have to want it."

The gray-haired man patted the younger one on the shoulder and walked out of the shop.

A half-hour later, Braxton lifted himself from the chair with legs that felt as if they weighed tons. Leaving the prescriptions on the table, he shuffled to the shop door on lead feet and exited. He fumbled with his car keys, and it took a couple of tries to find the right one for the lock. He opened the door, flopped into the driver's seat, and left the door open. After five minutes of sitting, he noticed the papers on the seat next to him. He closed the door and reached across the seat to find both Chickenhead's and Jamaica's sheets. He remembered there was a twenty-four hour copy center across the street from the city bus terminal. With one hand unconsciously scratching the quarter dollar-sized hives that covered his chest, he started the car. The defeated look was gone and was replaced by a serene composure and determined eyes that shone with a dead, cold light. Pulling away from the curb, the doctor drove to the corner of Central Avenue and Monroe Street and waited for the stoplight to change. A slight smile rested on his face. He dug hard into his rash and burst one of the lesions on his chest, spilling fluid onto his chest and shirt. He didn't notice. The only thought on his mind was getting relief...relief from the pain in his head...the pain that needed to go away. And he knew the two people who would help him find relief--relief from his pain through their pain.

Another sore erupted under his thrusting fingers. The light turned green just as the smile on his face got larger.

Chapter 12

Jeremiah Bitters sat on the edge of an overstuffed leather sofa in the Grand Suite of the Biltmore Hotel in Phoenix. The deep-blue color of his Italian silk tie and Egyptian cotton shirt matched the dark, violent mood surrounding him. Reading from a stack of 3 x 5 cards held in hands the size of small hams, he paused long enough to sip from a now-warm can of beer. He placed the can on a coaster atop the glass and rod iron coffee table in front of him and continued reading aloud from where he had left off. The only other person in the suite, Peter Driver, was across the room. Driver was standing at the door that opened to a balcony overlooking the nearby mountains. It had been two days since Peter had called him from the police station on his cell phone.

"Robert Stanley Gibbs a/k/a Chickenhead. Thirty-eight years old. Born and raised in Tucson, Arizona. Last real job was with Tucson City Fire Department. Worked with them from February '82 through November '91. Was a Paramedic with the same department from April '88 to November '91. Graduated at the top of his class in Paramedic training. Downfall began winter of '90. Was part of a crew that responded to an apartment fire. Records hint the owner set the blaze for insurance money. Problem was he didn't take the time to tell the twenty families living there that he was planning to cook them at two in the morning. Two of the people who died were Gibbs' friends."

He turned the card over and continued. "John and Patty

Brooks. Gibbs was the one who pulled them out of the building, damn near burned up himself trying to save them. Both dead at the scene. He got reprimanded for leaving other victims to work his people."

Bitters paused and took a sip of beer. He flipped to the next card.

"Took a one-month leave of absence for psychological counseling. Got wind of the arson aspect after he came back and started making inquiries on his own. Found out the arson report by the Fire Marshal was ruled inconclusive and hit the roof. Turns out the building was owned by the brother of a city councilman. Gibbs hired a lawyer and started suing everybody to reopen the case. Got copies of all the reports from his lawyer and started showing them to anyone who would listen. Right around that time, started getting shafted by the department...bad job reviews, the works. Ended up punching out his captain after his last evaluation. Got himself a two-week suspension with pay. Fired him on the last day of the suspension. Firefighter's Union never said a word."

Bitters looked up from the card he held to his employer. When Driver turned toward him and nodded, he continued.

"Gibbs couldn't get a job as a dog catcher after that. His marriage was on shaky ground before the incident and got worse as things progressed. She left him the week he was fired. Lost everything to legal fees and drinking. Was working eight months later as a bouncer at a strip club when the owner of the torched building walked in. Gibbs broke his jaw and two ribs. He left Tucson that night..."

"You can stop."

Bitters nodded at Driver and placed his stack of cards on the coffee table. He reached for the now-warm beer and sipped it slowly. Peter walked away from the balcony door to the chair opposite Bitters, stopping at the wet bar on the way to refill the tumbler he held with twenty-year-old Scotch. He moved the briefcase from on top of the chair down to his feet. Picking up bound copies of the police report and Chickenhead's notes from the coffee table, he flinched inwardly as he remembered paying a cop one-thousand dollars for the report and the notes. He tossed both to Bitters, who caught them easily.

"Have you been able to improve on anything in either of these?"

"Some. The cops had known about the killings from the last three years, but kept hitting a wall when they tried to get information. What little information they got they kept quiet about to the public. Their only real breaks were from Gibbs' call and the body in Mesa. Up 'til then, the only bodies found were weeks or months old. Also, the information in Gibbs' notes ID'd the body in Mesa. He also had info on two bodies the cops didn't know about. Using the info in the notes, I've come across two more killings in Tucson that happened in the last year. Both victims were transients. Both cases unsolved. M.O.'s the same...I'm fairly certain whoever is doing this is local."

Peter finished his drink and set the tumbler on the coffee table.

"I'm posting a $75,000 reward for information leading to the arrest of whoever did this. You'll be listed as the contact. The half-page ad will run daily in all the local papers starting Sunday."

Peter opened the briefcase at his feet and extracted a large manila envelope. He slid it across the table. Bitters didn't touch it. Peter got out of his chair and walked back to the bar. Taking a clean glass, he started to fill it with Scotch.

"All your local information is there, along with your fee. I want you to start immediately."

"Yes, sir."

Driver drank deeply from his glass.

"The police have lost track of Gibbs. The detectives working the case haven't heard from him in almost a week. I want you to find him."

"I know."

"I want you to find him in the next forty-eight hours. Can you do it by Sunday?"

"I'm already working on it. I'll have him for you then."

"Give him whatever he wants. I want him working for us."

"I'll take care of it, sir."

Opening the scuffed leather overnight bag beside him, Bitters placed the envelope on top of a holstered Glock 9mm handgun. He extracted two rubber bands from a side compartment, neatly bound his cards, and set them on top of the envelope. Zipping the bag closed, he rose from the sofa. Peter was back at the balcony, looking toward the mountains.

"I'll call you on Sunday with Gibbs, sir."

Chapter 13

Chickenhead stood in the open doorway of their motel room watching the Sunday morning sunrise burning away the early fog. His face was calm. He was wearing a thick black sweatshirt with matching pants and flip-flops as he stepped into the morning cold and quietly closed the door on his sleeping friend. With the money Braxton had given him, Chickenhead and Jamaica had spent the last two nights in a hotel. After a quick meal of hot dogs and coffee at the 7-Eleven, they caught the Number Three bus to the last Redline bus connecting into Mesa that night. It let them off almost an hour later on the corner of Apache-Main Street and Dobson Road, the seedier side of Mesa just across the border from Tempe. In the string of cut-rate hotels, motels, and trailer parks that lined these streets, finding a cheap room wasn't difficult.

While Jamaica took a shower in the tiny bathroom, grumbling constantly about holding his damaged arm outside the shower stall, Chickenhead left a twenty-dollar bill on the nightstand in between the twin beds with a note saying he'd be back late. Two-and-a-half hours had passed before he returned pushing a shopping cart full of food from the twenty-four-hour Safeway four miles up the street. While Jamaica put the food away in the kitchenette, Chickenhead showered and changed his chest and shoulder bandages. He stepped out of the bathroom in new sweatpants he had bought at the market, and Chickenhead accepted the fresh cup of coffee Jamaica handed to him.

"Thanks, bro. Sit over there," he pointed to the closest bed, "I need to check your dressings."

Sitting on the mattress, Jamaica held his arm out to his partner. Chickenhead looked at the bandages for a moment, then tapped him on the shoulder.

"It looks pretty good. You'll be cool with this for the night. I'll change it tomorrow sometime. I picked up some plastic bags and tape from the supermarket. You can put them on your arm when you shower next time."

"Thanks, doc. Your check is in the mail."

Chickenhead smiled at the memory.

Leaning against the wall next to their door, he watched the sun rise above the horizon. The last two days had been a godsend after the hell of the last few weeks. Sipping from the plastic mug of coffee, the world...at least this small piece...slowed down for a minute and gave him a chance to catch his breath. Pulling his small notebook out of his pants pocket, he set his coffee on the outside window ledge. He opened the book and slowly turned the pages. It felt as if it had been months instead of days since he had last viewed the notebook's contents. All of the information he found...all the hard work and pain wouldn't mean shit if he couldn't find the person who killed Mimi. And he knew he needed more help than just the two of them.

He put the book back in his pocket. Blowing the steam off of his coffee, he sipped it slowly. He and Jamaica had talked about it yesterday and kept coming back to the same wall that they couldn't get past--the cops. Chickenhead hadn't talked to them in over a week and really didn't want to, but he saw no way around it. They were the only ones who could help him, whether he liked it or not.

He dumped the half-full cup of coffee on the sidewalk. Tapping the upturned cup against the ledge, he watched the thick dredges fall downward. He loved Jamaica like a brother. He had been more than family to him for the last five years, but Jamaica's coffee was always terrible. And it probably didn't help that the pot had sat out all night.

He would call Proctor today. He didn't like it, but that didn't matter. He needed help. Opening the door quietly, he went back into the room. Jamaica was in his bed, tangled in the sheets and snoring loudly. Chickenhead locked the door and crossed the room to the bathroom, silently closing the louvered door. Turning on the water in the sink to wash up, he stopped and turned off the spigots. It wasn't often that he had the luxury of taking a real shower, and he wasn't going to waste it. Stripping and leaving his folded clothes on the sink, he turned the water on full blast in the stall before stepping in backwards so as not to disturb his chest bandages. He held a plastic bag he had brought into the shower to cover and protect his wounds, and he turned around and angled the showerhead to mid-back with his good arm. The doctor had done a good job sewing him up. He was very thankful and equally puzzled by the man. Two-hundred dollars was a chunk of money...more than he had seen in one place in quite a while. Turning his back to the stream of water, he let his mind drift as he enjoyed the wet heat. He stepped out of the bathroom ten minutes later and experienced the same sense of peace he had felt earlier. Jamaica was sitting up in the bed, lighting his first cigarette of the day.

"Man, those cancer sticks gonna kill you."

Jamaica took a deep drag before answering. "Shit, just livin' gonna do that eventually."

"You got a point. Light me up one."

Jamaica took another puff, then lit another cigarette off of his and handed it to his friend. They both smoked their cigarettes to the butt in silence. Crushing his out into a cheap tin ashtray on the nightstand, Jamaica rubbed the sleep from his eyes, then stared at Chickenhead.

"Guess you decided to call that cop, huh?"

"How'd you know that?"

"Man, I done told you, don't take no rocket scientist to read your ass...that and we need all the help we can get."

"Yeah, I'm gonna call him later on."

Jamaica got out of bed and crossed the small room to the kitchen area. He pulled off his tattered tee shirt and took one of the plastic bags off of the countertop. He tore a hole in the bottom of it and slid it over his bandage. Taping it closed with strips of duct tape, he squeezed both ends. After he was satisfied with his makeshift waterproofing, he entered the bathroom and closed the door. A minute later, Chickenhead heard the water in the shower turn on.

He leaned toward the nightstand, picked up the pack of smokes and matches, and retrieved what was left of their bankroll. Chickenhead lit a cigarette as he counted the bills. Eighty-two dollars and some change. Enough for a couple or three days at least.

What the hell, he thought, ya only live once.

Jamaica came out of the bathroom a few minutes later wrapped in towels.

"Yo, get your bony ass dressed. We're going to breakfast–my treat."

"Hey, that's mighty white of you. And a damn good idea."

"Get some clothes on your ass. I'll be outside."

Putting the room keys, cigarettes, and cash in his pocket, he left the room and closed the door behind him.

Better pick up a Sunday paper while we're out, he thought, as he leaned against the wall next to the door. I need to get a job.

He lit a cigarette just as Jamaica came out of the room dressed in the new sweats Chickenhead had bought for him on Friday.

"Robert, let's get ta steppin', 'cause I'm starvin' like Marvin."

"Yeah, and we both know how Marvin be starvin'."

They both laughed easily as Chickenhead passed the cigarette to his friend. As they were walking up the street talking, neither noticed the late-model Ford pull into the parking lot directly behind them. The driver watched them and waited until they had turned the corner down the block before leaving the car and walking to the office.

*   *   *   *   *

They both ate like kings at the Denny's restaurant and were pleasantly stuffed. Jamaica was sipping his second glass of apple juice and picking at what was left of his pancakes.

"So, what do you think?"

Chickenhead answered him through a mouthful of eggs.

"About what?"

"What do you think ties all of this together?"

"Outside of all of them being homeless prostitutes, I don't know…but I know what you're gettin' at. Gotta be more."

"Yeah, like why did he pick who he did? Are there others we don't know about? What do the cops know that they ain't tellin'?" Jamaica pushed his plate away and sipped his juice. "You gonna call them when you get back?"

"Might as well."

Getting up from their table to pay the bill, Chickenhead saw an older couple leaving a table across the room. They left behind a Sunday paper. He waited until they started for the door before he went to the booth and took it. He folded the paper under his arm and returned to their table. Chickenhead counted out the money for their bill, and he left it all on the table along with a tip for the waitress. Jamaica nudged him once they were outside.

"You get the funnies? The sports section?"

Chickenhead looked through the paper, pulled out the targeted sections, and handed them to him. Jamaica put the sports section under his arm and began reading the comics as the duo walked back to the hotel. Once they reached their room, Chickenhead threw the paper on his bed and made his way around it to the phone on the nightstand. Jamaica made a beeline for the bathroom.

"Man, don't be in there all day stinkin' up the place. Make sure you turn a fan on."

"Bro, I'm hurt. You know my shit don't stink."

They both laughed as Chickenhead reached for the phone. And both froze in place looking at each other when the loud knocking started on the door.

*   *   *   *   *

"Who's there? What do you want?" Chickenhead yelled through the door.

"Mister Gibbs? Robert Gibbs? Please open the door. I'm a private investigator. I'm working for Mimi's father."

Mimi's father, he thought. She never said anything about her father.

"You got some ID? A card or something?"

"Yes, I'll hold it up to the window."

Chickenhead made his way to the window and slowly pushed back the curtain. He saw the PI's license and card pressed to the glass on the edge of the lower glass. After a quick read, he let the curtain fall back. He stood next to the door.

"Are you alone?"

"Yes. May I come in?"

"What do you want?"

"To make you an offer."

Jamaica popped his head out of the bathroom door. Chickenhead silently shooed him back in. He turned around to face the door again and quickly unlocked it. He immediately took several steps back to the base of the beds.

"The door's open! Come on in," he yelled.

Bitters slowly opened the door until it rested against the wall. His other hand was palm up, facing Chickenhead. The first thing Chickenhead noticed was the size of the man's hands. Bitters was almost the same height as he, stocky, and his hands were huge. The second thing he noticed was the bulge on the left side of the half-zipped blue windbreaker he wore. Bitters stood at the doorway and quickly scanned the entire room. Chickenhead saw him look at the newspaper on the bed, then looked quickly back up. He still hadn't entered the room.

"Where is your friend, Mr. Rummains?"

He knew about Jamaica. He knew his full name. "I don't know what you're talking about. Are you going to come in or just let all the heat out?"

Bitters slowly lowered his hands to his side but still didn't enter the room. Just looking at this guy made Chickenhead nervous. Whatever he was, he was a professional. He could tell just by his demeanor.

"Mr. Gibbs, I know you're nervous. You've had a rough few weeks. So has my employer. I know it's hard to trust me...to trust anyone right now. If you..."

Bitters was interrupted by Jamaica's screaming. Chickenhead

turned to see him running out of the bathroom holding the shower rod over his head. He took three steps toward the door and stopped across from Chickenhead as if he had hit a brick wall. His eyes were wide open. Turning back to the door, Chickenhead saw why. The bulge was gone from Bitters' jacket, and in his hands was the form of a large nasty-looking handgun.

"I take it that you're Jamaica?"

Jamaica, staring at the gun, nodded twice.

"Good, you just made my job easier." Keeping the gun leveled at the man, Bitters slowly entered the room and closed the door behind him. He released one hand from the gun and locked the door. Backing up to the door, his eyes never left the two men standing eight feet in front of him. He nodded in the direction of the bed.

"Mr. Gibbs, that wouldn't happen to be today's paper, would it?"

"Um."

"Have you looked through it?"

"No, not yet. Why?"

"There is something that you'll find of interest on page four of the first section."

Chickenhead leaned toward the paper on the bed. His thought of throwing it was stopped by the chill in Bitters' voice. "Please remove that section slowly. I have a very light trigger on this thing."

Very carefully, Chickenhead made his way through the stack of papers. After some shuffling, he found the first section. "I've got it," he said as he held it up for Bitters to see.

"Well, open it."

Trying to keep one eye on Bitters, Chickenhead quickly glanced at the first three pages of the section, then turned to the fourth. On that page was a half-page picture of Mimi. She looked ten years younger.

"Oh...my...God."

"I thought you'd appreciate that. Now on the bottom of the page there's a phone number. See it?"

"Yes." She looks so young, he thought.

"Dial it."

Chickenhead walked over to the phone and dialed the toll-free number on the bottom of the page. Almost immediately, the pocket of Bitters' windbreaker began to ring. Again releasing one hand from the gun, he pulled a small cell phone from his pocket. He tossed it to Jamaica, who dropped the rod he was holding to catch it.

"Care to talk to your buddy?" he asked as he lowered the gun. He unzipped his jacket, holstered the pistol, and re-zipped the windbreaker halfway.

Jamaica looked sheepishly at the ringing phone in his hand, then gave it back to Bitters. He shut it off.

"Um, sorry 'bout that, Mister. Who are you, anyway?"

"Bitters, Jeremiah Bitters." He pointed to Chickenhead and said, "Your friend okay?"

They both looked at Chickenhead, who was still holding the phone and staring at Mimi's photo. Before either could move to him, he looked up at Bitters. The tension in his voice was laced with puzzlement.

"Who are you?" he snarled. "And what is this?"

Bitters stepped into the room, sitting opposite Chickenhead on the other bed. Jamaica sat on the edge of the same bed as his friend.

"I've already told you--I'm a private investigator hired by Mimi's father, Peter Driver, to find out who killed his daughter and why. That," he pointed to the newspaper, "is Plan 'A.' We're hoping you'll be interested in being part of Plan 'B.'"

Chickenhead looked at Bitters and then at Jamaica, who only shrugged his shoulders. He turned back to Bitters and nodded toward Jamaica.

"If I go, my partner goes with me."

"Fine with me." Bitters rose from the bed and walked back to the door. "But we need to be going."

"Hold it, you didn't tell me what Plan 'B' was."

Bitters slid the curtain open about an inch and looked out of the window. Satisfied with what he saw, he let the cloth drop back.

"Plan 'B' will be explained to you by Mr. Driver who, by the way, is very anxious to meet you, Mr. Gibbs. Again, we need to be going. Take whatever you need; we won't be coming back." Bitters unlocked and opened the door.

"Wait a minute! I paid for this room for two more days. I gotta check out..."

"Everything's been taken care of, sir. It's not safe here. If I can find you this easily, so can the person who killed Mimi. And as for any inconvenience..."

He pulled out a thick, folded envelope from his phone pocket and placed it on the inside window ledge.

"I'm going to get the car. Come out when you hear me honk twice. Lock this behind me." He stepped outside and closed the door.

They both looked at each other for a moment, not knowing where to start or what to pack. Chickenhead went to the door and locked it. He returned to the window and inched back the curtain to peek outside, then let the cloth drop. It dawned on him that he had no idea what he was looking for. With Jamaica behind him, Chickenhead picked up the letter-sized envelope that Bitters had left. His hand was shaking as he tore the envelope open. He glanced inside and handed it to Jamaica. Letting out a low whistle, Jamaica opened the packet wider to get a better look. There was at least a half-inch of bills inside...all fifty-dollar notes. Hearing the car horn, they looked at each other again and then examined the room. Chickenhead patted his pocket for his notebook, held the door open for his partner, and then walked outside. Before he closed the door, he threw the room keys inside.

*   *   *   *   *

The ride to the Biltmore was, for Chickenhead at least, surreal. No one spoke for most of the thirty-minute ride in the light Sunday morning traffic. Bitters made a quick, whispered phone call before they drove away from the hotel. Chickenhead watched and wondered if Bitters was reporting to someone. Both he and Jamaica, as instructed by Bitters, sat in the back of the late-model Ford Taurus.

The windows, both side and back, were so darkly tinted that the bright December sunlight looked nearer to sunset than midmorning. After they entered the car, Bitters had locked all of the doors from the button on his door panel. While Bitters made his short call, Chickenhead, out of curiosity, slowly slid his hand to the door release on his side and tried it. It wouldn't open.

They had been riding almost twenty minutes, taking mostly back streets, before Bitters spoke to them.

"In tracking you two down, I came across a couple of individuals with whom you've had some, shall we say, differences. A Mr. Jason Koppel and one Billy Cray."

Jamaica instantly recognized the names of the men who had tried to jump Chickenhead.

"There is no reason for you to be concerned about them any longer. They have been convinced that it is in their best interest to give you both a wide berth. Permanently."

Neither man wanted to ask him the details of the meetings.

Ten minutes later, their car was pulling into the long driveway of the Biltmore. Bypassing the lobby entrance, Bitters continued to the rear of the hotel grounds. He took a right turn into the second driveway and drove up to a large villa located away from the main hotel buildings. Bitters brought the car to a slow stop just behind the structure, switched off the ignition, and turned to the men in the back seat.

"Well, we're here. I'll get out first, then open the door on Robert's side. Jamaica, you'll slide out on his side. Go directly to the open door of the villa. There will be someone waiting for you. He's one of my men. He'll take you in."

Without waiting for any reply from either man, Bitters left the car and walked to the opposite side, opening Chickenhead's door.

"Step lively, gentlemen."

Both men followed Bitters' instructions to the letter. Once inside, they were met by a black man who, in another life, could have been an NFL linebacker. Closing the door behind them, he spoke into a small hand-held radio before turning back to his guests.

"Follow me, gentlemen, please."

Before he turned to walk down the hallway, Chickenhead noticed the same bulge in the linebacker's half-zipped gray windbreaker, just like the one Bitters was wearing. The stranger led them down the short hallway, and once they reached the end, they turned into a brilliantly sunlit living room more than twice the size of the hotel room they had just left. The man gestured around the room with a sweeping motion of his arm.

"Make yourselves comfortable, gentlemen," he said as he pointed across the room. "The bar is well stocked if you'd like a drink. Mr. Driver will be here shortly." With that, the stranger walked past them and down the hallway.

Both men stood in the entry looking into the huge, sun-filled room. Jamaica made his way across the room to the bar with his head on a swivel, trying to take it all in. Chickenhead followed doing the same. Stopping at the six-foot-tall, double-glass doors of the liquor cabinet, Chickenhead felt as if he were looking at every variety of alcohol known to man.

"'Cuse me, bro."

Chickenhead took a step back as Jamaica moved past him and opened the door to the case. He selected a bottle of Johnny Walker Black from one of the shelves and left the door open for his partner. Picking up a heavy crystal glass from the bar, Jamaica walked back to one of the large leather sofas in the center of the room and sat down. Chickenhead decided there were too many choices and picked up a glass on his way to the couch. Sitting down next to Jamaica, he felt as if he would sink to the floor in the soft, overstuffed leather cushions. Jamaica had opened the bottle and was pouring himself three fingers of whiskey. He handed the bottle to Chickenhead, who did the same. Jamaica held up his glass for a toast.

"Unfuckingbelieveable."

"I'll drink to that, partner."

Clinking glasses, they both gulped a good portion of their drinks in a single swallow. Setting his glass on the marble coffee table, Chickenhead saw Bitters enter the room. Behind him was a bear of a man with thinning silver hair. He instantly saw the resemblance to

Mimi in the older man's tightly drawn face. Peter spoke to them before he had finished crossing the room. His voice was stressed and all business.

"Thank you for coming, gentlemen. Thank you both. I'll make this short. I want you to work for me. I want you to help me find my child's killer."

He sat in a leather armchair diagonal to their sofa. He was leaning so close to the edge of his seat that, along with the wild look in his eyes, made Chickenhead wonder if he was about to pounce on them.

"I'm sure Mr. Bitters covered the basics, so I won't bore you with them. Just say 'yes' and we can get started. I'll give you whatever you need to succeed. Just tell me and it's yours. I want this bastard found."

Bitters, standing next to Driver's chair, placed his hand on his employer's shoulder. Driver glanced at him angrily but said nothing. Bitters removed his hand but remained close.

"I'm...sorry. I...I just want your help." The hard edge that had been in his voice moments before was replaced with an undertone of urgency that bordered on pleading. The sound of his pain was making Chickenhead squirm.

"I saw your notebook, Mr. Gibbs. You do good work. You found out more in four days than the police did in two years."

Driver was leaning so far out of his chair by now that Chickenhead thought he was going to fall onto the coffee table.

"Mr. Driver, look...I..." Chickenhead set his empty glass on the coffee table. "Can we stop with the 'mister' stuff? It makes me more nervous than I already am. Just call me Chick...call me Robert." He pointed a thumb to his partner. "He's Jamaica."

"Pleased to meet 'cha," Jamaica offered as he refilled his glass. Chickenhead, more than anything at that moment, wanted another drink, but wouldn't...couldn't bring himself to reach for the bottle in front of his host. The man's pain was too familiar...too close to his own. If he took the bottle on the table, he felt it would swallow him whole. His struggle to continue was evident in the beads of sweat covering his face, even in the cool room.

"I'll...we'll help you, Mr. Driver. I want this motherfucker, too. We'll do whatever it takes to get him."

The look of relief on Peter's face moved over his body as if it were a wave. Seeing him relax, Bitters walked from his side and sat in the center of a couch identical to the one on which Chickenhead sat. With all four men sitting down, the tension in the room slipped down a notch.

"Thank you, Robert. Thank you. I think we should get started as soon as possible, don't you?"

Man, don't waste no time, Chickenhead thought. "Um, yeah...I got a couple of questions, okay?"

"Of course."

"What is Plan 'B,' and how do we fit in?"

Bitters cut in. "Sir, would you like me to explain?"

"No, no. I'll be all right. Please get the reports." Driver settled back into his chair a bit. Bitters left his seat and disappeared down the short hall. He reappeared almost immediately with an aluminum briefcase. Seating himself, he opened it and handed both men a copy of the police investigation report. Driver continued.

"Part of this report you'll recognize...it was made from your notes. The bulk of it is information the police have gathered in the last two years. You'll both need to study it closely. The forensic report has all ten John and Jane Does who fit the M.O. of the killer and lists the sections of town where the bodies were found. You'll find that the report includes Mimi and the man in Mesa, a Jefferson Plate...the one you ID'd. You'll also notice that none of the other bodies have been ID'd, and the police haven't been able to get anything from anyone they've tried to talk to. It hasn't helped that all of the bodies were found weeks or months after they were dumped, leaving any surface evidence gone or contaminated."

Driver got out of his seat, walked to the bar, and removed a glass. He returned to his chair and poured himself a drink from the bottle on the coffee table.

"Plate was the only body they found with money...a twenty-dollar bill stapled to his forehead."

Chickenhead cut in before either man could ask the question.

"I found one on Mimi, sir... I have it. I want to make sure that that bastard gets it back."

"Robert," Bitters cut in, "it's not a good idea to keep that bill. As far as the police are concerned, you're withholding evidence and impeding the investigation of a felony. That assumption alone is enough to have you arrested."

Bitters and Chickenhead locked eyes across the coffee table.

"I know you don't want to, but it's imperative that you let me have that bill. If they find it on you, it could jeopardize all of our positions, especially yours."

Bitters and Chickenhead continued their staring contest. Abruptly, Bitters looked away. Folding both hands in front of himself, he leaned slightly across the table as he spoke. All eyes were on Chickenhead, who had unknowingly clamped his hand on the pocket that contained his notebook.

"Mister...Robert, we all know that you cared deeply for Mimi, that you want revenge for what happened to her. Well, we all do. But that's not going to happen if you're locked up. That's not going to happen if the police are dogging our and your every step. If they don't trust us, they'll become sidetracked and get in both of our ways. I'm sorry, but that's the way they'll see it. To them, that bill is evidence. I know that to you it represents a hell of a lot more," Bitters said and continued in a quiet voice as he shifted closer to the table. "I asked you to trust me when I met you this morning in your hotel room. Now is the time to bridge those waters. I promise that when this is all over, when we've caught that son of a bitch, I'll lay that bill back into your hands."

Chickenhead didn't move and didn't say a word. Jamaica brought him back by touching his clamped hand. Chickenhead turned to his friend.

"Robert, the man's got a point. We was talkin' 'bout this just this mornin', remember? Said we needed help." Jamaica pointed to Bitters and Driver, who was now back to the edge of his seat.

"Well, here is a hell of a lot more help than we ever thought we'd see. For this ta work, we gotta work together. To catch this mother-fucker, to do the shit we gotta do, we don't need no grief from the cops."

Jamaica released his hand and continued. "You know what

you gotta do, and it ain't easy...time's a wastin' if you're thinkin' 'bout anything else." Having said that, Jamaica reached across the table and poured himself another drink.

Chickenhead put his hand into his pants pocket and extracted the pocket-sized notebook. Turning to the last page, he removed the two paper clips that held the bill to the page. He held the bloody, folded bill in both hands and gently set it on the coffee table. His voice was low when he spoke to Bitters.

"You asked me to trust you," he whispered as he pointed to the torn note. "Well, there's my trust on the table. I want it back."

"You have my word, Robert."

Opening the briefcase at his feet, Bitters pulled out a plain letter-size envelope. He opened the flap and, using the end of a pen from the case, nudged the bill into the envelope. He folded the flap closed and then folded the envelope in half before placing it into a pocket of the briefcase.

"We'll need to run some tests on this in Houston. It may give us some hints about the killer."

Driver cleared his throat to get Chickenhead's attention. "Robert, you wanted to know about Plan 'B.' Well, you and Jamaica are it. Mr. Bitters is going to hand off to the police what comes off of the phone line we've set up...well, at least most of it. By doing this, they'll stay out of our way, and we'll keep some line of communication open in case they come across something on their own. I don't expect much from them. You and Jamaica are going to do what you've already proved you do very well--gather information. Get the people to talk, and if you need money or anything, let Mr. Bitters know, and he'll supply you with it. The other thing is that you need to go back to the police. Get in touch with Proctor...let him know you're willing to work with them again. Answer their questions, that will keep them happy."

Driver stopped and took a deep breath. He wiped the sweat from his brow with the back of his hand and looked at the two men hanging onto his every word. Shivering, he had a thought. Is this it? Is this what it comes down to? Is all of this in the hands of two bums off the street for less than an hour?

His hand trembled as he drained his drink. He slowly put the empty glass on the table.

"We'll need a place to stay...to work out of," Chickenhead replied. "We'll need driver's licenses, a car, something that's not new but reliable. You already gave us some money." Jamaica produced the envelope from his back pocket and gave it to Chickenhead. "I don't know how much this is, but we're gonna need ta hand it around. When it runs out, we're gonna need more."

"You have eight-thousand dollars in that envelope," Driver said. "Put it away. That's for the both of you. I'll have ten-thousand dollars in cash delivered to you by nine o'clock tonight."

Bitters picked up the conversation after Driver finished his sentence. "I'll take care of the car and apartment today. I'll also need to take pictures of you both for your driver's licenses. They'll be issued out of Houston...fewer problems that way. You'll have them in your hands tomorrow afternoon."

Bitters reached into his briefcase and pulled out a worn Bank of Houston moneybag. He unzipped it and extracted a plastic card, placing it on the table in front of Chickenhead. When Chickenhead picked it up, he saw that it was a Gold Visa credit card with his legal name embossed on it.

"I figured you both would need some things to get going. Clothes would be a good start, along with anything else for your apartment. Keep the receipts."

The look of disbelief on Chickenhead's face brought a slight upturn to the corner of Bitters' lips.

"I'm an optimist, Robert. I figured you'd say 'yes' to coming on board." His smile grew a fraction larger. "But you'll have to work for the Platinum card. Oh, and if you need a ride today, I'll get someone to ferry you both around."

Driver stood. The others followed.

"I have to go, gentlemen, I have city business that can no longer wait. I'm flying back to Houston this afternoon. I'll check back with you by week's end." Reaching across the table, he shook hands with both men. He hesitated releasing his grasp of Chickenhead's palm. Again, Chickenhead saw the pain, his pain, mirrored in Driver's eyes.

"Mr. Gibbs, remember... anything you need."

Chickenhead squeezed the mayor's hand in both of his and nodded. Driver turned away and left the room, but not before Chickenhead saw the water welling in the older man's eyes.

"Well, gentlemen," Bitters interrupted, "I think we've shocked you two enough for one day." Picking up his briefcase, he walked to the entrance of the hallway before turning back to the still standing men.

"This place is yours until you get the apartment. If you need anything, my room number and cell phone number are on my card. It's on the bar. I'll be back around five o'clock to take pictures for the licenses. Other than that, you're on your own the rest of the night. Don't get too drunk...we have an early day tomorrow."

Bitters turned to leave.

"Wait, hold up..." Chickenhead quickly walked around the coffee table and crossed the room to Bitters.

"Yes, Robert?"

"Back in the hotel room when you had the gun on us, you knew I was thinkin' about throwin' that paper, didn't you?"

The smile was hinting on Bitters' lips again. "I've been in this business for a long time, Robert. I certainly wouldn't have put it past you."

"Would you? Would you have shot us?"

Bitters' eyes practically sparkled as he replied. "Only to wound. If I'd killed you, I wouldn't get paid."

Chickenhead heard his chuckle as he walked down the hall. Chickenhead shook his head as he walked back to the sofa, where Jamaica was already reading the report Bitters had left. Chickenhead reached for the bottle on the table and poured his glass half full. Before he raised it to his lips, he decided he didn't want it and set it down. He picked up the other report, opened the cover, and started leafing through it. He was on page twenty-nine of the forty-page report when Jamaica called out to him from across the room, holding the phone in his hand. Chickenhead had been so engrossed in his reading that he hadn't noticed Jamaica crossing the room.

"Yo, I'm starvin' like Marvin. What you want from room service?"

Chickenhead looked around the room and then back at his friend. "Tell them to send me up a reality check."

Jamaica smiled. "You want that with or without mayo?"

Chapter 14

Proctor hadn't even closed the door to the lieutenant's office before LaPlante started ranting. He slammed down the phone to the desk.

"That was the third TV station this morning requesting an interview about this," he said as he shook the front section of the morning paper at Proctor, then threw it to the desktop. "I hope you had a nice weekend, 'cause this is gonna be a shitty week." He was interrupted by the sound of a ringing phone. Stabbing the "Hold" button on the console, he punched in his secretary's number. She answered immediately.

"Unless the world's coming to an end or it's the chief, don't call me for the next twenty minutes." He hung up before she could reply.

Proctor sat at the chair in front of his boss' desk.

"Thanks for the nice thought about the weekend. Mine definitely wasn't." LaPlante ignored the remark. "Where is Gibbs? Have you found him?"

"I don't know where he is yet, but I haven't had too hard a time tracking the broken bodies he and his buddy have been leaving behind." Proctor pulled a small notebook from his jacket pocket and flipped it open.

"Robert and Jamaica had a pretty bad altercation with a couple of guys at Robert's old flop last Friday. Turns out everyone got hurt. Took me 'til Sunday to track down the other men...a Jason Koppel and a Billy Cray. Found Koppel at the Savior's Soup Kitchen off of Adams Street on Sunday afternoon. Man was scared to death when I mentioned Robert's street name. Started sweating bullets and damn near ran me over when I showed him my badge. Same with Cray. Found him in the charity ward of Phoenix Lutheran Hospital. Left leg was wrapped up like a mummy. Said he slipped down some stairs and busted it. Almost died when I mentioned Robert. Same thing--didn't know anything," he growled as he snapped the notebook closed. "Said if I came back, he was gonna sue the department for harassment. Someone put a hell of a scare into both of 'em."

"Please tell me there's more."

"I'm sorry, boss. I've got Murphy down at the Columbus Clinic to see if Robert and Jamaica were treated for anything there on Friday."

The lieutenant's office phone rang.

"Shit," he mumbled before answering his phone. "Lieutenant LaPlante."

Proctor listened to his boss answer the caller in brief statements while writing notes on a pad. He wasn't on the phone more than a minute before hanging up.

"That was Murphy at the clinic. Both of them were there Friday night. He's talking to the doctor who treated Jamaica now. The doc who patched up Robert," he looked at his notes, "Howard, Braxton Howard, won't be in 'til tomorrow morning sometime." He directed his gaze at Proctor. "Make damn sure you're waiting for him when he gets there."

LaPlante picked up the section of the paper he had tossed away earlier. "I take it you've seen yesterday's paper and this morning's?"

"No. I didn't get in 'til half past hell last night and crashed. When I got up this morning, I didn't have time to read."

"This thing is going over like a lead balloon with the chief. The press is asking a ton of questions about the murder. They're sniffing around looking for more." He handed the page to Proctor. Staring back at the detective was a half-page photo of Mimi. The caption read:

Do you know this woman? Mimi Vivica Driver was murdered on or about December 1, 1999. Her body was found near the downtown section of Phoenix, Arizona, at approximately 7th Avenue and 13th Street. If you have any information, please call toll-free the number listed below. A $75,000 reward is being offered to the person or persons whose information leads to the arrest and conviction of those responsible for this heinous act. All replies will be kept confidential.

Beneath the picture was a toll-free number printed large enough to be read ten feet away, and the reward figure was even larger. Proctor set the paper back on his boss' desk.

"I've already called the phone company. Got the on-call supervisor to track down who set this thing up. Someone named Jeremiah Bitters is listed as the payer on the account," he said as he handed a sheet of paper to Proctor. "This is the contact info she gave me on him. Check him out."

"Did you call the number?"

"Yeah. Gave me a series of prompts, then asked to leave a way to get in touch with whoever called. Also has a prompt to talk to someone with a pulse. I pushed it, and someone came online pretty quick." He picked up the page Proctor had set down.

"You can best believe this isn't the only way Driver is gathering info...it's too obvious. And I'd bet my last dollar he's got both of them working with him."

The phone rang again.

"I'd better take this...the world's about to blow up. Get going." He picked up the phone.

Proctor wasn't halfway out of his seat when LaPlante gestured for him to sit.

"He's here? Now? Tell him he's on his way." He hung up the phone.

"Gibbs asked for you. He's waiting at your desk."

*   *   *   *   *

Proctor handed Chickenhead a cup of coffee from one of the vending machines in the second-floor break room.

"Thanks."

"You're welcome," Proctor said as he gestured to the closest investigation room. "Can we talk a bit?"

"Sure, detective. After you."

New clothes and shoes. Haircut, too, Proctor thought.

They sat across from each other with an air of adversaries. Proctor couldn't help but notice that Chickenhead looked calmer, almost to the point of being smug.

"Been out of touch for a while, Robert. What have you been doing with yourself?"

"Just tryin' to get my head together, ya know? The last couple weeks ain't been the easiest. Y'all disappointed me--didn't hear from you after I gave you a copy of my notebook...that's okay, though. I'm cool with that now."

Looking over his cup as he sipped his coffee, Chickenhead's eyes said otherwise.

"I'm sorry about that breakdown, Robert. That was my fault. Things got a bit sidetracked with the case for a moment. Mimi's father, Peter Driver, got involved with the investigation, and we dropped the ball on that one." Proctor paused to sip his own cup.

"You wouldn't happen to have met Mister Driver, would you?" Chickenhead saw no reason to lie.

"Yes. Jamaica and I are working for him."

"How so?"

"Same thing I came to y'all with. Finding out who killed Mimi."

"Well I wish you all the luck in the world. You have a hell of a man in your corner."

"Thanks," Chickenhead stood up from his chair, "I've got to be going. Just wanted to stop by...say hi. If I come across anything on the street you could use, I'll pass it on."

Proctor nodded and stayed seated, looking up at him.

"I was hoping to ask you a couple of questions. Are you in that much of a hurry?"

"Yes."

Both men stood their ground. Proctor, after almost a minute, was the one to break the stalemate.

"Robert, are you okay? You seem a bit...hostile."

"Detective, I'm fine, just in a hurry. You said you have some questions. What are they?" Chickenhead still made no move to sit.

"Why don't you have a seat...this shouldn't take more than a minute or two. Promise." Reluctantly, Chickenhead pulled out the chair he had just vacated and sat back down.

"Thank you." Proctor held up his empty cardboard cup. "Care for a refill?"

"No, thanks. The questions?"

"Yes, I'm sorry. Heard you and Jamaica had some trouble last Friday with a couple of guys at your flop."

"That's news to me, detective."

"So you don't know Jason Koppel or Billy Cray?"

"No."

"Were you at the Columbus Clinic last Friday evening?"

"Yes."

"Why?"

"Fell against a jagged piece of fence. I was collecting cans. Cut was bad enough for stitches."

"What about your friend? How'd he end up there?"

"Don't know. I saw him after I got there. His arm was pretty tore up, though."

"And you don't know how it happened? You didn't talk to him about what caused it?"

"No, I didn't."

"Seems kind of strange, don't you think? I mean, you two are pretty close, right?"

"Detective, I didn't ask, okay? He's my friend, not my wife." Chickenhead saw the wedding band on Proctor's finger. "Let me ask you a question, okay?"

"Fire away."

"When you get home from work, do you tell your wife every little thing that's happened in your day?"

"That would be really difficult for me to do, Robert. My wife's been dead for over a year."

All the aloofness left Chickenhead. "I'm...sorry."

"Apology accepted. No way you could have known, but you still haven't answered my question--how did Jamaica just happen to be hurt at the clinic at the same time as you?"

Chickenhead's voice wavered only slightly when he answered. "I don't know."

Proctor shifted in his chair, more to waste time than because of any discomfort. Picking up the empty coffee cup, he started tearing the paper away from the rim.

"Have you got a number I can reach you at? Someplace I can leave a message?"

"I'll be getting a beeper this afternoon. I'll call you with the number."

"You do that." Both men stood.

"Where are you staying? A hotel? Shelter?"

"At the Biltmore in Phoenix. Mr. Driver got us a room 'til we can find a place."

"Wow! The Biltmore? That's a helluva step up from Sunny Day, huh?"

"I guess so. Are you finished? I need to be going."

"I'm sorry. You're free to go after one more question. The night you found Mimi, you tore the plastic from around her head, correct?"

"Yes...we've covered this, Proctor. What's the question?"

"Money was found on Jefferson Plate's body in Mesa along with a picture in a plastic baggie similar to the drawing you made. Did you find any cash on Mimi?"

"No."

"Really? Nothing at all?"

"I said no, Detective, I was too busy freakin' out to check her fuckin' pockets! I didn't find shit."

"Robert, are you telling me the truth?"

"How many ways do you want me to say 'yes'?"

"So if I were to ask you, under oath, if you found money on Mimi's body, your answer would be the same?"

Dark red color rushed to Chickenhead's face.

"Under oath or any other way, my answer would be the same. I'm leaving."

"Maybe you should talk to me for a bit longer, Robert."
Chickenhead turned from Proctor and walked to the door of the
room. "Mr. Gibbs, I suggest you stick around a little longer," Proctor
repeated. Chickenhead whirled around to face Proctor.

"Cop, am I under arrest? 'Cause if I am, I get one phone call,
and I want it now."

"I could do that, Gibbs, but I wouldn't want to."

"And I would call my lawyer."

"What lawyer?"

"The one I have now...care to find out who that is, cop?"

Turning on his heel, Chickenhead left Proctor standing in the
room. After a moment, Proctor raised the heel of his hand and hit
himself on the forehead.

That could have turned out better, he thought.

*   *   *   *   *

Braxton Howard secured the last bright yellow tie-down to his
new Cessna 340-I single engine turbo-prop under the metal awning
of his parking slot at Scottsdale Airpark. Standing up from the short
metal pylon he tied the webbing to, he tested the tautness of the
straps. Satisfied, he stepped back from the slot and admired his new
toy. The color of the plane, a pearl base with an aqua underbelly,
glowed softly under the awning's fluorescent lights. Listening to the
hot engine tick as it cooled in the forty-degree night air, Braxton's
smile was wide and relaxed. It was an excellent idea to leave Phoenix
for the weekend, he thought.

After Gibbs' statement and his doctor's bad news, he needed a
break, a chance to catch his breath. Turning from his plane, he picked
up his overnight bag from the tarmac and headed for his car in the
parking lot. His mind wandered back to Gibbs. He would take care of
him tomorrow when he got to the clinic. After Gibbs stopped in from
his counseling session with the shrink, he would change his bandages
and talk to him for a bit. He needed to get him away from the
clinic...find out where he stayed. He beeped the alarm off on his car
with his key ring remote and opened the trunk, tossing in the bag.

Sliding into the driver's seat of the Mustang, he shivered as he started the car and turned the heat on high.

Before he had flown down to Texas for the weekend early Saturday morning, he had driven to the shelter where Jamaica stayed. He'd parked the Mustang across the street and had turned off the engine. He had sat in the darkness. After less than a minute, someone had detached themselves from the shadows in front of the building and had slowly walked across the street. As the stranger came to the passenger's side of the car, Braxton had pushed the button on his door to let that side's window down an inch. The stocky black man had leaned close to the window before speaking to Braxton in tones barely above a whisper.

"Nice ride you got here, my man. You lost? Lookin' for somethin'? Might be able to help ya out."

Braxton had talked to the dime-store variety drug dealer for ten minutes, and fifty dollars later (with a promise of one hundred more), they had exchanged pager numbers. This was the number that Braxton was dialing as he pulled out of the airport and into light traffic. Leaving a short message on voicemail that included his cell phone number, he placed the phone within easy reach on the front passenger seat. The man assured him that he would have Jamaica's room number by the time he got back from Texas and maybe even have his room key, too.

Braxton had decided the day before that Jamaica would die first, then Gibbs. He needed to find out what Gibbs knew, if anything, before he killed him...find out if he talked to anyone. Killing Jamaica in front of him might help to loosen his tongue a little.

His cell phone rang. He grinned as he let the ringing continue until it switched over to his voicemail. The wannabe drug lord would just have to leave a message. He would call back, of this Braxton had no doubt. His sorry, poor ass needed the easy money. All of their broke, whoring asses did. They always begged for money, and their stories were all the same...with the names changed to protect the stupid. And he loved to pay them...to meet them in hole-in-the-wall greasy spoons...buy them coffee, breakfast.

"I'll treat you good," they'd say while wolfing down forks full of soggy, sorry imitations of bland food scooped off of chipped plates.

"You ain't never had no pussy like this! You'll come back." They'd smile at him through red-rimmed eyes and open mouths with a gross lack of teeth, groping for him under the table as they grabbed the last roll...the last piece of toast to slop their plate.

"You a good man, a doctor even. Got somethin' special for you."

Looking over their files at the clinic, he had a plethora of choices. Occasionally it was a patient who he attended to, though more often it was someone from the other doctors' schedules. Spread the odds out a bit. There were always at least ten to twelve doctors on the clinic's roster. Sometimes up to six different doctors seeing patients a week. They'd come in once or twice a month...made them feel better about driving the Volvos to their second home on the weekends. They supplied a multitude of fodder to feed his fire.

"Where you wanna go? You got a house...a place nearby? If you wanna go in the car, I'm cool with that." Braxton would respond with, "No, I know someplace. It's just up the street--my dad's old store." Following him like puppies, high on the promise of money, mo' money, they'd get into his car, always one he'd stolen just hours before. He'd had a key made that was long and flat and would stick right into the destroyed ignition. They never even looked close enough to notice.

They'd touch him as he drove, their syrup-covered voices pleading. "Baby, you better hurry up. I'm so hot for some dick." They would be so close he could bathe in their funk...wash in their disease.

He was always ready for that, too. "Just hold on a minute, we 're almost there."

He owned a dilapidated, boarded-up storefront near the corner of Washington Street and 15th Avenue on the outskirts of downtown. Actually, a dummy corporation that was part of the Clinic owned the building. His name wouldn't be found on any of the paperwork. Some of them, seeing the shabby interior, would get nervous. The promise of money always calmed them. Despite the rundown appearance, the structure was a fortress. The plywood boarded windows and door were an almost three-inch thick sandwich of wood and insulating foam. The inside of the door was quarter-inch thick sheet metal painted black. The only light was a single sixty-watt bulb that hung from the ten-foot ceiling near the fifties-style refrigerator near the rear. Once the door closed, no one's scream could be heard on the street outside. They would always start to talk again when he took a thick wad of bills out of his pocket, smiling at them all the while.

"What do you want to start? A blow job? Anal? It's all good." He'd quickly respond with, "How about a drink? I'll get you one." Their answer was always "yes." He would walk across the wood floor to the full-size refrigerator. It was positioned so that when its door opened, they couldn't see into it. The fridge was stocked with cheap wine and beer, some liquor. And near the back of the first shelf, a small, nondescript bottle of plastic ampoules filled with liquid gamma hydroxybutyrate, better known as GHP, the date-rape drug, an odorless, tasteless batch of his own making. Bags of doped saline were in the bottom crisper with IV tubing and clean needles.

"Here's to a good time," he'd say, half closing the refrigerator door. He'd face them with a bottle in each hand, making sure they'd see and hear him twist open both bottles. Just as he would start to hand them the bottle, he'd stop, fumble a bit before turning his back to them, setting both bottles on a huge yellow-with-age Styrofoam cooler located behind him. He would turn back, taking the wad of bills out of his pocket. There'd always be a nervous laugh.

"I want to have a good time," he'd say as he'd peel off a twenty-dollar bill. "I hope this is enough to...to start," he'd continue meekly.

They would eagerly grab the bill, and their faces would break out in a smile, nearly threatening to split both lips in two. He'd turn back to the open drinks, and they'd never see him lance open the small plastic ampoule stashed in the space between his middle and ring fingers and drain the contents into their bottle. Feigning excitement, he'd turn quickly, swishing the drinks. Laughing.

"Oops! Spilled some," Braxton would say. "Guess I'm a little nervous." Then he'd hand them their spiked drink.

"Doctor, you 'd better drink up quick, 'cause I wanna make a lot of money tonight." She'd wink, grin like a fool, and raise the bottle to her lips, taking a long drink. With a forced laugh, he'd lead them to the slaughter like lambs.

Braxton pulled into the driveway of his gated community and punched in his password on the keypad near the front gate. Pressing the garage remote attached to his sun visor, he watched the door swing up as he made the turn into his driveway. He turned off the car engine as the overhead door closed behind him.

It took him almost a year of experimenting to get the right strength...the right dosage of GHP. Using it on waif-like, bottled blonde gold diggers in dark Scottsdale clubs with twenty-five-dollar covers, he would lance an ampoule into a drink at the bar, then move across the room to watch. He was ecstatic when he got them falling off their perches, unconscious, in less than nine minutes.

Picking up his cell phone from the passenger side front seat, he pressed the dashboard button for the trunk release and stepped out of the car. He took his bag out of the trunk, closed it, and hit his alarm switch on the key ring. Exiting the garage from the side door, he picked up both weekend papers lying on the stoop just as his cell phone chirped. He pressed the "talk" button.

"Yes?"

"Uh, I need ta talk ta...Clyde."

"This is he. Do you have my information?"

"Yeah, sure. When you wanna meet?"

Braxton looked at his Rolex. It was 6:49 p.m.

"Can you meet me outside the McDonald's on the corner of 17th and Van Buren at nine tonight?"

"Yeah...yeah, I can. You're lucky, Clyde, Monday nights been kinda slow past coupla weeks. If it gets busy, though, you'll have to wait for me."

"I can understand that. Tell you what...if you're on time, I'll throw in another hundred for your troubles, okay? But if I get there and you're not on that street corner, alone, at exactly nine p.m., I'll keep my two hundred dollars for someone else."

The man on the other end of the phone stammered as he answered.

"Hey, hold up, hold up...I'll be there, man. On time. Just jokin' wit' 'cha a little. Nine o'clock. On the dot."

"Thank you." Braxton clicked off his phone.

He opened the door to the condo, stepped over to the beeping alarm keypad, and punched in the deactivation code. After one beep, the keypad was silent. He didn't want to go out again tonight but thought it best to get this over with. Setting the overnight bag on the living room sofa, he dropped the two newspapers and plopped the cell phone beside them. He crossed into the kitchen, opened the refrigerator, pulled out a Bud Light, and popped it open. Draining the can as he picked up the overnight bag, he headed for the bedroom, wondering if he had time for a quick shower. He dropped the empty container in a small waste can near the bed and decided it was best to wait. Walking into the room-size closet near the master bath, he placed his luggage on the floor. After a brief moment, he selected black Levi's, a long-sleeved dark blue sweatshirt, and black penny loafers with no socks. He quickly changed out of his traveling clothes.

As he reached into the first drawer in a set of four, he moved aside rolled socks and folded tee shirts until he found a felt cloth-wrapped bundle lying at the bottom of the drawer. He unwrapped the cloth and pulled out a heavy, ivory-paneled, folded hunting knife, carrying it and the cloth into the living room. He extended the swatch of cloth out to arm's length. As he pressed a button on the knife, a five-inch stainless steel blade snapped open like a switchblade. Braxton took a quick swipe at the cloth and giggled as the entire bottom of it separated in a whisper of sound and fell to the floor. Folding the spring-backed blade closed, he put it in his back pocket. His informant would not live to spend any of his easy money.

Braxton picked up the newspapers from the sofa and walked to the alarm keypad. He pressed in the thirty-second delay and grabbed his keys from the kitchen before sprinting across the room and out of the door. Locking the door, he looked at the bundled newspapers, then sighed as he threw both into the blue recycle cans outside of the garage. Opening the side door to his garage, he pressed the key ring remote to disarm the car alarm. What the doctor really wanted to do was sit down and catch up with the news, something he didn't even think about during the weekend he bummed around Dallas. He started the car as the overhead garage door opened.

What the hell, he thought, bad as the Suns had been playin', they probably lost this weekend, anyway.

That thought brought a smile to his lips as he backed down the driveway.

Chapter 15

As soon as the nurse hung up the phone, it rang again. Swearing under his breath, he punched the "hold" button on the phone panel and stood up, looking into the clinic's packed lobby.

I didn't go to college for five damn years to be a friggin' secretary, he thought begrudgingly.

"The doctor can see you now, Detective. He'll be in the break room." The man gestured with his head as he stabbed the 'hold' button again, just as another line began ringing.

"End of the hall, then through the red door." Sinking into his chair behind the counter, the nurse went back to answering his backed-up phone lines.

"Thank you." Rising from his seat in the middle of the crowded lobby, Proctor stepped past the people sitting and standing beside his seat. It was like the parting of the Red Sea. The detective walked past the desk area, then proceeded down the hallway, passing four closed examination room doors. Proctor's stomach did a slow, bubbling roll. Since Carol's death over a year ago, anything that even looked like a hospital gave him an upset stomach. Pulling a half-gone roll of antacid tablets from his pants pocket (he had picked up a fresh roll on his way to the clinic an hour ago), he popped another one into his mouth and crunched it down as he came to the end of the hall and turned into the short hall in front of the red door. Standing in the middle of the room with his back to Proctor was a tall, trim man with tousled streaked blonde hair, his hands in the pockets of his knee-length lab coat. The doctor flinched at the sound of Proctor knocking on the open door.

"Doctor Howard?"

Braxton turned to face the doorway. Proctor could clearly see from the sour look on his face that the doctor was not in the mood for small talk.

"Yes, Officer," the doctor replied impatiently, "I'm really busy, so can we do this quickly? I have better things to do than this."

Testy motherfucker, Proctor thought. Who pissed in his oatmeal this morning?

"That's Detective, Doctor."

Proctor entered the room and placed his thin black leather briefcase on the end of the long tan folding table nearest the door. He didn't bother to offer his hand to Braxton to shake. The doctor followed Proctor's movements, turning slightly to keep him in sight. Proctor took his time pulling out one of the padded folding chairs, then sat down. Braxton made no move to follow.

"I apologize for the intrusion, Doctor. And this will be quick. I'd like to know a little about one of your patients. Did you see a Mr. Robert Gibbs last Friday night?"

There, he thought. He flinched again.

"I treated a lot of people on Friday, Detective. Could you be a bit more specific? Help me to remember?"

"This man is lying through his teeth...he knows Gibbs, Proctor thought."

"Skinny white guy, about six feet, maybe six one, red shoulder-length wild hair. That jog anything?"

"Yes, he was here on Friday. Came in late."

"What kind of condition was he in? Was he hurt?"

Braxton started tapping his left foot.

"Detective, have you ever heard of the 'doctor/patient relationship'?"

"Yes, I have."

"Good, then you know I can't discuss a patient's file unless the patient himself okays it. And Mr. Gibbs is not here." His foot started tapping faster. "Anything else? I need to be going."

"No...uh, yes." Proctor opened his briefcase and pulled out the front section of Monday's paper. He handed the page that was folded open to Mimi's picture to the doctor.

"Does she look familiar? Maybe you treated her in the past?"

Braxton almost snatched the paper out of Proctor's hand.

"Detective," he glanced at the photo, then back at Proctor sitting at the table. "I don't have time." Braxton stopped in mid-sentence and looked back at the photo.

"Doctor?"

This is the bitch I killed! In the paper? How?

"Doctor Howard?"

"I...need to get back to my patients, Officer. If you need to see any records, come back with a court order. Goodbye."

Braxton walked out of the room after tossing the paper on the table next to Proctor. He felt Proctor's eyes burning a hole into him as he turned up the hallway. Proctor sat at the table for a moment before picking up the paper. He looked at the half-page ad. That was one strange-ass encounter, he thought.

"Mimi," he said while looking at her smiling photo, "you're sure upsetting a bunch of folks, girl." Folding the paper, he put it back into his briefcase and popped another antacid. He picked up his briefcase and left the break room. As he walked to the front of the building, passing the same male nurse who was now arguing with someone on the phone, he tried to sort out what had just happened. Opening the clinic door and stepping into the street, he gently tapped the case against his leg.

"Let's go see if we can piss off a few more, girl."

*   *   *   *   *

Braxton never knew it was possible to vomit so hard without making a sound. After leaving the break room lightheaded, he walked to the front desk and told the nurse he'd be ready for his next patient as soon as he came back from the restroom. Turning, he reached into his pant pocket and calmly pulled out the key that opened the locked staff restroom. He twisted the lock, closed the door, and relocked the deadbolt. Braxton barely made it to the last stall before he lost his breakfast. After everything had emptied from his stomach, he dry-heaved for several minutes more before weakly reaching for the handle to flush. Climbing onto the seat, he pulled a long wad of tissue off of the toilet roll and wiped his smeared mouth. Dropping the soiled paper through his legs into the toilet bowl, he grabbed another handful to wipe the sweat from his face.

He had come to the clinic early, around 7 a.m., to replace the records he'd taken last Friday. Still euphoric from killing the informant (he had been stupid enough to bend over to pick up the bills that Braxton "accidentally" dropped at his feet the night before), the doctor recalled how he had pulled the knife out of his pocket and, in one stroke, had slashed the dealer's throat to the spine as he stood back up. The shocked man had died without a sound as Braxton walked away with Jamaica's room number on a piece of paper and a copy of his room key. He fed that feeling with a tablet of Demerol. By the time the clinic had opened at 8 a.m., Braxton was feeling great. He had treated several people before things started to go downhill. Loriann Blanco, the on-call psychologist for the clinic, called him at 9 a.m. to say that Robert never showed up for his session. Then right after that, that damn cop Proctor came by.

Hearing the bathroom door unlock, Braxton flushed the toilet again. He checked his stall and made sure it was still locked. He waited until the person exited the restroom before unlocking the stall and walking slowly to the bay of sinks. Taking a small plastic cup out of the dispenser over one sink, he filled it with water and rinsed his mouth several times. He heard the restroom door unlock again and straightened his crooked lab coat. The nurse from the front desk stuck his head into the room.

"Doc, you okay?"

"Yes, sorry. My stomach's upset a bit. Something I ate, I guess." He brought another cup of water to his lips.

"Yeah, those breakfast burritos do that to me sometimes.

Gimme gas like a son of a bitch. But they sure taste good. You gonna be out soon? We got a full house."

"Yes, just give me a minute more," he said. He watched the nurse nod in his direction and close the door behind him.

That bitch was in the paper! And Proctor showed it to him. Fuck! That cop couldn't have known...if he had, Braxton would have been talking to his lawyer from jail by now.

How the hell did she get into the newspaper? Braxton knew that he'd only chosen people who'd checked "none" in the next of kin box on the information form everyone filled out.

I need a newspaper, he thought.

Opening the door to the restroom, he walked to the desk in the lobby. Without looking up from the phone he was talking on, the nurse handed him a clipboard with a patient's information form attached to it. Braxton's mind was a thousand miles away when he called out the name on the top of the chart.

"Mark Carmela?"

An ancient, bent man with tufts of crinkly gray hair around his ears slowly rose from his seat at the farthest end of the lobby.

I've got to get out of here, Braxton thought. I've got to find Gibbs' friend today.

He watched the man of unknown ethnicity as he slowly made his way to the desk, holding his side.

I've got to get to him tonight...he'll get me Gibbs.

Taking the man's arm, Braxton guided him to the last examination room down the hall. Helping him to step through the narrow door, he steadied him as the old man sat on the low examination table.

"Sit here for a moment, Mr. Carmela. I'll be right back."

"Sure thing, Doc."

Braxton walked back to the front desk and tapped the nurse on the shoulder. Covering the mouthpiece to the phone with one hand, the nurse looked up at the doctor.

"What's up?"

"Did anyone bring in a paper today? Yesterday?"

"Um, yeah," the nurse responded as he reached into the

halfway open drawer beside him. "Yeah, here it is. Suns lost. Again." He handed a stack of newspaper to Braxton and returned to his conversation. While walking back to the exam room, Braxton sifted through two days' worth of papers. He opened the fourth page of yesterday's edition and saw her face again. Looking up and down the hall quickly, the doctor pulled out that part of the paper and headed for the break room. He set the stack of newsprint on the table and quickly folded Mimi's ad until it was small enough to fit into his back pants pocket. Leaving the mess of papers on the table in the break room, he headed back to his patient. He made an effort to steady himself before he opened the examination room door, a pained smile on his face.

"Mr. Carmela, I'm sorry about the wait. What seems to be the problem today?"

* * * * *

"Yo, Robert, let me off at the hotel. I wanna talk to a couple of people 'bout some of those Jane Does. I also need ta clear out my shit. I'll catch a cab or a ride back to the hotel."

Chickenhead pulled the car up to the sidewalk across from The Montovie Men's Hotel and cut the engine. Taking the key out of the ignition of the gray 1988 Ford Escort, he walked to the back of the car and opened the hatchback door. He removed a heavy, black backpack and a blue jean jacket. As he walked back to the front of the car, he tossed the keys to Jamaica, who caught them with his good hand.

"You take the car. You got a ton of shit to move. I'll catch the bus back if I need to. You got your pager?"

Chickenhead tapped the one he had on his belt.

"Yeah."

"I'm gonna head out to 35th Avenue. A body was found out that way 'bout five months ago. Old Pepper stays around here, near the wash. If anyone knows anything, he will. I'll beep you later."

"Be safe."

Jamaica crossed the street to the shelter. Taking the steps two at a time, he reached the top of the landing and opened the door, disappearing into the building. Chickenhead placed the backpack on the ground, then pulled on the jacket. He opened a pocket of the full backpack and took out a Phoenix bus schedule, leafing through the pages. Finding the page for the connection he needed, Chickenhead took his bus card out of his wallet to mark the spot. He closed the book and realized he had about forty minutes to kill before his first bus came. Pulling the backpack over his shoulder, he started walking down the street to a Quik Stop Market, got a large cup of coffee, and stood outside sipping it. Twenty minutes later he saw two people he knew walk by. The three talked for the next fifteen minutes with cups of soup in their hands, courtesy of Chickenhead, who also gave both of them a ten-dollar bill and almost missed his bus as he jotted down his pager number to give to the men. Neither had any information about any of the killings, but they said they would ask around. An hour and one transfer later, Chickenhead was standing in deep, dead weeds next to a trash-strewn squatter's camp near 35th Avenue and the dried-out Salt River bed. He walked against a steady wind that was blowing from the direction of a tallow-processing factory and was glad that he only had coffee for breakfast that morning. Chickenhead walked around the remains of a burned-out couch when a medium-size dog began barking loudly. Straining against its makeshift rope leash, the dog was given a wide berth. A tent made from cardboard boxes and two-by-fours in the size of a small garage leaned against the side of a rusted VW bus with no wheels. The flap that was the front door was pushed open and revealed a hugely fat man, his lower body wrapped in blankets. He had only one arm. For a moment, Chickenhead forgot the nauseous odor and smiled at his friend as he shouted at the still barking dog.

"Goddamit, dog! Shut the fuck up!" Wheezing, the man set the long stick he used as a cane on a pile of filled plastic bags lining the door. He picked up an old soup can and threw it at the dog, missing him by a mile. The dog stopped barking anyway.

"Who's there?" he asked.

"Put your glasses on, you fat fuck."

"Chicken, that you?" Pulling a taped-up pair of dirty glasses from the fold of his blanket, the old man squinted and then smiled when he recognized his old friend. Chickenhead crossed the short distance to the door and shook the extended right hand.

"Son of a bitch, Chickenhead! It's good to see you!"

"You, too, Pepper. It's been a while."

"Come on in. You hungry? I got some soup."

"Naw, bro, I'm good." Chickenhead slipped his full backpack off his shoulder and pulled open the zipper on the main compartment.

"Hope you're hungry, though. Brought you somethin'." Pulling out a plastic sack, he handed it to Pepper. Pepper set it on the ground in front of the door and opened it. Five Costco size cans of corned beef hash spilled out onto the ground.

"Hot damn! Chicken, you all right, man. I love that stuff. Thanks. Grab that shit and come on inside. Got a couple of seats and some beer."

Putting the cans in the plastic bag, Chickenhead carried them into the dim structure. He set them next to three plastic gallon jugs of water and pulled up a badly listing lawn chair that sat next to the mound of clothes and plastic bags Pepper was sitting on. Pepper handed him a beer out of a large pot of clear water. Chickenhead was surprised that the can was cold.

"How ya doing, Pepper?"

"Getting hard to walk...damn arthritis kicks my ass on cold days like this."

"I know what you mean. You doin' okay otherwise?"

"I'll live. Today. I think." Both men chuckled. In the dim light filtering in from the holes in the cardboard walls, Chickenhead saw Pepper's face become slack as he pushed the long matted gray hair from his eyes. He was grim when he looked back at Chickenhead.

"I'm sorry 'bout your woman, Chicken. Heard about her couple of weeks ago. Damn sorry."

"Thanks, Pepper. Maybe you can help me with somethin', okay?"

"Name it."

"'Bout five, six months ago, a body was found out this way, wrapped in black plastic...just like Mimi. You know anything about it?"

Pepper shivered as he pulled another blanket off the pile of clothes next to him and wrapped it around his huge shoulders.

"Yeah, I know who you talkin' about. Was Mandy...Mandy Jarrell. She been missin' couple three weeks when a guy I know found what was left of her. Found her in some bushes 'bout mile or two from here in the riverbed. When he showed me the body, I knew it was her 'cause she still had that thick, ugly-ass rope bracelet she always wore on her leg. That 'bout the only thing left you'd know...everything else was gone. Coyotes ate good for a coupla days. Ate right through the plastic wrapped around Mandy to get to her."

The smile on Chickenhead's face was a somber one as the men continued to talk. Pulling out his notebook, Chickenhead started to write. Pepper had given him his first name.

*   *   *   *   *

Chickenhead left Pepper's hut around two that afternoon, nearly three hours after he had first arrived. As he left he hugged the big man and slipped three twenty-dollar bills into his hand. Pepper stared at the money with wide eyes, then looked back at his friend.

"Damn, man, thanks a lot!" He slipped the folded bills into one of the many folds in the bottom set of blankets he wore like a skirt.

"I'll talk to Bobo and a couple of other guys I know...see if I can find out anything 'bout those other bodies."

"Thanks, Pepper. You hear anything, leave me a message at the number I wrote on the back." Chickenhead handed Pepper an envelope with a new fifteen-minute phone card inside. On the back of the plain white paper he had written his voice pager number.

"I'll get back with you as quick as I can," Chickenhead said as he left the campsite. Walking past the once-again barking dog, Chickenhead shook his head as Pepper screamed at the animal. A moment later, an empty can, the label of which was a picture of mixed vegetables, bounced past his foot.

*   *   *   *   *

Chickenhead got back to the Biltmore around 11:20 that night. As he walked up the pathway to his villa, he was greeted by a dapperly dressed waiter pushing an empty food cart down the walkway. Jamaica is really starting to like this room service thing, he thought. Using his card to swipe the door open, he was surprised to hear soft jazz playing. Once he cleared the hall, he saw Jamaica writing onto a pad of paper on the coffee table. Beside him were two covered plates and a liter bottle of orange soda. As he entered the room, Jamaica looked up at him.

"Damn, man, talk about timin'. I just ordered us some food. Cop a squat...found out a coupla things."

Chickenhead dropped his backpack and jacket at the entryway and looked around the room as he came inside. There were a few boxes of stuff, books mostly, that Jamaica had brought from his room at the shelter. He stopped at one of the four medium-size boxes near the far side of the room and opened the top box.

"This can't be all of your shit. Where's the rest of it?"

Jamaica took a swig of orange soda to clear the huge bite of pastrami sandwich from his mouth before he replied.

"Gave it away, mostly. Whole bunch of people back there doin' worse than me, I guess." How true, Chickenhead thought.

"How you like the sounds? Got us some music."

Chickenhead smiled at the sight of the new Sony CD boom box that was set up on the bar. Walking over, he looked through the stack of twenty or so CDs--all new--most still in the store wrappers. He saw Candy Dulfer, Luther Vandross, Babyface. Chickenhead chucked as he waved a Marvin Gaye's Greatest Hits CD in Jamaica's direction.

"You expectin' a booty call? Let me know beforehand, okay? I'll hit a movie. If you fuck anything like you snore, gonna be one noisy party."

Jamaica gagged on the sandwich he was chewing. He gave him the finger with one hand while wiping his mouth with the other.

"That's some cold shit. If this town had some decent radio stations 'stead of that country and yang shit, wouldn't need no records. Need some black ones, you ask me."

"Calm down, old man, you gonna blow a gasket."

Chickenhead flopped down on the sofa opposite Jamaica. Pulling the still warm covered plate to his side of the table, he took off the plastic lid and looked at a club sandwich that was almost as big as the plate upon which it sat. Starting to eat, he didn't look up until the plate was clean. Outside of countless cups of coffee today, this had been the first thing he had eaten. Drinking straight from the soda bottle on the table, he thought, Yeah, bunch of people out there doin' lots worse than us.

"Sonny James got killed sometime Monday night," Jamaica said.

"Sonny? The part-time dealer? What? He sell somebody baking soda again?" Chickenhead started picking fries from Jamaica's plate.

"Naw, man, shit was strange. Someone cut his throat. Musta used ah hatchet or somethin' 'cause his head almost fell off."

"Good riddance to bad people. World could stand to lose a few more like him." Chickenhead and Sonny had had several run-ins in the past, the last one over Mimi. Sonny had tried to "recruit" Mimi into his stable of cracked-out whores by slapping her around one day.

Chickenhead tracked him two days later to a rathole hotel in Mesa. The resulting fight put both men in the hospital for almost a week. Sonny had given him a wide berth ever since and looked the other way if Mimi was around.

"Singin' Man found him in that little park down from the McDonald's at 7th. Body was still warm when he got there. Here's the good part: he still had a pocketful of dope and cash. Singin' Man took it all and kept on steppin'."

"Like I said, good riddance."

"Check this out, though. He was askin' 'bout us the night before he was sliced."

That got Chickenhead's full attention.

"Who told you that?"

"Coupla guys at the hotel. Said he wanted to know if I still stayed there, where you stayed, shit like that."

"Think it might be Fatman? His buddies?"

Jamaica laughed.

"Oh, hell no, not those pussies. Saw Billy Cray when I was movin' out of my room today. He was limpin' up the street when I was going ta get a sandwich. Man saw me and ran into traffic. Took me five minutes ta stop laughin'."

The smile on Chickenhead's face at that mental picture was erased at the dead serious look that came over Jamaica's face with the next statement.

"I think we got someone else's attention, bro."

Chickenhead returned his partner's look with one just as formidable.

"Good. I'm looking forward to meeting the motherfucker."

The fire in Chickenhead's eyes let Jamaica know that he meant every word he'd said.

Neither man spoke for a couple of minutes, instead reflecting on what both had just said. Getting out of his seat, Chickenhead went to his backpack by the door and opened one of the smaller pockets. He removed his notebook and a pen, then returned to the sofa.

"Find out anything else? Any news about any of the bodies?"

"Oh, yeah," Jamaica acknowledged as he pushed his plate aside and reached for his own notepad. He leafed through a couple of pages before getting to the one he wanted.

"Talked to Singin' Man for a while today. Told me he remembered a guy in Glendale talkin' 'bout findin' someone that he fucked on a regular basis wrapped in plastic coupla days after he'd been with her 'round last Christmas. Took most of the day for me ta track him down. Then needed ta down a coupla six-packs with him to loosen his ass up...prove I wasn't some cop. Got her name, too. Debra... Debra Jenkins. She showed up right around the time of–," he glanced at his notes, "–Jane Doe Number Six on our list."

Chickenhead told him the information Pepper had given him earlier.

"Damn, man. We on a roll." Jamaica checked his notes,

turning three pages. "She sounds like she could be Jane Doe Number Two."

"Yeah, I thought that, too." Chickenhead closed his notebook and tossed it and the pen onto the coffee table next to the plates. Putting both hands behind his head and locking his fingers together, he leaned back into the sofa.

"I think we did pretty good for the first day. What do you think?"

Jamaica circled some lines on his tablet as he spoke. "Hey, two down, eight ta go." Chickenhead's pager buzzed. As he fumbled to get it off of his belt, the buzzing stopped and a number began flashing on the tiny screen. He looked at it upside-down, and by the time he righted it, the screen went blank, sending a jolt of fear down his spine. Oh, shit, he thought, I lost the number!

Jumping off the sofa, Chickenhead ran to his backpack and started looking through all of the pockets for the pager's instruction manual. He looked through several pockets before he turned the bag upside-down, dumping the contents onto the floor. The booklet was the last thing to fall out. Grabbing it, Chickenhead almost ran across the room to the phone. He quickly read how to retrieve a number and pushed two buttons on the unit. To his relief, the number returned to the re-lit screen. He dialed it immediately, and the phone on the other end rang three times before it was picked up. The noise in the background sounded like it was coming from a bar. The sound of blood rushing to his head didn't make it any easier for Chickenhead to hear, either.

"Chicken, that you?"

"Pepper?"

"Yeah, man, it's me. Glad you called right back. Got someone for you to talk to. Hold on, okay?"

"Yeah, yeah sure."

Chickenhead heard the phone bump something and listened intently as he heard Pepper talking loudly to someone. The line was picked up again.

"Chicken? You still there?"

"Yeah, Pepper."

"Okay..." Chickenhead heard Pepper speaking to someone and saying, "He's okay...he ain't no cop."

"Hello? Hello?" Chickenhead spoke into the phone. A woman answered.

"Um...hi. You Chickenhead? The guy askin' 'bout those killin's?"

"Yes, yes, that's me," he replied as he anxiously pressed the phone closer to his ear. "Could you speak up a little, please? I can barely hear you."

Jamaica jumped over the back of the sofa on which he was sitting and ran to the bar, quickly cutting off the boom box.

"Sorry, got a cold. If Pepper say you okay, I guess you all right..." She hesitated for almost twenty seconds before she spoke again.

"Pepper say you'll get me some cold medicine, coupla bucks maybe? That right?" Over the background noise, Chickenhead heard Pepper's loud groan.

"Give me your address...the address of the place you're in right now, and I'll be there tonight."

"Really?"

"Yes...I ain't gonna mess over you, ma'am."

She was quiet again, but only for a few seconds this time.

"Name's...Kitten...Kitten Robinson."

"Thanks, Ms. Robinson. Why don't you give me that address, okay?"

"You really comin'? Right now?"

"Yes, ma'am. What you have to say is very important to me."

She gave him the address of the bar. It was off of 92nd Avenue and Camelback Road, nearly an hour's ride away. Before they got off the phone, Pepper told Chickenhead that if the bar closed before he got there, they would both be standing two doors down at the 24-hour donut shop. Grabbing their coats and notebooks, Chickenhead and Jamaica made it across town in less than an hour, stopping only to get money out of an ATM and to run into an all-night Osco Drug Store. Since Jamaica didn't know what to get, he bought three boxes of the first cold medicine he came to and a bottle of cough syrup.

By the time the two friends pulled up to the parking lot of the Dime a Dozen Bar and Grill, it was 1:49 a.m. Jamaica pointed to the donut shop at the other end of the strip mall. Pepper, clad in a pair of bib coveralls, a dark sweatshirt, and laceless tennis shoes, was waving to them. He was standing alone. Parking the car, Chickenhead jumped out and left the key in the still running ignition. Jamaica reached across the console and turned off the engine. Seeing the fear in his friend's eyes as he ran to him, Pepper took a step away from the light of the donut shop and held his stump and hand in front of himself.

"Chicken, man, it's cool. She just had to go to the bathroom," he said as he nodded toward the donut shop. "She in there. No way I'd let her out of my sight 'til you got here."

Chickenhead let out a gush of relief. Pepper looked around him and squinted as he saw Jamaica coming from their car with the drug store bag in his hand. Jamaica switched the bag to his other hand in order to greet Pepper.

"Jamaica, long time no see." They all shook hands.

Before Jamaica could reply, all heads turned to the noise of the tinny buzzer that sounded as the door to the donut shop opened. A small mousy woman hesitantly emerged from inside. Wearing a man's army fatigue jacket that was big enough to fit two of her, she looked like a little girl who had gotten into her father's closet. Her tattered Phoenix Suns baseball cap barely kept her long, dark hair out of her face. The shoes she wore, at one time blue bathroom slippers, were caked in mud. She stopped in front of the closing door and looked at all of them. Pepper motioned for her to come closer. She took slow, small steps toward the men. She stopped just behind Pepper's shoulder.

"Chicken, Jamaica, this is Kitten. Kitten, these are the guys I was tellin' you about. They're okay."

She stood behind Pepper, looking at both men. Her eyes settled on the bag Jamaica was holding. Seeing her staring at it, Jamaica took a slow step toward Pepper, holding the bag in front of him as he closed the short distance between them. He stopped just in front of Pepper and reached out to her with the bag in hand. She took a quick step around Pepper and pulled the bag from Jamaica's hand, then stepped back behind Pepper. Jamaica stepped back as Chickenhead watched Kitten look into the bag. She took the bottle of cough syrup out of the bag and looked at Chickenhead. Even in the dim light of the parking lot, he could see her eyes brighten with the first hint of tears. Her voice was thick with congestion when she spoke.

"You got me some cold medicine. You didn't lie."

Chickenhead nodded at her.

"You said you needed it. I'm sorry it took us so long to get here. I'm not familiar with this part of town."

She put the medication back into the bag and stepped around Pepper. Holding the bag in one hand, she held out the other to shake first Jamaica's and then Chickenhead's hand. Chickenhead looked down on her and realized she couldn't be much older than in her early twenties, if that. She looked up at Chickenhead with eyes the size of moons.

"Could you buy me a cup of tea in the donut shop? I really would like to take this medicine with something hot," she whispered as she looked at her feet before softly adding, "Please?"

Jamaica tapped his partner on the shoulder, pointing to a Denny's restaurant across the street. Chickenhead nodded and then spoke softly to the woman-child in front of him.

"How about some breakfast with that tea? Is that okay?"

He pointed across the deserted street. "We can talk in there. Get out of the cold for a while."

Her tears fell this time as she looked up to him and nodded "yes." Taking Pepper's stump, she walked with the group of men as they crossed the street. After they were seated, Chickenhead ordered two large pots of coffee and tea. Everyone sipped their hot drinks, talking little while waiting for the food to arrive. When the waiter brought their orders, Chickenhead asked him to bring back two menus. Kitten's eyes never left Chickenhead as she opened the box of cough syrup and, taking her teaspoon, measured out two doses, sipping her tea afterwards. The waiter brought the menus to Chickenhead, who took them and laid them on the floor next to him.

The waiter asked if everything was okay, and Chickenhead nodded. Before leaving, the waiter said he would check back with them. As Kitten and Pepper finished their meals, Chickenhead, lifting both menus from the floor beside him, handed one to each of them.

"Why don't ya'll get something for the road, okay?"

Kitten started to cry softly as she kept her eyes focused on the table. She reached across the empty dishes in front of her and took Chickenhead's hand, squeezing it in both of hers with a grip that was surprisingly strong for someone so small. He gently squeezed back.

After the table was cleared and the boxed meals ordered, Kitten, still crying softly, excused herself to use the restroom. Remaining at the table, the men made small talk. The boxed meals came, and Chickenhead paid the tab. Another ten minutes went by. A light nervous sweat formed on Chickenhead's brow and he wiped at it. Just as Pepper stood to ask a waitress to check the restroom, Kitten turned the corner and headed back to the table. Her eyes, though red, had a thin line of mascara on them. Her thin face was lightly made up. And the baseball cap was gone. Her hair fell down her back in two long braids. She was smiling. Chickenhead hoped she didn't hear the slow sigh of relief escape his lips.

"I'm sorry I took so long. It's a woman thing."

She looked at Pepper. "May I sit there, please?" Pepper switched seats with her.

Moving the boxed meals aside, she reached across the short distance and held Chickenhead's hand, squeezing it again between both of hers.

"Thank you. Thank you very much, sir."

Chickenhead was too choked up to reply. She nodded for him, then cleared her throat with a small cough. She never released his hand.

"I want to tell you about my friend Shelly."

They talked for almost two hours. Shelly Mosley turned out to be Jane Doe Number Four on their list.

Chapter 16

Braxton had been pacing in the small hotel room for the last two hours, and all that movement was killing his Demerol high. After using his ill-gotten key to enter the room, he changed from his street clothes into long-sleeved navy blue hospital scrubs, complete with booties and two pairs of latex gloves that he'd taped to his sleeves. All the pacing back and forth across the small shabby room was making his outfit hot and uncomfortable for him. The small size of the room (the door was only two healthy steps from the twin-sized wood framed bed) was also starting to work on his already taunt nerves. He had left the clinic in South Phoenix early, around three o'clock, and had driven around for another half an hour before finding a hardware store for his supplies. He always picked a different one for each encounter, and he had used up all of those that were close to the clinic.

He picked up a forty-foot roll of duct tape, pruning shears, a spindle of twenty-pound test fishing line, and a box of twenty black plastic fifty-gallon garbage bags, all paid for at the counter in small bills. Stopping at the door, he turned back into the store and picked up a box of ten-penny nails, a small hammer, a metal file, and a Philips-head screwdriver with a five-inch shaft. He went back to the now smiling man at the counter. As the cashier started loading the items into another clear plastic bag, he gave Braxton a knowing grin and winked at him.

"Looks like the little lady got you busy this week. Don't let her work you too hard."

Braxton returned the clerk's grin with one of his own as the man handed him his change. "Got to bust your ass sometimes ta keep 'em happy," he said as he took his second bag from the countertop and grabbed the one he had placed at the door. He left the store for the short ride back to his condo in Scottsdale.

He was going to torture Jamaica before he got down to the business of finding out where his friend Gibbs was. It pissed him off immensely that this black piece of shit was making him work so hard to find his bastard buddy. Images of Jamaica screaming as Braxton first, with the pruning shears, clipped holes into his flesh and then hammered the five-inch nails into the openings, brought a large smile to his face and lightened his mood. This would hurt like hell but wouldn't kill him. He had something better planned for that scenario. Jamaica would tell him anything he wanted to know by then.

Arriving home, he placed his items into a dirty, scuffed green canvas gym bag that already contained his hospital scrubs and both latex and cheap cotton gloves. Braxton entered the kitchen and opened the refrigerator. He was careful as he reached to the back and pulled out a large mouth jar of Mexican salsa. The doctor returned to the sink and set down the jar as he opened one of the overhead cabinets and extracted a medium-size stainless steel bowl. Dumping the jar's contents into the bowl, he fished out a small, double plastic-wrapped 50ml bottle of Versed, an industrial-strength anesthetic. He donned a pair of latex gloves and began rinsing the tomato residue from the outside of the container before unwrapping it. Then he took a capped 5ml syringe out of his doctor's bag, uncapped the syringe, filled it, recapped the syringe, and tossed it into the gym bag.

Braxton returned everything to its place, changed out of the clothes he was wearing, and left for The Montovie Men's Hotel. He kept a bottle of Versed on hand just in case. A 5ml dose of the fast-acting drug would incapacitate a person the size of Jamaica in less than two minutes.

It was the capped syringe that he held in his double latex-gloved hand now as he paced. A door slammed down the hall. He stopped walking to listen. Someone was coming down the hallway toward the room. The sounds of various footsteps had been happening since he'd arrived earlier in the day, and he wondered if this person would also pass by. The steps stopped on the other side of the door, and Braxton tensed as he heard the jiggling of keys. The doctor moved quickly and quietly to the backside of the door, raising the syringe in his right hand as he listened intently at the key turning in the stubborn lock. When the door began to open inward, Braxton held his breath and took a small step backward at the same time the door swung toward him and away from the wash of light now flooding the room from the hallway overhead fluorescent lamps. Blocked by the door, he couldn't see who was there, but he could distinguish the frustrated sounds of the newcomer trying the wall switch beside the door. The man was still clicking the light switch when he looked up at Braxton.

"What the...?"

It wasn't Jamaica. This man was white.

Braxton's empty left hand shot out toward the surprised man's unprotected throat with a two-finger jab, connecting hard with the soft tissue. The force of the blow paralyzed the man's vocal cords. As the man instinctively reached for his bruised throat, Braxton dropped the uncapped syringe from his right hand and slammed the heels of both of his hands onto the man's ears, effectively rupturing his eardrums. As the bum's knees started to buckle, Braxton cupped one hand behind his victim's head, pulling him closer while simultaneously hitting the bum's jutting, unprotected jaw with a vicious upper cut. The unconscious man collapsed toward the doorway and into Braxton's outstretched arms. Spinning away from the open door while holding the man to him with his left arm, Braxton closed the door with his right. The enraged doctor locked the door behind his back as he held the man against him. Fighting the rage rising like steam within, Braxton dragged the limp body to the area next to the bed and slowly lowered the man to the floor. He reached across the body in the pitch-black room and slowly moved his hand over the surface of the bed until he felt the light bulb that he had put there earlier just after he'd removed it from the lamp. Standing upright, the doctor guided the bulb to the socket by touch and turned it twice into the opening. He stopped before he got to the final turn. Feeling his way to a dresser drawer against the wall behind him, Braxton opened the top drawer and pulled out three pieces of clothing that felt like tee shirts. He draped all three, one on top of the other, over the lampshade. He then reached under the shade and gave the bulb a final turn. The light blinked on, its rays barely showing through the layers of clothing covering the lampshade. Braxton removed the top shirt, a purple Phoenix Suns "Gorilla-for-hire" tee, and was able to make out the outline of the man's face as his victim wheezed on the floor. The doctor shook with rage as he pulled from his pants pocket the folded sheet of paper his now deceased informant, Sonny James, had given him. Unfolding it under the light, he checked the number written on it–214. Hell, he was in the right room all right, but this wasn't Jamaica, and he knew from asking that fat desk clerk that there was only one person per room in this dump.

The man on the floor started to stir. Braxton looked down on his victim's slight features, the thinning hair, and the second-hand mismatched clothes...and snapped. Raising one foot high, he slammed his size-eleven hiking boot down on the exposed throat, fully collapsing the bum's esophagus. As the man's body jerked beneath his grinding foot, Braxton almost tore open his back pants pocket pulling out his heavy, ivory-paneled knife. Snapping it open, he fell on the man and was blinded by rage. Every blow to the man's chest reminded Braxton that he was no closer to finding Gibbs, and that thought enraged him even more. And with every convulsion of the man's body beneath him, the out-of-control doctor would stab him again. Braxton was shaking as he became soaked in the man's blood and gore and finally regained enough control to move away from the mutilated figure. He had stabbed the man forty-nine times in less than a minute. Lightheaded from his rage, Braxton stood up and held onto the dresser drawer behind him until his breathing slowed to close to normal. Looking down at the mess beneath him, the doctor cursed softly and hotly. He tried to clear his racing thoughts...tried to think. Staring back toward the man, he saw his knife sticking out of the bludgeoned chest. He bent down slightly and pulled it out of the body. It made a soft, slurping sound as it came out of the flesh.

Holding the dripping blade in his hand, Braxton got an idea. He reached down and opened the front pockets of the bum's pants. Nothing there. He rolled the body over. As he cut the back pockets open with the knife, a well-worn wallet fell out. The doctor kicked the body onto its back as he lifted the wallet closer to the light, absentmindedly wiping the knife's bloody residue on the shirt covering the lampshade. Braxton wiped his blood-slick gloved hands on the same shirt and parted the wallet open with the tip of the blade. Seeing papers inside, he placed the wallet on the desktop, folded the knife and stuck it back into his back pocket, and then reopened the wallet with both hands. He held it under the light and pulled out four ten-dollar bills, laying them on the desktop. The top bill had a slight red mark from the wet blood on his gloves. Opening the wallet even wider, Braxton saw a folded sheet of paper and took it out. He unfolded it and read the contents. He gasped when he saw the name under the local number—Jamaica Rummains.

Suddenly a door slammed, and someone ran down the hall cursing loudly. The noise startled Braxton, and he backed into the desks. The money on top fell soundlessly into the space between the bed and the nightstand. Braxton looked at the body again, then toward the door. It's time to go, he thought.

Forgetting about the money, he shoved the piece of paper with Jamaica's number into a side compartment of his green gym bag. He moved back to the dresser he had opened earlier, pulled out the top drawer, and dumped the contents on the floor around the body. This will have to do, he thought. I've got to get out of here.

He walked back to his gym bag, took out a plastic garbage bag, and spread it open on the floor. Then he stood on the bag and carefully undressed, placing all his clothes, gloves included, around his feet. He reached into the gym bag again and pulled out a clear plastic bag containing his other clothes and a pair of black cotton mittens. Braxton balled all of the gore-splattered clothes into the first bag and quickly dressed in the fresh clothes. The doctor took out a clean pair of bargain basement sneakers from the gym bag and put them on as he scanned the dark room. He saw a radio and an old army jacket on the chair near the door. He grabbed them both and stuffed the radio into his bag. Braxton looked near the door and squinted his eyes in the low light, trying to spot the syringe he had dropped earlier. He didn't see it.

Braxton crossed the room back to the nightstand and stayed as close to the dresser as possible. He didn't want to bloody his shoes. Angling the shade slightly toward the door, he returned to the base of the bed and looked again. He still couldn't find it. The door at the end of the hall opened, and he heard several voices talking loudly. One voice was shouting a name that he couldn't quite make out.

He heard another door open closer to him and the men entered. Braxton determinedly continued his search as he went to the other side of the bed and felt around on the floor. No syringe. Close to panicking, he felt a rush of relief when he looked back to the door and saw a slight glint of metal near the baseboard. The frantic doctor moved closer to the object and got on his knees to get a better look. In the dim light he made out the battered surface of the mesh floor grate. Running his gloved hand across it, he felt gaping holes in the mesh, any of which were big enough for the thin syringe to have fallen through. He put his face close to the grate and felt the hot air blowing upward. Running his hand across it again, he counted four screws fastening the grate to the floor.

Braxton stood up. He forced himself to think. When he dropped the syringe, he wasn't close to the grate, but he could have kicked it there when he'd been in the throes of attacking the man earlier. The door at the end of the hall opened again and broke his concentration. I've got to go!

For a moment he was tempted to take the tee shirts off of the lamp...but no, he realized that wouldn't be wise. The gap under the door was a space of a couple of inches. If someone saw the light...a friend of the unconscious man, perhaps—no. Bad idea. Mumbling under his breath, Braxton grabbed the man's jacket and put it on before he retrieved his gym bag. He took the room key out of his pocket and flipped the wall light switch off. Bag in hand, Braxton felt the pockets of the jacket and found a woolen stocking cap in one of the pockets. He pulled the cap low over his head. Ear pressed against the door, he listened. He heard only quiet. It was time.

Braxton slowly released the deadbolt and, taking a deep breath, opened the door and stepped out into the hallway. Room key in the same hand as the bag, he quickly locked the door. He tilted his head down and hurried to the far end of the hall. Opening the door to the stairwell, the man who now looked as much like a bum as any other inhabitant of The Montovie Men's Hotel descended to the first floor and quietly exited the building.

*   *   *   *   *

Do a mutherfucker a favor, he thought. Barry Jewell, the night clerk for the hotel, was severely pissed as he climbed the steps to the second floor of the hotel. Breathing hard, he stopped on the landing for a moment to catch his breath before opening the door to the second floor.

Mutherfucker knows I don't like climbin' these goddamn steps, he thought as he entered the hallway and walked slowly up to Room 214. Barry had let his sometime drinking buddy, Darnell Nabwell, move into the room Jamaica had vacated that very morning because Darnell had promised he'd have the twenty-dollar deposit at the front desk before Barry came on shift at 8 o'clock. And here it was–ten past nine. Barry was winded, mad as hell, and dragging his ass down the hallway. Barry's boss--an aged Korean immigrant who chain-smoked cheap cigarettes and owned a string of fleabag hotels from here to Las Vegas--had just called. He was coming over to pick up the day's receipts. Barry wasn't about to spot a twenty to anyone, especially to an alky like Darnell. Oh, he'd always say something like "Thanks, I'll get it right back to you." Yeah right, Barry thought. That son of a bitch'll drink it up and then claim fuckin' amnesia or somethin'.

Barry knocked on the flimsy door loud enough to wake the dead. He was still mad and still out of breath. "Darnell, open up. Your ass gonna get me in trouble."

No answer. He knocked harder.

"Bitch, I ain't playin' wit' you. I know your ass got off work at four." He put his ear to the door. Didn't hear anyone moving inside.

Fuck this, he thought. Taking a thick ring of keys off a clip on his sagging belt, he looked through several before trying one in the door lock. It took two more tries before he found the duplicate to the key he had given Darnell at his job that morning, working the night shift at the Circle "K" up the street.

Bastard tryin' ta play me for ah fool, he thought. Fine. I may be a fool all right, but this fool's gonna throw his shit in the street.

As soon as Barry opened the door, the scent hit him full force. The same God-awful smell that used to greet him at the start of his shift when he used to, years ago, work at the Barrow's Tallow Works out past 35th Avenue. Blood and shit.

"Godfuckin' damn," he mumbled and choked as he covered his mouth with one hand and flicked the light switch on the wall near the door with the other hand. The light on the nightstand across the room came on, but he could barely make it out. It looked like it was covered with something.

The small hairs on the back of his arms and neck stood straight up as he stepped very slowly into the room.

"Darnell?"

The smell got stronger with each measured step he took into the room. Trying to look all ways at once, Barry willed himself to see through the darkness as he made his way to the nightstand and stretched his arm toward the lamp. He stepped into a puddle of something just as he reached the nightstand and pulled the wet tee shirts off of the lampshade. That's when his bulging eyes got a good look at the clothes-covered body of his ex-drinking partner.

"Sweet-Mother-Jesus!"

Barry's off-balance backward leap carried his six-foot, two-hundred-seventy-pound bulk to the door. Almost. Again landing off balance near the foot of the bed, his foot slipped on a pool of congealed blood as he back paddled into the edge of the doorframe, cracking the old wood and rotten drywall like twigs under his weight. His momentum carried him through the edge of the wall into the hallway. His shoulder dislocated when he hit the wall opposite the room from which he had flown. Half of the doors on the floor were flying open in a symphony of angry curses.

"Take that shit outside!"

"Fuck you bastards! Fight outside!"

"Goddammit, keep it down, man!"

Barry appeared to hear none of the shouts and saw none of the half-dressed men walking toward him from down the hall. Even the pain of his sprained foot and dislocated shoulder couldn't take his eyes off of the grizzly scene in the room before him. One of the residents, a tall Hispanic man covered with tattoos across his shirtless chest, walked up to the babbling big man and looked in the direction Barry was pointing with his good arm. The cigarette in the man's mouth dropped to the floor as his jaw went slack.

"Jesus-in-a-go-cart." The barefoot man took off running, bowling people out of the way as he sprinted to the stairway and headed for the pay phone on the first floor.

Barry, still sitting against the hallway wall, couldn't move his eyes from the body. As shock started to settle into his system, even the noise of people around him began to soften...to dissipate into a gray background. As his head started to drop forward onto his chest, his eyes caught a sharp twinkle of light near the base of the bed. Distracting him from the carnage in front of him, the sharp, bright shine caused him to focus his mind. As the distraught man leaned forward, the searing pain in his shoulder made him sit upright. It also cleared his head. Barry looked again at the sparkle he recognized by now. Sticking straight up out of the threadbare carpet just in front of the left post of the rickety bed, the metal shaft of a hypodermic needle was reflecting the hall light like a beacon.

*   *   *   *   *

Proctor took the steps two at a time as he ran up the stairwell to the second floor of The Montovie Men's Hotel. Opening the door at the top of the stairs, he saw that all the doors lining the long narrow hallways were open and cops, both plain-clothed and uniformed, were talking to people standing in front of them. He had been at the LA Fitness gym off of Southern Avenue in Mesa, fresh out of the shower, when he heard his pager go off in his locker. Digging it out from under some clothes, he turned on the unit. He looked at the backlit number on the tiny screen and was surprised to see a "911" message followed by his boss' number. In the two years that he had been a detective under LaPlante, his boss had never called him after work hours.

Proctor hurried into his street clothes and cursed his timing—he had left his cell phone in the glove compartment of his car. Stuffing his wet workout clothes into his gym bag, he slammed his locker door closed and was out of the dressing room before the echo died. He stopped at the front desk and cleared his throat loudly...twice...trying to get the attention of the deeply tanned, chisel-featured counterperson. The man ignored him as he talked a mile a minute to the most anatomically correct set of brunette-haired womankind Proctor had ever seen. After another thirty seconds of watching the body builder drool on the desktop, Proctor slammed the flat of his hand hard on the wood countertop. The sharp sound caused all three people to jump. The attendant looked at Proctor for the first time, obviously pissed. The plastic smile on his face didn't mask the daggers shooting from his eyes. Both women offered big smiles in Proctor's direction and showed two sets of flawless teeth.

"Yes, sir, is there something that I can help you with?" the attendant said in a singsong voice as he looked back at the women and winked.

"I need to use your phone, please."

The man's smile got bigger as he pointed past Proctor to the front door of the gym.

"Pay phone's out front, buddy. Desk phone's not for personal use. Sorry."

The attendant was already turning back to the beaming twins. Proctor's detective shield was out and the flap opened before the man completed his turn.

"I'll only be a minute, sir. Police business."

Both women pivoted as one and exited when the attendant suddenly became attentive and fumbled for the desktop phone. After he sat it on the counter in front of Proctor, he excused himself and took off in the same direction his ladies had gone.

Quickly dialing his boss' cell phone number, Proctor heard LaPlante pick up on the first ring. He frowned as he listened to his boss. Hanging up the phone a moment later, he was searching his pants pockets for his car keys even as he was running to the gym's street exit.

*   *   *   *   *

Proctor passed small groups of cops who were talking to the hotel residents remaining on the floor and stopped at the broken doorway just as Murphy's head popped out of the room. Proctor pointed to the splintered doorframe.

"What happened here? Fight?"

Murphy shook his head as he exited the room.

"Naw, just a big fat chicken-eatin' mutherfucker panickin'. Tried to make a new exit as he back paddled out of the room. The wall won. Busted his shoulder." Murphy pointed to a couple of boxes on the floor just on the other side of the door.

"Better put on some gloves and booties 'fore you go in. Place is a mess. Oh, and good news—Lieutenant's waitin' for you inside."

After putting on the protective gear, Proctor stepped into the room and was immediately claustrophobic. Including LaPlante, there had to be four other people squeezed into a room that on its best day could only fit two. And that wasn't counting the sheet-covered body bag that was loaded on a gurney and on its way out. Stepping out of the way of the morgue technicians who were wheeling the corpse through the cracked doorway, Proctor wished he had something to cover his nose and mouth. The smell of blood and excretions were making him nauseous.

LaPlante stepped out from the far side of the twin bed when he saw Proctor come inside the room. A small rodent-looking man whom Proctor thought he knew followed him. All of the portable lights set up in the room had raised the room temperature enough to make Proctor break out in a thin sweat. Didn't help the smell of the room, either. LaPlante touched Proctor's arm and introduced him to the man standing slightly behind him.

"Proctor, this is Eric Downly. He's one of the head guys over at the Medical Examiner's office."

Proctor remembered where he had seen him now. He was at the scene when they found Mimi's body in Little Beirut.

"Eric, Detective Proctor's heading up the investigation on the Driver homicide." Proctor and Eric shook gloved hands. A tired, knowing smile painted Downly's small hard features.

"Looks like you've got your hands full on this one, Detective."

Proctor glanced around the room, now empty save for them. "That's an understatement if I've ever heard one."

"Let me show you a couple of things, Detective. Might help you out a bit."

All three men stepped around the narrow bed to the side where the body was found. The area the corpse rested on was void of carpet. The bare floorboards showed up through the gaping hole that had been left when the carpet on which the body laid was removed. Downly moved to the top of the opening near the nightstand and, after adjusting the closest portable light to flood the area, kneeled down. He pointed at the scarred floorboards as Proctor and LaPlante looked on.

"This is where the body was found. I counted forty-odd puncture wounds to the chest and abdomen areas, several of them overlapping. Maybe more. I'll be able to give you a more definite number later. Half of the wounds were so forceful they completely penetrated the body into the wood of the floor. Almost any of the blows individually would have been fatal. Size of the cut suggests the blade used was big-about an inch and a quarter, inch and a half across." Downly stood up and stepped back about a half foot.

"Angle of the cuts says the perp was on the right side of the man, and he's also right-handed. Found severe trauma to the throat region. The perp had literally crushed the esophagus with his shoe. We might be able to extract a print of the shoe by the shape of the bruise. He crushed his throat first, then stabbed him."

"How can you tell?" Proctor asked.

"Amount of blood around the wounds and on the floor. The man..." Downly hesitated as he looked to LaPlante, "What's this guy's name?"

"Nabwell. Darnell Nabwell."

"Nabwell's cardiovascular system was already in distress. The blow to the throat tore one of his carotid arteries open. The other one, the one closest to the front of the perp's foot, was sealed shut from the blow. Blood started to pool in the abdomen, with his heart going a mile a minute, vessels wide open, and the blood's got nowhere to go. First couple of knife blows hit the heart, stopped the pumping, and released the pressure. First few wounds spurt, then just ooze."

Proctor really wished he had that facecloth now. Downly continued in a tone of voice akin to someone making conversation about the weather.

"Had some head trauma, too. Both ear canals were full of blood and fluid. At first glance I think that twin blows ruptured his eardrums. Whoever this person was, he wanted to put Nabwell out quick, fast, and in a hurry. And the perp knew exactly how to do it."

Downly moved closer to the bare spot on the floor. "Perp was very pissed, too. Used enough force to have killed Nabwell four or five times over."

A cell phone chirped. Both LaPlante and Downly reached for the phones on their belts.

"It's mine, Bryan," Downly said.

The room was quiet save for Downly speaking softly into his phone. About a minute later, he shut the unit off and reattached it to his belt.

"The body's at the morgue. That was McAffy. I gotta get down there. He's ready to cut." Downly stepped closer to Proctor and offered his gloved hand again. Proctor shook the man's hand.

"Hope some of what I've told you helps you out."

"Thanks. At least I have a better idea of what we're up against."

Downly turned to LaPlante. "Bryan, I'll have the preliminary report on your desk this morning, and everything else as soon as I can."

"Thanks, Eric." Both men watched Downly leave the room, then turned back to the spot where Nabwell had lain. LaPlante suppressed a shiver as he stared at the bare floor. He looked at Proctor, who seemed to be lost in his own thoughts. The lieutenant tapped Proctor's arm.

"Let's step outside and get some fresh air. Got a couple of things I want to run by you."

Both men walked into the hallway. Several police were still in the corridor talking to the residents. A uniformed officer was standing just outside of the room they had left. LaPlante nodded at them as they cleared the doorway. The lieutenant turned toward the officer and spoke to him in a strong voice.

"No one, and I mean no one, is in that room unless I've okayed them. There's a crime lab team that'll be here soon. Let them in. You stay here until you hear different from me."

"Got it, sir."

LaPlante guided Proctor to the less populated end of the hall. He lowered his voice even though there was no one near enough to hear him.

"Bastard that killed that poor slob tried to make it look like a robbery gone bad. Found forty dollars in ten-dollar bills in the space between the nightstand and the bed. Empty wallet was on the bed, and you saw how the room was torn up. The money was smeared with blood. Either he's the most inept crook in Phoenix, or something else got his attention. Found something even more interesting sticking up out of the floor at the end of the bed—a syringe full of some kind of clear fluid. Talked to the guy with the broken wing, and he said Nabwell was a straight boozer...no drugs. Crime lab's got the syringe now. They'll let me know as soon as they find something. Now here's the kicker–that's Jamaica's old room. He moved his shit out this morning."

Proctor didn't bother to hide his surprise.

"There's more. Local patrol found the body of a lightweight dealer in Liberty Park on Van Buren late Tuesday morning. Guy's throat was damn near cut through to the spine. No wallet or ID on him. Ran his prints and came up with a name--Sonny James. Since people are dropping like flies in Little Beirut nowadays, I decided to do a little research. Pulled his sheet and read it over lunch. Lost my appetite real quick when I came across Chickenhead's name. Seems that couple of years ago they got into a fight over Mimi. Both said the other started it, but neither would press charges."

Proctor held up one hand to stop his boss. "You don't think Gibbs killed Sonny, do you?"

Looking past Proctor to the room, LaPlante shook his head.

"After what I saw tonight...no. But I do think it's no small coincidence that both these people are dead, one just for being in Jamaica's old digs."

They both looked up as they heard the door at the far end of the hall squeak open. Several police technicians, all of them in dark blue jumpsuits and carrying pieces of equipment, came into the hall. Murphy was behind them. The cop at the door of Room 214 looked toward LaPlante and Proctor. The lieutenant nodded. The cop stepped away from the door and let the men enter. The officer moved back to the door after the crew and their equipment were inside. Murphy joined LaPlante and Proctor at the end of the hall. LaPlante pointed to Proctor when he spoke.

"I want you to get the both of them and bring them in. I want it done tonight, right the fuck now. Take a squad car with you to the Biltmore."

He turned to Murphy. "You stay here and babysit everyone else. Call me if anyone gets anything useful."

"What's the charge?" Proctor asked.

"I don't need one for twenty-four hours. I'll think of something after I lose their paperwork. Just get them. Tonight. If they get killed, this case is done."

LaPlante walked back to the room, looked inside, and then spoke briefly to the officer at the door. He then continued down the hallway to the door that led to the steps. He opened it and was gone.

Murphy looked at his partner. "They're not gonna like this."

"No shit, Sherlock," Proctor grumbled. Walking to the door of the now-closed room, he asked the officer standing guard to lend him his radio. Using it he requested backup to meet him at his car downstairs.

*   *   *   *   *

After leaving The Montovie Men's Hotel, Braxton got on I-10 and headed toward Tucson until he got to Ray Road, where he exited the highway and turned east on the surfaced street. Making his way into Chandler, a bedroom community fifteen miles from downtown Phoenix, it took him another fifteen minutes to get to his destination. He drove slowly down Sunny Cactus Lane, an almost deserted cul-de-sac of a new home development called Wanamakca Estates. Save for the six homes on the street, all in various stages of development and none occupied, Braxton was alone. He moved slowly around the circle, spotting what he was looking for and pulling up next to it. He turned off the car's headlights but left the engine running. The doctor popped the trunk of the stolen car by using the lever under the dashboard. Jumping out of the car, he looked all around as he walked quickly to the open trunk, lifting the lid. He pulled out the double-bagged bloodied clothes and tools. Kneeling down to the open storm drain next to which he had parked, Braxton pushed the parcel through the five-inch opening and heard it bounce off of the walls before splashing into the water at the bottom. He returned to his car and quickly drove away. Fifteen minutes later, he was back on the interstate heading toward Phoenix.

Now that the incriminating package was gone, Braxton began to relax. Half of the storm drains in the new Valley of the Sun housing developments held the remnants of his killings over the past five years. Crossing over to the I-17 Expressway, Braxton drove to the 7th Avenue Exit and left the highway. He made a right turn two miles up at the BankOne Ballpark on Washington Street and drove through two stoplights before making two quick right turns, ending up in the deserted back parking lot of the Esquire Barber Shop off of 12th Avenue. Braxton pulled into the space farthest from the sole flickering street lamp. He parked the front end of his car facing the four-foot wall surrounding the lot. Scanning the area while still in the car, he twisted the flathead screwdriver sticking out of the ignition and killed the engine. Braxton pulled the tool out of the key slot and dropped to the floor of the vehicle. Ten minutes later he was pulling off the black leather and spandex Isotoner gloves he'd been wearing and, just before walking across 7th Avenue in front of the ballpark, stuffed them into a nearby corner storm drain. Head down and hands in the pockets of the pea green fatigue jacket he had "borrowed" from Nabwell's room, Braxton walked through the streets of downtown Phoenix for another fifteen minutes before he reached his red Mustang. It was parked across the street from the Hyatt Regency Hotel. He started the car, made a U-turn, drove back to 7th Avenue, and turned left. Once he reached the intersection, Braxton turned onto Van Buren and headed east until he came to a convenience store with a bank of pay phones lined up outside. Careful to turn on his signal, he veered left onto the side street and parked at the far end of the store. He sat in his car for several minutes, waiting for two cars to leave the lot. While he sat there, he dug into his back pocket for his wallet. He pulled it out just as the last car left the parking lot. Taking a pair of latex gloves from the glove compartment, he put them on before exiting the vehicle. A moment later, he was dialing the number he had taken out of the dead man's wallet hours ago. Jamaica's number rang three times before it was picked up.

"Um, hi...this is Jamaica."

It's a voice mail system, Braxton thought.

"If you have any information about the murder of Mimi Driver or know about any of the Turkeystuffer killings, leave me a name and a way ta get a hold of you. Me and my partner will keep your name out of it, and we're willing to pay good money for information. We ain't no cops. Leave your message at the beep. Peace."

Braxton hung up the phone but kept his hand on the handset. I can use this, he mused.

Still holding the phone, he wondered how best to use this new information against them and how he could lure them in. Though deep in thought, he was still aware of the two men who had walked up to the far end of the parking lot. Both men were standing next to his car trying to look like they weren't watching him. After a couple of minutes they started to walk toward him, both looking up and down the deserted street. Braxton pretended to concentrate on the phone in front of him, his right hand still on the handset. His other hand, the one facing away from the thugs, tightened on the ivory panel knife in his jacket pocket.

As the goons looked both ways up the street and ambled toward him, Braxton lifted his hand slightly out of his pocket and clicked the knife open. He kept the open blade in his pocket and moved closer to the phone, taking the receiver off the hook and lifting it to his ear just as the baggy jean-wearing men—one black, one white—reached him. Braxton gave them a quick look over. Both were shorter than he and moved with the arrogance of thugs who had done this routine before. The one closest to him—the black one--looked stocky under the green satin FUBU jacket he wore. The smaller one stayed a few steps behind.

Braxton moved closer to the phone and spoke softly into the dead mouthpiece. The brother stopped at the phone down from him and nodded at Braxton before he spoke.

"Yo, man, whassup?"

Braxton moved the dead phone away from his ear as the man's shorter, skinny partner took a quick look at Braxton, then turned his back to him to look out to the street.

"I'm sorry," Braxton replied, "I didn't hear you."

"I said whassup...got a smoke?"

"No...nasty habit, I think." Upon Braxton's reply, the kid's chest muscles tightened under the skin-tight, white tee shirt he wore under the open jacket.

Jesus, punk can't be more than twenty-one. Braxton tightened his grip on the phone, knowing what was coming next. *Fucking amateurs,* he thought in disgust.

"Give it up, white boy."

As fast as the brother moved, it looked like slow motion compared to Braxton. As the doctor stepped toward him, his hand—the one holding the phone—shot out, and using the top edge of the earpiece, slammed it down hard on the bridge of the approaching thug's nose. It broke with a sharp, hollow pop. Blinded by tears at the instant pain, the goon opened his mouth, and his outstretched left hand bounced off of Braxton's right shoulder. In two quick smooth moves, Braxton pulled the handset away from the thug's face and rammed the entire top half of the phone into his open mouth, turning it clockwise all the while. The force of its entry and the twisting action broke most of the man's upper and lower teeth. The trauma of the blow to the man's face and jaw caused the thug's jaw to clamp down solid around the unit in his mouth as Braxton pushed him aside. The entire scenario took less than seven seconds.

By the time the man's partner casually turned to Braxton, he saw two things simultaneously—his friend flopping like a fish on a hook, the lower part of the handset sticking out of the bleeding hole which used to be his mouth, and Braxton a scant few inches from him, smiling like the devil. With a nasty-looking, thick-bladed knife in his left hand, Braxton caught the wrist of the kid's hand before it cleared his baggy pants pocket in a grip that almost buckled the boy's knees. Ripping the hand upward and smashing it against the corner of the aluminum box housing the phone, the back of the boy's now broken hand split open. The cheap switchblade he had held in that hand dropped to the ground. He had the nerve to cry as Braxton held the thick blade to his thin throat.

"I'm s...sorry, man! We was just playin'! Don't hurt me..."

There was no joy in the smile that painted Braxton's face. "The only thing you're sorry about is not fucking me up."

Braxton glanced at the boy's trembling, bleeding hand. His smile got bigger.

"Hope you're not right-handed." Stepping back slightly, Braxton's hand quickly released its grip on the boy's wrist and slid back to the two outer fingers of the quaking hand. Grasping both fingers, he pulled them quickly and savagely backward and down, bringing the boy to his knees. As the boy's body followed his hand down, Braxton brought the knife to the fold between his middle fingers and, with a hard fast jerk, cut off the two fingers nearest the thumb. Braxton stabbed him in the throat to stop his scream.

The doctor walked quickly past the front door of the store and made it back to his car in seconds. He slowly pulled out onto 12th Avenue. As he started down the street, a low rider white Honda Civic pulled up beside him and turned into the lot he had just exited. Cursing softly, he turned his face away from the car and continued into the dark neighborhood behind the store. He then headed straight for the I-17 Expressway, watching his rearview mirror all the way.

He didn't dare stop anywhere in the Mustang. Braxton needed to get the car home and into his garage, then come out and make his call to Jamaica. Thirty minutes had passed before the Mustang was sitting next to the Mercedes SLK Roadster in his garage. Running inside the house, Braxton quickly changed his clothes and grabbed his other set of car keys. Ten minutes later, he was driving the streets of Scottsdale, looking for a pay phone. He pulled up to a pay phone in a closed gas station and sat in the car for a minute mulling over what he was going to say. It wasn't until he picked up the handset that he noticed he wasn't wearing any gloves.

"Fuck it," he said aloud.

Dialing the number, he listened to it ring three times before switching to an answering service. After it beeped, Braxton left a detailed message with his beeper number. He hung up the receiver and looked at his ungloved hand on the handset. After some thought, he untucked his shirttail and half-heartedly wiped down the phone. He looked at the phone with a huge grin on his face.

"I've got your black ass now," he muttered as he turned to walk back to his car.

Chapter 17

Luther Vandross singing in the background wasn't helping an increasingly nervous Jamaica to calm down one bit. Actually, the soft crooning brought to a very sharp point his present situation—this was the first date—a real date—in forever. He had almost finished lighting the twenty-odd candles he had spread around the large front room of the two-bedroom villa he shared with Chickenhead when his apprehension got the best of him and he had to stop for a smoke. Lighting the cigarette, he watched the match shake slightly in his trembling hand before he shook it several times to put it out.

This is fucking ridiculous, he thought as a smile crept onto his lips. After ten years of walking the streets of Phoenix, living hand-to-mouth among the decadent, demented lost souls who became his neighbors, here he was shaking in his boots in a four-hundred-ninety-five-dollar-a-day suite while waiting for a thirty-nine-year-old divorced mother of two girls to get off of work from her job at a Home Depot in Tempe. He had stared down death several times over the years, seen sights that would drive most men crazy, but none of them held a candle to the scare this woman was putting into him.

"Gee-manetti-and-my-name-ain't-Freddy," he muttered. "Nigger, get a grip. Breathe!"

He tapped the cigarette into the heavy crystal ashtray and pinched the ash off at the tip. As he placed the half-smoked Pall Mall back into an almost full pack, his smile returned. After a week of living high off the hog, some old habits were dying hard. He busied himself with double-checking the pot of seafood gumbo he was preparing in the lavish kitchen area. Cynthia, his soon-to-be date, said she loved seafood.

He let his mind drift as he stirred the simmering pot. Jamaica had come to Phoenix, via Newark, New Jersey, almost eleven years ago, running from his loss. Wayne, his fourteen-year-old son and only child, was dead, eaten alive over a three-year battle with testicle cancer. The sickness had killed his boy as well as his sixteen-year marriage.

His wife, Mattalynn, died in a more difficult way. Four days after the couple watched the doctors pull the plug on their only child's life support system--the cancer had spread to his brain, resulting in an irreversible coma that lasted the remaining seven weeks of his short life--she walked off her job as an insurance broker for Prudential Life Insurance in downtown Newark, gone two blocks down the street to Houston's Pawn Shop, and bought a .38-caliber, snub-nose revolver. She then walked up two more streets to purchase a box of shells from another pawnshop. Jamaica was working as a short haul trucker for Vibrant Electronics, delivering and setting up custom data processing systems over a five-state area for clients of the company. He was about to leave on a three-day run when she walked out of the door of their home off of South Orange Avenue. Without a word, she led him back into the house...back to their bedroom. Jamaica remembered all too well the tears that fell from both of their eyes as she undressed first him and then herself and then slowly made love to him for the first time in months. Afterwards, she showered with him. He asked her if she was all right...if she wanted him to stay. She kissed him and helped him dress, telling him to have a safe trip. Sometime that night after he left, she killed herself with a single gunshot to her heart.

He found her lying across Wayne's bed in one of his old Rutgers University sweatshirts. He had come home early because he couldn't get in contact with her. She was clutching the last family picture they had taken two years earlier at a picnic at Branch Brook Park in Newark. He buried her next to his beloved Wayne exactly ten days after he had buried their son. Returning to the home in which they had shared all of Wayne's life, he packed an overnight bag and walked out, leaving the front door standing wide open. He hailed a cab and rode to the downtown Greyhound Bus Station in silence.

That's when his living death began. That's when he started his two years of hell. That's how long it took him to remember that he was still alive.

A loud knock on the door brought him back to the here and now. The pager beeped on his belt, and he absentmindedly reached for the unit and switched it to vibrate mode. Turning down the heating element on the flat-top, ebony-colored stove, Jamaica crossed into the living room while checking the time on his watch...it was 9:12 p.m. Cynthia said she would be around by 10:00 that evening. The knocking on the door started again, but this time it was harder and louder.

"Hold your damn horses, I'm comin'!" he yelled from halfway down the short hallway. When he arrived at the door, he looked through the peephole and frowned.

Cops. One uniformed, the other a big black guy in a badly fitting dark sport coat. Jamaica unlatched the deadbolt and opened the door about a third of the way.

"What the fuck y'all want?"

The black cop took a step closer to the door before he spoke. "Mr. Rummains? Jamaica Rummains?" Proctor asked. "Can we talk to you for a few minutes? It's very important."

Jamaica opened the door a sliver more. "Why? Is something wrong with Robert? Is he hurt?"

"No, no. But it does concern both of you. We have reason to believe your lives may be in danger."

Jamaica stood at the doorway and laughed aloud. He made no move to open the door farther.

"Y'all mutherfuckers slow on the uptake if you just figurin' that out. Thanks for the warnin'. Bye." He slammed the door closed.

The knocking restarted immediately.

"Jesus H. Christ," he muttered as he turned back to the door and reopened it.

Proctor quickly stepped to the doorway and put his foot in the space between the door and the frame. "Mr. Rummains, please. We just need a little of your time."

Jamaica looked down at Proctor's foot. "You gonna need a lot more than a little time if you don't remove that boot from my doorsill. Might accidentally get it smashed when I shut this heavy motherfucker closed."

The uniformed cop quickly stepped forward. He dropped his hand to the butt of his gun.

"Who the hell do you think you are? You can't talk to us like that!"

Both Proctor and Jamaica looked at the young officer and spoke at the same time.

"Shut the fuck up!"

The startled cop looked back and forth between the two men, speechless. Proctor stepped back from the door and within inches of the uniform's face. "Go down to the fuckin' car and wait, Officer. I'll handle this."

"But, Proctor..."

"You have a hearing problem, Officer? Step to the car. I'll deal with this."

The cop looked at his superior with a beet-red face as if he wanted to say something, then thought better of it. Turning, he stomped to the squad car at the end of the driveway below. Proctor turned back to Jamaica, who still hadn't moved out of the doorway.

"Look, we can play this game all night. I, for one, would rather not. How about a truce?"

Jamaica moaned aloud. "Look, bro, anything to get you out of my hair. What's on your mind? I've got a date tonight."

"Ten minutes of your time, inside, then I'm gone if you want. Deal?" Proctor pointed to his watch, then inside the door. Jamaica cursed, then opened the door and stepped aside.

"Shit, I knew you were gonna say somethin' 'bout inside." Jamaica started motioning for Proctor to come in. "Come on, dammit. Ain't got all night ta talk ta ya. The clock is tickin'."

Proctor was barely through the door when Jamaica continued to hurry him.

"What ya got ta say?"

"Damn, can we at least get out of the hall before you kick me out? And the name is Proctor, Stephen Proctor."

"I know who the hell you are. Robert described you to me. 'Sides, ain't that much color on the Phoenix PD with your kind of badge."

Jamaica walked past Proctor and down the hall. Proctor followed him into the front room. Jamaica pointed in the general direction of the sofas as he walked to the kitchen area.

"Cop a squat. I gotta go check my gumbo on the stove."

In the few minutes it took Jamaica to add seasoning to the food and stir it, Proctor started leafing through, then reading, both notebooks sitting on the coffee table. He was totally engrossed when Jamaica, can of Bud Light in hand, re-entered the room and turned on the overhead lights. Choosing the sofa opposite Proctor, Jamaica frowned and reached across the table, taking the notebook out of Proctor's hand and closing it. He also grabbed the other pad on the coffee table and sat both of them next to him. He took a sip of beer before speaking.

"Proctor, you one nosy mutherfucker."

Proctor put up both his hands. "Hey, it's part of my job." He pointed to the notebooks that were now sitting beside Jamaica.

"How about you let me finish reading those? Looks like ya'll been busy."

"Yes, we have, and no, you can't...we'll get you a copy in a couple-three days," Jamaica retorted as he sat forward on the edge of the sofa.

"Your time's a'wastin.' I got things ta do, and you need ta go."

Proctor sniffed the air. "Damn, what you're cooking smells good. What is it?"

"Goddammit, this ain't no restaurant, and you 'bout three seconds from gettin' booted the fuck outta here. For the last time, what do you want'?"

Proctor put both hands up in surrender. Leaning slightly forward, he reached into the back pocket of his jeans and pulled out a sealed, clear plastic baggie of instant Polaroid photos. Breaking the seal on the bag, he tossed the contents on the coffee table.

"Take a look--see. Anybody you know?"

As hard as ten years of living on the streets of Phoenix had made him, the bloodbath in the crime scene photos still shook him to the core. If Jamaica's dark ebony complexion had been a few shades lighter, Proctor would have noticed the blood leaving his face. Jamaica looked at each of the fifteen photos again, then placed them back into the baggie. Sealing it closed, he put it back on the coffee table. He reached for the beer he had left on a coaster in front of him and drained the three-quarters full can in one long swallow. He placed the empty can on the coaster and looked at Proctor.

"Fuck a duck."

"Thought you'd like that. Notice anything about that scene?"

"What, other than that poor slob was cut up like sushi?"

"That's your old room at The Montovie."

The look of surprise on Jamaica's face would have made Proctor laugh at any other time.

"Get the fuck outta here."

"According to the hotel records, you just did. By about four or five hours."

Jamaica could only stare at Proctor.

"I checked the hotel records. You gave your room key back at eleven-thirty this morning," Proctor continued as he reached across the coffee table and picked up the baggie of photos. He waved them in the air as he spoke.

"Mister Hamburger here, better known as a Darnell Nabwell, moved into your old room, per those same records, at 12:10 p.m. this afternoon. Best we can figure right now, he was cut to hell around four or five o'clock today. Whoever did it tried to make it look like a robbery. Too bad after going through his wallet the perp left the money there. We found it in the room." Proctor waved the photos again, then tossed them back onto the table.

"You wouldn't happen to know this guy, would you?"

Jamaica reopened the bag of pictures still lying on the table. Out of fifteen photos, only six had a clear view of the dead man's face. Jamaica shook his head. Placing the photos back on the table for the second time, he wiped his hands on his pant legs as he answered Proctor's question.

"I don't think so...his face looks familiar, though. I might have talked to him. Been talking to a ton of people recently." Jamaica's beeper vibrated on his belt. Without looking at it, he shut it off.

"Was one of them Sonny James?"

"Nah, but we heard about him. Got killed sometime Tuesday morning at Library Park. Found out from a guy I know that he was askin' 'bout us couple days before."

Proctor sat up at attention.

"What kind of questions? Asking who?"

Jamaica mentally kicked himself for letting out that bit of news.

"Look, Proctor...we can handle this. We're okay."

The stupefied look on Proctor's face would have been hilarious under other conditions. The calm in his voice was gone, replaced by a tone reserved for a man talking to the village idiot.

"Are you nuts? Two people have been killed in the last three days with ties to y'all--one stabbed so many times his chest was mush, and you say you can handle this? Are you fucking insane?"

Before Jamaica could answer, there was a knock on the door. Jamaica got up from the sofa. Proctor had a somewhat less dumbfounded look on his face by then.

"Excuse me. Unlike you, that's someone I'd really like to see." Jamaica gestured to the hallway with his thumb. "Your time's about up." Proctor stood up as he walked past him to the entryway. Proctor spoke rapidly to Jamaica as he sped past him.

"Jamaica, listen to me. You're both out of your element and in way over your heads. Just give..."

Jamaica disappeared down the hall. A moment later, Proctor heard him open the door. That sound was followed by a small female voice. As he listened to them getting closer, Proctor took the crime scene photos off of the coffee table and, placing them back in the baggie, put them into his back pants pocket. Jamaica re-entered the room as Proctor adjusted his jacket. With Jamaica was his date--a tall, slender almond-skinned black woman with closely cropped gray-streaked brunette hair. Jamaica introduced her to the now standing detective.

"Cynthia Winaford, Detective Stephen Proctor, Phoenix Police Department." She extended her hand to him with a smile.

"Nice to meet you, Detective. It's good to see one of us in a position of importance." They shook hands politely.

"Thank you, ma'am. It's nice to meet you."

Releasing his hand, she turned to Jamaica.

"Timothy, may I use your restroom? I'd like to freshen up a bit, please?"

Jamaica gave her directions to the bathroom. She had barely left the room when he turned to Proctor and nodded toward the hallway.

"That's your cue, my brother."

"Jamaica, please, this is serious. Whoever this son of a bitch is wants to kill you and Robert."

"Cop, the only thing gettin' killed 'round here is the fuckin' mood. You've had more than your ten minutes. Now go."

"Jamaica..."

"Proctor, I'll talk to you in a couple of days, okay? You satisfied? Now get the fuck out of here."

"Jamaica..."

Jamaica's date came back into the room. He smiled in her direction and nodded. He also grabbed the elbow of Proctor's arm and began to guide him to the door.

"I'll walk you out, Detective," he said with a smile. As they moved down the hall, Proctor pressed a business card into Jamaica's hand. Jamaica put it into his front pants pocket without looking at it. Proctor lowered his voice when he spoke.

"Look, call me tomorrow. Better yet, why don't both of you just come down to the station with your information? All of my numbers are on the card. I'll be waiting for your call, okay?"

Jamaica was hissing words through his teeth. "Yeah, yeah, right. I'll call you."

"Jamaica, both of you need our help...our protection. Call me tomorrow."

"Right now I need you gone. Have a nice night." Jamaica opened the door and ushered him out.

"Make sure you call me tomorrow. Early." Proctor stepped through the opening just as the front of the rapidly closing door hit his heel. Turning around, he looked at the door for a moment, then shook his head.

These poor bastards don't have a clue, he thought.

Turning away from the door, he made his way down the walkway. He knew that there was gonna be hell to pay for him not arresting Jamaica like the lieutenant had told him to do. He also knew that if he had done so, what little civility that existed between him and the two friends would have been destroyed. Robert and Jamaica were key to this investigation. And they knew it.

As he got closer to where his car and the squad car were parked, he saw the officer leaning against the blue and white, talking on the car radio. The pang of remorse he felt for chastising the officer in front of Jamaica was crushed by Proctor's dislike of the young cop's arrogance. The man saw him coming down the trail and waved him over to the squad car. Proctor broke into a jog as he approached the vehicle. The officer handed him the car radio when he got there.

"Sir, I just got a call from your partner. He wants to talk to you."

Proctor pushed the button on the side of the hand-held unit. "Murphy, you still there?"

His partner answered his call immediately. "Stephen, can you talk? Do you have your cell with you?"

"It's in my gym bag in the car. What's up?"

"Get it. I'll call you back in five minutes."

Proctor had his phone out and was sitting in his car when Murphy called back.

"Were they there? Did you arrest them?"

"Jamaica was there, and no, I didn't. I've got another idea that I think will work better. I'll talk to you about it tonight. What's up?" Proctor heard his partner's loud groan.

"Jesus, man, do you like pain or something?"

"Murphy, later. Now what's up?"

"Found something that may mean something from a patrol near downtown. Couple of gangbanger wannabes messed with the wrong person or persons at a bank of phones outside a Circle K near downtown and got truly fucked. One died at the scene."

"How?"

"Stabbed in the throat. That was either before or after he had ah coupla fingers cut off. The other guy's still alive...looks like he's got a busted nose and--get this--half the business end of a pay phone stuffed halfway down his throat. Jaw was frozen shut around it, and he was thrashin' like a mackerel on a line when a coupla kids drivin' up to the store saw him. Girl in the car called 911."

"Goddamn...is he gonna make it?"

"Don't know yet...he was still alive when they carted him off. Whatever happens, he won't be chewin' nuts for a while."

"Did anyone see anything? A person? Car?"

"Couple remember a late-model Mustang pullin' out as they pulled in. Guy says it's red, girl says it's burgundy. Neither saw the plate or who was drivin'."

"The phones?"

"Already checkin' 'em. I'll have a list of outgoing calls within the hour."

Proctor rubbed his throbbing temples with his free hand--one side and then the other. The headache just starting was going to be a bad one...that much he could feel already. Proctor heard his phone click silent for a second. Someone was trying to call him. He ignored the signal.

"What about the other guy, the phone guy? Is he awake?"

"Hell, no! Paramedics and the doctor on site had to put him under just ta move him. Cut him and ran a tube through his throat to help him breathe. Cut the phone cord and rushed the whole package to Good Sam Trauma Center. He's probably in surgery now gettin' Ma Bell outta his mouth. Even if he does come around anytime soon, he ain't gonna be talkin' for a month of Sundays."

Proctor heard Murphy's phone click quiet for a moment.

"Hold on, Steve. You can guess who that is."

Murphy was off line for all of a minute. When he came back on, Proctor heard the loud gush of air his partner expelled before Murphy spoke to him again.

"Well, that was fun," he mumbled. "The lieutenant wants me to hunt you down and relay a message. Call him. Now. I played dumb about Robert and Jamaica. You owe me dinner for a month...that is if you still have a job after you talk to LaPlante."

"Thanks, pal. All of my food stamps for the first month will be yours." Proctor wondered just how true Murphy's last statement could be.

"Steve, all kiddin' aside, the lieutenant is fuming. What you gonna tell him?"

"I'm putting a 'File Stop' out on Robert. If a blue and white sees him, they can keep him there 'til they can contact me. I'm also requesting four cops for a very discreet 24-7 on the both of them. These idiots wanna be bait, least we can do is to watch 'em and see what turns up."

Proctor sighed before he continued. "This thing may give soon, and I want to make sure we have a front row seat when the shit explodes. I'm gonna have a unit camp out here 'til Robert gets back. Like it or not, all three of us are gonna have a little talk tonight."

Murphy was quiet for a moment and then began to chuckle.

"What?" Proctor asked.

"Can I have your desk when you get bused down to dogcatcher?"

Proctor shut off his phone as his partner's raucous laugh echoed through the small earpiece.

*   *   *   *   *

Jamaica looked at the back of the door through which he had just ushered Proctor out. I need to call Robert, he thought. He needs ta know how deep this shit is gettin'. He had told Chickenhead earlier about his date for the evening with Cynthia. Chickenhead had laughed and said he would make himself scarce.

"Timothy?"

Jamaica turned around to face Cynthia. She was standing at the entryway to the room.

"Is everything okay? With the police and all?"

Jesus, he thought, this is just what I need on a first date. "Cynthia..."

"Call me Cindy," she said with an easy smile. "All my friends do."

Mentally, Jamaica breathed a sigh of relief. "Cindy, how about I explain this to you over dinner? Then, if you want to run away screaming, you can do it on a full stomach. Besides, I made some seafood gumbo that'll make ya call yo' mamma's name in vain."

She leaned against the wall of the entryway, a smile still planted on her face. "Damn. Good lookin', mysterious, and can cook? This just might be one interesting night."

Jamaica felt a warm ball of something tighten in his stomach. Immediately, he was nervous and sweating. He tried to appear calm as he walked Cynthia to the nearest sofa.

"Uh, do you want a drink? Wine or something?"

"Yes, a glass of blush or Zinfandel would be nice, if you have it."

"Right away."

Quickly moving past the furniture to the bar, Jamaica found several bottles of Robert Mondovi Napa Zinfandel. He picked the bottle closest to him, uncorked it, and poured both of them a glass. His hand only shook a little. Picking up two coasters from the bar, he set them both on the coffee table and then placed the crystal wine goblets on top. Cynthia touched his hand as he put her glass before her. He barely succeeded in not sloshing her drink.

"Timothy...is it all right that I call you Timothy? I heard the detective call you Jamaica."

"Jamaica's my middle name. You can call me whatever you like."

"I like Timothy. Now, can you do me a favor?"

"Sure. Name it."

She gently squeezed his hand. "Breathe. I won't bite. Yet."

She let go of his hand and smiled up at him. He couldn't help but return the smile with an almost goofy grin.

"I'm sorry. This is my first date in a very long time."

"I know the feeling."

"I need to check the food. I'll be right back."

"And I'll be right here," she responded with a wink.

OhGodOhGodOhGod, he thought feverishly.

He forced himself to walk casually to the kitchen. He opened one of the overhead cabinets, pulled out two sets of plates, and set the small table. Just as he put down the last plate, he heard Luther Vandross' voice get a bit louder. He happened to glance into the living room and saw the lights dim a notch.

I'm okay. I'm cool, he thought as he closed his eyes.

Moving to the stove, Jamaica stopped dead in his tracks in front of the huge pot. He slowly lifted the lid off of the large kettle and smelled the stew. He nearly panicked. He had left the gumbo on too long, and it was slightly but definitely scorched. He quickly replaced the lid on the pot and frantically looked around the kitchen. Cynthia called to him from the living room.

"Is there anything I can help you with?" He found it.

"Uh...no. I'm okay. Uh, Cynthia...there's been a slight change of plans."

She appeared at the door to the kitchen and smiled at him as she leaned against the frame of the entryway. "Oh, really? How so?"

A nervous tick started on the corner of his mouth as Jamaica raised the hotel's menu in front of him like a shield.

"I kinda burned dinner...how do you feel about room service?"

They both stared at each other for a moment before they cracked up laughing.

*   *   *   *   *

Chickenhead watched Proctor and the cop from a wall of eucalyptus bushes almost forty feet in front of the villa. Though most of the leaves were gone, the density of the eight-foot plants, along with the early evening darkness, gave him perfect cover as he leaned into the side of the bushes. Chickenhead had been standing in the foliage for nearly thirty minutes...watching. After he saw Jamaica's date go up the walk and watched Proctor join the cop at his cruiser about ten minutes later, he began to relax a little. He just knew that they were there to question or arrest the both of them. He saw Proctor get out of his own car and walk back to the squad car. Watching for a moment longer, Chickenhead slowly backed away from the bushes as quietly and quickly as he could. He walked backwards for several yards while keeping both officers in sight and staying close to the bushes. Then he turned around and started up the long lane that led to the Biltmore's 24th Avenue entrance. He was smart enough to stay well back from the road.

It took him nearly fifteen minutes to return to the street. Turning south, he kept his pace slow as he walked back in the direction of the bus stop at Camelback Road--the same one he had left an hour and a half earlier.

Chickenhead was coming back to the villa for a change of clothes when he saw both cop cars parked next to the Escort. After chasing a lead on a body all the way to Tucson for the last two days, Chickenhead had to acknowledge that the trail panned out when his connection never showed up at the Ronstadt Bus Station in downtown Tucson. He had waited two hours before he caught two buses that took him to the Tucson International Airport, where he bought a ticket on the next flight back to Phoenix. He was in the air forty minutes later. Chickenhead had time on the trip back--both on the plane ride and the bus ride from Phoenix's Sky Harbor--to peruse his notes of the last week. In that time he and Jamaica had matched six bodies to names: Shelly Mosley...Jane Doe #4, Debra Jenkins...Jane Doe #2, Mandy Jarrel...Jane Doe #9, Patricia Carmel...Jane Doe #7, Tonya Wiannes...Jane Doe #1, and Bobbi Moore...Jane Doe #3.

Chickenhead was beginning to have doubts about finding anything on the ones that were left. People had moved on. The ones that were left either didn't know anything or refused to talk to him. The Tucson episode was the third dead end he had encountered this week, and he was getting antsy. He wanted to go on to the next step, whatever that might be.

Chickenhead wished he knew more about why the cops had been paying a visit to Jamaica. Finally arriving at the corner, Chickenhead switched his backpack to his other shoulder and turned left into the Biltmore Fashion Park, a very upscale group of stores and boutiques, instead of going back to the bus stop. He walked under a huge arch of multicolored blinking Christmas lights and walked through the mall as he watched the assortment of passing people. He stopped in front of a small coffee shop and looked through the plate-glass window at the crowd inside. A group of older people caught his attention given the holiday garb they were wearing. One couple in that group stood out from the rest. Both were bearing the same outfit--a baggy green and red sweater bright enough to stop traffic and dark, loosely fitting blue jeans. The green reindeer pattern that encircled their midriff looked like it would bound off the clothing if it were any brighter.

Chickenhead opened the door to the shop and stepped into the noisy, festive atmosphere. Moving to the counter area, he again looked at the couple. He smiled when he saw that they were holding hands. A pimply-faced kid, wearing a tiny nose ring and blue velvet antlers, smiled at him from behind the counter.

"Happy holidays, sir. Can I help you?"

"Yes. Let me have a hot chocolate, please."

"Right away, sir."

The group of people standing next to Chickenhead burst out in loud laughter, and their joviality startled him as he paid for his drink. Chickenhead looked at the older man as he gently pulled his mate closer to him and kissed her on her flushed, wrinkled cheek. Chickenhead was standing close enough to see the sparkle in the man's eyes when his lips touched her cheek...and to see the woman close her eyes, smiling, when her mate kissed her. Pulling slightly away from his woman, the man looked at Chickenhead as the smile remained, on his lips. It didn't surprise Chickenhead that when the man spoke, his voice was a deep, rolling baritone.

"Happy holidays, son. How are you doing?"

Chickenhead had to stop and think before he replied.

"I'm doing better, sir. But you...you look really happy. Why's that?"

The man positively radiated goodwill as he kissed his companion's hand before he answered the question.

"It's Maggie's birthday today. And our forty-ninth wedding anniversary." Releasing her hand, he put his arm around his plump, silver-haired wife. She looked up at Chickenhead and beamed like a schoolgirl at her first prom.

"I'm tryin' to figure out if I should keep her for another twenty-thirty years, or what?" Turning to her husband, she playfully hit his arm, then kissed his cheek.

"Uh, oh, she's gettin' riled up. Better to shut up and keep the peace."

Her voice was like the beauty of a gentle night rain. "Monty Fant, you'd better behave!" She looked to Chickenhead as she continued. "Don't mind him, child. I don't let him out much."

The group they were standing with laughed aloud at their good-natured repartee. Even Chickenhead, looking at them, saw the ease they had with each other and felt the love they shared. It made him not ever want to leave the coffee shop. He wanted to hold onto this space in time.

"Mister Fant, can I get you and your wife something? Hot cider maybe? Just to say congratulations?"

The man's smile grew wider as he nodded a discreet "yes."

"Why, thank you, son. That's very nice of you," he boomed as he looked at his wife. "Sweetie, would you like something?"

"A hot tea would be nice. Thank you so much, young man."

Chickenhead ended up buying drinks for all six people in the group. Chickenhead talked to them for a few minutes more, then said goodbye. Looking back through the plate-glass window of the shop as he left, he noticed the entire group raise their drinks to him. He waved back at them with a smile on his face. The group's parting waves and Maggie and Monty Fant's aura kept him warm in the chilly night air as he walked back to the Biltmore.

Twenty-five minutes later he was walking up the long driveway to the villa he shared with Jamaica. The cop and Proctor were standing outside of the squad car talking when he cleared the row of bushes from which he had watched them earlier. They noticed him immediately.

Proctor turned to the cop and spoke briefly to him, then with a fast walk moved away from the squad car as the officer got into the vehicle. Proctor met Chickenhead before he was halfway up the path.

Before Proctor could open his mouth, Chickenhead held up his hand to stop him.

"Can we talk? Away from here?" He pointed to Proctor's car. "You got me blocked in. You drive."

Proctor looked stunned. "Uh, sure. Where to?" Proctor was already pulling the keys from his pants pocket.

"Can you do me a couple of favors first, Proctor?"

"I'll try. What are they?"

"Your partner," Chickenhead pointed to the cop watching them from the squad car. "If he has to stay, could you at least get him to go down the driveway a bit? Jamaica's got a date tonight, and he's nervous as hell about it. He don't need to look out the window and see your guy lookin' through the glass at 'em. Give my bro' a break, please?"

Still wearing the confused look, Proctor turned and walked to the squad car. Two minutes later, the blue and white slowly pulled away from the front of the villa and past Chickenhead. The cruiser stopped at the entrance to the driveway, well back but still within sight of the building. Proctor met Chickenhead at his unmarked police car.

"Good enough for you?"

"That will be fine, thank you." They both got into Proctor's car.

"Anything else I can do? That second favor?" Proctor started the car.

"Yes. There's a Denny's at Camelback and 7th Street. Let's head there. I could use some...hot chocolate."

"Anything else?" Proctor asked as he pulled down the driveway. He waved at the officer as he passed the blue and white. Thinking Chickenhead hadn't heard his question, Proctor was about to repeat himself when he looked over at his passenger. He was surprised to see a calm smile on the man's face. As they drove by the intersection of Camelback and 24th Street, Chickenhead's smile was broken by a short laugh. To Proctor it looked like Chickenhead was looking past him to the Biltmore Fashion Square. Chickenhead spoke as the light changed and they turned onto Camelback Road, heading west to the restaurant.

"The other favor is gonna be a bit tougher for you. If you could do it, though, it would help me out a lot."

"Hey, I'll do my best. What is it?"

"I need you, just for tonight, to act less like a cop and more like the person who got me a cup of coffee when I almost lost it the first time we met."

Chickenhead stared straight ahead and looked at traffic with the smile still firmly planted on his face. Proctor was quiet until the car rolled to a halt at a red light above the intersection of Camelback and 22nd Street.

"That may be hard, but doable. I'll give it a try."

Proctor was surprised again by Chickenhead's good-natured laugh. Proctor smiled to himself although he didn't have a clue as to why.

"Proctor, if you can loosen up your tight ass a bit, I might like you enough to buy you breakfast."

As the light changed, Chickenhead laughed again at the uncertain smile painted on Proctor's face. And as the laugh subsided to a smile, Chickenhead said a silent heartfelt "thank you" to two old people on their forty-ninth wedding anniversary...

Chapter 18

Proctor was trying to keep from nodding off at his desk. He had stayed up talking to Chickenhead until the early morning hours. Murphy was reading aloud the preliminary report they had just gotten from the crime scene at Jamaica's old room at The Montovie Men's Hotel. Proctor sat up straighter when he heard the excitement in his partner's voice.

"Check this out! The drug in that syringe we found was a controlled substance."

Murphy leafed through the pages of the folder that had just been delivered to his desk. Proctor reached for an identical folder on his own desk.

"Something called Versed. Says it's a class three drug, right up there with Valium. This shit is kept under lock and key at hospitals and pharmacies."

Proctor caught up to the page from which Murphy was reading.

"Not something your average Joe's gonna carry around."

"Naw, this shit's potent. Used as a general anesthesia during surgery. Dose that was in that syringe was enough ta knock you on your ass in less than a minute. Keep you down for an hour or two." Murphy turned to the next page in the report. "Also has an amnesia effect. You get hit with it, you're out like a light...and ya wake up not knowing what the fuck happened. Nice thing ta use if you want ta knock someone out and move 'em."

Proctor finished the thought that Murphy was thinking. "Move 'em someplace where you could do what you wanted with 'em."

Proctor picked up the folder containing Mimi's forensic data from the pile of folders in his in-basket. He pulled out the toxicology report that had been done on her. Reading it, he shook his head.

"This shit wasn't found in Mimi. She was pumped full of Valium and something called Haldol, enough to keep her high as a kite and disoriented as hell. Both of 'em aren't on the shelves of Circle K, either."

The yawn that came of out Proctor's mouth was long and hard. Murphy looked over at him and chuckled. "How long were you and Robert buddy-buddy last night?"

Proctor gave him the finger before he answered. "Talked for a couple of hours last night. Hate to admit it, but he's an interesting guy. Him and Jamaica are gonna come in around two o'clock with all their info to see if we can put two and two together."

"What did the lieutenant think about your tailing idea?"

"Well, after he finished chewing on my ass, he said he'd try it for a couple of days to see what happens. Got a couple of guys following them today. We'll hear something from both teams later today."

The phone rang on Murphy's desk as Proctor left to get a cup of coffee from the hallway vending machine. He came back with two cups just as Murphy hung up the phone. He put one on Murphy's desk.

"That was the hospital. Kid with the busted mouth is in intensive care, but he's stable. We can forget about talking to him for at least a week, maybe more. Lost a lot of teeth and had to cut away part of his tongue to reduce the swelling. Fuck!"

Proctor's phone rang. "Detective Proctor speaking."

"Hello, Detective, this is Eric Downly, Medical Examiner's Office..."

Their conversation lasted only a couple of minutes. Proctor was wide awake when he hung up the phone.

"Downly's got a match on the size of the blade used to kill Nabwell. Said it was more than likely the same one used on the kid at the phone. Did we get the numbers back on those phones yet?"

"Oh, shit! I forgot," Murphy muttered as he dug through the folder in his own overflowing in-basket. He removed a manila envelope marked as interoffice mail. Opening it, he extracted a thin envelope with the address of the local carrier. The time stamp on it was from the day before. He tore open the telephone company's package and pulled out eight sheets of letter-size paper. Each sheet was covered from top to bottom with telephone numbers.

"The phone company screwed up. Gave us all the calls that went out that day 'stead of the block of time we asked for." Murphy handed Proctor the last four sheets from the list.

"You got Robert and Jamaica's beeper numbers?" Murphy asked.

From his shirt pocket, Proctor pulled the card listing the pager numbers that Chickenhead had given him the previous Monday. He copied both numbers onto a sheet of scrap paper and handed it to Murphy.

"Start lookin'," Proctor urged.

Twenty minutes later, Proctor circled Jamaica's beeper number. "Found it! A call went out to Jamaica's beeper from the Number Three phone at 7:26 p.m. It lasted about thirty seconds. What time did the 911 call come in from the couple that found those kids?"

Both detectives dug through the papers and folders on their desks looking for the scene report. Murphy found his copy first.

"Says here that the call came in at...7:31 p.m. Shit! That son of a bitch has Jamaica's beeper number!"

Proctor was already dialing the line to Chickenhead's room at the Biltmore before Murphy finished his sentence.

*   *   *   *   *

"What time ya wanna meet at the police station, Robert? I got a coupla people I need to see this morning."

"Told 'em we'd be there around two this afternoon, Jamaica." Chickenhead looked up from his notes as he spoke to his friend. "That cool with you?"

"Yeah. I should be finished by then." Jamaica grabbed his notebook off of the coffee table and stuffed it into his backpack. "What you got planned today, bro?" Jamaica asked as he pulled one strap of the backpack over his shoulder.

"Not much. Chill out here, talk to Bitters. Ain't heard from him all week. See when we gonna move out of this dump," Chickenhead said with a grin. Jamaica laughed.

"Man, this kinda dump was made for me. I'll catch ya later."

"You need a ride?"

"Naw, I'll catch the bus."

Chickenhead couldn't stand it anymore. "Jamaica?"

Jamaica stopped at the hallway and turned to his friend. "Whassup?"

"How did everything go last night? You been floatin' 'round here on a cloud all mornin'. I was tryin' not to be nosy, but..."

Jamaica laughed out loud, then turned down the hall. Chickenhead heard the door of the villa open just before his friend shouted down the hallway.

"Try harder, my brother." Jamaica was still cackling as he closed the door.

"Son of a bitch," Chickenhead mumbled through smiling lips.

*   *   *   *   *

Chickenhead was on his way out the door to meet Bitters when the phone rang in the villa. It was half past nine, and Jamaica had been gone for almost two hours.

"Hello?"

"Robert?" It was Proctor. "Robert, is Jamaica there?"

"Naw, he left a couple of hours ago. Had a couple of people ta see...what's up?" Proctor's string of curses surprised Chickenhead.

"Robert, we think the killer has Jamaica's beeper number."

Proctor quickly explained the information he and Murphy had just put together.

"Do you know where he was headed...who he was going to see this morning?"

"No, we hadn't talked about it."

"Did he take the car?"

"No, I've got it today. He's on the bus. Fuck, Proctor, why the hell you just now callin' me about this?"

"Robert, we just now put everything together."

Chickenhead's mind was going a mile a minute. He knew that Jamaica could take care of himself, but could he take care of this? His arm was better, but what if he were walking into something blind...

Proctor's brain was in overdrive, too. As of that morning, both Robert and Jamaica had a plainclothes officer assigned to discreetly follow each of them. Proctor, after waking up LaPlante the evening before, had gotten the lieutenant's okay. He knew someone was following Jamaica because he had radioed the man just before he called Robert. His dilemma was now a moral one--should he tell Robert? He was still wrestling with his conscience when Chickenhead spoke again.

"I need to page Jamaica and then call Bitters. Get over here."

"I'm on my way."

*   *   *   *   *

Jamaica was finishing his second cup of coffee at the Denny's restaurant on the corner of 7th Avenue and Camelback Road in Phoenix. The first guy he talked to was a bust--basically a bum who wanted a free meal. After several minutes of useless information intermixed with lies, Jamaica made a deal with the old man: Go sit somewhere else in the deserted diner, and he'd buy him breakfast. Jamaica was now watching the man. From across the dining room, the old guy kept looking up from his plate and was giving Jamaica a thumbs-up as he finished his second plate of pancakes and eggs. Looking at the clock behind the counter—it was a little before nine o'clock–Jamaica hoped that the next person he was supposed to meet would be on time.

He looked out the window that ran the length of the restaurant and watched the morning traffic go by as his mind drifted back to his date with Cynthia the night before. She had stayed. After the shit with Proctor and after his burning dinner, she had still stayed. While they had waited for room service to bring their late dinner, Jamaica had slowly unraveled the reason why he and Robert were at the Biltmore. In the thirty minutes it took for the meals to be delivered, she had only interrupted him once. That was when she had asked him to come back into the living room and sit beside her on the leather sofa. By the time the meals arrived, he had started to relax a bit. Placing her covered plate in front of her, he'd asked her what she wanted to drink as he moved to take the plastic lid off of her food. She had stopped him by touching his hand.

"Timothy, dinner can wait. I want to hear the rest of your story," she had said in a soft voice as she handed him her glass. "And I could use some more wine, please?"

The food sat untouched for the next two hours as they had talked. Well, he had talked...she had mostly listened. By the time he'd finished his tale, Jamaica felt as if he'd run a marathon. And she had been silent. There had been almost two minutes of dead air between them before she'd spoken to him.

"Timothy?"

The hesitation he had heard in her voice made his empty stomach do a slow roll and had instantly dried out his mouth.

"Yes, Cynthia?"

She had picked up her drink, sipping it slowly while looking at him over the rim of the crystal goblet. Gently setting it down, she had moved closer to him on the sofa and took his hand.

"Damn! Good-looking, can order room service, and now twice as mysterious! If this is what you're like on the first date, the second one must be incredible! When can I see you again?"

Jamaica reluctantly looked away from his memory to return to the present. Coming through the entrance was a tall white guy wearing a torn, black woolen skullcap pulled low over his blond-streaked hair.

That had gotten Jamaica's attention. The stranger was wearing an oil-stained green fatigue jacket that, save for the oil stain on one side, appeared new. Looking toward Jamaica, the man nodded. Jamaica returned the gesture. As the man approached the table, Jamaica looked him over. His light blue jeans, like the jacket he wore, had several large oily stains on them, but they, too, looked new. And the man's shoes--some surface dirt on both low-cut white sneakers, another oil stain on one but fully laced up and tied. Jamaica caught a glimpse of brilliant white socks--on both feet--as the man cleared the last bit of distance to the table.

This guy must be new to the streets, he thought. Cleanest bum I've ever seen.

"Jamaica? Are you Jamaica?" Both of the man's hands were shoved deep into the pockets of his jacket.

"That's me. Are you Clyde?"

"Yes...may I sit?"

"Cop a squat."

Hooking one foot under a chair, Braxton pulled the chair out enough to slide into it. When he was finally seated, he removed both hands from his pockets and folded them in front of him on the tabletop. Jamaica glanced at his hands and suppressed a frown--the short clean nails were cut perfectly.

Who is this guy? he wondered.

"A buddy of mine said you were looking for information about the killings. Said you'd pay for it. I got the number from him. Is that true?"

"Depends on what you got ta tell me, bro. You called me. Now what you got?"

"I found a body about five-six months ago near the Salt River bed out by 35th Avenue...I was camping out that way..."

Jamaica listened to the man sitting across from him as he described the scene of a body that they'd already identified. He watched the man's face as he spoke. Perfect white teeth. Clean-shaven. Jamaica observed as one of the man's hands, his right one, slowly left the table. Saw the cloth of his jacket pull downward on that side. Braxton had put his hand into the pocket. Jamaica slid the palm of his right hand to the table's edge in front of him.

"...I didn't want to call the cops–they're assholes. I just kept my mouth closed. When I heard you and Gibbs were looking for info on this, I got your number and called."

He said Robert's last name! Oh fuckin' shit...

"Hey there, buddy, wanna thank ya for the meal...ya think ya can spare a coupla bucks for some butts?" The old man turned to Braxton and slapped him on the back. He pointed to Jamaica across the table.

"Buddy, this guy is okay."

It was the bum from the first interview. While Jamaica was concentrating on Braxton, the grateful bum had walked up to the table. Braxton was looking up at the old man with daggers shooting from his eyes.

"Sure, partner," Jamaica answered quickly. "Why don't you have a seat for a minute?"

Jamaica watched as Braxton's hand came out of his pocket very slowly and returned to the tabletop. The irritation in his voice was obvious when he spoke.

"Hey, hey...I thought you were talking to me. Who's this guy?"

Jamaica's pager beeped just as the smiling bum pulled out the chair closest to Jamaica and sat down. Jamaica looked at the flashing four-digit number on the tiny screen: 7373. That was Chickenhead's code to call him pronto. As Jamaica looked at the unit in his left hand, it beeped again and showed the same number. A third time...same number. Uh-oh.

"Hey buddy, how about that change?"

Jamaica looked up and saw that both of Braxton's hands were gone from the tabletop and had been placed in his pockets. And the "informant" was staring holes in him as he began to stand up.

Fuck-a-duck, Jamaica thought.

Dropping the pager, Jamaica palmed the edge of the table with both hands and pushed it as hard as he could into Braxton's legs. Braxton's right hand tore out of his pocket to steady himself and a thin, uncapped syringe went airborne as Jamaica's coffee cup, notebook, and everything else on the table flew in every direction. Braxton screamed as the edge of the table slammed into his thighs and he started to fall toward Jamaica. Braxton's left hand came out of his other pocket and was clutching the open ivory-paneled knife. Off balance, he swung it in a wide arch, the tip of the stainless steel blade slicing to the bone the forehead of the bum sitting at the table. The bum screamed at the top of his lungs as he fell backwards and tumbled out of the chair. Jamaica flipped the table upward as he dove underneath it and barreled into Braxton, who was now falling backward and away from him.

Scampering to his feet, Jamaica looked over his shoulder as he ran in the opposite direction. Braxton was untangling himself from the table.

"Halt! Police!"

Jamaica looked up into the two-foot muzzle flash of a .38-caliber Smith and Wesson Police Special at point blank range--directly in front of his face. He felt a searing pain in his jaw...and saw darkness. The last thing he remembered was the sensation of spinning.

*   *   *   *   *

Officer Matthew Woods replaced Officer James Winzer at the last minute when Winzer called in sick.

"We need a body, rookie, and you're it," the desk sergeant had said. "Change back into your street clothes and get back here on the double. Got a cherry assignment for you."

Matt returned to his locker dragging his feet. He hated this job with all his heart but needed to hang on for at least another week. That's how long it would take him to find out if he got the sales rep position at the IBM district office in Phoenix. He had sailed through all three interviews over the last two weeks and knew they needed to fill five openings. His college roommate had told him so. Dalton had been with IBM since they'd both graduated from the University of Arizona two years before and had worked his way up to the #2 salesman for the region.

It bothered the hell out of Matt that Dalton was doing so well. Matt used to kick the guy's ass in school, his GPA had been higher, and he was much better with people than Dalton. Matt had no doubt that he could do it again given the chance.

Back in his street clothes, he returned to the desk. "I'm back, sir."

Suppressing a frown, the twenty-four-year veteran of two police departments looked up at the rookie who was younger than his own time in service. The sergeant pushed a thin folder across the desk.

"Okay, rookie. What's your name, anyway?"

"Woods, Matt Woods, sir."

"Okay, Woody, you're relieving Officer Steinbeck over at the Biltmore. The guy you're following's picture is in the folder along with all you need to know. Got it?"

"Yes, sir."

"Good." He handed Woods a sheet of paper. "Go to the garage and sign out a car. Give 'em this. They'll take care of you. You got your piece?"

"I left it in my locker...sir...you...you didn't tell me to bring it, sir."

"Thing ain't gonna do you much good in there now, is it, son?"

The sergeant looked Matt up and down, wondering how he ever made it out of the Police Academy. Reaching into the bottom drawer of his desk, he pulled out a battered shoulder holster. He handed it to Woods.

"Put your piece in this and wear your jacket over it. Make sure your radio has a fresh battery in it and ya got another one chargin' up in the car. Keep your radio volume low. This is an all-day thing, and ya don't want ta nut it up, got that?"

Woods shook his head "yes."

The desk sergeant looked Woods over again. He hated to send a rookie--no, he hated to send this rookie on this particular assignment, but he had little choice in the matter. For whatever reason, there had been a rash of sick call-ins over the last two shifts, and people were tight.

Hell, he thought, he'll just be followin' this guy. Probably be drinkin' coffee all day...

The sergeant grabbed his shift report and opened the thick folder. He sighed when he saw the ton of paperwork inside that he knew would keep him busy for hours. He glanced back at Woods, who was clumsily trying to figure out how to adjust the shoulder holster.

"On yer way, rookie! Steinbeck's been up all night."

Woods took a step back and then stopped. Turning back to the desk, he hesitated for a moment before stepping up close. The sergeant didn't look up from his paperwork when he spoke to Woods.

"You forget something, rookie?"

"Sergeant...my name is Woods. Matthew Woods. Not 'rookie,' sir."

The sergeant glared up at Woods with enough heat to make the young officer take a half-step back from the desk. Rising from his chair to his full six-foot-six-inch, two-hundred-eighty-pound bulk, Woods instantly regretted his attempt to grow balls.

"Your name and ass is gonna be shit if you don't get the fuck out of my station and to your assignment, rookie. You earn the right to be called by your name on my watch, boy. And you got a helluva ways to go." The big man sat back down, then looked back at the now-pale officer in front of him.

"Get your sorry ass out of my face. You're keepin' a real officer waitin'. Oh, and don't forget your fuckin' piece!" He waved Woods away as he returned to his mound of paperwork.

In the empty locker room, Woods shoved his service revolver into the shoulder holster and slammed his locker door shut twice before it stayed closed.

"I hate this goddamn job," he mumbled softly as he left the building to pick up his car.

*   *   *   *   *

Sitting in the nearly deserted Denny's restaurant, Woods drank his umpteenth cup of coffee and seethed. When he had gotten to the Biltmore, Steinbeck had barely grunted a hello before shoving a copy of his night report to him.

"Somethin' for ya ta read. They're both inside. If Robert comes out...he's the white one... Spacey's got 'im," Steinbeck grumbled as he pointed across the way to a thicket of bushes. Woods looked but couldn't see the other officer. Steinbeck continued to gather his stuff and handed Woods a pair of police issue binoculars.

"Jamaica's short and black. If he comes out, take your time. Give him a little room. If he's drivin', stay three-four car lengths behind him. If he's walkin', stay in your car and give 'im about a block head start. Piece of cake. Later, rookie."

It was mid-morning, and Woods had been following Jamaica since he left the Biltmore a little after 7 a.m. It wasn't as hard as he thought it would be. When Jamaica left the villa, he headed down the gentle slope of the driveway to the street. Following the road to the resort's 24th Avenue entryway, Jamaica exited and turned left. Woods used his field glasses to keep his target in sight from his own vantage point–a parking lot about a quarter-mile from the villa's front door. Woods waited until Jamaica was almost to the resort's entryway before starting his car and slowly driving to the entrance. He crept past the tall row of bushes that lined the avenue entrance and saw Jamaica walking up the block toward Camelback Road. Waving out his driver's side window for the two cars behind him to pass, Woods waited until Jamaica crossed 24th Avenue going west before driving onto the same street heading north. He made a U-turn around the divider and drove back up the block to the intersection, finally stopping at a red light. Woods looked out the passenger side window and saw Jamaica sitting at the bus stop's open shelter. Jamaica appeared to be calm as he read from a notebook.

The light changed to green, and Woods drove through the intersection. He turned into the parking lot of the Circle K on the southwest corner of Camelback Road and 24th Avenue. Quickly entering the store, the rookie cop went to the low rack of newspapers in front of the store and picked up a USA Today, all the while watching Jamaica across the street through the store's large plate-glass window. Woods had been standing in the same spot for almost ten minutes when a greasy-headed, squat duty manager approached him and tapped him on the arm.

"Excuse me, sir, can I help you with something?"

Woods fumbled for his badge and pulled it from his back

pants pocket. Flipping it open—upside-down—he showed it to the man, then shoved it back into his pants pocket.

"I'm on important police business. I'll be out of here in a few minutes, sir."

"Hey, sure thing. No problem, officer. That will be fifty cents, though."

Woods looked away from the window with an annoyed look on his face as he glared at the little man. "Fifty cents? For what? Staring out your window? I told you--I'm on official police business."

The smirk on the shorter man's face got larger as he answered Woods. "Standing is free, officer. Tearing up my merchandise isn't."

The man pointed to the morning newspaper in the cop's hand. It was then that Woods noticed, red-faced, that he had been twisting the paper between his hands. Bits of the tattered newsprint littered the floor around him like snow. Woods groaned out of embarrassment as he removed his wallet and gave the man a ten-dollar bill--the smallest note he had. As the man walked away, Woods saw Jamaica stand up across the street as an approaching bus slowed down. Woods edged to the door of the store as the bus stopped in front of the bench. The cop turned to the man behind the counter.

"Hey, buddy, where's my change? I have to go."

The man looked at Woods, then pointed to the line of early morning clientele standing in front of the counter. As if on cue, all four of them turned to Woods.

"I'm sorry, sir, give me a minute to finish with these people, and I'll be right with you."

Turning his head with a quick jerk to look out of the plate-glass window, Woods saw the bus pull away from the bench--the empty bench. Running through the door, he jumped into his car and grinded the gears as he started the engine twice. In an attempt to catch the departed bus, Woods pulled into the intersection against the stoplight and crossed three lanes of traffic as horns blared. The man behind the counter watched the commotion through the storefront while he waited on his customers. As the last of the people in line left the store, he laughed and pulled out a half-gone pack of cheap cigarettes. The smile was still on his face as he folded Woods' ten-dollar bill and stuffed it into the crumpled cellophane wrapper surrounding the smokes...

*   *   *   *   *

Woods watched as Jamaica talked to the tall bum with the oil-spotted army jacket.

This shit is a waste of time, he thought begrudgingly. Feeling as if his bladder was about to burst from the three cups of bad coffee he had downed since he sat down, Woods got up from the table located three rows behind Jamaica and went to the men's room. He heard his name being called over the radio just as he unzipped his pants.

"Shit!" he grumbled as he removed the unit from the holster on his belt.

"Officer Woods here."

"Woods, this is Lieutenant LaPlante. What's your 10-20?"

Woods gave the lieutenant his location, omitting the fact that he was in the men's room trying to pee quietly while holding the radio.

"Anything unusual? Any trouble this morning?"

Woods relayed all he had seen in the hour and a half he'd been watching Jamaica--his target eating breakfast--his target talking to a couple of bums.

"Fine, Woods. Keep this frequency open, and if anything happens that looks interesting, call me at my cell phone number." The commander gave Woods the number.

"Yes, sir."

Woods turned down the radio's volume and holstered it before he washed his hands. He left the restroom and looked at the bank of pay phones on the wall as he glanced around the corner toward Jamaica's table. He noticed that the bum Jamaica had talked to earlier was standing next to a cleaner-looking bum who was seated. Woods quickly dug some change out of his pocket and fed it into the pay phone. When he got a dial tone, he punched in the number to the personnel department of IBM's Regional Sales Office in Phoenix.

Once the IBM operator answered, Woods asked if he could speak to Wesley Snails, the manager Woods had interviewed with the previous week. The operator put him on hold.

"Hello, this is Wesley speaking. How can I help you?"

"Hello, Mr. Snails, this is Matthew Woods. I spoke to you last week about the sales position. I was wondering if you--"

Woods heard a loud crash and dropped the phone. Reaching for the gun in his shoulder holster, he struggled to pull it free as he sprinted around the corner to the diner's main room. He saw Jamaica scampering to his feet at the same time he finally freed the pistol from its leather holster. That's when he saw Braxton untangle himself from the overturned table. When he noticed the huge knife in Braxton's hand, Woods stopped dead in his tracks.

Oh, shit, he thought, that's him! He's gotta be the guy who's killin' everyone!

"Halt! Police!"

Woods raised the gun and pulled the trigger before he realized Jamaica was in the line of fire. Everything seemed to slow to half speed as he watched the right side of Jamaica's jaw explode in a wide spray of blood. The force of the bullet that glanced Jamaica's face spun his now unconscious body directly into Woods. Woods raised the gun high as he attempted to catch a collapsing Jamaica by grabbing him with his free arm. The dead weight of the slack body pushed both men into the table behind them.

A second later, Woods was startled to see Braxton almost on top of them--with a large, gleaming knife held high over his head. That's when a falling Woods pulled Jamaica closer to him and, off-balance, fired his gun again. The last thing Woods remembered was the sound of a scream as he himself fell backwards over the table and caused several chairs to scatter in all directions. Jamaica was still cradled against him as Woods' head hit the floor...

*   *   *   *   *

He knows who I am! Braxton thought as he uncapped the 5ml syringe of Versed that was still in his fatigue jacket pocket and rose from the table. Before Braxton could fully stand up, Jamaica surprised him by slamming the table into his legs. Braxton felt himself falling, first forward, then backwards as the table plowed into him. When he lost the syringe as he fought to keep his balance, he pulled the heavy ivory knife from his pocket, opened it, and tried to slash the top of Jamaica's hands as they gripped the edge of the table. One of his wild swings caught the forehead of the bum sitting next to his prey.

The bloodied bum fell backward screaming. Braxton pushed the table off of his legs and snarled as he jumped to his feet. He sprinted over the body of the squirming bum who was piteously holding his bleeding forehead.

Fuck this, he thought. I'm gonna gut this nigger right now!

"Halt! Police!"

Braxton saw the plainclothes officer level the gun at him a split-second before Jamaica scampered to his feet that put him in a position between Braxton and the officer's shaking gun. In that instant, Braxton sidestepped just as the officer fired his revolver. Overturning the fallen furniture in front of him, Braxton tried to stay behind Jamaica's falling body as he closed the gap between himself and the cop.

I've got to kill them both now, he thought. They've seen my face.

Raising the knife high over his head, Braxton had almost reached Jamaica when he heard a second gunshot. The surprised doctor was rocked by an instant hammering pain in his right side. The force of the bullet buckled his knees and sent the knife flying out of his left hand. Sliding to a stop, Braxton watched Jamaica and the cop fall backwards over several tables and chairs--still far out of his reach. The doctor breathed hard, and with his hands pressed tightly to his wound, spun around and ran to the emergency exit two tables beyond the overturned furniture. He hit the door hard with his bad side and fell to the ground with a scream that was muffled only by the hand he had thrust over his own mouth.

Braxton jumped up and raced to the stolen car that was parked in the restaurant's lot. Starting it, he backed out too quickly and slammed into another parked car. His bloody hand ground the gears as he shoved the shifter into first, shot into traffic, and headed south down 7th Avenue. The last thing he saw as he sped out of the parking lot was a skinny kid wearing chef's whites and running down the street behind him--writing something in the palm of his hand...

*   *   *   *   *

Chapter 19

The police radio in Proctor's unmarked police car blared to life as Proctor backed the unit out of the driveway of Chickenhead's villa at the Biltmore. Chickenhead was shifting in the front seat with Bitters sitting in the back.

"Officer down—I repeat—officer down! Shots fired at Denny's Restaurant, 5002 North 7th Street, northwest corner of 7th Street and Camelback Road. Any available units please respond."

Proctor's blood ran cold as the radio was instantly filled with units calling in to dispatch. That location was where the commander had said Woods was.

"Unit 482 responding."

"Unit 360 en route to Denny's."

"Unit 401 responding. We'll be there in three minutes."

Proctor's hand shot out to the radio and pressed the button on the hand-held unit as he pulled it to his face and almost screamed into the microphone.

"Dispatch, Detective Unit 211 on its way to Denny's. Eight minutes out." Proctor's hand shook as he slammed the red plastic globe to the roof of his car. He looked over at Chickenhead as he slapped the toggle switch on the dashboard to activate the siren and bubble light. "No matter what happens, both of you stay in the car."

Chickenhead reached for the door handle to steady himself as Proctor gunned the car through the red light at the corner of Camelback Road and 24th Avenue.

*   *   *   *   *

Proctor got to the scene just as one of two ambulances in front of the restaurant pulled away with its siren screaming. He parked his car onto the sidewalk across the street and shut off the car and siren. The parking lot of Denny's was full of police cruisers and swarming with cops. Half of the street ahead of them was already shut down to one lane of traffic with an officer hastily directing people through. Proctor briefly watched the business being overrun with his people, then turned to face both Chickenhead and Bitters.

"You both stay put. I'll be back in a few minutes." He grabbed his mobile radio from the charger between the front seat and opened his door. Before he was fully out of the car, Proctor leaned back in and punched his code into the keypad of his car radio to disable it. The last thing he wanted was for either of them to hear what had just happened. Proctor slammed the car door closed and ran toward the bustling restaurant.

They both watched him disappear across the street into the sea of blue uniforms. Bitters leaned forward toward the front seat and tapped Chickenhead on the shoulder to get his attention.

Let's step outside--get some fresh air. It looks like he may be in there for a while."

As the two men leaned against the car, Chickenhead pulled the pager from his belt and checked the tiny display window. Nothing. Jamaica still hadn't returned any of his pages from almost twenty minutes earlier, and now he was starting to worry. He was just about to ask Bitters to use his cell phone when he heard the private eye's phone ring. Chickenhead watched as Bitters spoke into the unit, abruptly stop his conversation, and look directly at Chickenhead. Turning his back to him, Bitters quickly finished the conversation and immediately dialed another number. He rapidly spoke into the mouthpiece in a language Chickenhead couldn't make out. Bitters talked for less than a minute and then shut the phone off. He put it into his pocket and surprised Chickenhead by grabbing his arm.

"We need to go. That was an informant of mine in the police department. Jamaica's been shot. I know where he's at. Let's go."

Chickenhead understood the situation instantly. He felt his heart jump painfully in his throat. "Is he...?"

Seeing a cab across the street at the corner gas station, Bitters waved it down. He answered Chickenhead as he watched the cabbie wave back at him through the driver's side window.

"He's alive and being prepped for surgery," Bitters said as he led Chickenhead by the arm through the backed-up traffic to reach the waiting cab. Opening the door of the cab, Bitters felt Chickenhead tense and begin to pull away. When Bitters looked across the street, he immediately saw why--Proctor was standing outside the Denny's Restaurant with both of his hands against his forehead as he shouted at two officers who were standing at the front door. Looking half-crazed, Chickenhead was almost free of Bitters' restraining hand.

"I'm gonna kill that son of a bitch!"

"Not here, Robert," Bitters said calmly.

Bitters tightened his grip on the stiffened arm and quickly turned Chickenhead so that his back was facing him. Bitters' free hand rose in a blur, and the edge of his hand slapped down hard, slightly left of the base of Chickenhead's neck, effectively knocking him senseless. Bitters poured his friend into the back seat of the cab and pushed in beside him. The cabby's view of what had happened seconds before had been blocked by Bitters' wide shoulders. He looked at Chickenhead's slumped body through his rearview mirror.

"What's the matter with your friend? Is he sick?"

"Yes. He forgot to take his seizure medicine. We need to get to the hospital as quick as possible." A hundred-dollar bill appeared in Bitters' hand. "Good Samaritan Hospital is up the street. Take us there and this is yours." The note fell out of Bitters' hand and fluttered to the front seat, landing next to the driver. Masking his astonishment, the cabby leaned over, turned off his meter, and looked both ways before slowly turning into traffic. He drove in the opposite direction of the backup and quickly found a side street, speeding up as he entered it. The cab made the twelve-block trip, hitting all the lights, in less than seven minutes. All the while Bitters was talking on his cell phone in rapid-fire Japanese...

*   *   *   *   *

Bitters handed Chickenhead a can of soda from a hospital vending machine and watched as his angry friend rubbed the sore spot on the back of his neck with the ice-cold can. Sitting across from Chickenhead in a private waiting room, Bitters sipped a Diet Coke. It was almost four o'clock in the afternoon.

"Guess you want to kick my ass right about now, eh, Robert?"

Glaring at Bitters, Chickenhead winced as he shook his head "no." "Thanks for not letting me get my stupid ass arrested or shot back there."

A slight smile played on Bitters' lips for a moment, then was gone. "You're very welcome." Bitters continued to sip his drink.

Chickenhead put the can of soda on the table next to him and rubbed his neck as he spoke. "Have you been able to find out when Jamaica gets out of surgery?"

The door to the small waiting room began to open before Bitters could answer the question. Chickenhead was amazed at the speed in which Bitters stood up, gun drawn, before the door completely opened. Bitters reholstered the weapon just as Proctor and a uniformed officer cleared the doorway. Neither had seen the gun. Proctor looked at Chickenhead, then turned to the cop hovering at his shoulder.

"Wait outside and don't come in unless I call for you."

The cop gave Proctor a questioning look, then nodded and exited the room. Proctor closed the door behind him. Both Bitters and Chickenhead noticed then that Proctor's shoulder holster was empty. Proctor looked at Chickenhead, then looked away. The look on Proctor's face made blood rush to Chickenhead's already throbbing temples.

"I'm...sorry this happened, Robert."

Chickenhead launched himself across the room at the cop, arms swinging wildly, raining blows to Proctor's head and stomach.

The cop barely kept his arms up to protect himself. Chickenhead pushed Proctor back to the door with blows that shook his body as they landed, but it was a kidney punch Proctor couldn't deflect that tore open several of Chickenhead's chest stitches. Chickenhead, breathing hard with his hand over the reopened wound, stared at the detective with a wishful look of death. Proctor--outside of a busted lip and an aching kidney--was no worse for the wear. Bitters casually looked from one man to the other as both limped to opposite ends of the room and flopped into chairs.

"Well," Bitters said with a mild look of amusement, "now that we know y'all still love each other, can we get back to business?" Bitters watched Chickenhead as he huffed in his seat and gave him the finger. Bitters turned to Proctor, who was holding his side and gingerly touching his swelling and bleeding lower lip. Bitters shook his head and continued.

"Detective?"

"What?" Proctor grumbled as he grabbed several tissues from a box on the small table beside his chair. He pressed them to his lip.

"How the fuck did your man shoot Jamaica?"

"He was a rookie...he made a mistake."

"A fuckin' mistake that almost killed Jamaica, you piece of shit!" Chickenhead spit out.

Bitters quickly glanced at Chickenhead. Seeing that the man was staying seated, Bitters returned his attention to Proctor.

"What's Jamaica's prognosis?"

"The bullet grazed the outside of his jaw on the right side, breaking it. The doctors are operating on him now to realign it. So far it looks like—outside of his jaw and some bumps and bruises—he'll be okay."

Proctor bent over the wastebasket beside his chair and spit out a dribble of bloody saliva. "The doctors are gonna keep him knocked out for a couple of days to be on the safe side," Proctor added as he looked at Chickenhead. "He'll have 'round-the-clock police protection."

Chickenhead laughed and winced at the same time. "Yeah, that kind of protection we all need."

"Detective, for Mr. Driver's own piece of mind, we'll be keeping some of our men here also."

Proctor shrugged his shoulders.

"Did anyone make an ID of the guy that got away?"

"A cook got his license plate and a good description of the car. The officer on the scene is being debriefed. He got a good look at the perp. We're hoping to have a composite soon."

Proctor looked at Chickenhead, who was still glaring at the detective. Looking back to Bitters, Proctor rose and went to the door, opening it. He called out to the cop standing slightly down the hall and waved him over.

"Jeez, sir, your lip! It's bleeding!"

"Don't worry about it...had an accident. Do me a favor--go take a ten-minute break and get a cup of coffee or something, okay?"

"Um, yes, sir."

Proctor watched the officer walk down the hall before going back into the room. He closed the door behind him and settled back into his chair before speaking again. Proctor pointed to Bitters.

"You didn't hear this from me, understand?"

"Yes."

"We have the knife the perp has been using. Found it at the restaurant this morning. We also recovered a syringe, the second one we've found that's connected to this guy. If it's anything like the first one we found a few days ago, the fluid inside it is Versed, a controlled substance that's used as a general anesthesia. We're dusting both items for prints along with the overturned furniture. We also believe the perp was wounded. He was hit at least once by our man."

Chickenhead moved to the edge of his chair. "How bad was he hit?"

"We don't know. The cook who saw him running away said he was holding his right side. We found spots of blood on the emergency door he ran out of and a splotch on the sidewalk outside the door where he must have fallen." Proctor paused for a moment to wipe a trickle of blood from his oozing lip.

"We think this guy is in the medical profession or knows someone in it. The M.O. of the last few killings, the anesthesia...this shit can't be a coincidence."

"Have you checked the clinic–the Columbus Free Clinic? Guy might be from there," Chickenhead offered.

"Yes. We've talked to the doctors and some of the nurses. Still checking out one of them. Out of all the people who have worked there, only this one has been there for the entire time of the killings over the last few years. Bastard almost freaked when I showed him Mimi's picture in the paper."

Chickenhead sat up immediately. "Who was it?" he asked in an urgent tone.

Proctor gave Chickenhead a pained look that had nothing to do with his now swollen lip. "Robert...you know I can't tell you that."

"Goddammit, Proctor, who was it?" Chickenhead shouted. "Was it the doctor who saw Jamaica? Was it the doctor who saw me–Dr. Howard?"

Proctor tried to appear calm at the mention of Dr. Howard's name. Waiting for a moment, he took several deep breaths to slow down his heart.

"Why did you mention Jamaica's doctor? Why did you mention the doctor who saw you–Dr. Howard?"

Bitters instantly knew Chickenhead had stumbled onto something and where Proctor was headed.

"'Cause those are the only doctors I know, dammit!"

"But why, Robert? Why those two? Did something happen? Did either of them ask you anything or do anything that was strange?"

The revelation that hit Chickenhead was almost like a physical blow. "Oh...oh fuck..." Chickenhead put both hands to his head.

"What, Robert? What?"

"I told Howard about Mimi, about my nightmares, how I couldn't sleep. I was 'posed to come back to the Clinic last Tuesday to see one of their shrinks. He made arrangements for me ta shortcut the list they had, ta move to the top of the list. And he gave me some money...two-hundred dollars...and said he felt sorry for me...said he had a sister who was killed a few years ago..."

Chickenhead's voice trailed off as he hugged himself and began rocking in his seat. The room was quiet for a moment as Proctor, unsure of what to do next, stood up and took a half-gone pack of antacid tablets from his pocket and crunched two into his mouth. He glanced toward the door and sat back down. His eyes darted between Chickenhead and Bitters before they settled on Chickenhead.

"Robert, I...I talked to Howard on Tuesday. His reaction to my questions made me dig deeper...check out his background. Robert, Howard has two brothers. He's never had any sisters."

The howl of pain and anger that came from Chickenhead caused both Bitters and Proctor to cringe in their seats. It also caused the cop stationed outside the door (he had just returned from his break) to rush into the room with his gun drawn. Proctor and Bitters both jumped to their feet. Proctor quickly walked to the door.

"Jesus Christ! Detective, are you okay in here?" the cop asked as he stared at Chickenhead, who had lowered his head into his hands and had begun sobbing.

"Yes, yes, I'm fine. Leave. Go back outside. Please."

Proctor pushed the confused officer out the door and closed it. Bitters knelt next to Chickenhead and spoke to him in monotones. "Robert...Robert, I need you to talk to me. Can you understand me?"

Chickenhead raised his head and looked at Bitters with eyes drowning in pain.

"Robert, can you hear me? Can you talk to me?"

Chickenhead stopped rocking and slowly nodded twice.

"We're gonna get this guy—you, me, and Proctor. His ass is ours. I need to know if you can hang. I need to know if I...if all of us can count on you. Can we, Robert?

Looking a bit steadier now, Chickenhead wiped the tears from his eyes and nodded again.

"Good. You need something? A cigarette?"

Sitting up a bit straighter, Chickenhead ran his fingers

through his bright red hair before he spoke. "Fuck a cigarette...I need a drink."

Bitters reached into his inside sports coat pocket, pulled out a slim silver whiskey flask, and handed it to Chickenhead. Uncapping the flask with shaking hands, Chickenhead took a long draw from it before handing it back to Bitters. Before he put it back in his pocket, Bitters gestured to Proctor. Proctor shook his head.

"Thank you, no. I'm on duty."

"Hey, man, might take the edge off of that swelling lip."

Proctor gave a short laugh but still refused the drink. Bitters put the flask back into his inside breast pocket.

Chickenhead surprised both of them when he spoke. "I've got information that will help you, Proctor."

Leaning forward, Chickenhead opened the main compartment of his backpack and took out two slim notebooks. He handed one to Proctor, the other to Bitters. His voice was getting stronger as he spoke to the detective.

"These are copies of all the information we've found on the street people who were killed in the last year and a half. Out of ten, we were able to ID six. Their names, the locations their bodies were found--it's all there. You might wanna check them against any records they might have at the clinic."

Proctor looked at the notebook in his hand, then back at Chickenhead. "Robert, thanks...thank you," he stammered for a moment before he continued. "I need to go. I'm going to put out a warrant for Howard's arrest and subpoena any and all records that the clinic may have on any of the names in this book."

Proctor turned to the door he'd been leaning against, hesitated for a moment, then opened it and left. Bitters pulled the flask from his pocket and took a deep swallow, emptying it. As he capped the lightweight flask, he looked at Chickenhead and made a mental note to call Driver when he got a minute alone. Leaning forward in his chair, he tapped Chickenhead's leg.

"Partner, we need to be going. You up for this?"

Chickenhead looked back at Bitters with eyes the color of the sky and with a gaze as cold as ice. "I'm ready to kill this fuck."

Bitters smiled. "Can't let you do that, bro...but I will let you beat the shit out of him for a minute if it makes you feel better."

"Problem is if I start, I don't know if I'll be able to stop."

Bitters stood up, a smile still on his face. "That's why I get paid the big bucks, Robert-to keep your ass out of trouble." Bitters walked to the door and opened it. Stepping into the hallway, he looked back into the room at his friend. Chickenhead was still seated.

"What you waitin' for, bro? The rabbit's a'runnin'...let's go catch it."

*   *   *   *   *

"Are you okay, Mr. Howard?" the bank teller asked the pale, sweating man in front of her as she counted out the last of the nine-thousand-dollar withdrawal. "Do you need any help? I could call my manager."

"No, that's fine. Thank you, ma'am. I just have a bit of the flu. Can I have that in an envelope, please?"

"Of course, sir." With practiced hands, the teller quickly placed the thick stacks of twenties and fifties in a large manila envelope and slid the package through her window to Braxton. "You have a good day, sir, and make sure you rest, okay?"

"Thank you again, ma'am."

The wound in Braxton's side radiated pain throughout his entire body like a rotten tooth as he tried...and failed...to walk normally out of the bank. He had driven the stolen car back to the Mustang and left it parked in the back lot of an abandoned church off of Adams Street near downtown. He had accomplished that without passing out. Barely.

Changing out of his shirt and jacket had taken him several agonizing minutes. He had known better than to try to remove his pants. Once he'd gotten his shirt off, he got a good look at the wound and almost fainted at the sight of the purple, bloody flesh. The bullet had ripped a deep ravine through his side, tearing a line of flesh just above his belt line but hadn't entered his abdominal wall. Standing close to one of the Mustang's side view mirrors that he'd angled up to get a better look at the wound, he'd seen the imbedded scraps of fiber from his jacket and shirt. He chewed tablets of Demerol and packed the wound with gauze from the first aid kit he kept in the Mustang. He had whimpered in pain when he'd slowed the blood flow to his side, but he'd been thankful that the spilled blood was slight.

God, he thought, another inch and my gut would be full of blood and shit.

He knew he had to run. Now. His knife and the syringe were somewhere in that restaurant, both covered with his prints. Prints that were on file with the State Medical Board. Gingerly, he had slowly put on a mid-length black leather coat from the change of clothes he'd stashed in the car. The designs of the jacket hid the bulge of the bandaging beneath his shirt and disguised the spots of blood near his waist while he stood in line at the bank. Getting back to his car Braxton tried to slow down the near-panic rushing of his mind. Thoughts jumped in and out with a rapidity that threatened to frighten him into a standstill. Moving carefully, he slid behind the wheel of his car and felt his wound reopen. He started the car and drove for almost ten minutes before he pulled to the side of the road and turned off the engine. He reached into the glove compartment, pulled out his cell phone, and quickly dialed the number of his friend, Tony Norwood. He forced himself to breathe slowly and deeply. The phone rang once, then switched over to Tony's answering service.

Good, he thought, he's talking to someone.

Braxton left a message for Tony to call him back as soon as he got the message. Putting the phone on the dashboard in front of him, he re-started the car and five minutes later was on the highway. Braxton was ten minutes from his exit when the phone sprung to life. He checked the number before he answered and let out a sigh of relief when he saw it was Tony.

"Hey, Tony, whassup?"

"Don't know. You called me. Make it quick 'cause I'm on my way to a procedure."

"Anything interesting?"

"Nah, routine shit. What you need, buddy?"

Braxton shifted in his seat and bit his tongue to keep from screaming. Stay focused, he thought.

"Yo, Braxton, you still there?"

"Yeah, sorry 'bout that. Got cut off in traffic. Bro, I need some party favors for a very special lady. Think you can help me out?"

Tony's chuckle was loud and clear through the digital unit in Braxton's shaking hands. "She got any sisters?"

"Sorry, man, this one's solo. I'll tighten you up the next time, though."

"Yeah, right. What ya need?"

Braxton took a deep breath and tried to think past the pain. "Coupla 'scripts of Percodan. We're gonna have a little party at her place in Denver this weekend. I wanna make sure neither of us will be feelin' any pain."

Tony's laugh was loud and long over the phone before he answered. "You are one sick puppy, Braxton. Yeah, I can fix you up. Gonna cost you dearly, tho', my boy. I want all the gory details on Monday. When you need 'em?"

"How 'bout after you get out of surgery? I'm flying out this afternoon."

"No prob. I'll have this bitch bagged and tagged by noon. I'll give you a holler when I got it. Gotta go. Later."

The connection broken, Braxton switched off the phone and dropped it to the floor of the car. Almost weeping in relief and pain, he didn't know what he would have done if he hadn't been able to get in touch with Tony. He didn't want to write the prescriptions for himself...that would have given way too much information. Someone would remember something. He could imagine the scenario: What, Officer? A tall white male? Looked kind of pale? Yeah, I remember him, sir, I sure do. He got two prescriptions of Percodan filled, 120 tablets. I got his paperwork right here...

Braxton pulled off the highway at his exit and waited for the light to change. As he turned into surface traffic, he saw a Scottsdale police cruiser on a side street ahead of him, waiting to merge into traffic. Clamping both hands on the steering wheel as he drove past, Braxton unconsciously let out a moan as the cruiser slid into the opening behind him. The doctor stopped at a red light at the intersection, and time stopped as he stared straight ahead and tried to concentrate on the traffic signal.

There is no way they can know anything yet, he thought.

The light changed, and he slowly moved forward. Just as he pulled through the intersection, the cruiser's lights and siren came on. Braxton almost slammed on the brakes as he saw the police car in his rearview mirror closing the space between them. A car length behind him, the cruiser veered to his left side and sped past him with sirens screaming. Braxton slowed down gradually and pulled into the first side street he came to. He parked well down the block, turned off the car's engine, and shook for almost five minutes. He reached down to his wound and drew back his hand—damp with blood. Although the bleeding had slowed, he needed to change his bandages. Once his heart rate slowed to a more life-sustaining level, Braxton started the car and made a U-turn at the end of the block. Looking for cop cars, he pulled back into the main thoroughfare. It took him another twenty agonizing minutes to get home.

*   *   *   *   *

Braxton's cell phone rang just after he finished re-bandaging his wound. He checked the number displayed and saw that it was Tony calling. He answered with, "Hey, buddy, ya got my poison?"

"In my dirty little hands as we speak. Want me to bring it over? I'm on my way out of the hospital now."

"Tell ya what, why don't you meet me at Sky Harbor? I'll be out of here in about twenty minutes. Can you meet me at the Executive Terminal by–," he looked at his watch, "–by 3:15?"

"No prob, my druggie friend. Just remember you owe me big time."

"Thanks, Tony. I'll see you there." Braxton clicked the unit off. As quickly as he could, he packed an athletic bag with clothes and extra bandages and placed the envelope containing the money he had withdrawn on top. He zipped up the full bag and grabbed his medical bag, quickly scanning his condo for anything more he might need to take with him. Nothing jumped out at him—nothing caught his eye. He needed to leave, but he hesitated to move out of his front room.

I've got to throw them off the trail-buy myself some time.

Entering the kitchen, he picked up the Yellow Pages from under the wall phone and turned to the airline listings. He picked the first one he came across and dialed the toll-free number. After a series of automated prompts, he finally got a reservationist.

"American Airlines. How can I help you?"

Braxton gave the woman his credit card number and booked a roundtrip flight in his name. As far as anyone knew, he was flying to Denver at six o'clock that evening. He completed the transaction, thanked the lady, and hung up the phone. He grabbed his coat and bags, headed for the door, and stopped only long enough to pick up the keys to the Mercedes. He didn't look back as he left his condo for the last time...

*   *   *   *   *

Having followed his friend into the men's restroom, Tony handed Braxton a small brown paper bag. The large goofy grin on Tony's face irritated the hell out of Braxton, who was finding it increasingly difficult to maintain his cool.

"Don't get too buck wild tonight with these. You may need some more tomorrow," Tony said with a chuckle as he gave Braxton a hearty, playful slap to the doctor's bad side. Braxton's knees almost buckled and his face lost all its color. Tony stood up straight and stared at his friend as Braxton leaned against one of the sinks for support.

"God, Braxton, are you all right? You look like shit!"

Braxton hoped the weak smile on his face was somewhat convincing. "Hey, I'll live. Nothing that a six-foot blonde can't take care of, ya know what I mean?" He followed his weak smile with a wink. Tony continued to stare at his friend with a look of unease.

"Seriously, Braxton, what's wrong?"

"Look, things got kind of out of hand last night with a

coupla girls I picked up. I'm still a little sore, okay? There. Now you know."

Tony's concerned look was replaced by a knowing smirk. "You dog, you! Anyone I know?"

"Naw, but you'll get to meet one of them tonight if you want. I already got a roundtrip ticket for you to join me in Denver."

"Get the hell outta here! Really?"

"Yeah, thought you'd like to see first-hand what's whuppin' my ass. You're gonna love her. Besides, I owe you one."

"One my ass! This will do for now, though."

"Your ticket is on American Airlines Flight 406. It leaves tonight at six. You can pick up the ticket at any American counter whenever you're ready. You interested?"

"Hell, yeah, I'm interested! I'll grab it before I leave."

Braxton walked to the door of the restroom with Tony on his heels. They both walked to the door leading to the tarmac where Braxton's plane was parked. Braxton held the door open with one foot as he turned to Tony.

"I gotta get going. I need to pick up...Debra. She lives in Tucson. I'll get her there, then we'll fly up to Denver and meet you at your gate tonight, okay?"

Tony was bouncing like a puppy with a new toy. "Hey, I wouldn't miss this for the world! I'll see you tonight!" Tony said as he waved to his friend.

Braxton exited the terminal and hurried over to his plane. Quickly going through his checklist for takeoff, he paused for only a second to dry-swallow two Percodan tablets. He started the engines to the Cessna and thought about the lie he had told Tony. He wondered how Tony could have been stupid enough to swallow the story–hook, line, and sinker. Calling his flight number into the tower, Braxton waited for his slot for takeoff.

Asshole's in for a hell of a surprise when he gets to the airport tonight, he thought. *This should buy me a few hours' head start.*

Receiving clearance from the tower, Braxton taxied his plane behind two others waiting to take off.

Dumb son of a bitch always did try too hard, he thought.

Watching the plane in front of him speed down the runway for takeoff, Braxton revved his engines up a notch and pulled into the slot that had just been vacated.

Damn! I'm almost out of here!

After receiving final clearance from the tower, Braxton opened the throttle full bore and rushed down the runway to the open sky. A smile plastered his face as he left the ground at 4:12 p.m....

Chapter 20

"My God...all of these people were treated here within three weeks of being killed!" Proctor looked down the list of names Chickenhead had given him hours ago as he sat in the medical record archives of the Columbus Free Clinic. Piles of medical records were stacked in front of him on the only table in the small room. The nurse he'd brought into the room with him kept adding to the steadily growing pile. Proctor looked at Murphy, who was standing in the doorway.

"Out of the names Robert gave us, Braxton actually treated three of them–including Mimi. Mutherfucker's been shoppin' this place like a goddamn supermarket."

Warrant and subpoenas in hand, Proctor, Murphy, and a small army of uniformed and plainclothes officers had descended on the clinic less than an hour before. In less than five minutes, they'd cleared out the homeless people and shut the clinic's doors. Everyone who worked there–all the doctors, nurses, and the secretary who had just been hired that day to answer phones–had at least two officers interviewing them. None of the detainees were happy, to say the least. Two of the doctors had loudly protested the clinic's blanket raid. Proctor had both of them arrested immediately, especially after they began yelling about calling their lawyers. They were hauled away, handcuffed, in the back of the filthiest police cars at the scene. Seeing their co-worker and supervisor handled like cattle did what Proctor hoped it would do–it made everyone there think a little bit harder and answer questions a lot quicker. Grabbing the first person he saw in scrubs, Proctor shoved a copy of the list of names Chickenhead had given him earlier under the frightened nurse's nose.

"Where are your records kept? Are they here?"

"Yes, sir. They're right here, sir. We have a room in the back where we keep them." Proctor called over to the nearest uniformed officer and then turned back to the wide-eyed nurse. "Let's go," he said forcefully as he rammed the piece of paper into the nurse's hand. "You're gonna find these people's records. Now."

Proctor was sitting in front of those very documents, pissed to high heaven and beyond. Pissed that Braxton, working less than three blocks from the Phoenix Police Headquarters, had been killing and butchering people under their noses for God knows how long. Pissed that, with all the resources the Phoenix PD had at its disposal, two street people--Chickenhead and Jamaica--had broken the case in one week that his department hadn't put so much as a dent into in three friggin' years. And pissed that Jamaica was laid up in the hospital after almost losing his life at the hands of the most inept cop Proctor had ever met.

"F-U-C-K!" Proctor yelled loud enough to startle the nurse as he threw the folder he was holding to the floor. Murphy pushed the nurse out of the room and told the uniformed cop standing at the door to leave as well.

"Hey, buddy, you okay?"

"Do I look the fuck okay? Jesus, I talked to this guy four days ago, Murphy! Four fuckin' days ago! I had that son of a bitch in the next room and let him walk!"

Murphy leaned against one of the floor-to-ceiling file cabinets that lined the wall and shook his head at his partner. "Man, you can't blame yourself. There's no way in hell you coulda known then..."

"Tell that to Jamaica. Because of me, he's lying on a goddamn operating table gettin' his face put back together."

"Steve..."

Before Murphy could console his friend, a uniformed cop

stuck his head into the room. "Hey, you two Proctor and Murphy?"

They both nodded. The cop turned and yelled down the hall. "Lieutenant LaPlante, over here."

The commander entered the room a moment later carrying a slim manila file folder. He had a solemn look on his face.

"Braxton's our man. Lab lifted prints off of the knife, table, and a loaded syringe found at the restaurant. They all matched prints we got from the State Medical Board. Also, blood residue on the knife and the size of the knife matched the kid and the bum at the hotel. Matched Sonny James, too."

LaPlante threw the folder on top of the pile of records on the table in the middle of the room. It slid off the stacks of medical documents and opened, spilling papers as it fell to the floor. No one moved to pick them up.

"Can you believe this shit?" LaPlante grumbled as he stood in the doorway. "A doctor... a fuckin' doctor..."

Bending down, LaPlante started to gather up the papers as he spoke to Proctor and Murphy.

"Got police at his practice in Scottsdale and at his house. Found a half-gone bottle of Versed hidden in a jar of salsa in the fridge--gotta be the same one he's been using on everybody. Shit was all over the place when we got there. Had bloody bandages in the bedroom, so our boy's hurt. Hurt and on the run."

The cell phone clipped to LaPlante's belt rang insistently. He answered it and talked for a minute before clicking it off. "Son of a bitch withdrew nine-thousand dollars from his checking account this morning. Teller remembers him from the withdrawal amount and the fact that he looked like shit. Guys at his place also found records of a plane he bought two weeks ago. They're working on getting the dealer on the phone."

LaPlante looked at his watch. It read 6:08 p.m. "Probably safe to say he's in the air some fuckin' where."

LaPlante's phone rang again. He was on the phone for only a moment when a grim smile appeared on his face. He clicked the unit off, motioning for Proctor and Murphy to follow him.

"Guys, we're on our way to the airport. Some stupid ass just tried to fly out under a ticket Braxton bought this afternoon. Airport police are holding him for us."

*   *   *   *   *

Bitters had all of the same information the police had within minutes of their receiving it, courtesy of the mole he was paying within the Phoenix Police Department. He had just taken the week's notes, which included the fiasco that had happened in the restaurant earlier that same day, and relayed all of his findings to his employer, Peter Driver, via his suite's phone at the Biltmore. Bitters watched Chickenhead as he paced the floor in front of him, downing his second beer in the last twenty minutes. Driver's shouting on the other end of the line had become so loud that Bitters had to hold the phone away from his ear. Chickenhead stopped walking in circles and finished in one long gulp what was left of his beer while he stared at Bitters.

"Mr. Driver, please..."

"I want this piece of shit, Bitters! I'm paying you a ton of money to get the son of a bitch! I want results, and I want them right fuckin' NOW!" The line went dead before Bitters could say anything else. The Mayor had hung up on him.

Chickenhead opened another beer as he spoke. "What did he have to say?"

"He's...disturbed to find out a doctor is suspected of the killings. Doesn't set well with his conservative views."

"So what do we do now?"

"We wait. I have a couple of deliveries on the way; they'll be here within the hour. And you need to pack a bag. Throw enough stuff together for the next few days. I've got some calls to make. Be back here in twenty minutes. Go." Bitters pointed to the door behind Chickenhead as he picked up his cell phone and dialed. Chickenhead stopped dead in his tracks when Bitters started speaking Japanese into the phone. Curious, Chickenhead stood at the door drinking his beer while he watched the man. Bitters stopped speaking and looked up from his conversation.

"Robert, you need something?"

"What's with the Chinese talk?"

"It's not Chinese. It's Japanese. Old army habit. You never know who's listening over the airwaves. Anything else?"

"No...well, yeah. If you were in Japan and talkin' to someone, what would you use?"

Bitters shook his head before he answered. "Probably an African dialect. Swahili more than likely. Is this leading somewhere?"

"No."

"Then go get packed."

Bitters watched Chickenhead as he closed the door to his suite. Shaking his head again, he returned to his phone conversation...

*   *   *   *   *

It had been almost an hour since Chickenhead had left Bitters' suite, and he wasn't even close to finishing his packing. His half-filled duffel bag leaned against the bed in his room while Chickenhead drank another bottle of beer. He had lost count as to how many he'd consumed. Actually, he did have a distinct pattern--when he'd finish one, he'd open another. The routine seemed to be that he'd pick up something (a toothbrush, a roll of socks) and then look at the item as if it had just fallen from outer space. The more he walked through the villa he shared with Jamaica, the slower he got. After a half-hour of going in and out of all the rooms of the suite and not knowing why, Chickenhead went to the bar, opened another beer, and sat on one of the barstools.

He wasn't drunk--didn't even feel so much as a buzz from all the alcohol he'd downed. From his vantage point at the bar, he could see into the kitchen. With regret, he saw the pots that Jamaica had cleaned that morning and had left on a drying rack next to the sink. Sipping his drink, Chickenhead remembered their short conversation earlier that day and how happy Jamaica had been about his date the night before--and with amusement recalled how Jamaica had tried not to show it. That brought a short-lived smile to Chickenhead's face. It had been a long time--hell, it was the first time he could remember in forever that he had seen Jamaica so happy about anything. Setting his beer aside, Chickenhead pulled out a cigarette from an open pack on the bar and lit it. When the phone rang at the other end of the room, he took his time walking over to it.

"Hello?"

"Hello. Is this Robert?"

"Yeah, who is this?"

"Hi, Robert, this is Cynthia...Cynthia Winaford. I was hoping that Timothy was in. Is he there?"

Chickenhead felt his stomach constrict in a knot. "Ma'am...Cynthia...Jamaica's in the hospital. There's been an accident."

It was nearly a full minute before Cynthia spoke. "Wh--what happened? Is he going to be all right?"

"He...he was shot this morning. Doc said he was lucky...that he'll pull through okay."

More silence. Another minute. When she spoke again, Chickenhead could hear the concern in her voice. "Was it about the case you two are working on? Finding the man who killed your girlfriend?"

"Yes."

"Can I go see him? Would that be all right?"

"Cynthia, I think he would really like that. He would like that a lot."

Chickenhead gave her the hospital information and the address. "I don't know the room number yet, I'm sorry. When you call, ask for Detective Proctor. I'll leave a message with him to make sure you can get to see our friend."

"Thank you, Robert. And how are you doing? Are you holding up all right?"

"I'm...here. I don't know, really."

"Jamaica and I talked about you for a long time last night. Quite a bit of it was about you. I'm so sorry about your girlfriend."

"Thank you, ma'am."

"He really loves you, Robert. And I can only imagine that you're blaming yourself for this trouble, but you shouldn't. You can't.

Timothy and I talked about what might happen. He said he would help you, anyway. He would give his life for you."

He almost did, Chickenhead thought dejectedly.

"Cynthia, I've got to go. Will you check up on Jamaica? Let me know how he's doing? I would do it myself, but I may be out of town for a few days."

"Of course." She gave him her home and work numbers.

"Thanks. I'll call and give you my number as soon as I can. Will you go see him tonight?"

"I'll leave as soon as I get off the phone. And Robert--be careful. Timothy told me the man you're looking for has killed a bunch of people."

"One of them was almost Jamaica," he interrupted. Chickenhead was instantly sorry he said what he had just then. "I'm sorry. I really didn't mean to say that."

"No apology necessary. You have my numbers. Call me when you get yours."

"Yes, I will. I gotta go. Thanks for calling."

"Robert...be careful!"

Chickenhead, not knowing what else to say, softly hung up the phone. He looked at his drink and, carrying it to the sink at the bar, poured what was left of it into the drain. He watched the amber fluid foam as it hit the stainless steel bowl and felt ashamed of himself for feeling the strength flowing back to him—strength fueled by anger. Jamaica had believed in him...had believed in him so strongly that he'd put himself in the middle of something that had nearly killed him. And here he was, crying in his drink and feeling sorry for himself. Sorry wasn't going to bring Mimi back...nothing could reverse her death. Sorry wasn't going to help Jamaica. The best he could hope for—the best he could do—was to catch Braxton. To bring him back here...

Leaving the bar, Chickenhead walked to his bedroom and grabbed his half-filled bag. Into the bag he threw whatever clothes were near it and quickly closed it. With a newfound resolve, he threw the bag over his shoulder as he exited the villa. His moves no longer stunted, Chickenhead practically ran back to the main building of the resort. He jabbed the button to the lobby elevator and fidgeted with the clasp on his bag as he watched the digital display count down the floors.

I'm gonna catch this son of a bitch, he thought as he watched the elevator's numbers descent. I'm gonna drag his ass back here and throw him to the cops if it's the last friggin' thing I do.

Chickenhead stepped through the doors of the elevator before they were fully opened and pushed the button to Bitters' floor three times before the unit began to ascend. He began rocking from foot to foot as he stared at the panel of flashing numbers. When the doors opened on Bitters' floor, a newly determined Chickenhead pushed through them at a dead run.

I'm gonna hand him over--give him to the cops all right, he thought just before he got to Bitters' suite, just after I beat him to this side of death.

He pounded on Bitters' door. It opened immediately.

"About time you got back. I got a lead on Braxton. His plane touched down about forty minutes ago in Dallas." Bitters handed Chickenhead a new cellular phone complete with belt clip.

"Keep this with you. If we get separated in Dallas, we'll need to stay in touch. My new number is on a sticker on the back of your phone. I'll explain the rest once we're on the way to the city."

Bitters closed the door to his suite, and they started toward the elevators. Chickenhead used his new phone to call Proctor, who answered on the second ring.

"Detective Proctor. How can I help you?"

Chickenhead quickly told Proctor about Cynthia and her plan to visit Jamaica. Proctor promised to see to it that she got in to see him. Before Proctor could ask any questions, Chickenhead broke their connection. He clipped the phone back to his belt while Bitters held the door open to the elevator. As the door closed behind Chickenhead, Bitters looked at him with a sly grin.

"Glad to see you're back in the land of the living."

"Not now, Bitters. Let's just go get this fuck."

Bitters laughed. He patted the phone on his belt. "You'll

appreciate the special qualities of this phone, my man. Totally digital with satellite uplink, one-hundred percent encrypted with a wavelength that's non-traceable by the cops."

Chickenhead looked at the descending numbers on the elevator panel.

"You've got three days talk time, a week-and-a-half standby, and an open-end police scanner. This baby does it all."

The door opened on the ground floor. The two men exited the lobby and Bitters waved over a cab.

"We've got the next flight out on United at 8:10 tonight. We'll be in Dallas in a couple of hours. There'll be some of my people at the gate waiting for us. I know it's tough, but you might try to get some sleep on the flight. Once we hit the ground..."

"I'll be ready."

The cab pulled away from the resort and moved toward the street. At the entrance to 24th Avenue, the cabby asked for their destination.

"Airport, United," they said in unison.

They were halfway to the airport before Chickenhead spoke. Bitters, his eyes closed and head back against the seat cushion, answered him without opening his eyes.

"How did you find out where Braxton was?"

"His plane's transponder. Cop I'm paying passed on the plane info they found in the house to me. Braxton filed a phony flight plan to Denver, took off in that direction, then circled around to Texas. Even set up one of his friends to make it look legit. Kind of a weak ploy, actually."

"What's that?"

"Transponder's coded. Air traffic radar picks it up like a phone number. Braxton either didn't know...which I doubt...or didn't care that they could. Boy's been runnin' scared."

"Why Dallas?"

"Don't know. But I do know he's been there four times in the last few years. Last time was only a week ago. Checked out his credit card transactions over the last three years. Probably feels familiar with the town. Maybe knows someone there. We'll find out soon enough."

"How'd you get his credit card files?"

"Not hard to do if you have his Social Security Number and know where to look on the Web."

Neither man spoke again until they left the cab and picked up their tickets at the United counter. Walking down the concourse, Bitters stopped Chickenhead and directed him toward a bank of phones. He pointed to the half-filled duffel bag Chickenhead was carrying.

"Robert, before we go through the metal detectors, you wouldn't happen to have anything in there that could get us in jail, like say...a bazooka?"

Chickenhead snatched his bag from the floor and headed for the short line at the detectors.

"Well, I didn't think so," Bitters mumbled to Chickenhead's back.

The plane was boarding by the time they got to the gate. Moving to their seats in first class, they both quickly settled in. As the plane pulled away from the gate, Chickenhead pushed the button for the flight attendant. She appeared smiling a moment later.

"How can I help you, sir?"

"I'd like to order a drink. A Bud Light."

"If you'll give us a few minutes to reach cruising altitude, I'll be happy to get that for you. I'll be back in a jiffy."

Bitters tapped him on the shoulder after she left. In his hand was his whiskey flask. "Care for a drink?"

Taking it, Chickenhead took two swallows before handing it back. "Thanks."

"No problem. Couple of FYIs. I cancelled all of Braxton's credit cards–labeled them stolen–just in case the police hadn't gotten around to it. The only funds he has are the nine grand he took out this morning, unless, of course, he has something hidden in Dallas. His other bank accounts are frozen. Even as we speak his plane is being impounded by the Dallas PD. The cops are onto him, so he knows he can't walk up to the Hilton and get a room. He's gonna go underground, try to think, try to heal up. Our best chance to get him is in the next two days while he's trying to figure his next step."

"I know."

"We're gonna hit the ground running when we get to Dallas. If you have trouble hangin', you'll get left behind."

"No shit! Don't worry about me."

"Just wanted to let you know." Reclining his seat back, Bitters closed his eyes.

Ten minutes later, the attendant reappeared with Chickenhead's beer and a chilled glass mug.

"Thank you, ma'am. You can keep the glass."

Sipping the beer, Chickenhead settled back in his chair for the two-hour flight. And wondered if he would have enough strength not to kill Braxton if he found him first...

*   *   *   *   *

"Have you been able to contact Mr. Bitters yet, Kelly?"

Peter Driver's secretary bit her lip to stop herself from screaming at her boss. This was the third time in the last half-hour he had paged her at her desk via the intercom wanting to know about Jeremiah Bitters.

"I'm sorry, sir. I'm unable to connect with his cell phone. I'll continue trying and let you know as soon as I do."

Driver broke the connection before his secretary had finished her second sentence and let out a loud string of profanity. Spinning his chair around, he looked out of the second-story picture window of the Mayor's office, which overlooked downtown Houston, and saw nothing but his thoughts. It had taken him almost two hours to calm down after Bitters had talked to him earlier that day. He recalled the conversation with total clarity.

Mr. Driver, the police have evidence that a doctor, one Braxton Howard, may be responsible for the murder of your daughter as well as the other killings in Little Beirut. They have his prints as evidence and can directly connect him to several murders in the last three days. He also was involved in the accidental shooting of Jamaica Rummains by a policeman this morning...

Driver was beyond furious. A doctor! A goddamn doctor killed and gutted Mimi?

There was a sharp knock on his office door. "What?" Driver yelled.

Opening the door to the mayor's office, his personal aide, Daniel Jacobs, entered the room.

"Good afternoon, Mayor. We need to be going soon. Your meeting with the fire chief and his staff is within the hour."

Driver looked at Jacobs as if he were from another planet. "Cancel it. Better yet, you go and tell him I understand his needs, concerns, whatever. I'll get back to him sometime next week. I'll call him."

With a look of concern, Daniel stopped in front of the massive cherrywood desk the mayor sat behind. He put down his slim aluminum briefcase and moved to sit in one of the two chairs in front of the island of wood.

"But, sir..."

"Don't sit down and don't 'but sir' me," Driver grumbled. "Go. Handle them. I'll call you later."

Driver swung his chair back toward the window. Dismissed, Jacobs picked up his case and walked to the office door. Before he reached it, he turned to face Driver from across the room. "Your Honor, if I can be frank, I'd like to talk to..."

Driver exploded out of his seat, knocking it backwards as he jumped to his feet. "Jesus, do you understand goddamn English? I said GO!"

The swiftness of Jacobs' departure was evidenced by the door still swinging open, well after Jacobs had run through it. Driver stabbed the button to connect him to his secretary.

"Kelly?"

"Yes, sir?"

"Please try Mr. Bitters again."

"Right away, sir."

Grabbing the overturned leather and chrome executive chair, Driver slammed it upright and shoved it under his desk. He stomped around the slab of wood as he took his jacket off of the suit tree in the far corner of his office. Pawing through the inside pocket, he found his cell phone and worn leather phone book. The intercom on his desk buzzed. He made it across the room in four running steps.

"Yes, Kelly. Is it Mr. Bitters?"

"I'm sorry, sir. It's the superintendent of schools. He's on line one. I still haven't been able to contact Mr. Bitters. I'll keep trying, sir."

"Tell Ralph I'll call him back in a half-hour. And keep trying with Mr. Bitters." He released the button on his desk console, then pressed it again a second later. "Kelly, hold all my calls for the next twenty minutes. If you get in touch with Mr. Bitters, put him through immediately."

"Yes, sir."

Driver looked through his leather phone book and flipped the pages until he came to the letter "M." Using his cell phone, he dialed the number to the Mooreman Detective Agency and waited for the connection to be made. The line rang four times before it was picked up.

"Mooreman Detective Agency, George Mooreman speaking. How can I help you?"

"George, this is Peter Driver. How have you been?"

"Mayor Driver! Nice to hear from you! Can you give me a moment? I need to put you on hold."

"Of course." Driver heard the soft hiss of the line for several seconds before Mooreman came back on.

"Mr. Mayor?"

"I'm here, George."

"Sorry 'bout that, sir. Staff meeting. Had to clear out my office. What can I do for you?"

"I want some of your people--and you--to help me with a personal situation I want finished--and finished quickly."

"Of course. How can I help?"

It took Driver ten minutes to give Mooreman an abbreviated version of the events of the last week. "I'm expecting updated information any time now. As soon as I get it, I'll pass it on to you."

"Can you get me hard copies of everything we discussed? I'll need them to inform my people."

"I'll have a courier to you within the hour with all that I have."

"Thank you. But I do need to ask you something, Mayor. You never mentioned who else was working for you on this case. Anyone I need to know about?"

"Jeremiah Bitters."

The silence on the other end of the line lasted all of fifteen seconds.

"Is there a problem with that, Mooreman?"

"No...no, not at all. Bitters is a good man. We'll stay out of his way."

"I'm not paying you to stay out of anyone's way, Mooreman. I'm handing you this case on a fucking silver platter. Bitters and his team have flushed this bastard out. I don't give a shit who catches Howard as long as he gets caught. And soon."

"I understand."

"I'll pay your expenses plus $50,000. I want you to bring him to me--NOT to the police. I'll add another $50,000 if you find him--alive--in the next two days. Do we have an understanding, George?"

"Yes, sir. I'll be waiting for your information."

Driver smiled as he disconnected the call.

*   *   *   *   *

George Mooreman sat in his office, a second-floor walk-up across the street from Jackson's Appliances on Westheimer Road in the low-rent district of Sharptown just southwest of downtown Houston. His hand still cradled the phone that he had hung up a minute earlier.

Feeling as if he had just won the lottery and been told he was going to the electric chair—simultaneously–he tried to process the information given to him by Peter Driver.

Fifty-thousand dollars to catch this guy? he thought. And another fifty to deliver him to Driver and look the other way? Goddamn.

The thought of turning the other cheek while Driver did whatever to Howard didn't faze Mooreman one bit. From what Driver told him, Howard deserved to burn in hell, and slowly. Also, as an ex-cop (he'd been busted quietly off the Houston PD after fourteen years for rolling pimps and penny-ante dope dealers), George's morals fluctuated depending on the size of his paycheck. For one-hundred-thousand dollars and the goodwill of the Mayor of Houston, he'd blow up the Dallas Cowboys.

But Jeremiah Bitters was a different matter all-to-fuckin'-gether. Bitters was the ex-CIA, ex-State Department, ex-go-to-small-Third-World-countries-with-revolving-door-names-and-bring-back-really-bad-motherfuckers kind of trouble that Mooreman wanted no part of. Not for a measly hundred grand. Maybe half a million or so. With a howitzer thrown in. But a hundred—hell no. He liked his balls right where they were, thank you. He didn't have the resources, the manpower, or the guts to go up against someone the likes of Bitters...still...a hundred-thousand was an awful lot to be leaving on the table. And Driver was sending him all the information Bitters and his team had collected. That in and of itself would put him at the head of the pack. He could fake a little work, pad his expenses...

Someone tried to open the door to Mooreman's outer office. It was locked. The neighborhood he worked out of wasn't the best in Houston. It took a moment for whomever to read the small sign on the wall that directed them to the intercom unit beside the door. Mooreman heard the tinny buzz shortly before the nasal voice of the person identifying himself.

"Uh, this is New Dawn Courier Services. Package for George Mooreman. It's from Peter Driver."

George's mouth fell wide open as he stared at the cheap Rolex knockoff he sported on his chubby wrist. It had taken Driver less than thirty minutes to get the package of information to him.

This man is serious as a heart attack, he thought.

He buzzed the messenger in with the button on the side of his desk. The door opened, and the messenger entered the room. Meeting him in the outer office, Mooreman signed for the thick parcel, gave the man a five-dollar tip, and let him out. While walking back to his fire sale desk, Mooreman began a mental list of who might be available for a few days' work on such short notice. He sat back at his desk and tore open the large package, spilling an assortment of folders and papers on the scarred wooden desktop.

It was a letter-sized envelope sitting on top of the pile of documents that got his attention. The envelope was embossed with the seal of the City of Houston and contained the address of the Mayor's office. Mooreman's name was written on it in the tight, small style he instantly recognized as Driver's handwriting. Opening the seal, Mooreman pulled out a handwritten note:

> **George,**
> **Here is the information as promised. Put your team together and start now. I expect to hear something back from you by midnight tonight. I have yet to be contacted by Mr. Bitters. As soon as I am, I will relay any and all information to you via your office phone number.**
>
>
> **Peter Driver**
> **P.S. An incentive is enclosed.**

Putting down the note, George picked up the envelope and looked inside. There was nothing in it. Puzzled, he pushed aside several folders before spotting, on the bottom of the mess of papers, another larger manila envelope. It was much thicker than the first one and was marked "Incentive."

How original, he thought.

The documents that were inside the envelope knocked the wind out of George and brought fear--hot and thick--to his throat. Suddenly finding it hard to breathe, Mooreman looked through several duplicates of evidence sheets--sheets that should have no longer existed. Evidence tampering was one of the scams he and his ex-partner of five years had schemed on together. Thoughts of old Joe Langley (a short black piece-of-shit sergeant in charge of evidence storage who was now doing fifteen years hard time in Bofield State Penitentiary outside Gasson, Texas, for busting a pimp's head open in a shakedown gone bad) made George's stomach turn into an acid pit.

He remembered that for a price, cocaine held in their lockup would change to cornstarch and heroin to sugar. Mooreman would go to the lockup during Langley's watch, sign out evidence "to be checked by the lab," and depending on the size of the haul, would exchange sugar for shit in three or four trips over a few days time. George would sign the sheet and give them to Langley just in case anyone stopped by in the brief time he was in and out. Mooreman always made sure he got the filled-out paperwork—all copies—back from Langley when the exchange was completed. Hell, they'd only pulled the scam five or six times. They both agreed, though it paid very well, that it was way too risky to do over the long run. Langley got popped on the aggravated assault charge a year to a year and a half later. Driver had been the judge who sent him up the river. Looking closely at the signatures on the copied forms, the lump in Mooreman's throat got much bigger. There was no mistaking that they were his.

OhShitOhShitOhShitOhShitOhShit! he thought repeatedly.

Mooreman looked at the last sheet of Xeroxed paper and saw the words "turn me over" written in red marker. With his hands shaking, George did as he was instructed. A large Post-it note was stuck to the back of the paper. It read:

George:
Now that I've gotten your attention, you know why I've chosen you for this job. An old acquaintance of yours--Joe Langley--brought these documents to my attention at his trial. He tried to cut a deal for leniency. He didn't get it. Currently he is serving a fifteen-year sentence with no hope of parole. I'd say--and I'll put it delicately--that he's not able to take his sentence sitting down, if you catch my drift.

Complete your assignment to my satisfaction, and these records--in their original form--will be discreetly delivered to you. The only copies are the ones you now possess. If your results do not satisfy me, be warned! There is no statute of limitations on evidence tampering crimes that involve an officer of the law in a felony case. I will see to it that justice is done.

Peter Driver

Mooreman was shaking like a leaf in a windstorm. He was convulsing so hard that the large Post-it note attached to the copy from hell loosened and then fell off the paper he continued to clutch. Behind it was a small, folded square of paper. He put the Xerox page down on the desktop, and it took him several seconds to steady his hand enough to remove the slip of paper taped to the top end of the copy. Mooreman opened it and discovered a check for fifty-thousand dollars written out to him. On the small line to the left of Driver's signature was the inscription "get to work." Quickly picking up the phone and dialing one of his employee's numbers, a deeply disturbed George Mooreman did just that...

Chapter 21

Within minutes of taxiing his plane into the private aircraft area of Love Field in Dallas, Braxton knew he needed to find somewhere to rest and change his bandages—and the sooner the better. The weakness he was feeling, along with being half-high from all the meds he had been chewing like candy, slightly distorted the world around him. Colors were a bit too bright—sounds a bit too crisp. Inside the main terminal, he carefully and slowly put one foot in front of the other as he shuffled along. He kept his medical bag on one arm and his overnight bag containing his clothes and money tightly grasped in the other as he searched for a men's restroom. He stopped in the middle of the concourse and looked up and down the row of shops and boutiques, scanning for a break in the early evening crowd so that he could detect a sign anywhere that would point him to a restroom facility. Buffeted on all sides by hurrying travelers scurrying to their flight connections or bopping in and out of shops on both sides of the terminal, Braxton weaved through the fast-moving river of humanity as he became a slow-moving part.

People bumped him as they passed, some grumbling at his timid pace. Seeing a sign across the hall for a men's restroom, Braxton angled toward the facility in a fast walk. Four steps from the entry he was jostled, then hit from behind on his bad side. The world whited out from the wave of pain that seemed to fill every cell of his abdomen. His knees buckled and he fell forward.

Miraculously, he seemed to stop falling in mid-air. It took a second for him to realize that a pair of small, strong hands were holding him up and guiding him to the nearby wall. His vision went from triple to double to near normal as he leaned against the glazed brick wall. A moment later his vision had cleared enough to focus on who had rescued him from his fall. A short, stocky and well-dressed Hispanic male about his own age supported him as he continued to lean against the wall. Standing directly in front of him was a strikingly beautiful black woman as tall as Braxton himself and lusciously full-figured. She wore a dark blue pinstriped business suit that covered her like a second skin. She set her large black handbag at her feet as she helped to steady him.

"Sir, are you all right? I'm...I turned my ankle and fell into you. This was all my fault," she continued as she touched Braxton's face with one hand and straightened his clothes with the other.

"Senor, you okay, yes?" asked the man who was close enough that Braxton could smell his cheap cologne. He handed Braxton the overnight bag that had fallen from his hand moments before. Both the man and woman were so close that he suddenly felt claustrophobic. He made an effort to lock his knees and stood up straight.

"Yes, yes, I'm fine...just a little woozy," he managed to say. Mindful of the stares he was attracting, Braxton pushed away from the wall. He steadied himself and looked at the men's restroom now just a few feet away. Both of his rescuers gave each other a quick glance.

"Thank you both...I, uh, have to go. Thanks again." Braxton's pace quickened as he entered the opening to the restroom directly in front of him. The Good Samaritan gentleman quickly turned, walked halfway down the concourse, and entered the men's restroom at the Fly-Time Bar. The woman entered the adjacent ladies restroom just moments later. She emerged after a short time with her large black shoulder bag in hand. She was wearing baggy blue jeans, a billowing Dallas Cowboys sweatshirt, and a baseball cap embroidered with "Don't Mess With Texas." Included with her new duds was a smile the size of a small planet. When her partner came out of the men's room, he was dressed in new blue jeans with a red and black flannel shirt and carried a black plastic garbage bag under his arm. It contained the clothes he had just changed out of. Before he could speak, she let out a loud squeal, grabbed him by his collar, and bent down to give him a loud kiss on the lips. He pushed her away while nervously looking up the short hallway in which they stood.

"Damn, woman! Are you crazy? What if someone saw you do that? Let's get the fuck outta here!" Quickly leaving the bar, the man looked both ways before double-timing it to the south exit that led to ground-level parking. Going two rows down, he opened the door of a primer-colored 1976 Grand Prix that had truly seen better days. He opened the passenger side door from the inside, and his girlfriend was sitting beside him a moment later. She looked at him with her smile still intact. He just shook his head and started the car, carefully backing out of the parking slot. As he began pulling forward, his lady leaned back in her seat and started hammering her feet on the floor as she laughed like a mad woman. Hector Cruz had had enough.

He stopped the car in the middle of the parking lot and looked at his girlfriend, Margo Harris. He tried to sound calm as he watched her stomp the floorboards on her side of the car.

"I give up, Margo. Please tell me why you're so goddamn happy! This ain't the first time we've done this, ya know."

Reaching under the clothes she had just changed out of in the bar's restroom and jammed into her shoulder bag, she pulled out the large manila envelope that Hector had slipped into her bag earlier during their "rescue" of Braxton. Still laughing but no longer stomping, she turned the envelope upside-down and dumped into Hector's lap Braxton's nine-thousand dollars along with his bulging wallet. Hector propelled himself out of his seat and promptly knocked himself senseless on the now-dented interior roof of the vehicle. He held his head in both hands and tried to squeeze the stars he was seeing back into his head as he looked at the piles of bundled twenties and fifties that lay in his lap and were strewn on the floor. Margo started shrieking again, then abruptly stopped. She leaned across the seat, kissed Hector's forehead as he rubbed the top of his head, cupped his chin in one hand, and angled his face to hers. In her other hand she held a bank-bundled stack of fifty-dollar bills.

"Honey, can we go to Red Lobster? I think this calls for a seafood celebration."

Hector nodded his aching head as Margo started to cover his face with kisses...

*   *   *   *   *

His money and wallet were gone. Braxton fingered the razor-made slit in the side of his overnight bag and felt a hate so strong that his physical pain and weakness were momentarily forgotten. Fingering the clear piece of tape that Hector had used to secure the tear, Braxton sat in the back stall of the men's restroom and wanted to kill them both with his bare hands. At least his medical bag was intact so he still had all of the Percodan, bandaging, and med tools—just no money.

He went through his pockets and found two twenty-dollar bills. Forty lousy dollars. That's all that stood between him and broke. The irony of his situation threatened to incapacitate him.

I kill bums. Now I am one, he thought.

Shutting his mind down to the panic that was trying to grab hold of it, Braxton, after flushing the toilet several times, methodically cleaned his wound with the water. He wiped down his tender wound and re-bandaged it, then slipped back into his shirt. He decided against any more Percodan or Demerol...at least for the time being. It dawned on him that if he hadn't been so high, he wouldn't have been robbed.

He pulled on his jacket, opened the door to the stall, and with quick determination moved out of the restroom and to the front of the terminal. Braxton exited the building and stopped at a coffee stand just outside the main doors. Buying a small cup for a dollar, he asked the elderly proprietor where the closest bus stop was while he sipped on his hot drink. The old man pointed with a mitten-covered hand, and Braxton followed his finger to a spot directly behind him.

"Over yonder is the closest one. Better hurry, tho'. I think the next one leaves 'round 7:45-8:00."

"How much is the fare?"
Buck fifty or thereabouts, I think."
Damn, Braxton thought, thirty-seven dollars left...

*   *   *   *   *

Braxton rode on the bus for almost an hour and a half trying to weigh his options. With his wallet and money gone, Plan "A"--him finding a nice out-of-the-way place to rest for a couple of days--was out the window. Thirty-seven dollars wasn't about to find him anything with great room service. For that price he'd be lucky if the bed had sheets. He couldn't go anywhere near any of his old haunts-- the police had to know who he was by now and were sure to be looking for him. He knew he needed to leave the bus--he'd already been on it for too long--but fear and indecisiveness kept him glued to his seat. He looked out the window on his side and saw that the bus had made the turn to retrace its route to the airport. Braxton reached for the side-panel buzzer strip and pressed down the thin plastic covering. He heard a faint hum and felt the bus slow immediately. Gathering his things, he made his way to the back door of the nearly empty vehicle and waited for the bus to stop. The door opened and let in a wall of cold air as he stepped off the platform onto the wet broken concrete of the sidewalk. He watched the bus leave until it was a bright dot of light in the distance.

Braxton shivered in the wet cold of the Texas night. He ignored the pain in his side and dug through his overnight bag until he came to the thick black sweatshirt he had packed. Taking off his jacket, he pulled the sweatshirt over his head. When he put his arm through the left sleeve, it exited out of a long slit that Hector's razor had left in the cloth. He looked down at the hole and welcomed the wave of anger that enveloped him. Braxton jerked his hand out of the hole and into the opening of the sleeve, putting his jacket back on as he looked around the area to get his bearings. He saw a brightly lit convenience store about a block up the street. Next to it was a shabby parking lot full of cars and several buildings dark save for large illuminated signs outside of them that he couldn't read from where he stood. Picking up his things, he started walking toward the light...

*   *   *   *   *

Thirty minutes later Braxton was sitting barefoot and bare-chested on a bed in Room 268 at the End of the Runway Hotel. This hotel was definitely bottom-of-the-barrel lodging at its worst at nineteen dollars a night with a bathroom down the hall. When he checked in, the albino desk clerk with a terrible case of adult-onset acne glanced up from his paperback novel as he took Braxton's money and gave him a dollar's change. He never asked to see any ID.

"Check out time's noon. You ain't out the room, you pay another nineteen--no discussion. Got it?" the thin man asked as he scratched one of the lumps on his face with one hand and threw a tarnished key attached to a plastic tab at Braxton with the other.

"If I hear any complaints, your ass is gone–no refunds," he continued. He licked the tip of the finger he was scratching with and used the moist digit to turn the page of his book.

"Bathroom's at the end of the hall on your floor. One towel in your room. Have a nice stay."

Braxton turned on the TV for company and watched green-tinted people with the set's volume turned down low. Before he had locked himself in for the night, he had visited the community bathroom hoping to at least get washed up before bed. The room smelled like an open sewer and looked slightly worse. Soaking his only towel in the tepid water from the single-spigot sink, he carried the sopping cloth back to his room and wiped the edges of his wound and aching chest. He dried off with one of his tee shirts and took inventory of his supplies. He had enough bandages and antibiotics for the next four or five days. His Demerol was down to fifteen tablets, and he had one-hundred-and-eight Percodan tablets left. He split the Percodan into two small piles, put twenty-five tablets of the drug in with the rest of his Demerol, and closed the plastic bottle. The rest of the Percodan he figured he could sell, though he had no idea what the drug was going for on the street. He chewed on a tablet of Percodan from the "For Sale" pile and took out his travel alarm clock. He was only mildly surprised to see that the face of his digital clock had also been damaged by the razor slash. Setting the alarm for 10:08–two minutes from the time his watch showed–he was too tired to be relieved when the clock, despite the deep groove cut in its face, still worked. He reset the alarm to 7:00 a.m. and set the clock next to his bed on the nightstand. Walking to the door and pulling the only chair in the room behind him, Braxton wedged the straight-back chair under the doorknob. He turned off the overhead light using the wall switch by the door and returned to his bed, turning off the TV before climbing in. He pulled on a tee shirt he'd left on the bed and got under the thin, scratchy covers. The doctor was asleep in minutes.

*   *   *   *   *

It was several hours later when Braxton was jerked awake by the pain and itching of his wound. Groggy from exhaustion and the drugs still circulating in his system, he gingerly placed his hand on his wound to feel if the bandages had come off under the tee shirt he still wore. He awakened instantly when he felt tiny lumps under his shirt–tiny lumps that were moving. He tore the covers off and jumped out of bed, stumbling over his own feet as he tried to reach the wall switch. He flipped the switch several times. Nothing happened.

Running to the TV, he felt for the power switch and turned it on. His side was on fire, and he turned his body to the tinted light of the set. As the tube got brighter, Braxton stared down, horrified, at a moving mass of bedbugs that were feeding on the blood seeping from his wound...

*   *   *   *   *

"Damn! Platinum American Express, Gold MasterCard, and VISA--y'all had a good day ta-day."

Margo and Hector smiled through the haze of good food and drink that they'd just consumed at a Red Lobster twenty minutes from

Love Field. Their fence, Willie "Two Tone" Anderson, held the handful of credit cards below the edge of the table as he went through Braxton's wallet. He pulled out Braxton's driver's license and his doctor's ID card as he let out a low whistle.

"Shit, you guys're movin' up in the world! How old are these?"

"'Bout hour and a half, two at the most," Hector mumbled through a mouthful of fried shrimp.

"'Kay. I need ta book before the good doctor reports all of these gone." Anderson pressed three bills into Hector's hand under the table, then got up from his seat. "If I get a chunk out of this, I'll sweeten your take later. In a minute, y'all."

"'Bye, Two Tone," Margo said in a slightly inebriated singsong voice. She picked up her half-empty glass of beer and raised it for a toast. Hector joined her with his wine glass and clicked it to hers.

"Baby," she said, "a thanks to the medical profession. And thank God for rich doctors, crowded airports, and profitable HMOs."

Hector coughed white Zinfandel out of his nose, laughing, as Margo motioned to their server to order another round of crab legs...

*   *   *   *   *

"Robert, this is Regina Parkell and Dane Childress. Everyone, this is Robert Gibbs."

Chickenhead shook both of their hands, lingering on the tall black woman. She had to be six four with model good looks and eyes the color of copper. Her close-cropped hair was the same hue as her eyes. The thick blue sweater showed every curve of Regina's upper body, including the expansive girth of her breast. Chickenhead forced himself to look away from the melon-sized orbs directly in front of him.

Regina spoke first. "Glad to finally meet you, Robert. We've heard a lot about you."

The deepness of her voice surprised Chickenhead and as he

looked up at Regina, he wondered how the hell a woman could have a voice like...and that's when he saw an Adam's apple bigger than his.

Regina, at one time, had definitely been a man. Of that Chickenhead was certain. He smothered the urge to wipe the hand he had shaken hers with on his pants. He stopped staring at Regina's amused face at the moment Bitters tapped him on his arm. He turned to face Bitters.

"You'll get used to it," was all he said.

"Guys, we need to get," Dane interjected. "Word out of Love Field is a guy matching your boy's descript took a bus into town 'round eight o'clock tonight. I dropped Pinky by there on our way over here. She's gonna try to talk to the bus drivers 'round there-see what she can dig up-see what bus he took."

Given Regina's little "surprise," Chickenhead was already apprehensive about meeting Pinky.

"I've got us rooms at the Westin Hotel," Regina continued. "Our ride's outside." She handed Chickenhead a thin folder as the group began to walk through the terminal in the direction of the elevator.

"Here's some information about your boy in case you want to read it."

Chickenhead opened the thin cardboard and looked at the face of Braxton Howard as the face stared back at him from the glossy, four-color sheet. He closed the folder quickly and stuck the papers under his arm. The small group rode the elevator to the parking garage in silence.

"Chill out for a minute here. I'll get the car," Dane instructed. A moment after he left, Bitters' phone rang.

"Jeremiah here."

"Where in the hell have you been?" It was Driver.

"I've been doing the job you're paying me to do, sir."

"Where the hell are you? What have you learned?"

"Braxton is here in Dallas. Gibbs and I have just gotten here, and my team is on this, sir. I'll call you later with more information when I have it, sir."

"Wait! Where in Dallas? Has anyone seen him?"

"His plane landed at Love Field about two hours ago. I already have people checking for leads. I'll call you when I have more, sir." Bitters disconnected the call.

"Shit! I knew I shouldn't have programmed my old number into this phone," Bitters grumbled. Pushing several buttons on the display panel, Bitters erased the call-forwarding feature from his old phone number.

Dane pulled up in a late-model black Chevy minivan just moments later. Bitters opened the sliding side door and motioned for Chickenhead to get into the middle bench seat.

Chickenhead threw his duffel bag over the back of the seat and slid over as Bitters climbed in beside him. Regina was settling into the front seat and was already banging away on the keys of a laptop computer that had been sitting on the floor.

"Give me a minute, boss," she said as she stuck her arm out of the passenger side window and stuck a portable, magnetic antenna to the minivan's roof. "I'll have a printout of all the hotels and motels in the Love Field area."

"Make sure you include all of the overnight spots on every bus route," Bitters mentioned quietly.

"Already on it."

Someone's phone rang. In the vehicle's close quarters, everyone reached for their unit.

"It's mine," Dane announced.

Pushing a button to receive the call, Dane talked for a couple of minutes before clicking off the unit. "Boss, that was Pinky. She still has a couple of drivers to talk to. She's gonna go to the bus yard after she's finished at the airport and see if she's missed anyone."

Chickenhead looked at all the busy-ness going on around him with a sense of helplessness. He was beginning to feel like a fifth wheel.

"Um...has anyone thought about Dallas International Airport? The Greyhound bus stations?" Chickenhead offered.

Regina answered his question while pounding on her keyboard. "Cops are crawling all over those places, at least that's what I noticed when we got here this afternoon. Dane checked out the bus and train station, too. Same thing. Anything that moves out of this burg--plane, train, or automobile--is gonna be looked at real close. Driver carries a ton of weight in this state. The cop that fucks this up is liable to have a real short career in law enforcement 'round these parts."

Chickenhead felt even dumber after Regina answered his question.

"Got it!" Regina said. Opening the glove compartment, she pulled out a new package of floppy disks. She balanced the computer on her thighs and tore open the package, extracting a disk and shoving it into the laptop.

"I've got all the hotels and motels--at least the legal ones--on a grid. I'm downloading the information now. When we get to the hotel, I'll print up copies in the business center."

Ten minutes later the van pulled off of the LBJ Freeway into the expansive elegance of the Westin Galleria Hotel. Looking up at the towers that were brightly lit with multicolored Christmas decorations, Chickenhead shook his head as they pulled up the service road to the hotel.

Does this guy ever just stay at a Motel 6?

Regina jumped out of the van, laptop in hand, before it came to a full stop. She yelled over her shoulder to the group. "I'll be upstairs in a few minutes." She disappeared into the hotel at a brisk walk.

A smiling valet appeared beside the driver side door as everyone emptied out of the van. Dane handed the keys to the valet and then turned to Bitters and Chickenhead. He handed them both envelopes with the hotel's name embossed on the front. Chickenhead opened his and saw it was a magnetic key the size of a credit card.

"Boss, I'm gonna hang out here for a minute, get something to eat. Either of you want anything?"

"Yeah," Bitters answered. "Couple of steak and cheese sandwiches would be great. Get extra mustard and relish. You want anything, Robert?"

"What you're having sounds good. Thanks."

"No prob. I'll be upstairs in a bit." Dane turned to the valet who had just parked their van and gave him a sheepish grin as he handed the young man a ten-spot to turn around and go get the vehicle again.

Chickenhead and Bitters entered the hotel and walked across the lobby toward the bank of elevators. Bitters pointed to the card Chickenhead was holding in his hand.

"Your room number is taped on a slip of paper to the back of your card."

The elevator they were standing in front of dinged as the doors slid open. A slew of people poured out. Once they entered their elevator, Bitters continued his conversation after the doors closed. They were the only ones on the elegant elevator. He pushed the button to the sixteenth floor.

"Now might be a good time to take a shit, shower, and shave if you want. After we grub and get our maps, we're out of here, understand?"

"Totally."

The elevator opened to their floor, and they both exited. Chickenhead followed Bitters down the lushly carpeted hall that led to his room. Stopping in front of Bitters' door, he swiped his card through the door unit. It opened with a soft click as Bitters turned to face him. He reached inside his inner breast pocket and pulled out a thin envelope, handing it to Chickenhead.

"There's a couple grand in there in case you need to spread some around to loosen a few tongues tonight. See you in a few."

Chickenhead looked at the back of his key for his room number as Bitters' door closed. Walking down the hall until he found the right number, he unlocked the door and entered the elegant room. It was nearly as big as the villa he had shared with his partner at the Biltmore.

Jamaica would love this shit, he thought sadly.

Thinking of Jamaica reminded him that he needed to call Cynthia. He got her number out of his wallet and dialed her home number from the hotel phone. It rang twice before it was picked up.

*   *   *   *   *

"Winaford residence. It's your dime on my time." The chorus of high-pitched giggles that followed let him know that he had to be talking to one of Cynthia's kids.

"Hello, this is Robert Gibbs. Is your mother there?"

"Oh, hi, Mr. Gibbs. I'm sorry. I thought you were a friend of mine. Momma's still at the hospital. She told me to tell you to call her there if you called here before she got home from there."

Given that the young girl had run the words into one long fast sentence, Chickenhead caught only the last part of the jumble of words. Before he could ask her to repeat the message, she breathlessly continued.

"Here's the number momma gave me to give to you. Are you still there?"

"Yes."

"'Kay." She read off a phone number to Chickenhead. He was thankful that she took a breath this time.

"Thank you very much, young lady. Do you have a pencil and paper nearby? I've got a number for your mom."

"Kay."

Not knowing if that meant she had the paper or not, he waited a second and then repeated his question.

"'Kay. I'm ready."

Chickenhead read his cell phone number off of the back of his unit and gave her his room number as well as the hotel number off of the back of his key. He had the girl repeat both phone numbers, thanked her, and then hung up the phone.

She sounds like a handful, he thought as he dialed the hospital's number. The line rang once, then was picked up.

"Hello?" It was Cynthia.

"Hi, Cynthia. It's Robert. How's Jamaica?"

"Hi, Robert. Timothy is sleeping. The doctor said he's going to be fine. He's going to need some plastic surgery. He's..." He heard her crying softly over the phone.

"Cynthia! What's wrong?"

"I'm sorry...you don't need this...it's just that he's all bandaged up. They said it was best to keep him unconscious for another day or two. He just looks so helpless. I'm sorry, Robert."

The emotion and concern in her voice for his friend brought a huge lump to Chickenhead's throat.

"Hey, hey, Jamaica's tough, and he'll be fine, Cynthia. Really. Besides, he likes scars...it'll give him something to talk about. By the time he's out of the hospital, he'll be braggin' that he was shot by a tank."

The small laugh from her end of the line made him feel much better. Robert's reassuring words were exactly what she needed.

"Thank you."

"Hey, no problem. Just look after my bro 'til I get back, okay? I left my number with your daughter. I gotta go."

"Wait! Robert, you left a message with my daughter?"

"Yeah, that was all right, right?"

"Robert, you don't have any teenagers. Do you?"

"No."

"Well, they can't remember my name unless food or allowance is involved. That or tickets to an *NSYNC concert. You'd better give me those numbers again."

Chickenhead dutifully repeated the information, then said goodbye and hung up the phone. As he stripped for a quick shower, he relaxed a bit knowing that Jamaica was in good hands with Cynthia watching over him...his buddy was probably in for a hell of a ride, tho' when her daughter got a hold of him...

*   *   *   *   *

"Everyone got their maps and phones?" Everyone on Bitters' team and Chickenhead nodded "yes" to his question. "Good. I faxed Pinky a map. She's got the area north of Love Field bordered by Royal Lane to the North and overlapping into y'all's section," he said as he pointed to Dane and Regina.

"People, this is by the numbers. This guy is hurt and may be armed. If you find him, keep him in sight. Stay out of view and call in. No heroes here, folks."

When Bitters completed the last sentence, he made sure he had eye contact with Chickenhead in particular. He chewed his bottom lip when Chickenhead quickly broke his stare and looked at the map he was holding in his hand.

"We also have some unsolicited help in the form of every cop on duty and off in the Dallas-Fort Worth area who wants to get in the good favor of Mayor Driver. I'm also sure Driver has another agency or agencies out there looking for Howard. Keep your eyes open, people! It's gonna be crowded out there with some itchy-fingered cowboys. Call in on time. Now GO!"

Everyone grabbed their rental car keys (Bitters had had the vehicles delivered downstairs during the meal break) and headed for the door. Bitters waved Regina over to him before she left the room. After Chickenhead exited, Bitters spoke quietly to her.

"Keep your equipment ready and running. If we get surprised, I'm gonna need your talented fingers to work their magic. Stay awake and sharp."

"I'm all over it like a chicken down the road," was her instant reply.

Bitters had no idea what her saying meant. And, after working with this Amazon's crazy California-bred attitude for the last seven years, he knew she was hoping he'd ask.

"Okay, on your way. Break a nail and cover Robert's ass."

"Oh, that I most certainly will." Regina winked and blew Bitters a kiss on the way to the door. Bitters couldn't help but smile. He knew exactly what that statement meant...

*   *   *   *   *

Howard's in Dallas. Find him.

Those words echoed through George Mooreman's mind as the van he was driving slowed slightly. He pulled the van off of Loop 12 and onto Lemmon Avenue–the road leading to Love Field Airport. Making the five-hour drive from Houston in just over three hours, Mooreman chewed what was left of his fingernails on his left hand as he looked into his rearview mirror. He shuddered as he recalled his furious attempt to hire halfway competent investigators to work the case. One of Mooreman' s rapidly filled slots was taken by a mousy, sandy-haired, part-time drunk named Tanner Brice, who now sat in the back seat. Mooreman had been watching him throughout the trip to Dallas as Tanner checked, cocked, loaded, and drooled on the small armory of weapons loaded in boxes on the rented minivan's rear floorboard. Mooreman would liked to have flown to Dallas and saved two hours on the road trip, but the last he'd checked, such things as concussion grenades, sawed-off shotguns, and semi-automatic firearms weren't things the airlines approved as carry-on baggage. And he thought it was a waste of money to charter a plane for a one-hour flight.

Mooreman scowled as he saw Tanner's nervous hands toying with a sawed-off shotgun that lay on the back seat. He lost it when he saw the little man reach for a box of shells.

"Goddammit, Tanner! For the last time, leave that shit alone!" Mooreman practically screamed as he picked up a folded map of Dallas from the dashboard that was littered with fast-food wrappers. He threw the map over his shoulder toward the back of the van. It bounced off of Tanner's head and landed in the pile of shotgun shells the jerk had been reaching for.

"Open that fucker up and tell me where the hell the nearest hotel is. The ones close to this excuse for an airport are marked in red."

Brice turned on another overhead light in the van and fumbled with the map. "Hey, boss," he said brightly, "how about, ya know, when this job's over, you let me check out a coupla these things, maybe buy some of this shit from you at, like, a discount?" Mooreman almost swerved the van into the neighboring lane of traffic as he turned and yelled at Tanner.

"Jesus Christ! Just find a fuckin' hotel!"

"Jeez. Damn. I was just askin'," Tanner mumbled as he unfolded the map—upside-down. He wondered if Mooreman had inventoried the boxes of weapons piled in the back seat and on the rear floor of the van. He was thinking that if he had, then he was surely going to miss the Smith and Wesson .357 that Tanner had stuffed down the back of his pants and pulled the loose sweatshirt he wore over it. Righting the map after a short struggle, he put his finger on the first red spot he saw.

"There's a Motel 6 off of Hopkin Avenue and Roper. Ain't too far from here." Half folding the map together, Tanner tossed it to the van's floor.

"Is that the closest one to the airport?" Mooreman asked as he changed lanes.

"Yeah, looks like it," Tanner lied.

Mooreman turned to the other man in the van. He was sitting beside Mooreman in the front passenger seat and was reading a paperback novel with a small lamp he'd attached to the top of the book.

"Call your guys and tell them to meet us there in an hour," Mooreman commanded as he looked at his watch. It read 1:42 a.m. "Tell them to be there at 2:30 and don't be late."

The blond fat man turned off the small lamp on his book and placed both on the dashboard.

"No problem." Digging into the front pocket of his loose-fitting khaki pants, he pulled out a small cell phone and started to dial a number as Mooreman looked at the road in front of them. Driver had pasted on all of the information Bitters had given him moments after he received it. Mooreman knew that Howard was hurt and that he had been spotted leaving the airport on a bus. He hoped Driver would get a call from Bitters telling him which one.

"Yo, Moony and McPorth are on their way."

"Huh?" Lost in his thoughts, Mooreman didn't know what the big man next to him was talking about. The man picked up his pulp novel from the dashboard and switched on the tiny lamp again before he answered Mooreman's question.

"Those guys I told you about. The bouncers. They're gonna meet us at the hotel." He turned several pages in his book and began to read again.

"Oh, yeah, right. That's good," Mooreman stuttered as he went back to staring at the road ahead of him and tried to sort through his jumbled thoughts.

I've gotta find this son of a bitch, he thought miserably. I ain't put together to do time. Those fuckin' animals inside will eat my ass for lunch...

Seeing a street sign for Hopkin Avenue, Mooreman switched on his turn signal and moved closer to that side of the road. He came to the intersection and turned up the road heading toward the hotel...

Chapter 22

"Pinky's got a lead," Bitters said over the phone. "Guy matching Howard's description was on the Route 72 bus. The driver remembers him getting off around an industrial park near Wycliff and Bower Avenues. Pretty shitty part of town the way he described it. Should be right up your alley, Robert."

Chickenhead, sitting at a stop sign, turned on the car's overhead light to check his location on a map. It took him a minute to match the two positions.

"Looks like I'm about three or four miles from there now. Gimme a few to head over that way."

"I've already called Regina and Dane. When you get to that corner, find somewhere to park and wait for us." Bitters hung up the phone.

Shutting off the dome light in the rental car, Chickenhead turned east on Record Crossing Road and sped toward Lemmon Avenue, barely staying below the posted speed limit. He had no intentions of waiting for anyone once he got to that side of town.

Motherfucker picked the wrong side of the track to hide out in, Chickenhead thought.

Moving past Dallas Market Center, a huge shopping mall off of Interstate Highway 35, Chickenhead pulled into the breakdown lane, slowed to a stop, and put his car into park. He took the cell phone Bitters had given him from the passenger seat and again turned on the overhead light. Searching the front panel of the unit, he found the button he was looking for. He switched the phone off, strapped the unit to his belt, put the car into gear, and pulled back into the light stream of traffic. He turned onto a connecting artery of the Dallas North Toll way and figured he was about two miles from Lemmon Avenue. The large grin on Chickenhead's face never warmed the chilling blue of his eyes.

Bitters gonna be waitin' a long time if he's expectin' me on that corner, he thought.

*   *   *   *   *

Reluctantly, Bitters made a quick call to Driver. He had been at the corner of Wycliff and Bower for the last few minutes and wondered why he was the only one there. The mayor answered his phone before it could complete the first ring.

"Driver here. Is that you, Mr. Bitters?"

"Yes, sir. I believe we've narrowed the search on Howard. One of my team has a lead that's only a couple of hours old. I'll call you back once we get a chance to check it out."

"Good! Where are you?"

"Still in Dallas."

"I thought as much, Mr. Bitters. Where in Dallas?"

Bitters gave him the location from the street signs on the corner where he was parked, then immediately disconnected the call. Five minutes after he'd hung up he was joined by the first of his crew. Pinky pulled her rental car into the parking lot beside him and waited for further instructions.

*   *   *   *   *

"GoGoGo! Get the fuck up! MOVE!" Mooreman yelled at the four men as they all sat at the counter of the Night-Drop 24-hour donut shop down the street from their hotel. Everyone grabbed what was left of his donuts and coffee and exited the warmth of the bakery. Looking at the crumbled map in his hand as he clipped the cell phone to his belt, Mooreman followed his men outside. He stopped them when they got near their cars.

"We caught a break. Bitters' team is only–," Mooreman looked at his map again under the parking lot's bright sodium lights and quickly located the stop he had marked inside, "–a couple of miles from here." He turned to the two newest additions to his crew. "Moony, McPorth–you lead. They're on the corner of Wycliff and Bower Avenues. Tanner, Greene–you're with me."

The fat man and Tanner jumped in the van as Mooreman walked the newest two hulking head busters to their screaming yellow late-model Camaro. "Y'all packin?" he asked.

Simultaneously both men patted the left side of their dark winter coats. Mooreman nodded in approval.

"Like I said earlier, a thousand each for the night's work, and another grand when we catch this fucker. He has to be alive. Anyone else around him I don't give a shit about." Both men nodded as they reached the Camaro.

"Remember, just drive by that corner–nothing else for now. I need to see who's with Bitters. Keep the radios on that I gave you."

Nodding again from opposite sides of the car, both men squeezed into the front seat. Moony started the engine just as Mooreman got into the driver's seat in the minivan. Mooreman turned to talk to Tanner and Greene and froze in mid-motion. He stared at Tanner, who was now sitting in the bench seat behind him. The frown on Mooreman's face became an angry scowl. A moment later, he lost any semblance of control and started screaming at Tanner.

"Goddammit, you moron! We're not going to fuckin' war! Take all that shit off! Your dumb ass is gonna get us all killed!"

Moping and grumbling, Tanner started to take off one of two shoulder holsters–both complete with .357 Magnum handguns, a web belt with six concussion grenades attached to it, another pistol stuck in the front of his pants, and a sawed-off shotgun strapped to his thigh in a black nylon holster. Out of his baggy khaki pants side pocket, Tanner pulled a police-issue Taser he had no business having and began whining as he spoke to Mooreman.

"Can I like, ya know, hold on ta the Taser? We might, like need it, ya know?"

Grinding his teeth, Mooreman would have shot him to death and back right there and then if he hadn't needed him tonight.

The Camaro flashed its headlights twice and slowly pulled out of the strip mall parking lot and onto the street. Mooreman noticed the other car moving and turned the key in the van's ignition to follow the yellow vehicle. What had really scared the hell out of him was seeing the armament on Tanner and realizing that all of that firepower was exactly what Mooreman wished he'd have on him when he met Bitters. With enough weaponry in the van to supply a medium-sized gang war, Mooreman still felt naked going up against Bitters. As best as he could, Mooreman pushed the fear he felt to the back recesses of his mind. He tried to concentrate on the Camaro as it picked up speed in front of him. Mooreman listened to Greene and Tanner make small talk from the bench seat as a frightened Mooreman wished he were anywhere but here...

*   *   *   *   *

Bitters looked at his watch. It read 3:41 a.m. He thought of how much pleasure it would give him to strangle Chickenhead right about now. He and his crew had been at the corner of Wycliff and Bower Avenues waiting for Robert for almost thirty minutes. Bitters had called him twice with no success. By now it was a foregone conclusion that Chickenhead wasn't coming. Bitters turned to Dane, who was smoking a cigarette while he leaned on his rental car.

"Dane, take two miles up the road and double back this way. If it looks like a hotel, stick your nose into it. Regina and I will cover this end of the bus route. Pinky, you go with him. Call in every half-hour."

Both got into Dane's car and were gone in seconds.

"'Gina, you got your laptop?"

"As close to me as a third tit."

"Fire it up."

Regina pulled the computer out of her leather backpack and

attached the portable antenna to the roof of her car. The computer beeped as it began booting up. Moments later, she was working her way into cyberspace. She looked up at Bitters.

"I'm online."

"Please find Shithead."

"Damn, boss! You're touchy tonight."

Fingers moving in a blur across the keyboard, Regina typed in various commands and code words to access her satellite uplink. One of the special features Bitters had purposely neglected to mention to Chickenhead was the GPS--Global Positioning System--chip imbedded in the motherboard of the cell phone he had given him. All members of Bitters' team were connected to the satellite system via their cell phones, and the system was accurate to within nine square feet anywhere in the world. Less than ninety seconds after typing Chickenhead's phone code into her system, Regina spoke to Bitters.

"Got Mister Man. He's not far from here."

"Find him and follow him. Call me every fifteen minutes. I'm heading west."

Bitters turned and walked to his car.

"I'm on him like mustard on a melon," Regina said as she headed for her vehicle.

*   *   *   *   *

From almost a block away, Mooreman watched Bitters' team through night-vision goggles he had picked up at Costco earlier that day. When Dane and Pinky drove off, he grabbed his walkie-talkie and spoke rapidly into it. Mooreman's voice was picked up by the two musclemen parked across the street. "Moony, ya'll follow the first team. Ya see 'em?"

"Yeah, we got 'em."

Mooreman watched for another ten minutes before Bitters walked to his car and Regina turned to hers. Quietly he cursed long and hard for not thinking to get a rent-a-car for the imbecile brothers sitting in the van smoking cigarettes. He watched both cars' headlights come on and then ran the short distance to his van and started it. As he strapped on his seatbelt, he decided to follow Bitters himself. Mooreman had met Regina on two occasions--neither of them happy ones--in the last three years. As frightened as he was of Bitters, Mooreman was downright terrified of Regina. She reminded him way too much of the hardcore transvestite whores whom he had avoided at all costs when he was a cop. Way too freaky for him. Giving Bitters a one-block head start, Mooreman looked both ways before slowly pulling into the light early-morning traffic...

$$*\quad *\quad *\quad *\quad *$$

In the thirty minutes Bitters and his crew had stood in the winter cold waiting for their disappearing team member to show up, Chickenhead had hit two flop houses and one rundown hotel--none of them appearing on the map Regina had give him. All of them were across from a huge industrial park a few miles south of Love Field. Chickenhead drove into the parking lot of Elroy's Pick-It-Up 24-hour convenience store and shut off the rental car. He exited the vehicle and walked into the store.

"Pack of Old Gold Menthols and some matches."

The old man behind the thick pane of Plexiglas that shielded the counter took Chickenhead's five-dollar bill through the slot at the bottom of the plastic. Getting the smokes, he slid them along with change back to Chickenhead. Chickenhead lifted the cigarettes from the tray, left the change untouched, and added another ten-dollar note to the pile, pushing it back through the opening. The clerk looked at the money with a puzzled expression on his face, then took a wary step away from the counter.

"Can't sell you no booze, son. Way past cut-off time."

"Don't want none, Pops. Just a little info, that's all."

"In that case, I don't know nuthin' 'bout nuthin'."

"Relax, bro, all my questions are easy, and I ain't no cop."

Chickenhead took two twenties off of the thick wad of money he was holding and placed them on the counter just shy of the opening. Returning the roll of money to his back pocket, he kept his hand on the twenties as the man took a step closer to the counter.

"Not that I'm all that interested, but what you askin'?" the man asked as he grabbed the change and the ten Chickenhead had left in the slot, all the while eyeing the forty dollars that lay just out of his reach.

"Make it quick and go."

Chickenhead pulled out of his denim jacket pocket the folded sheet with Braxton's picture on it. It was the paper that Regina had given him earlier. He held it up to the plastic.

"Seen this guy? Someone that might look like 'im?"

The man glanced at the photo, then back to the twenties. "Can't say I have. That all?"

"Naw...any hotels around here? Any dumps that I could spend the night at that don't exactly cater to the tourist trade?"

The man stepped closer to the plastic wall and nodded at the money. Chickenhead pushed the notes through the open slot toward the man. The man's thin twisted fingers quickly surrounded the notes. The bills disappeared into the front pocket of the patched, faded green jeans. The clerk pointed past Chickenhead's right shoulder toward the store's front door.

"Got a flop house up the way 'bout two blocks up on Holland and Lucas Avenues. Called Mackie's Place. Ain't got no sign or nuthin', just a green light in the front window on the ground floor. Better bring your piece if you got one--if you're going there and all." Chickenhead knew the place the man had just described; he had just left it ten minutes before.

"You can try next door," the man said as he jerked his head in that direction. "Ain't as bad as Mackie's...still a shithole, tho'."

Chickenhead thanked the man as he folded Braxton's picture and put it back into the breast pocket of his jean jacket. He turned toward the door and halted in mid-stride when the clerk called out to him.

"Hey, man..."

Chickenhead turned back to face the man behind the plastic wall. "What you need, Pops?"

"Why you lookin' for that guy? What you want him for?"

The evil contained in the look on Chickenhead's face made the man step back from the counter. It was several seconds before Chickenhead spoke. "I got somethin' for him...a gift from a couple of friends of mine."

Turning, Chickenhead walked out of the small store. He looked across the broken asphalt of the parking lot to his car. Approaching the vehicle, Chickenhead first made sure it was locked. Satisfied, he crossed the short distance toward the flickering vacancy sign that hung in the front-gated window of the End of the Runway Hotel. He pushed past the sagging door and walked to the front counter. The albino clerk put down the huge burrito he was eating and wiped his mouth with a napkin he had picked up from the floor. The crumpled, soggy napkin left a green streak of guacamole that stretched from one ear to the other across the clerk's volcano-cratered face.

"You need a room?"

"No...need some of your time...a bit of information."

The clerk picked up his burrito. "Ain't in the info business. Bye now," he mumbled as he took a huge bite of the overstuffed burrito and began chewing loudly. For a brief moment, Chickenhead looked at the man as he ate with his mouth open. Containing his anger, he stepped closer to the counter. It was when Chickenhead casually took his hand out of his pant pocket that the clerk stopped his open-mouth chewing frenzy and looked at the roll of bills in Chickenhead's hand. He almost forgot to swallow as he watched Chickenhead peel off a fifty-dollar note.

Putting down his lunch, the clerk smiled at Chickenhead, proudly displaying a set of large, stained-with-food yellowed teeth. Chickenhead tossed the bill the short distance to the surface of the dirty countertop. The clerk leaned forward as the money came to a stop next to his meal.

"How can I help you, sir? What kind of information are you looking for?"

Though no one was in the small, cold lobby, the clerk scanned the area with a nervous sweep of his eyes before he leaned across the counter toward Chickenhead. When he finally spoke to Chickenhead, his voice was barely above a whisper.

"You lookin' for some pussy? Some dope? I know a coupla people, can have 'em here in 'bout ten-fifteen minutes."

"Naw, thanks anyway. I'm lookin' for...a friend."

Taking the folded glossy paper out of his pocket, Chickenhead handed the picture to the suddenly attentive clerk. The man grabbed the photo with one hand and the money on the counter with the other. The width of his smile increased greatly as he looked at the picture and shoved the money into his back pocket.

"Shit! I know this guy. He's here. Came in a coupla hours ago. Looked like shit warmed over..."

Chickenhead closed the one-foot space between him and the counter so quickly that the clerk flinched backward. The cold deadness of Chickenhead's voice, along with the blank look in his eyes, made the now-paler clerk take another step back. Chickenhead pointed to the picture that was still in the man's hand.

"This man is here? Now?"

"Yes...sir."

Chickenhead peeled off six fifties from the roll of bills in his hand and let them drop to the countertop. The clerk, his face so pale that the lumps of acne stood out like red mountains, kept his ass plastered to the wall behind him.

"These are yours. Now where is he?"

Looking at the money on the desktop and then back at Chickenhead, the clerk didn't move an inch. Without saying a word, Chickenhead peeled off four more fifties, dropping them one at a time to the scarred surface. The clerk was suddenly shaken by a thought that he hoped to hell wouldn't be true: If I don't tell this skinny mutherfucker what he wants to know, he's sure as shootin' gonna come over this desk and beat the shit out of me...

Chickenhead peeled off another fifty and dropped it to the pile. Slowly the clerk detached himself from the wall and crept to the counter against which Chickenhead stood flush. He kept one eye on Chickenhead and opened the ledger that Braxton had signed earlier. Gingerly he placed a finger on the line Braxton had scribbled on hours before.

"Room 268...sir, second floor," he whispered as he pointed a shaking finger to the stairwell that led to the upper-level rooms. Chickenhead stared at the man for a moment as his thin, quivering arm fell slowly to his side.

"Are you sure that's him?" Chickenhead asked impatiently.

"Oh, hell, fuck yeah."

Chickenhead backed away from the counter a step, then turned toward the stairs. Before he made it across the small lobby, he turned back to the counter, retracing his steps there.

I'm gonna fuckin' die, the clerk thought.

Standing at the counter again, Chickenhead reached into his pocket and pulled out the roll of bills. The clerk's eyes widened as Chickenhead tossed the wad of bills onto the counter. "No calls. No cops. Got it?"

"Y...yeah. I got it."

Chickenhead turned and without looking back walked to the stairwell leading to the second floor and started up the steps. The now dumbfounded clerk watched Chickenhead disappear up the corridor. It took him a moment to look back at the loose pile of money that lay on the desktop. Snatching up the notes, he hurriedly folded the money in half and, pulling up his left pant leg, stuffed the currency into the side of his sock. He pulled his sock up and lowered his pant leg in one swift motion.

Jesus, he thought, gotta be a grand or two that dude dropped...

Even more shaken now, the clerk glanced at the phone and the baseball bat resting behind the counter. He quickly walked to the opposite end of the short enclosure. Grabbing a week-old, half-filled pack of generic cigarettes from under the counter, his hand trembled as he lit one of the stale smokes.

No fuckin' way I'm callin' the cops, he thought as he looked toward the now-empty stairwell. That son of a bitch got mob written all over him, and I ain't no idiot...

*   *   *   *   *

Regina watched as Chickenhead disappeared into the dark doorway of The End of the Runway Hotel. Parked across the street in a vacant field steps from the bus stop where Braxton had stood just hours before, she reached across to the passenger seat to get her map and opened it. She used a penlight attached to her key chain to look over the hotel locations circled on her map. This dive wasn't marked off. Frowning, she turned the light off and refolded the paper, placing it back on the vacant seat beside her.

Gotta remember to update my software when we get back to Houston, she chided herself.

Regina watched the door to the building for another ten minutes while the frown on her face deepened. Suddenly she experienced that sick, excited feeling--the one she always got in the pit of her stomach just before shit was about to hit the fan. Regina stepped outside of the car, locked the door, and pulled the cell phone off of her belt clip. She had barely put the phone to her ear when Bitters answered her call on the first ring.

"Bitters here."

"Boss, 'Gina. I think this is the place. Robert's been inside 'bout fifteen minutes, and I just started feelin' sick." She gave him the address and directions.

"'Kay. Go in and be careful, 'Gina. I've picked up a tail. Gonna try to drop it before I get there. I'm about ten minutes out. I'll call the others." Bitters hung up.

Clipping the phone back on her belt, Regina reached behind her back and extracted a 9mm Glock handgun from the holster near the small of her back. She clicked off the safety, reholstered the piece, and walked to the rear of her rental car. Regina opened the trunk with a key and took out a black mid-length leather coat. She put it on after she closed the trunk and looked both ways before crossing the street and entering the hotel.

*   *   *   *   *

"Sweetie, I was wondering if you could give a girl a hand," Regina purred to the pale clerk behind the desk. "I'd really appreciate it, honey."

It was at that exact moment that the clerk chalked up his evening as the weirdest night he had ever experienced in his six years at that very front desk.

"Um, what can I do to help you, ma'am?"

This is the biggest bitch I've ever seen, he thought miserably.

"Well, it's kind of embarrassing...my boyfriend...he's tall and skinny with bright red hair...well, he's kinda jealous. He found a note from my man on the side telling me to meet him here tonight." Leaning across the counter as she opened her jacket, Regina's size 44DDs strained against the thin fabric of her turtleneck shirt as they almost touched the countertop. She batted her eyes at the man in front of her as he stared at her breasts.

"Um...uh..."

"Honey, all I want is a room number. I can make it worth your while...in so many different ways." Taking a fifty-dollar bill out of her pocket, Regina kissed it before handing it to the perspiring clerk. She squeezed his hand before releasing it and the bill.

"Um, he went upstairs to 268 'bout ten minutes ago. He looked really pissed. Is he really, ya know, um, your boyfriend?"

"Yes, baby, but don't you worry, I've got plenty ta go around." Regina winked as she dropped two fifties on the desk. She turned toward the stairs and ran up them two at a time. The clerk looked at the lipstick-stained money in his hand for a moment longer before picking up the other two notes on the desk and jamming all three into his bulging sock.

This shit's gettin' way too freaky for me, he thought as he walked to the far end of the counter. He reached behind the phone and pulled out a half-gone bottle of vodka from a brown paper sack. Looking toward the stairwell, he opened the bottle and took a long swallow.

*   *   *   *   *

Standing on the landing just below the hall that led to the second floor, Regina wasted no time calling her boss. Bitters answered before the phone stopped its first ring.

"Regina?"

"Boss, get your ass here. Robert's found Braxton."

"I'm in the parking lot outside right now. What room is Braxton in?"

"Second floor, number 268. Look for a stairwell on your left as you come in the door. I'm on the landing just beneath the hall. One clerk on duty–he's on your right–scary-looking albino with a pizza complexion."

"'Gina, we may have company," Bitters grumbled as he crossed the street to the hotel. "I don't think I lost my tail. Be ready."

"Hey, more fun for our party."

Bitters looked through the door of the hotel toward the desk area. It was empty. Thankful for this small miracle, he opened the door and moved unseen up the stairs. A moment later he was beside Regina on the dark landing.

"'Bout time you got here. What's the play?"

"I'll take point; you've got the rear. Cover my ass and please, for once, be quiet."

"Shit, you want me ta make your coffee, too?" Regina hissed as Bitters silently passed her on his way to the top of the stairs while hugging the wall. Regina, dialing the backlit pad of her cell phone, stayed close behind. As they entered the dimly lit second-floor hallway, they both saw that it was empty. They were looking toward the end of the corridor when Bitters noticed the open bathroom door.

"Shit," he whispered. He turned to Regina as she clipped her phone to her belt. "Move!"

Hurrying down the hall, the duo stopped in front of Room 268. They tried the door, and Bitters felt it move inward when he turned the knob. A loud thump made him stop for just a second. Bitters quietly and quickly eased the door open an inch and saw Chickenhead straddling Braxton. He turned and whispered to Regina.

"Go down the hall. Keep an eye open for company. And kill that bathroom light." Unholstering his gun, Bitters entered the room as Regina ran to the community bathroom down the hall.

*   *   *   *   *

Mooreman got to the hotel just in time to see Bitters slide through the front door. He parked next to Bitters' car, and all three men piled out of the van. Mooreman turned to Greene.

"Stay with the van. Tanner, you're with me." Running across the street, both men stopped at the door to the hotel. Mooreman glanced inside and saw that the front desk was empty. Both men grabbed for the door, opened it, and ran to the counter. Tanner swung his legs over the dirty countertop and dropped behind it. It took him all of four seconds to find the hotel registry lying behind the desk. As he opened it, he heard a toilet flush.

Dropping the ledger to the floor, Tanner grabbed the baseball bat he saw lying on the floor and flattened himself against the wall opposite the restroom. The door slowly opened, and the clerk hitched up his pants as he walked out of the tiny restroom. He stopped when he saw Mooreman smiling at him from just a few feet away.

"You need a room, bud–?" His question was cut short by almost three feet of Louisville Slugger connecting to his midsection, doubling him over. Tanner kicked him on the way down and was about to hit him with the bat again when Mooreman jumped the counter and ripped the wood out of his hands.

"What you tryin' ta do, kill him? Stand back, fuckhead!"

Tanner obeyed. Leaning down to the doubled over clerk, Mooreman grabbed the collar of the man's shirt and jerked him to a sitting position. He brought his gun to the man's temple and pressed hard into his bulging flesh.

"Okay, I ain't got no time for games, asshole. Where is Braxton Howard?"

Still nursing his bruised ribs, the clerk looked up at Mooreman. "Ain't no one come in here tonight named Howard."

Mooreman smashed the butt of his gun against the clerk's forehead, tearing away an inch-long gash of flesh. The man's scream was cut short by the shaft of the gun being jammed against the side of his throat. Tanner laughed and hopped from one foot to the other as he watched with glee.

"That refresh your memory any, freak? Now where is he?" Mooreman persisted as he raised the gun again.

"I...don't...Room 268...Room 268 upstairs! Don't hit me!"

"Too late, snowman." Mooreman's gun crashed home just behind the clerk's ear and knocked the terrified man out cold. Tanner kicked the clerk's prone body before jumping the counter. Mooreman joined him moments later. They both ran up the stairs and stopped at the top of the narrow hallway. Using his gun and pointing through the dim light to a door ajar at the end of the hall, Mooreman spoke to Tanner as they hurried down the hall, glancing at the numbers on the doors as they passed.

"Go in there. If anyone tries to come in behind me, take care of their ass."

The little man sprinted down the hall and into the darkened community bathroom just as Mooreman kicked in the door to Room 268.

Chapter 23

Chickenhead stood at the bottom of the landing and looked down the hallway to the light coming out of the partially opened community bathroom door. He was tall enough to stand on the bottom of the six steps that led up to the landing, and standing flat against the wall, still had a clear view down the dimly lit corridor. Chickenhead watched the door open and caught his breath when he saw a bare-chested Braxton Howard walk out of the bathroom, his right side covered in bandages. Carrying a dark towel in one hand and holding his side with the other, Braxton shuffled to his door like an old man. The doctor opened the door to his room and went inside.

Chickenhead had to force himself to slow his breathing—to try to keep his head from exploding. He walked close to the wall opposite Braxton's room and stopped once he'd passed the door to Room 268, pausing to listen to the sounds around him. He heard a TV playing softly and nothing else. He bent down, unlaced his shoes, and took them off. Chickenhead flattened both of the cheap low-top sneakers, loosened the belt around his waist, and then stuffed both of the shoes midway down the back of his pants. He tightened the leather strap before he silently padded back to Braxton's door and gently put his ear to the warped wood. The TV he had heard was the one playing in Braxton's room. Chickenhead backed away from the door a bit and looked at the flickering light coming from beneath the door jam itself. He knelt down to get a better look at the lock and was unsuccessful at suppressing a grim smirk.

Chickenhead took out his wallet and extracted the credit card Bitters had given to him almost a week before. He returned the wallet to his back pocket and moved closer to the door. Quietly and with a gentle grip he grasped the ancient wooden doorknob and turned it slowly counterclockwise until he felt the knob stop. He pulled the door toward him and eased the edge of the plastic card past the warped door seal. Chickenhead felt for the outward-pointing grooved notch in the door bolt that he knew all too well was there. Having lived on the streets and in fleabag hotels like this one for more than seven years, Chickenhead had learned to become quite adept at breaking into rooms exactly like the one he was now targeting. Usually he used a flathead screwdriver. In this case, a credit card would have to do.

Slowly adding more pressure to the card as he turned the knob, Chickenhead felt the bolt give with a soft thump. He turned the doorknob slowly as he continued to pull the door toward himself and stopped only after completing half a turn. The door was unlocked, and the only thing holding it closed was Chickenhead's strong grip.

Chickenhead slid the card into his pant pocket and took several deep breaths before flinging the door open and bolting into the room. Braxton, sitting on the edge of the bed with his head resting in his hands, jerked his head up in surprise. His eyes were the size of teacups as he stared at Chickenhead uncomprehendingly. The doctor scurried backward across the single bed to the nightstand that held his medical bag. He intended to grab his scalpel but fell over the side of the narrow bed as he reached for the bag. Chickenhead, taking a running leap over the piece of furniture, landed fully on Braxton's upper chest with both feet, knocked the wind out of the doctor, and cracked the man's sternum from his ribs. Braxton was lying on his back with his legs still on the bed as he tried to grab Chickenhead's legs and gasp for air at the same time. He got a fistful of Chickenhead's pant leg and tried to push his attacker off balance. Chickenhead easily tore away from Braxton's flailing hands, and his legs were a blur as they rained hard, stomping blows on Braxton's face and chest, breaking his ribs, nose, and clavicle like dry twigs. Unable to take a deep breath under the barrage of blows, the only sound coming from Braxton was a high-pitched whine—that and the wet snapping crack of his ribs breaking.

Chickenhead moved away from the side of the bed, his socks bloody, grasped one of Braxton's twitching legs, and pulled him out of the small space between the bed and the wall and into the middle of the floor. With his face totally blank, Chickenhead grabbed the only chair in the room—a straight-backed wooden dinosaur as old as the crumbling hotel itself—and raised it over his head. He smashed it down onto Braxton's right side as he lay curled up on the floor. Once. Twice. The scream that escaped Braxton was a pitiful excuse for expelled air. Placing the undamaged chair upright, Chickenhead was still breathing hard as he turned the shaking mass of broken bones that was Braxton's body onto his back and straddled him. He raised his fist high and began punching Braxton faster and faster—directly in his face.

"Robert!"

His knuckles bleeding and his fingers breaking on the floor as his hands slid off of the gore-covered facial bones, Chickenhead began to hit Braxton even harder.

"Gibbs!"

With the doctor's splashed blood dripping from his face, Chickenhead put both of his hands around Braxton's neck and started to strangle him.

"CHICKENHEAD!"

He looked up to see Bitters' fist coming straight for his jaw. Bitters had to hit him twice to knock him out. Even unconscious, Chickenhead's fingers stayed around Braxton's neck until Bitters pried them open. Jeremiah began dragging his now-limp friend to one side and leaned him upright against the bed, then went back to the bloody mess that was Braxton. He felt for a pulse on Braxton's blood-drenched neck and was mildly surprised to find a weak but steady one.

"Well, doctor, I guess it's your lucky day." Circling behind

Braxton, it took Bitters a moment to get a good grip under the arms of Braxton's slick, broken body. Finally wrapping the bulk of his arms around Braxton's caved-in chest, Bitters almost had the unconscious man upright when the door to the room exploded open.

In a half-upright stance, Bitters was caught flat-footed with Braxton in his arms. He stared down the barrel of a Beretta complete with a six-inch silencer. The gun and its owner were less than six feet away.

The man at the door looked quickly at Bitters, at Braxton, and finally at Chickenhead. Nervously, Mooreman moved a half-step into the room, leveling the weapon at Bitters' head. "Not a motherfuckin' sound out of you, Bitters."

Bitters let go an easy chuckle and lifted Braxton a bit higher in front of him. "My man, you've gotta be jokin'. If you'd stop shaking so much, I might take you seriously."

"Shut the fuck up, Bitters! Put Braxton down and back away from him." Mooreman motioned to the wall behind Bitters with the tip of his quivering gun.

"Sorry, no can do," replied a grinning Bitters. "I've got a date with the Phoenix PD tonight. Sleeping boy here is the party favor I'm 'spose to bring."

Where in the hell is Regina? he wondered.

"This is one party you're not gonna make. I'll make sure Driver gets his package, though. Now put the doctor down or your buddy gets a new nostril." Mooreman motioned the gun toward the still unconscious Chickenhead, then pointed it back toward Bitters. As Bitters started slowly lowering the doctor, he saw a huge smile spread across Mooreman's face.

"Jeremiah Bitters...your ass ain't shit...where's your team now, huh? Where's your black he-bitch?"

Appearing in the doorway behind Mooreman, Regina tried to crush the base of his skull with the butt of her gun as she slammed it into Mooreman with both hands. Clamping his hands closed, Mooreman squeezed the trigger on his weapon as he fell and discharged the gun with what sounded more like a hard cough. Regina smashed his head again as Mooreman's limp body, gun still clutched in his hand, sank to the floor. Regina looked up from Mooreman's bleeding head and saw that Bitters was still holding Braxton, who was now convulsing violently. She understood why when she saw the hole Mooreman's gun had shot into Braxton's left side. Bitters dropped the dying doctor and scooped up a stirring Chickenhead as he ran out the door.

Following her boss out, Regina stopped at the door, took a disposable camera out of her leather jacket, and quickly used up the twelve-picture roll before putting it back into her pocket. She stepped back to the door and kicked Mooreman in the head with her three-inch block heels. His low moan brought a sweet, child-like smile to her lips.

"By the way, asshole," she whispered at Mooreman's prone figure, "I had my operation years ago. It's just plain 'bitch' now." Giggling like a schoolgirl, Regina ran down the stairs and tried to catch up to Bitters. When she reached the bottom of the stairs behind Bitters, Regina scanned the lobby, her eyes stopping at the vacant counter. Bitters sat Chickenhead on the bottom step and reached into his jacket pocket to pull out a small vial of smelling salts. He was waving the bottle under Chickenhead's nose when Regina touched his shoulder.

"Boss, when I first came in the hotel, there was a clerk on duty..."

Chickenhead started to put up a weak struggle as he came to. Bitters held him in place with one hand as he pocketed the medication with the other. Bitters jerked his head in the direction of the desk. "Make it quick, 'Gina. We need to roll."

Regina walked to the counter in a wide arc with her gun drawn. Hesitating only a second, she carefully leaned over the structure and saw the beaten clerk stirring as he lay on the dirty carpet. Regina reholstered her gun, climbed over the desk, and knelt beside the groaning man. He flinched when she touched him but didn't resist as she gently sat him upright. His forehead and face were covered with dried blood.

"Who? Wha...don't hit me!"

"Easy, baby, easy. It's gonna be okay. Let me clean you up a bit, okay?"

The man shook his head as he shivered. "I...I can't see you," he whined miserably.

"Hold on a second. I'm going to get you some towels." Regina entered the tiny restroom off to the side and returned with a handful of paper towels she had found near the sink. She carefully wiped down his face, freeing his blood-caked eyelids and clearing most of the blood from his frightened face. She took his left hand, placed a soggy mess of paper towels in his palm, and raised his hand to his head wound.

"Press this to your head for a minute. It will help to stop the bleeding. I'll get more towels."

Regina returned in seconds, her hands full of water-soaked paper towels. Again she gently wiped his face and neck clean of blood. Less shaken now, the man looked up at Regina.

"Thanks...thanks for the help."

"No problem, sweetie. We didn't mean for you to get hurt. I'm really sorry."

"'Gina!" Bitters yelled from across the lobby. "Let's hit it!"

Standing up, she looked over the counter and saw that Bitters was still supporting Chickenhead. She bent down close to the clerk, took out a roll of twenties from her jacket pocket, and pressed the bills into the now-alert clerk's hand.

"I gotta jet, honey. See you in your dreams."

The pained smile on the man's face as he held his cut head almost made him look attractive as he answered her. "Only if they're nightmares."

As Regina cleared the counter, the clerk called out to her. She peeked back over the desk and saw him attempt to stand. He held onto the counter to steady himself.

"The two guys that hit me—they still here?"

A bright smile radiated from Regina's face as she pointed toward the steps where Bitters and Chickenhead were standing. "The tall one's in Room 268. The short guy is in the bathroom down the hall. Both are down for the count for awhile." She blew him a kiss and then winked. "Give 'em my best, sugar."

Regina turned and rushed to the door as Bitters walked out, still supporting a wobbly Chickenhead. The clerk slowly bent down, seeing stars all the way, and pushed the wad of money Regina had given him into his overstuffed left sock. As he regained his composure, he had only one thought in mind. Without a moment's hesitation, he grabbed the baseball bat lying on the floor. Although he had to wince in pain, he carefully climbed over the countertop. He leaned the bat against the desk as he fished into his front pants pocket. Pulling out a worn set of keys, he walked over to the front door of the hotel and locked the door after turning off the flickering neon "Vacancy" sign. He held the bat in front of him as he walked up the stairs as quickly as his throbbing head would allow. Fortunately, his anger seemed to help abate the pain somewhat.

The clerk looked down the hallway as he reached the top of the stairwell and saw what looked like an arm sticking out of a partially open bathroom door. He was able to move quicker now and arrived at the open door of Room 268. Looking inside, he saw a crumpled Mooreman lying in front of the TV. By the light of the muted set he saw that Mooreman was starting to move. He rushed into the room with the bat raised over his head and brought the piece of wood down as hard as he could. A sickening thud sounded as the bat made contact with the elbow of the semi-conscious Mooreman's gun hand. The force of the blow that shattered Mooreman's arm caused the gun he held in his hand to discharge again. The stray bullet was stopped shortly after it entered Braxton's body, bouncing off of bone fragments from his broken ribs. Braxton regained consciousness for a sliver of a second when the bullet lodged in his heart, stopping it forever. Braxton's body shuddered once more as the clerk, for the fourth time, slammed his favorite bat onto the battered head of George Mooreman.

*   *   *   *   *

Tanner Brice moaned softly when he recognized that he was actually awake. Lying on the filthy floor of the second-floor bathroom, he tried to move as carefully as possible. All he could see were bright flashes of light mixed with pinpoint stars. The fireworks behind his eyes lasted throughout his struggle to sit upright. The last thing he remembered was opening the door to the dark restroom, and then...well, nothing. Moving upright, he leaned against the mildew-encrusted, dark-wood cabinet housing a rust-stained sink. He gingerly touched the growing lump on the left side of his head and winced. Someone had knocked the hell out of him, and he had no idea who it might have been. Standing upright, he turned on the sink's single spigot and splashed the chilled water on his face. It was then that he noticed the light in the bathroom was on.

This shit can't be good, he thought. Time to blow this joint.

Tanner opened the door to the bathroom and looked dead into the eyes of the clerk he had beaten earlier. Reaching for his gun, he realized it wasn't in his holster at the precise moment the bat in the clerk's hands connected to the lump on the left side of Tanner's head.

*   *   *   *   *

Glancing over the top of the paperback novel he was reading, Greene watched the three figures leave the hotel. It wasn't until they got closer to the van that he was able to determine that the dark streaks on both of the men's clothes was blood. Unsure of what to do, he turned off the tiny book light attached to his paperback and tried to shrink his considerable mass as low into the car seat as possible. He observed that one of the men was supporting a tall skinny guy and was helping the wobbly man into the car parked right smack beside Greene's van.

Of all the freakin' luck!

It was at that moment that the tallest woman Greene had ever seen scared the living daylights out of him when she appeared next to his window--smiling of all things--and pointed at him the ugliest gun he ever wanted to see. Still smiling, the woman lightly tapped the tip of the weapon on Greene's window, then motioned for him to open it. Greene obeyed.

"Hi ya, Blondie. Do me a favor, huh? Reach over real slow-like and take the keys out of the ignition, okay?"

Again, Greene obeyed her request to the letter. He handed the van's keys to Regina through the open window. After she palmed them, she backed two steps from the van's door.

"Step out of the car, baby boy. And leave the door open."

Greene got out of the van. Not knowing what else to do, he plastered himself against the side of the vehicle he'd just exited. Taking a step toward him, Regina motioned with her gun hand for Greene to turn around.

"You know the procedure, sugar. Spread 'em."

Quickly relieving him of his gun, Regina turned him back around with her free hand. She stepped up to the shorter man and looked down into his frightened eyes as her gun lightly rested on his trembling chest.

"Might want ta boogie on out of here, baby. Things 'bout ta get real busy 'round these parts."

Greene turned away from her as slowly as he could and began walking away. He stopped just on the other side of the car in which Bitters and Chickenhead were sitting when he heard her call out to him.

"Turn around, sweetness. I've got something for you."

This fuckin' bitch is gonna shoot me, he thought anxiously.

Turning back to her with his eyes closed, Greene let out a short yelp when he felt something hit him square in the chest. He fell to the ground as if he'd been hit by a rocket. Opening one eye and then the other, he looked up at Regina, who seemed to be covering her mouth with her free hand to stifle a giggle. Then he noticed the paperback book on the ground in front of his feet. Sitting up, then standing, he picked it up and switched off the book light that had snapped on during its flight. He turned away quickly now and sprinted away a lot faster, hoping all the while that Regina didn't see the growing wet stain in the front of his pants...

*   *   *   *   *

While Regina closed up the van next to him, Bitters called Dane. The man answered the phone on the first ring.

"Boss?"

"Dane, head back to the hotel and close us out. We're done in Dallas."

"Right. Thought you'd like to know--had a tail for a minute. Lost 'em about ten minutes ago."

"I'm not surprised. See you in Houston in a few hours."

Clicking off his cell phone, Bitters tossed it on the dashboard. He looked over toward Chickenhead, who was staring at the now-dark hotel across the street. Bitters tapped him on the arm. Chickenhead didn't respond.

"How you holding up? You okay?"

Silence.

"Robert...I couldn't let you kill him."

More silence.

Sighing, Bitters turned away from Chickenhead as Regina opened the door and jumped into the rear seat. She took off a pair of latex gloves as she settled into the soft leather.

"She's locked and definitely loaded. Cops gonna have a field day on those poor slobs inside--at least what's left of them." Looking at Bitters and then at Chickenhead, she put her hand gently on Chickenhead's shoulder as he started to sob.

"Robert, hang in there. I know it's rough right now..." Her voice trailed off as she ran out of things to say. Chickenhead shook his head at her and kept crying, although softer now.

"'Gina, go across the street and get Robert's car. Call Pinky and tell her to hightail it out here with Dane and get your car. Park all of them at the hotel. I'll have the company pick them up later."

"On my way." Regina squeezed Chickenhead's shoulder and took the key out of his shaking hand as he gave it up without a struggle. As Regina pulled out of the convenience store's parking lot, Bitters started his car and followed her into the street.

*   *   *   *   *

Peter Driver paced the Oriental rug-covered wood floor of the dimly lit office in his home in the Tanglewood section of Houston.

He'd had no contact—with either team—since he'd called Mooreman with Bitters' street corner location in Dallas. Stopping his marching for a moment, he looked at the two-hundred-year-old, hand-carved mahogany grandfather clock in the near corner. It read 7:54 a.m. It had been almost six hours since anyone had contacted him.

As the judge grabbed one of the two glasses he had alternately refilled with whatever bottle of liquor was closest to his grasp, he continued to trot about the room, stopping only to refill the glass with Scotch. He was now beginning to wonder if he had done the smart thing by putting Mooreman on Bitters' trail. He wondered if this particular move would come back to haunt him. Knowing from experience (Driver had used Bitters on two other occasions in the past three years), Bitters was never someone to be taken lightly. The judge hoped the information he'd passed on to Mooreman allowed the ex-cop to take care of Bitters should their paths cross-permanently if need be. With a very real prison sentence hanging low over his head, Mooreman wouldn't let anything stand in the way of his getting Braxton back to Houston. Driver knew that for a fact. Yes, no one would stand in Mooreman's way--even someone as formidable as Jeremiah Bitters.

The judge circled back to this paper-covered desk and flopped into a leather and chrome office chair. The now-empty glass slipped from his hand and fell to the floor. He didn't even hear it shatter. He sat behind a desk that was identical to the one he had in his downtown office and rubbed his sleep-deprived eyes, as much to clear his mind as to rest his sight. When his hands fell from his face into his lap, he had to blink twice in the sparse light to believe what he was seeing.

Jeremiah Bitters. Standing in the doorway to his office.

Oh…my…God.

Unhurriedly, Bitters walked into the spacious room and stopped several feet from the sitting Judge. Both of Bitters' hands were in the lower pockets of the dark windbreaker that was only partially zipped. His face blank, Driver saw the dead shine of Bitters' eyes—even in the sparse early morning light that was filtered by the closed blind on the bay window. The Judge didn't have to think twice about not reaching for the loaded gun he kept in the top right-hand drawer just inches from him.

"Judge, we have some issues we need to clear up." The casual tone of Bitters' voice frightened Driver far worse than any scream could have. Very deliberately and slowly, Driver lifted both hands from his lap to the desktop and placed them flat on the paper-covered desk in full view of Bitters. Just as cautiously, he angled the oversized executive chair to face the man who stood in front of him. A thin smile touched Bitters' lips for a moment before the blank look returned to his face.

"Glad to see you haven't lost all of your mind. Yet." Bitters took his right hand out of his jacket pocket and unzipped the windbreaker, exposing the shoulder-holstered silver gun that looked as big as a cannon to Driver. Still moving easily, Bitters unholstered the weapon, clicked the safety off, and chambered a round. He folded both hands in front of him–gun hand on top–as the judge followed every move with wide eyes.

"Braxton is dying–or dead–killed by the fool you had shadowing me. You'll get copies of the photos that will be delivered to you in the next few days. By now Dallas PD is having a very interesting conversation with what's left of your man and his weasel-faced partner--that is if the clerk they beat half to death left the police anything to talk to. I don't think he took too kindly to them trying to behead him while they questioned him."

Bitters took one step closer to the desk, and Driver suppressed a moan of terror by almost biting his lower lip bloody.

"By the way...what was fuckwad's name?"

"Mooreman-George Mooreman..."

Bitters took a step back from the desk, gun tapping lightly against his thigh. The look of disgust on his face was plain to see.

"You're making this way too easy, Judge. At least lie. You know, hold back a little information? That would give me a good reason to knock the shit out of you."

The papers that Driver's hands rested upon began to dimple from the sweat that was pouring off of his hands.

"I'm...uh, Bitters..." he stammered.

"Shut up, Judge. I'm not finished yet."

Driver's mouth closed with an audible "clack."

"Your intervention killed Braxton and almost killed me and a member of my team. That doesn't sit well with me, understand?"

Driver nodded "yes" very slowly.

"Good! We're communicating here. Couple of things--because of your idiot, Dallas is gonna be a mess. A mess I will come out of smelling like a rose, by the way. Take care of it."

Bitters stared at Driver and watched the man nod a little quicker this time.

"My fee just increased by $400,000. Gibbs and Jamaica need a bit more for their troubles, too, don't you think?"

Bitters waved his gun toward the desk and stopped Driver in the middle of yet another nod.

"Start writin', or have you forgotten that your dirty-business checkbook is in the lower right-hand drawer?"

Driver was too afraid for his life to think about how Bitters knew that bit of information. Until this meeting--actually until that very moment and to the best of the judge's knowledge-- Bitters had never set foot in his home. Keeping one moist hand on the desktop, the judge shook the other one to dislodge the wet paper that stuck to his palm. He lowered his hand to the drawer and saw, for the first time since Bitters had entered the room, that the gun was pointed directly at his head. And a smile was on Bitters' face.

Driver slowed his movements to a crawl as he raised his hand from the drawer. He was clutching a leather-bound checkbook as if his life depended on it, an assumption he didn't doubt for a moment. The judge dried his hands on the front of his button-down, long-sleeve shirt and picked up a pen. He wrote out three checks totaling well over a half-million dollars. All were made out to "cash."

Driver dried his hands on his shirt again before he pushed all three checks to the edge of the desk closest to Bitters. Stepping to the desk, Bitters took the checks in his free hand, folded all of them in half, and placed them in his jacket pocket. He leaned across the massive desk as Driver tried to lean away from him. The blank look and dead eyes burned a hole in Driver's memory.

"It has not been a pleasure doing business with you. Lose my fucking number."

Holstering his gun, Bitters zipped his jacket halfway before he backed out of the room. For a solid five minutes, Driver stared at the doorway through which Bitters had left. He was shaking slightly even after the minutes had passed. Summoning all the courage he had, Driver stepped out into the opening and walked to the front room. The door leading to the street was closed and locked. Driver looked at the state-of-the-art alarm system's keypad that was mounted on the wall. Every area of the house showed "ready." Anger started to replace the fear Bitters had left him with as he walked back to his office. He stepped into the room, approached the desk, and leafed through a large Rolodex on his desk until he came to the number he wanted. Before he dialed it, the Judge crossed the room to the bar. He took out a fresh bottle of booze, opened it, and drank from it in a long swallow. Taking the sloshing bottle with him to his desk, he dialed the direct line to the watch commander of the main precinct of the Houston Police Department. The phone rang twice before it was picked up.

"Captain Priest speaking. How can I help you?"

"Captain, this is Mayor Driver. I need the direct line to the watch commander at the Dallas Police Department headquarters. How soon can you connect me?"

"If you hold the line, Your Honor, I think I can get you right through."

"Thank you."

"I'll have to put you on hold for a bit, sir." Recorded music played as Driver took another swallow from his bottle. Less than a minute later, the captain came back on the line as Driver set down his already half-empty bottle.

"Mr. Mayor, I have the Dallas watch commander on hold. I'll patch you through, sir."

"Thank you, Captain."

As Driver listened to music again, his anger smoldered just beneath the surface of his still-clammy skin. He knew what was angering him now. This entire mess was Mooreman's fault. If that weasel was still alive, the mayor was going to make him pay for his mistakes. Of that he was certain.

"Captain Alan Long, Dallas Police Department. How can I help you, Your Honor?"

A smile cracked the granite of Driver's damp face. Mooreman was going to pay and pay dearly for his mistake...

Chapter 24

Chickenhead grimaced as he took a sip of his first cup of coffee for the day. Jamaica's coffee was horrible, as usual. Ought to call this stuff "black death," he thought as he poured first his cup and then the remaining contents of the half-filled pot down the kitchen sink. Rinsing out the glass unit before refilling it, Chickenhead carefully measured out two level scoops of ground java, dumped both into the paper filter, and poured the water into the black plastic unit. Minutes later, he was blowing on the hot beverage in his mug to cool the liquid that was far less likely to give him heartburn for the rest of the day.

"There ya go," he mumbled, pleased with the flavor as he walked out of the kitchen and entered the large living room of the two-bedroom apartment he had shared with Jamaica in Mesa for the last two months. He sat down on the sofa in front of the TV and saw a sheet of notebook paper taped to the middle of the 27" screen. Setting his drink on the coffee table in front of him, he crossed the room to the TV. He took the paper off of the glass and brought it closer to read.

Bro,

I put the car in the shop today before going to work. Brakes are dead. Should be fixed by one o'clock or so. Pick it up, and while you're out, swing by the supermarket and grab some steaks. I'm cooking for Cynthia and us tonight. The card for the garage is on the table in the kitchen. Oh, and get your ass a job! Ha! Ha!

Jesus! Mutherfucker's worse than a wife, he thought with a grin.

After returning to Phoenix, Chickenhead had checked himself into the psychiatric ward of the same hospital in which Jamaica was recuperating. Three days of people telling him what was wrong with him and wanting to pump him full of drugs whose effects scared even him made Chickenhead sign himself out. He was actually in worse shape than when he'd come in. It was Proctor who had guided him to the police psychologist that Proctor himself had been using since the death of his wife over a year before.

Chickenhead talked to Doctor Amber Bennet for almost two hours the first time he'd seen her. He immediately began seeing her on a weekly basis during the first month he was back in town. His life consisted of visiting Jamaica in the hospital and crying his heart out to both Jamaica and Doctor Bennet, neither one of whom ever uttered a single complaint. At the end of the last session he'd had with the doctor two weeks before, Chickenhead had asked her how much he owed for her services. The doctor looked at him a bit puzzled before she answered his question.

"I'm sorry, I thought you knew. There is no charge for my services to you, Robert. All of your fees are being paid for courtesy of the Phoenix Police Department. Detective Proctor insisted on it and Commander LaPlante agreed."

Chickenhead still remembered the barely suppressed giggle she'd tried to cover up at the look of astonishment on his face. Bitters had called him and Jamaica almost every day for the first month he was back--sometimes just to say "hey." It helped Chickenhead in ways he couldn't explain.

Crossing the room to return to the sofa, Chickenhead sat down and looked at the neat but thick stack of newspapers--dailies from Dallas, Houston, and Phoenix--that Jamaica had refused to get rid of. It wasn't until weeks afterward that Chickenhead realized that everybody and their mamma had–or wanted–a piece of Braxton' s story as well as theirs. The "Turkeystuffer" killings had been front-page news in Arizona and in Texas for weeks along with requests for interviews from it seemed like anybody who knew how to hold a microphone. Both Chickenhead and Jamaica greatly appreciated Proctor and LaPlante running interference for them while both of them healed-mentally as well as physically.

The Phoenix Police Department continued to surprise the shit out of Chickenhead with the way they handled the situation with Woods. After a written apology from the department (signed, it seemed, by half of the police force), the department had covered all of Jamaica's injuries and rehabilitation costs. And very much to the two friends' surprise, two-hundred-thousand dollars had quietly been deposited into Jamaica's bank account, an account that was already bulging from the one-hundred-thousand-dollar check from Driver.

Driver…he was the reason they had both agreed on getting an answering machine. After Bitters had handed Chickenhead a check for two-hundred-thousand dollars (and suggested it was best to let this sleeping dog lie), Driver had called every day for almost a month. The conversation was always the same:

"Do either of you need anything? Anything at all?"

"No, thank you, Mr. Driver."

"I can get you both houses, jobs…anything. Just name it, Robert."

"Right now, sir, I…we just need some time. Thank you for everything, tho'."

"You let me know if I can help, son. Call anytime, day or night…"

*   *   *   *   *

The stories the paper told about Braxton's capture and death were far different from the one Bitters had supplied the both of them. According to the papers, it turned out that some guy named Mooreman had found Braxton at the hotel before any of them got there and had kidnapped the fucker. The Dallas cops had found the bodies of Mooreman, Braxton, and another man, Tanner Brice, a week later in an illegal garbage dump three miles east of The End of the Runway Motel. All of them had been beaten and shot--Mooreman and Tanner at point-blank range behind the ear. Twice. Dallas PD was still investigating, but to this day, there hadn't been any leads that went anywhere, at least in the newspapers. The security guard who found them while taking a shortcut across the field to work got a ten-thousand-dollar reward--and a nice job with the City of Houston--for stumbling across the bodies and reporting his find to the police. Chickenhead laughed every time he looked at the Houston Bee front-page color picture of Driver handing a huge foam-board check to the smiling albino clerk from the hotel...

The phone ringing brought Chickenhead back to the present. Letting the answering machine pick it up, Chickenhead opened the closet next to the front door and pulled out his denim jacket. He returned to the kitchen and poured another cup of coffee into a huge plastic travel mug. He snapped the lid on the cup, put on his jacket, and patted his pocket to check for his wallet and house keys. Satisfied that they were both there, he locked the door behind him as he sipped his coffee.

Might as well head out to the garage, he thought distractedly. He buttoned up his jacket against the mid-morning cold as he began the ten-block walk to their car.

*   *   *   *   *

When Chickenhead drove up to the apartment two hours later, he saw a petite woman bundled up in a bright yellow parka. She was sitting on the two steps in front of his door. She stood up and smiled cheerfully at him as he made his way up the walk to his front door. Chickenhead paused and shifted the two bags of groceries that were propped in his arms. He was in no mood to return her radiant smile.

Jesus, I hope this ain't no reporter, he thought to himself.

"You need a hand with that, Robert?" She reached for one of the bags as Chickenhead groaned.

Shit! She knows my name!

Holding onto his groceries, he shook his head as he tried to maneuver around her to the front door. He set both bags on the sidewalk while he fumbled for his house key.

"Um, ma'am, thanks for the offer. Look, I don't wanna talk to any reporters right now, okay? Just leave me your card and when I get a minute, I'll call you."

Chickenhead had no intention of carrying through with his hastily made-up promise. The small woman's smile stepped up a notch as she took a step closer to Chickenhead, her right hand rising from her side. Chickenhead couldn't help but notice that she was knockdown drag-out cute.

"I can't stand those bastards, either. Too nosy and never know when to shut up. I didn't get a chance to meet you in Dallas. I'm Pinky."

The smile erupted into a genuinely pleasant laugh as Pinky saw the look of complete surprise on Chickenhead's face. And she watched his eyes drop to examine her throat.

*   *   *   *   *

"I'm in town for a couple of days to see my dad. Thought I'd stop by and introduce myself."

They both sat on opposite ends of the sofa in the living room, nursing cups of coffee Chickenhead had hastily prepared.

"Both Bitters and Regina said 'hey.' And I have something for you and Jamaica." She started fishing through her large shoulder bag. Chickenhead ignored his coffee and stared at his guest.

This is who I missed in Dallas? Man, this woman's a knockout!

"Um...I'm sorry about staring when we first met. It's just that...you know..." Chickenhead stammered badly as he began blushing. Her infectious laugh brought an embarrassed smile to his lips.

"No apology needed. Everyone does that to me after they meet 'Gina. Ah, there it is," she said exuberantly as she pulled out two slim white boxes from her bag. She handed both to him and stood up. She zipped her parka up halfway. It wasn't until then that Chickenhead noticed that she hadn't taken her parka off when she'd first come in.

"I've got to be going. Going fishing with my dad today, and he'll kill me if I keep him and the fish waiting."

Chickenhead walked her to the door and opened it. She turned to him after stepping down to ground level.

"That was a nice piece of detective work y'all did. Here and in Dallas. You should be proud. See ya."

She turned and walked down the path to the apartment's parking lot. Chickenhead watched her get into a late-model Volkswagen Beetle that was the same color as her parka. She waved to him as she pulled out of her parking spot and was gone in a yellow flash. Closing the door behind him, Chickenhead leaned against it for a moment before glancing across the room. He focused on the two small boxes Pinky had left for him and Jamaica. Chickenhead crossed the room and sat down on the sofa, grabbing the nearest box and opening it. He was again surprised when he held in his hand the exact replica of the phone Bitters had given him in Dallas. Turning over the trim unit, he saw a small placard taped to the bottom of the phone. On it was a typed phone number and the words "think about it…"

*   *   *   *   *

It was 2:48 a.m. on March 3rd and raining cats and dogs in the Little Beirut section near downtown Phoenix. Chickenhead and Jamaica stood in a doorway a few feet from their car and looked into the wall of water falling from the sky. After about ten minutes, Jamaica reached out and touched his friend's shoulder.

"How you doin', bro?"

Chickenhead looked at his friend and brother. The wetness around his eyes had nothing to do with the water falling from above. Chickenhead squeezed Jamaica's hand in his while a sad smile struggled to his lips.

"I'm cool, bro. Thanks for coming with me tonight."

"I'm here for you, Robert. Always."

Stepping out into the downpour, Chickenhead walked the few

steps to the place where he'd found Mimi's body months before. Rain soaking his long hair into a dripping pelt, he didn't feel the cold river of water falling on him as he stared at the cracked sidewalk in front of him. Both men looked up as a car passed in front of them, slowly making its way down the slick street. Chickenhead watched in silence as the car turned left at the end of the block. He reached into the breast pocket of his now-sodden denim jacket and took out the twenty-dollar bill he had removed from Mimi's body forever ago. He squeezed it tightly in his right hand, opened his fist and in the diffused glow of the streetlight he stood under, saw the blood on the bill run into his palm. He looked a moment more, and one brief hiccup escaped his mouth as he brought the note to his lips. Chickenhead kissed the bill before dropping it into a fast-moving stream of runoff water. As he watched the balled-up bill disappear underground into a storm drain, Chickenhead unclipped a slim cell phone from his belt. He walked back to the shelter of the doorway and looked at Jamaica, who nodded once.

In the darkness of the alcove, Chickenhead slowly dialed a number that he had, in the last few weeks, surprised himself by memorizing. The phone rang once before it was picked up on the other end...

The End

Acknowledgements

Gee-manetti-and-my-name-ain't-Freddy.

Okay…this is to say "hey" to all (or at least most of, I'm gettin' old and the mind goin' quick) the people whose shoulder's I've cried on (feel free to send the dry-cleaning bills) when I went temporarily insane writing this novel. Well, here it is (and I'm still young enough to smile at pretty women with my natural teeth)…upward onward and movin' down the road..Dr. Carl Wulfsberg, Meg Files and Dave Powers-all at one time or another a part of the Pima Community College writing program-thank you (only took me nine years), Amina Sonnie, girl, WHERE'S THAT BOOK! Kimberly Crockett, sorry I fell out of touch with you while going nuts but hey, not bad for a poor boy from East Orange, NJ huh? Whatta concept…Justin Rouse, my brother of another mother, you made Costco a lot easier…now, READ THAT BOOK. Shalaon, honest, I can cook. Larry Mancient, thanks for everything (including my old job). Phil (Dad) got that twenty? Art Thompson, you're all right in my book (now will you please call Kim). E.J. Haddad of the Scottsdale Police and James Acosta of the General Investigation Bureau of the Phoenix PD, thanks for the ton of info on police procedure…donuts for everybody (okay, bad joke)!!! Super RN Cathy Haddad, your info and sources were the bomb. Monica Cooper, without your magic this brother woulda been hard up (you got my thanks and a LOT more books). Greg Arnett, Pharm. D., thanks for all the drug info. Zane, thanks for taking a chance on the new guy on the block. Momma and Daddy...what can I say? I love you and Mom (with any kind of luck and a million years) I hope to be half the writer you are. My friend and mentor Sandra Kitt, are we in NY yet? All my brothers, sisters, nieces and nephews-thanks for putting up with my REALLY bad chicken jokes over the years (yes, now it's gonna get worse)...and finally to my big brother Butch, thank you for-all those years ago-opening the door and letting me stay...I'm out.

Mark T. Crockett

About The Author

Mark Crockett has been writing fiction for over ten years. "Turkeystuffer" is his first novel. The one time romantic greeting card company owner has written several short stories for many magazines. This one time EMT, IBM chemical analyst, TV cameraman, radio talk show producer and used car salesman is from East Orange, NJ. He currently lives in Phoenix, AZ.

ORDER FORM

Use this form to order additional copies of *Strebor Books International* Bestselling titles as they become available.

Name: _____

Company _____

Address: _____

_____

City: _____ State _____ Zip _____

Phone: _____ Fax: _____

E-mail: _____

Credit Card: ☐ Visa   ☐ MC   ☐ Amex   ☐ Discover

Number _____

Exp. Date: _____ Signature: _____

ITEM	PRICE	QTY.
1. *Shame On It All by Zane*	$15.00	
2. *Luvalways by Shonell Bacon & F. Daniels*	$15.00	
3. *Daughter by Spirit by V. Anthony Rivers*	$15.00	
4. *All That and A Bag of Chips by Darrien Lee*	$15.00	
5. *Blackgentlemen.com*	$15.00	
6. *Turkeystuffer by Mark Crockett*	$15.00	
7. *Nyagra's Falls by Michelle Valentine*	$15.00	
8.		

SHIPPING INFORMATION		Subtotal	
GROUND ONE BOOK	$3.00	*shipping*	
EACH ADDITIONAL BOOK	$1.00	*5%tax (MD)*	

Make checks or money orders payable to
Strebor Books International LLC
Post Office Box 1370
Bowie, Maryland 20718